ALL BETS ARE ON...

BOOKS BY C.M. STUNICH

Romance Novels

HARD ROCK ROOTS SERIES
Real Ugly
Get Bent
Tough Luck
Bad Day
Born Wrong
Hard Rock Roots Box Set (1-5)
Dead Serious
Doll Face
Heart Broke
Get Hitched
Screw Up

TASTING NEVER SERIES
Tasting Never
Finding Never
Keeping Never
Tasting, Finding, Keeping
Never Can Tell
Never Let Go
Never Did Say
Never Could Stop

ROCK-HARD BEAUTIFUL
Groupie
Roadie
Moxie

THE BAD NANNY TRILOGY
Bad Nanny
Good Boyfriend
Great Husband

TRIPLE M SERIES
Losing Me, Finding You
Loving Me, Trusting You
Needing Me, Wanting You
Craving Me, Desiring You

A DUET
Paint Me Beautiful
Color Me Pretty

FIVE FORGOTTEN SOULS
Beautiful Survivors
Alluring Outcasts

MAFIA QUEEN
Lure
Lavish
Luxe

DEATH BY DAYBREAK MC
I Was Born Ruined
I Am Dressed in Sin

STAND-ALONE NOVELS
Baby Girl
All for 1
Blizzards and Bastards
Fuck Valentine's Day
Broken Pasts
Crushing Summer
Taboo Unchained
Taming Her Boss
Kicked

BAD BOYS MC TRILOGY
Raw and Dirty
Risky and Wild
Savage and Racy

HERS TO KEEP TRILOGY
Biker Rockstar Billionaire CEO Alpha
Biker Rockstar Billionaire CEO Dom
Biker Rockstar Billionaire CEO Boss

BAD BOYS OF BURBERRY PREP
Filthy Rich Boys
Bad, Bad Blue Bloods
The Envy of Idols
In the Arms of the Elite

STAND-ALONE
Football Dick
Stepbrother Inked
Glacier

BOOKS BY
C.M. STUNICH

Fantasy Novels

THE SEVEN MATES OF ZARA WOLF
Pack Ebon Red
Pack Violet Shadow
Pack Obsidian Gold
Pack Ivory Emerald
Pack Amber Ash
Pack Azure Frost
Pack Crimson Dusk

ACADEMY OF SPIRITS AND SHADOWS
Spirited
Haunted
Shadowed

TEN CATS PARANORMAL SOCIETY
Possessed

TRUST NO EVIL
See No Devils
Hear No Demons
Speak No Curses

THE SEVEN WICKED SERIES
Seven Wicked Creatures
Six Wicked Beasts
Five Wicked Monsters
Four Wicked Fiends

THE WICKED WIZARDS OF OZ
Very Bad Wizards

HOWLING HOLIDAYS
Werewolf Kisses

OTHER FANTASY NOVELS
Gray and Graves
Indigo & Iris
She Lies Twisted
Hell Inc.
DeadBorn
Chryer's Crest
Stiltz

SIRENS OF A SINFUL SEA TRILOGY
Under the Wild Waves

Co-Written

(With Tate James)

HIJINKS HAREM
Elements of Mischief
Elements of Ruin
Elements of Desire

THE WILD HUNT MOTORCYCLE CLUB
Dark Glitter

FOXFIRE BURNING
The Nine
Tail Game

OTHER
And Today I Die

BURBERRY
PREPARATORY ACADEMY

EST 1883

MAP KEY

A. Marnye's Dorm
B. The Towers
C. Amphitheater
D. Lakeside Lodge
E. Yacht Harbor
F. Cemetery

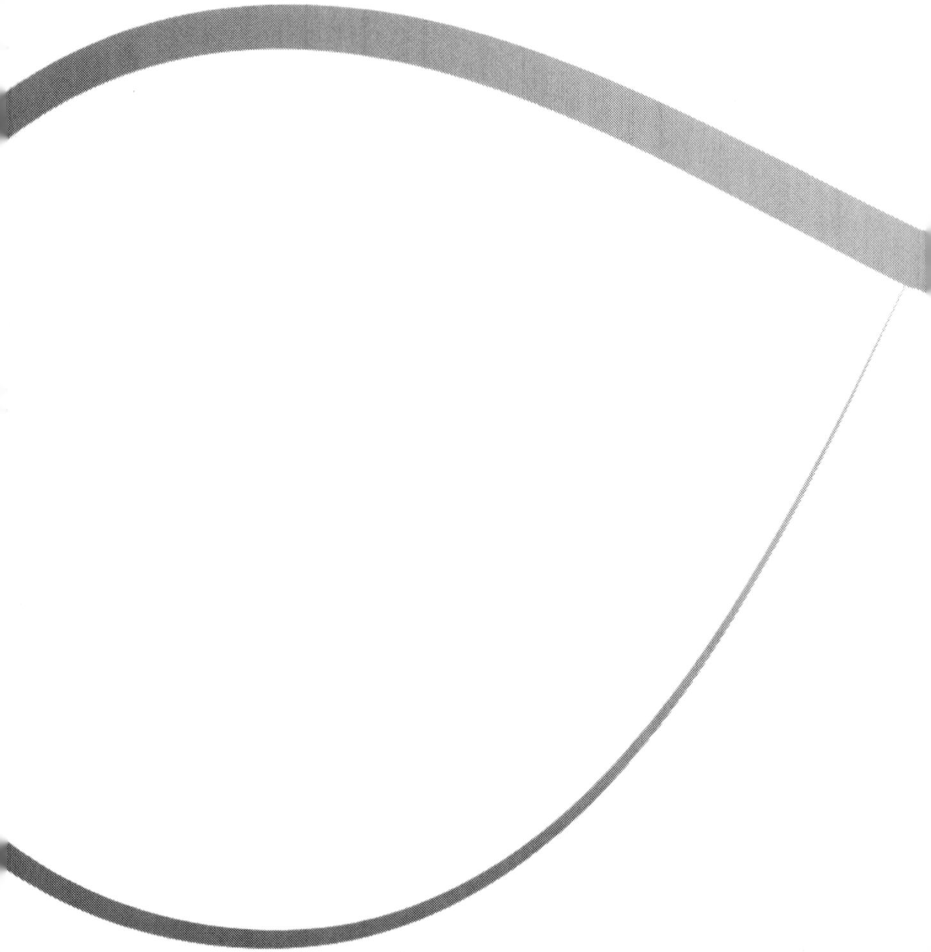

RICH BOYS OF BURBERRY PREP, YEAR ONE

FILTHY RICH BOYS

C.M. STUNICH
INTERNATIONAL BESTSELLING AUTHOR

Filthy Rich Boys
Copyright © 2019 C.M. Stunich
ISBN-10: 1092390413 (pbk.)
ISBN-13: 978-1-092390415(pbk.)

All rights reserved. No part of this book may be used or reproduced in any manner whatsoever without written permission except in the case of brief quotations embodied in critical articles or reviews.
For information address:
Sarian Royal, 89365 Old Mohawk Road, Springfield, OR 97478

Contact the authors at
www.cmstunich.com

Cover art © 2017 Amanda Rose Carroll

The characters and events portrayed in this book are fictitious. Any similarity to real persons, living or dead, businesses, or locales is coincidental and is not intended by the authors.

this book is dedicated to Amanda and Rhea.
thanks for taking me to that drag show, ladies. I really needed it.
this one goes out to all our future travel endeavors. Bon voyage!

Author's Note

Possible Spoilers

Filthy Rich Boys is a reverse harem, high school bully romance. What does that mean exactly? It means our female main character, Marnye Reed, will end up with at least three love interests by the end of the series. It also means that for a good portion of this book, the love interests quite literally bully Marnye. This book in no way condones bullying, nor does it romanticize it. If the love interests in this story want to win the main character over, they'll have to change their ways, accept her revenge, and embrace her forgiveness.

Karma is a bitch, especially when it comes in the form Marnye Reed.

Any kissing/sexual scenes featuring Marnye are consensual. This book might be about high school students, but it is not what I would consider young adult. The characters are brutal, the emotions real, the f-word in prolific use. There's some underage drinking, sexual situations, mentions of past suicide attempts, and other adult scenarios.

None of the main characters is under the age of fifteen. This series will have a happy ending in the fourth and final book.

PROLOGUE

My uniform—and my dignity—are in tatters.

My eyes scan the gathered crowd, but there are three faces in particular that catch my attention. Cold, cruel, beautiful. *An ugly sort of beautiful,* I think as I meet a narrowed silver gaze and catch the faintest edges of a smirk. Tristan Vanderbilt thinks he's beaten me; they all do. But what they don't understand is that I'm not the nervous, eager little charity case I was when I first started at Burberry Prep.

Lifting an arm up, I swipe a bit of blood from my mouth. My bra is showing through the torn remnants of my white blouse, and it's the pretty red one I wore just for Zayd. He made me believe he cared about me. Flicking my eyes in his direction, I can see quite clearly now that he doesn't. He isn't smiling, not like Tristan, but the message in his green eyes is clear: *you don't belong here.*

"Had enough yet?" Harper du Pont purrs from behind me. I don't bother turning to look at her. Instead, I let my attention slide to the last of the three guys. My three biggest mistakes; my three greatest betrayals. Creed is frowning, like this whole confrontation is a necessary evil. Get rid of the lower-class trash, clean up the school.

The wind picks up, the ragged red pleats of my academy uniform billowing in a salty breeze. In the distance, I can hear the sea. It crashes against the rocks in time to the frantic beating of my heart. A storm is coming.

Tristan moves toward me with predatory grace, his expensive loafers picking up droplets of dew as he comes to stand toe-to-toe with me, as close as he was that first day when he insulted me and then laid out the challenge: *how long do you think you'll last?* Well. It's the final day of freshman year, and I'm still standing here, aren't I? Tristan, though, he thinks that while I've won the battle, he's going to win the war.

I stay stone-still as he lifts his fingers and tangles strands of my paint-splattered hair through them, giving the short rose gold locks a light tug. Red paint smears across his perfect skin as I meet those gray eyes of his with a defiant glimmer in my own.

"I take it you won't be coming back next year, will you, Marnye?" he whispers, his voice like whiskey over ice. Tristan thinks he's the master of this school, a veritable god. The other boys think of themselves like that, too. I'd like to be a fly on the wall when a confrontation finally comes. They think their money will buy them the world. Maybe, in a way, it will.

But it won't buy them true friendship, and it won't buy them love. It definitely won't buy them me.

I glance past Tristan to Zayd and Creed, and then I refocus

Filthy Rich Boys

my attention back on the asshole that started it all. From day one, he went out of his way to make my life a living hell. He succeeded. And Zayd and Creed, they loved every horrible, filthy second of it.

"Just go home, Marnye, and it'll all be over," Tristan says, the softness in his voice edged with cruelty. He's like a predator who's too cute to be afraid of. I made the mistake of letting him get too close, and now I'm cut and bleeding—physically and emotionally. I'm fucking shattered. "You don't belong here."

Zayd listens to the whole conversation, and then slides his tattooed arm around Becky Platter, putting the final nail in my coffin. He's chosen her over me. He's chosen her and her cruelty and her mocking laughter over me. My hands curl into fists so tight that my nails dig crescents into my palms.

I meet Tristan's haughty, self-assured stare. There are tears on my face, and when he removes his fingers from my hair, he touches one with his knuckles, bringing it to his lips for a lick. It's a derisive, awful move, like a knife in the back. I can feel the blade beside my heart, but it's just missed. I'm not broken yet.

"I've already enrolled in my classes," I state, and the entire courtyard goes silent. Nobody is expecting this, the poor girl, the lamb in a pack of wolves, standing up for herself. What they don't know is that the hardest hearts are forged in fire. With their cruelty and their jokes and their laughter, they've forged me into something spectacular. "Come September, I'll be the first in line for orientation."

"You wouldn't dare," Tristan says, still cold as ice, still full of wicked triumph for what he thinks he's done. His dark hair flutters in the breeze, softening some of his hard lines. It's all an illusion though. I know that now, and I won't make that same mistake again. "I'll make your life a living hell."

"You can try," I retort, reaching into my pocket and pulling out my registration form. I'll be back at Burberry Prep come hell or high water. This is *my* opportunity, and I won't let three handsome faces, three pairs of hot hands, three sets of ardent lips destroy that. "Because what you don't know …" I take a deep breath, and then bend down to grab the handle on my ratty, old duffle bag. Everybody else here has hired help to carry their luggage. Not me. Straightening up, I lift my chin in defiance and Tristan scowls. "Is that my life outside of these walls was already a living hell. This is just another level of Dante's inferno, and I'm not afraid." My gaze flicks past Tristan and back to Zayd and Creed. "Not of any of you."

I move around Tristan, intent on the school gates and three months of freedom from these jerks, but he puts his hand around my arm and holds me back. Glancing down, I stare at his fingers pressed against my flesh, and then look back up at his face. He's smiling, but it's not a pretty smile.

"Challenge accepted," he purrs, and then he releases me.

As I head down the path in my torn uniform, I keep my chin up and my fears pushed back.

Challenge accepted is right. I won't be driven away from the best opportunity in my life. Not by Tristan, not by anyone.

As I walk, I can feel three sets of eyes on my back, watching, waiting, plotting.

I'll have to make sure I stay one step ahead.

CHAPTER 1

The impressive stone façade of Burberry Prep hides a host of wicked souls with pretty faces. I don't know that yet, standing at the bottom of the wide, worn steps with my heart thundering in my throat. My school schedule is clutched in my right hand, wrinkled and well-loved; I've been staring at it since the fourth of July.

Deep breath, Marnye. My red, pleated skirt is freshly-pressed and fluttering around my thighs as I move across the old brick walkway towards the front entrance. According to the orientation email, I should be meeting my guide just inside the inner courtyard. *I wonder if I look poor?* I swallow hard against my own paranoia, but it's not easy. The dean assured me that my scholarship status would not be advertised; that doesn't mean nobody knows about it.

I hear the trickle of a fountain before I see it, a soft tinkling sound, like wind chimes. As I come up the last step, the sound's matched to a bronze statue of a stag, water spouting from the rocky base he's standing on. There's a sitting on the edge of the fountain, wearing a uniform that matches mine. *So he's a first year, too,* I think, reminding myself that most of the students here have been attending the academy since preschool. Different buildings, same campus. So a first year guide isn't totally out of the question. In fact, only two percent of new students enroll during their first year of high school.

Good for me, I muse as the boy stands up and I catch a glimpse of how incredibly handsome he is: silky chestnut hair with blond highlights, bright blue eyes, full pink lips. *Always working outside the box.* Now if I can only keep the rest of the students here from finding out just how outside the box I really am, like wrong side of the tracks sort of out.

"Tristan?" I ask hopefully as my new loafers clack across the intricate brick patio. I'm already holding out my hand in invitation, a bright smile tracing its way across my lips. I've decided that if anyone asks me about my family, I won't lie. No, I'm not shamed of where I come from. Actually, I'm proud of myself. Not only am I going to be the first person in my family to finish high school, but I'm going to do it at a prestigious academy usually reserved for the filthy rich.

"Actually, no," the boy says as he takes my hand with a smooth, dry palm. He smells like coconuts and sunshine, if that's even possible, to smell like sunshine. "I'm Andrew Payson. Tristan should be ..." Andrew trails off for a moment, and I catch the briefest flick of his eyes in the direction of a janitor's closet. "Around here somewhere." Andrew's gaze switches back over to me and for a split-second, I see a flare of interest before he blinks, and it's gone. *Or maybe I just imagined it?* I wonder, realizing for the first

Filthy Rich Boys

time that my dating life here ... is probably gonna be pretty slim.

Guys might show interest at first, but no loaded teen wants to date someone without two nickels to rub together.

"I'm guessing he's your student guide?" Andrew adds, dropping my hand. He gestures for me to take a seat on the fountain beside him, and I oblige, hissing a little at the cold of the bronze against my thighs. Wearing a skirt like this is going to take some serious getting used to. But I asked about wearing pants and was given a very firm no. Like in many elitist endeavors, there's a very prevalent sense of gender roles regarding uniforms.

"Yep," I reply with another smile, flipping up the tag around my neck. My name's on one side; the name Tristan on the other. "I'll be shadowing him all day." Andrew smiles back at me, but there's a slight grimace to his expression. Uh-oh. I have a feeling Mr. Payson doesn't much like this Tristan guy. "Why? Is there something I should be worrying about?"

"You'll see," Andrew says, leaning back on his palms as he studies me. In the rafters above, a flock of birds lands, scattering feathers. The wind catches them and sends them dancing around my face along with the brunette waves of my hair. "He's an interesting sort of guy." Andrew cocks his head slightly, chuckling under his breath. "He's damn lucky to be paired with you though."

"Sure thing," I say with a laugh, holding the handle of my new leather book bag in my left hand, being careful to keep it from falling into the water. This thing not only holds my new laptop and tablet, but it also cost the scholarship foundation a small fortune. Frankly, it's worth more than my dad's car. I nod my chin in Andrew's direction. "What's your girl's name?"

"Girl? Nah." Andrew shrugs. "I'm not quite that lucky." He reaches up and flips his badge over, revealing the name *Rob*. Ah. I grin as sunlight streams between the four bell towers that surround the courtyard, turning Andrew's hair a generous gold. "And I'm definitely not that gay—unfortunately. Between you and me, most of the girls here are already engaged." I raise an eyebrow, but Andrew just smiles. "Old money, you know."

Right.

"How about you?" I ask, and even though I don't mean to, I end up flirting with the guy. Great. My mother's daughter, I guess. "Are you engaged?"

"I," Andrew begins, his eyes twinkling, "am perfectly single."

We both pause as a boy in the red pants, black jacket, and white shirt of a first year comes up the steps and pauses awkwardly, raising his hand in a hello. After he introduces himself as Rob Whitney, I step back and lean against the cool stone walls of one of the bell towers, excited that classes are actually still held in these narrow buildings. I'm trying to give the boys a little space, so I tug one of the books from my bag, crack it open, and wait for my guide to show up. Normally, I'd be all over my phone, but the academy is super strict about electronics: school-issued laptops and tablets only.

Before Andrew and Rob even get a chance to start their own tour, the door to the janitor's closet flies open and a girl in a fourth year uniform—black skirt, black shirt, black jacket

Filthy Rich Boys

—comes out, one shoulder of her top falling down, her lipstick smeared.

A boy comes out behind her, a boy with silver eyes and an awful, awful smirk. The moment I see him changes everything. Hell, it changes my whole life, rearranges my past, dictates my future. When I first lay eyes on Tristan Vanderbilt, I become a different person.

Heat rushes through my body, and it feels suddenly hot, like I should take off my jacket and loosen my tie. Tristan's fixing the buttons on his white first year shirt as he makes his way over to me with long, confident strides, his hair glossy and raven-black, his mouth too dangerous to be tempting. My fingers curl tight around the side of my book bag and my heart races, sweat beading at my temples.

What a reaction.

What the hell is wrong with me?! I wonder with increasing panic as Tristan marches right up to me, towering a good half a foot over me. He takes the jacket that's lying over his arm and shrugs into it, fixes the two center buttons, and then leans forward, putting his forearm on the wall above my head. I can smell him, too, like peppermint and cinnamon. It's damn-near intoxicating.

"You're the charity case, huh?" he asks me, his smile growing even wider. There's nothing at all nice about it. Tristan looks downright vicious. I open my mouth to respond, wishing I'd never made the decision not to lie. It'd feel good right now, to deny this boy's accusation. But it's true, isn't it? I *am* the charity case. But how the fuck does he know?

"My name is Marnye Reed, and yes, I'm the scholarship recipient." *Jesus, I sound like a school teacher or something.*

So much for acting cool. Not that it would matter to this guy: he's already made up his mind about me. It's written all over his face, a dash of disdain drowning in haughty arrogance.

Tristan scoffs and shakes his head, immediately refocusing his gaze on mine. I'm not sure how long I can maintain that stare without losing part of my soul. It's absolutely terrifying … and thrilling, all at once. I've only ever met one guy like this before, and that didn't turn out so well.

"Scholarship. Trash talk for free money handout." His smile turns into a nightmarish grin. "My family actually built this school, and yet, we still pay to be here. What makes you so special that you should get to come here for free?"

I'm so not ready or expecting this attack that it blindsides me, and I'm left gaping as he reaches out and teases a strand of my loose hair around his finger. He gives a little tug on my brunette waves and leans even closer, brushing my ear with his mouth.

"Pretty enough though, for white trash." Without thinking, I reach up with both palms and shove this stranger back with everything I've got. One bonus of growing up on the wrong side of the tracks, you learn to stand up for yourself. Tristan barely moves, his expression never changing. It's like shoving at a mountain of bricks. Completely and utterly immovable. "How long do you think you'll last?" he continues, cocking his head slightly to one side. I reach up to push his hand away from my hair, but he's already leaning back, dropping his arm —and his smile—with a sudden change in expression. His lids go half-lidded as he studies me. "Not long, I don't think."

Filthy Rich Boys

That beautiful mouth of his purses. "Shame. I was looking forward to a challenge."

Tristan turns away from me, like I'm the one who's done something wrong when he was late to meet me *and* he was ... well, doing something with an older girl in the closet. What, exactly, he was doing, I don't want to know. *And yet some dark, messed-up part of me really does.* Damn it.

Even though I don't want to, I take off down the open air hallway with the blooming jasmine, and catch up to my 'guide' for the day. Fantastic. I've clearly been paired with the rudest—and probably richest—boy at this school. *And probably the best looking, too.* My heart flutters in my chest, but I push the feeling away. I try to be nice to everyone, but I'm not going to simper at some guy just because he's hot.

He doesn't wait for me to catch up, so I have to run, panting by the time we're shoulder to shoulder. Tristan doesn't seem to notice or care that I'm short of breath. Nor does he seem to notice or care that he's supposed to be showing me where the dorms—sorry, *apartments*—are, the classrooms, the cafeteria.

"You're my guide for the day," I say, cheeks flushed with heat from running, my fingers lifting the badge up for Tristan's inspection, flashing his name on the backside. "Whether you like me or not is irrelevant, you have a job to do."

Tristan pauses just outside a door with beautiful stained glass panels stretching from floor to ceiling. My instinct is to gape at it, and then snap a picture for my dad, but I'm going to have to get used to the idea of not having a phone. That, and my gut instincts are telling me it'd be a mistake to let this

Tristan guy learn anything about me, even something as small as my fascination with historical architecture.

"A job?" he scoffs, taking a step back and looking me up and down with a slow sweep of silver eyes. They cut across me like a blade, making me bleed. Unconsciously, I cross my arms over my chest and he chuckles. It's not a pleasant sound, not even close. Instead, Tristan's laughter is mocking, like he thinks I'm some cosmic joke thrust upon him by an uncaring universe. "Listen, Charity," he starts, and I open my mouth to tell him off when his palm slams into the stained glass panel behind my head. "No, don't talk. There's nothing you have to say that would interest me." Reaching out, Tristan runs his fingers down the side of my jaw, and I slap his hand away. He snatches my wrist and holds it there, like he owns me. Looking at the guy, I get the impression that he thinks he owns the whole school. "Do you know what my last name is?"

"After the way you've treated me," I start, lifting my chin, nostrils flaring. "I don't think I care to."

At my last school, we had metal detectors, drug dogs, and an on-campus police force. If Tristan thinks he can intimidate me, he's got another thing coming. What I don't know in that moment is that rich boys are far more dangerous than poor ones. The poor ones might join gangs and pack heat, might rough you up for walking in the wrong neighborhood, but the rich ones have all the same instincts wrapped up in pretty faces and designer shoes, white smiles and genteel manners. The thing is, with infinite resources comes the ability to inflict infinite pain.

Filthy Rich Boys

"If you want to survive even a single day on campus," he continues, leaning in and putting his mouth so close to my ear that his breath stirs my hair, raising goose bumps on my arm. I can't decide if I like or hate his proximity, his long, lean body brushing up against the front of me, one knee between my legs. My breasts just barely brush his chest, two crisp white shirts teasing one another with each breath we take. "Then you best learn it—and quick."

Tristan releases me and steps back. The arrogance in his handsome face is staggering, his high cheekbones and full mouth a waste on such a haughty face. He's too full of himself to be pretty. *Liar,* my mind whispers, but I brush that aside. The guy practically assaulted me. If he thinks I won't report his ass, he's got another thing coming.

"That girl in the closet ..." I blurt before I can stop myself. There's a morbid fascination brewing in me that I know I should tamp down. Play with flame and get burned. That's a hard fact of life I learned long ago, so what the hell am I doing?

Tristan slides long fingers through his lush, raven-colored hair, looking down at me like I'm gum on the bottom of his shoe. I'm not surprised. By the time lunch rolls around, the whole school will be calling me Charity.

"Want me to tell you how I fucked her?" he asks as heat rushes up the back of my neck and burns my cheeks. "If you last the week," he continues, reaching up to adjust his black silk tie, "maybe I will."

He turns then and leaves me standing alone on the walkway. On either side of the awning, rain begins to fall.

That's not a good omen, not a good omen at all.

CHAPTER 2

Without a guide, Burberry Preparatory Academy is like a labyrinth of old stone hallways and spiraling staircases. It's haunted by a melancholy beauty that makes the hair on the back of my neck stand up, like I can sense the history crouching inside the building, eras long past watching from shadowed eyes.

"Hey." A voice sounds from behind me, and I jump, stifling a small scream as I spin and find a girl with bright blond hair and a wide smile. If it weren't for the genuine warmth in her blue eyes, her beauty would be intimidating, almost cold in its perfection. She bears a striking resemblance to the marble statue in the corner, carved infallibility and plaster pale skin. "Are you lost?"

Filthy Rich Boys

"Am I that obvious?" I ask, risking a small smile and hoping like hell she's nothing like Tristan. "I've been wandering around for half an hour, but I'm too embarrassed to ask for help." *Embarrassed? More like too anxious.* The looks I've been receiving from the other students haven't exactly been welcoming. That, and the staff I've seen have all been running around in that panicked first-day-of-school state, prepping lesson plans and greeting students they've known since preschool. I've never felt like more of an outcast—and trust me, I've been a pariah before.

"You're the Cabot Scholarship Award winner, right?" the girl asks, her voice like bells. Wow. Her voice is as pretty as she is. But also, looks like the whole school already knows my socio-economic status, huh? "Oh, no, no," she continues, waving her hand in my direction, "it's not what you're thinking. I just ... my mother is Kathleen Cabot."

My mouth pops open, and I lean forward, my leather school bag clutched in two hands.

"Your mom is Kathleen?" I ask, feeling this sharp sense of relief wash through me. Kathleen Cabot is a self-made *billionaire.* Yep, you heard it right: billionaire. She was born in the same neighborhood as me, raised by a single mom in a studio apartment, and ended up becoming a tech mogul. I met her twice: once at the award ceremony, and then later at the celebratory dinner. She's a freaking saint—and the only reason I'm standing here at Burberry Prep.

"I take it she made an impression?" the girl asks with a wry smile. "Good or bad? She can go either way, depending on the weather, the position of the stars, whether it's a full moon or not ..." A grin takes over my face.

"Good impression, definitely. I've spent the last three weeks trying to write the perfect thank you letter." The girl smiles back at me, holding out a warm, dry palm for me to shake.

"She'll be happy with anything you send her," she says as we clasp hands. "Miranda Cabot. And you're Marnye Reed." Miranda takes a step back and looks me over. "I hope you're made of tough stuff," she says, but not unkindly.

"And why's that?" I ask as her blue eyes lift to my face and one pale brow goes up.

"Because Burberry Prep is a hellhole dressed with money." Miranda gives me a big, wide smile and then reaches out a hand. "Give me your schedule, and I'll tell you which demons to avoid." She pauses and gives me another critical look. "Mostly though, you'll want to stay away from the devils."

"The devils?" I ask, digging my wrinkled schedule out of my pocket and passing it over to Miranda. She scans it, chewing her full lower lip and smearing sparkly pink gloss. When she glances back up at me and reaches out to spin my nametag over, her mouth tightens into a thin line.

"The devils," Miranda says with a sigh. "Nobody calls them that but me. Looks like you already met one this morning?" She's looking at me with pity now, like she's well-acquainted with Tristan and his bullshit.

"What does everyone else call them?" I ask, and she sighs, looping her arm through mine and pulling me down the long, wide hallway. It's big enough to drive a truck through, small tables with lemon-cucumber water and cups placed every so

Filthy Rich Boys

often. Sometimes there's fresh fruit or pastries, too.

"Oh, girl, you and I have a long talk ahead of us. Stick with me. We have Monday classes together. By the time we're done, you'll know everything you need to know about the Idols."

The Bluebloods of Burberry Prep
A list by Miranda Cabot

The Idols (guys): Tristan Vanderbilt (year one), Zayd Kaiser (year one), and Creed Cabot (year one)

The Idols (girls): Harper du Pont (year one), Becky Platter (year one), and Gena Whitley (year four)

The Inner Circle: Andrew Payson, Anna Kirkpatrick, Myron Talbot, Ebony Peterson, Gregory Van Horn, Abigail Fanning, John Hannibal, Valentina Pitt, Sai Patel, Mayleen Zhang, Jalen Donner ... and, I guess, me!

Plebs: everyone else, sorry. XOXO

"Why am I holding a list of names in my hand?" I ask as we walk down the hallway, pausing for coffee at one of the side tables. My old school never served coffee to students.

C.M. STUNICH

Sometimes, kids would break into the teacher's lounge and steal some, but that's as close as we'd ever get.

"Memorize that list like your life depends on it," Miranda says, lifting a mug of black coffee up to her lips.

"Miss Cabot," a stern voice says, plucking the white cup from Miranda's thin fingers. "You know that the coffee stands are for staff only." I turn and find a tall, brunette woman in a skirt suit watching us with a raised brow and a wry half-smile. She looks like she'd be more at home in Washington D.C. than in a rural prep school in central California. "There's a sign, after all. And I know you can read. Your mother promises she taught you herself."

My mouth twitches as Miranda tosses her hair in a haughty gesture that doesn't seem to quite fit her personality. And that's a good thing. I've known a lot of hair-tossers in my life, and none of those girls were pleasant. They made my middle school years a living hell with the help of a guy named Zack Brooks. *Zack* ... I'm not going to let myself think about him. This is my chance at a fresh start and new, better memories.

"Ms. Felton, I see the war against caffeine is still on," Miranda grumbles, waiting for Ms. Felton to turn her back, so she can flip her off. "It's a losing battle—like the war on drugs."

"Why don't you wait until tomorrow, and we can discuss politics in class?" Ms. Felton dumps the coffee into the drain of a water fountain as we turn the corner and Miranda rolls her blue eyes at me.

"Sorry, that's Ms. Felton. She's a bit of a rule Nazi. She

Filthy Rich Boys

can get away with it, too, since she was an Idol once upon a time. It's like, that shit never fades." Miranda pauses and then peeps around the corner, like she's checking to see if Ms. Felton's following us. She's not. Miranda grins and then gestures at my belly with loose fingers. "Roll it, or be forever dubbed a Pleb."

"A ... what?" I ask as Miranda untucks her shirt, and then proceeds to roll the waistband of her red pleated skirt until it's dangerously short, like *can't bend over or reach for too high of a shelf* short. A light breeze is liable to blow it right off. "Pleb? Like ... Plebeian?"

"Yep," Miranda says with a sigh, tucking her shirt back in and then looking at me like I'm crazy. When I don't move to copy her, she groans and steps forward, tugging the crisp white blouse from my waistband. I sort of just stand there and let her do her thing. It's exhilarating, naughty but in an innocent sort of way. "It's stupid, I know, but it's how it is here."

Once my skirt's the appropriate level of, well, inappropriate, Miranda leans over and taps the piece of paper she wrote out for me. On the bottom, there's the term *Pleb* with the words *everyone else* written after it.

"Plebeian means, like, commoner or peasant," Miranda continues, huffing and tucking loose strands of platinum blonde behind her ears. It's so pale, it's practically white, but when the sun leaks in through the stained glass windows and bathes her in light, it's angelic, glowing as golden as a halo. "If you're not an Idol or in the Inner Circle, then you're a Pleb. Once a Pleb, always a Pleb." Miranda pauses and lifts her eyes to the ceiling, long dark lashes fluttering. I think she's got eyelash extensions, but it would be rude to ask. Hell, maybe I'm just jealous and she's just pretty? "Well, except this one time when Karen Evermeet screwed the soccer coach, and shared the video with the whole school." Miranda flashes me a model-esque smile. "She went from Pleb to Idol in a day. But that never happens." Miranda pauses again and then reaches out to ruffle up my hair with her fingers, curling one brunette ringlet next to my face. "I mean, unless you're into forty-year-old married athletes."

"Not quite that adventurous, I'm afraid," I say as Miranda gestures with her chin, and I study the paper again. Tristan Vanderbilt, huh? When I look up, I catch sigh of a bronze plaque labelled *Vanderbilt Study Hall*. Right. *"My family actually built this school, and yet ... we still pay to be here. What makes you so special that you should get to come here for free?"* Guess he wasn't joking about that first part. The rest of it ... that asshole has no idea how hard I worked to get here.

"Hey, don't sell yourself short. You have other, more important traits and talents. My mom and I read over a thousand essays before choosing yours." Miranda studies me as we walk, the rain beating a rhythmic pattern against the stone walkways outside. Somehow though, even though this building's big and drafty, it's nice and warm in here. "Must've been a lot of hard work, jumping through all those hoops." Miranda sounds a bit detached when she says that, like her mind's already long gone to somewhere else.

Me, I'm flushed, and my skin feels suddenly hot. I stop walking and Miranda pauses next to me, blinking the fog

Filthy Rich Boys

from her vision. I knew my essay would be read by 'qualified student judges' but ... Our eyes meet, and her expression softens. This girl now officially knows everything there is to know about me. She knows my darkest memories, my greatest fears.

"I loved your essay," she says, reaching out to squeeze my hand, "and I won't tell anyone what I read. Not only am I seriously desperate to make friends with you, but my mom would kill me. You've met her: she's terrifying."

My lips curve up in a slight smile, and I squeeze her hand back before letting go.

"I appreciate that," I say, feeling this new sort of comradery simmer between us. There are things in that essay that could destroy me at Burberry Prep.

We turn another corner, and I wonder if she's going to get to this piece of paper in my hand before we reach the chapel for the morning announcements. Or, like, if we're even going to *get* to the chapel at all. *How far did I wander? And how big is this place?!*

I mean, I studied the map of Burberry Prep religiously, lying in the hot white heat of summer on my dad's sun-dead lawn, shades on my eyes, headphones on my ears. I memorized the entire layout, and yet ... I'm so turned around I don't even remember which door I came in. Looking at a flat illustration of something, and walking it in person are two completely different things.

Lifting my head up, I see something that takes my breath away.

Or ... more like some*one*.

"Who the hell is that?" I choke out as my eyes catch on

the platinum blond head of the most beautiful boy I've ever seen. He's lounging in a chair with insouciant disregard, an air of entitled laziness captured in his long limbs. The way he sits there, boneless, bored, but with bright, piercing eyes, it all reminds me of a cat. A lazy, spoiled housecat.

His hair shimmers in the light from outside, bits of sun breaking through the clouds. Outside, there's a rainbow stretching across campus that I can just barely see through the glass, but it's nowhere near as beautiful as the guy in the loose tie and half-tucked shirt. He's still crisp, still polished and put-together, but with an air of effortlessness that Tristan Vanderbilt doesn't have. Nah, that guy has a stick shoved so far up his ass, he could never *luxuriate* across a chair the way this one does.

"That," Miranda starts as the boy's ice-colored eyes swing our way, "is my twin brother: Creed Cabot."

My mouth opens, and then snaps closed when I realize that I have absolutely nothing productive to say. I'm enthralled, held by that sharp gaze as Creed makes his way over to us. He's tall, sure, but he feels even taller by the way he stands, his fingers just lightly tucked into his pockets, the top two buttons on his shirt undone. His jacket is nowhere to be seen.

"Mandy," he says by way of greeting, looking at his sister's skirt with distaste. Creed Cabot ... he doesn't even give me the time of day. *Rude much?* I raise an eyebrow and cross my arms, waiting for him to acknowledge me. "Was wondering where you'd disappeared to. Andrew's looking for you." Miranda nods and then holds out a hand to indicate me.

Filthy Rich Boys

"Are you going to say hi to the new student?" she asks, those ice-blue eyes of Creed's sliding over to me. I swear, even from here, I can smell him. He's got this crisp linen scent with just a hint of tobacco, like he's been hanging out with someone who smokes but isn't a smoker himself.

"Am I?" he asks, looking me up and down with a calculating coolness to his gaze. "And why should I?"

"Oh for shit's sake, Creed, this is Marnye Reed." Miranda raises her brows and waits for him to make the connection. Apparently, he already has.

"Yeah, Mom's pet peasant. I already know that." Creed looks at me, his skin like alabaster, his expression as haughty as Tristan's. "Charity work is her thing. Doesn't have to be mine." Creed turns away as Miranda sputters, and I do my best to come up with a quick retort.

"Charity isn't what got me here, Mr. Cabot. It was hard work and dedication."

He doesn't even slow his stride to acknowledge that I've spoken. Somehow, that's worse than having him come at me with a verbal assault the way Tristan did. What is wrong with these people? Is everyone at this school an arrogant jerk?

"Don't let him get to you," Miranda explains, but she doesn't sound particularly sure of herself. "He's an asshole to everybody." She takes my wrist and pulls me along, toward a crowd that's bottlenecking the entrance to a cavernous chapel. "This way," she continues, nodding with her head as we move up to a small door on the left of the main entrance. Miranda uses a key to open it and then lets me into a narrow hallway with beautiful rose red transom windows situated near the high ceiling.

"Whoa, how do you get invited to this club?" I whisper, following Miranda down the hall and then up a set of stone stairs. The smell of cigarette smoke wafts over to me, and we pause at the first landing. Without skipping a beat, Miranda answers me and plucks a cigarette from the fingers of the boy who's smoking it.

"Only Idols, Inner Circle, and staff are allowed back here," she tells me, cocking out a hip as the dark-haired boy sitting on the edge of the windowsill turns to glare at her. "Are you fucking kidding me, Gregory Van Horn? If Ms. Felton catches you smoking on day one, you're in for a world of trouble."

"Don't be such a fucking pastor's daughter," the guy responds, leaning despondently against the stone, and then glancing over at me. His gaze is assessing, but much less judgmental than my previous two acquaintances. "Who's this? The charity case?"

"Everyone knows?" Miranda asks, and my heart plummets into my stomach. It does seem that way, doesn't it? That everyone knows I'm the only person at this school whose family doesn't have a net worth equivalent to the GDP of a small country? "How bad is the damage?"

"Girl from the wrong side of the tracks, short, chubby, dull hair, not even fuckable. If she were fuckable, maybe she could be a Pleb. As of right now, Harper's already started calling her the Working Girl."

My cheeks flush, but I'm not stupid enough to miss the connection. Admittedly, it's a clever play on words: working girl, like blue-collar working girl … and working girl, like

Filthy Rich Boys

prostitute.

"What do you mean, *maybe she could be a Pleb?*" Miranda asks, pausing at the sound of the door slamming behind us. We both turn around to find one of the most beautiful girls I've ever seen staring right at me. How is everyone in this school pretty?! Boys and girls alike. Must be the personal chefs, chauffeurs, maids, personal stylists, and plastic surgeons. Life must be so easy when you barely have to live it. My hands curl into fists; I'm expecting a confrontation.

The girl at the bottom of the stairs is already looking at me like I'm public enemy number one.

"Kesha Darling is a Pleb," the girl says, her voice high and cultured, a soprano just waiting to sing. "And her father owns a chain of pharmacies valued at over a hundred and sixty million dollars." The girl—I'm guessing this is the infamous Harper?—crosses one arm over her chest, resting the elbow of the other in her palm. She gestures dismissively in my direction. "So why on earth should some penniless bitch from the ghetto be ranked right up alongside her?" Harper moves toward me, her glossy mane of chestnut hair swinging, her skirt even shorter than Miranda's, makeup professionally done. She pauses in front of me, several inches taller. Several inches skinnier, too. We both notice. My hands tighten on my schoolbag. "Do you know what Social Darwinism is, Working Girl?"

"The name's Marnye," I say, my voice edging dangerously close to a growl. I can take a lot of shit, but I've already had my fill for the day. "And yeah, I do know what that is: a bunch of bullshit propaganda perpetuated by the super-rich to explain why they eat cake and everyone else suffers."

"Aw," Harper purrs, pouting her perfectly painted pink lips, "look at you, so smart, using a Marie Antoinette reference." She leans in toward me, her sweet vanilla-peach smell making me sick. "If you think you've got what it takes, bring your pitchforks, peasant, and take my head." With a laugh like sparkling water, Harper stands back up and flips her hair over her shoulder.

And there it is, the supreme hair flip. She executed it perfectly; it suits her.

I knew we were never going to get along.

Harper brushes past me, glancing down at the guy on the windowsill, Greg.

"No Working Girls in the Gallery," she says, and he nods, raising his eyebrows at Miranda as she sputters and flushes. When she turns to me, I hold up a hand to stop her from trying to explain.

"It's okay," I tell her, stepping back. "I get it." I turn around and head back down the hallway, leaving the way I came and making for the crowd jostling to get into the chapel.

"Hey!" Miranda calls after a moment, running after me and pausing to pant when she catches up. Her face is firm with resolve. "I'll sit with you today."

A smile lights my face and warmth fills my chest.

That's when I know we're going to be friends for sure.

Based on how things are going, she very well might be the only one I'll have.

CHAPTER 3

Burberry Prep isn't a religious school, but it used to be, and while the crosses have been removed, a bit of Catholic flair remains in the rows of pews, the raised dais, the stained glass windows, and the nooks that used to house saints and now house kissing teenagers.

With so many people crammed into the church-turned-auditorium, the air feels charged with excitement and anticipation for the upcoming school year. I wish I could share in it, but all of my enthusiasm has been snatched away—and fast. I didn't expect to get my spirit crushed for a few weeks yet.

"I'm really sorry about how the morning's gone," Miranda whispers, her jaw clenched tight, fingers teasing the hem of her skirt. She glances over at me and forces a smile. "Honestly, it's my fault for drawing their attention to you. I'll get them off your back though, I swear it."

"Your fault?" I ask, raising both brows. "This is nowhere near your fault. That Tristan guy started it when he decided to be a jerk to me this morning." *Don't think about that girl's swollen lips, her clothes all askance, Tristan's triumphant smirk ...* "And don't worry, I expected it." Pausing, I give Miranda a critical look. I'm not judging, but I'm curious to understand why she's so keen on making friends with me when her peers act like they'd enjoy seeing me drawn and quartered. "Could I ask you why you're so interested in being friends with me anyway?" Raising my hands, I continue before Miranda can get her feelings hurt. "Not that I'm not grateful or anything. Seriously, meeting you has been the highlight of my week."

Just before I packed up and got shipped out here, I had a pretty shitty birthday week at home. Dad was drinking again, so badly that I almost didn't leave. I almost stayed to take care of him, but I guess I'm too selfish to give up an opportunity like this. *It was Mom's fault,* I think, resisting the urge to give into that old anger. First time in almost a year that she shows up at our doorstep and it's right before I leave. Every time he has a chance encounter with that woman, Dad falls off the wagon. She told me to thank her for redshirting me as a child (delaying my start in kindergarten until age six), handed off a stack of presents for my fifteenth birthday, and scattered like leaves in the fall wind.

"I ..." Miranda starts, pausing briefly and exhaling. She lifts her blue eyes to mine. "Did Mom tell you her story?" She asks, and I nod. I know all about Kathleen Cabot and her rise to the top of the tech industry *and* the Forbes Most

Filthy Rich Boys

Powerful Women in America list. "How about the part where she had Creed and me, and then moved into Grenadine Heights and sent us to public school?"

My eyebrows go up, and I think my mouth opens in shock. Kathleen Cabot is worth *billions*, and she moved to Grenadine Heights? Sure, compared to the train car my father lives in (don't ask, long story), it's a little ritzy, but most people would call it straight-up middle-class. And public school, huh?

"Political statement?" I ask, and Miranda shrugs, tucking some of that beautiful platinum blonde behind her ear. Her brother's hair was just as light, maybe lighter, almost white but with an unmistakable gold sheen in the sunlight. *Another useless rich asshole*. I banish him from my thoughts. Well, I mean, if I were alone in my bed then maybe I might think about him ... My cheeks heat, and I refocus on Miranda.

"She wanted us to grow up well, but with enough sense to ..." Miranda gestures in the direction of the Gallery which, apparently, is the name for the balcony on the second floor, to the left of the stage. Rows of comfortable chairs line the space, and even though I try not to, I just have to glance up and see who's sitting there.

Tristan Vanderbilt is front and center, impossible to miss with that dark smirk of his, like shadows under the guise of a full, ripe mouth. Creed Cabot sits beside him, but not like a flunky or a sidekick, more like a rival. That bitch, Harper du Pont, is on Tristan's left, with a tow-headed girl next to her. Andrew's up there, too, and when he sees me staring, he waves.

A small smile teases my lips. Okay, fine. I have enemies

in Tristan, Creed, and Harper. Maybe that guy that was smoking, too (Gregory, was it?) but I have allies, too. So the Idols and the—I check the page still clutched in my fist—Inner Circle, they can't be all rotten. I can deal with a few bad apples.

"Enough sense not to act like Creed acted today," Miranda finally says, completing her thought. "Guess the trick didn't work with him, but maybe it worked too well on me." She looks down at her bare knees for a moment. "I've never felt comfortable going to school with these people. I miss my old school, to be honest with you. If I could go to Grenadine Heights High, I would transfer in a second."

"So what you're saying is that I'm the only normal person on campus?" I ask, and Miranda lifts her head, flashing me a grin.

"Pretty much. Everyone else here is too busy loving themselves to waste energy on anyone else." She shrugs her shoulders and leans back in the pew, taking in the room with a critical eye. I've never been so grateful for uniforms in my life; it's impossible to tell the billionaires from the millionaires from the … charity cases. Sigh. There are little touches here and there though that give off hints of personality: a black bow covered in skulls, an armful of wooden bangles, bright red shoelaces. All of which are technically against the dress code, but it's the first day; students are pushing limits.

"I'm happy to be your one normal friend in the whole school," I say with a grin, "but I'm nowhere near Grenadine Heights High. More like … if I'd stayed home, I would've

Filthy Rich Boys

been going to Lower Banks High." Miranda's brows go up, and I give a half-smile. I know the reputation of LBH. My middle school, located right across the street, doesn't have a much better one.

"I'm not sure the students at LBH are any worse than the ones here," Miranda hedges, eyes lifting up to the Gallery where the uh, *Idols* are sitting. Three male, three female Idols. What a strange social hierarchy, and so structured. As we're sitting there, Miranda pulls the paper from my hand, drawing lines between names. "The solid lines mean they're dating. Broken lines mean they're on-again, off-again. Wavy lines means they're rivals."

"How screwed am I?" I ask finally, just as the crowd begins to settle down and a group of administrators takes their positions on the dais at the front of the room. Miranda won't meet my eyes, flicking hers up to Ms. Felton as she takes center stage and starts the commencement speeches. We might be at a school for the world's wealthiest students, but I swear I've heard this very same speech a million times in my life.

"If all the Idols are against you ..." she starts, swallowing hard and tapping her pen against the paper on my lap. "Then I have to admit that I'd be worried about you. Seriously fucking worried. The odds are not good, Marnye."

Nodding, I focus my attention on the front of the room and try not to think the worst.

I've faced bullies before, and I survived; I can do it again.

What I don't know then is that these guys ... are nothing like the ones at my old school.

Things are about to get much, much worse before they get

better.

REED, MARNYE – 1st YEAR, BURBERRY PREP ACADEMIC SCHEDULE

MONDAY/WEDNESDAY/1st FRIDAY:
    Homeroom: Mrs. Felton, Room T112
    Period 1: Academic Literature, Room CH7
    Period 2: Trig/Pre-Calc, Room CH9
    Lunch Period
    Period 3: Beginning Japanese, Room T210

TUESDAY/THURSDAY/2nd FRIDAY:
    Homeroom: Mrs. Felton, Room T112
    Period 1: AP Chemistry, Room SB1
    Period 2: Art, Music, and Dance, Room MM1
    Lunch Period
    Period 3: Government, History, and Civics, Room CH3

MANDATORY FOR ALL FIRST YEARS:
Physical fitness and health class is held in the gym every other Friday after school unless the student is participating in team sports. Absences require a coach's written approval. This is compulsory beginning the second week of class.

Tucking my schedule in my pocket, I follow Miranda to

Filthy Rich Boys

our shared homeroom class on the twelfth floor of the first of the four towers I saw in the courtyard this morning. Based on my own life experiences, I'm already dreading walking up twelve flights of stone steps. But once we get inside the ancient looking stone structure, it's all modern luxuries: including an *elevator*.

An elevator, in a high school. Wow, so this is how the other half lives? Of course, if it were up to me, I'd scrap the elevators and offer the money needed for their maintenance and installation to more scholarship students, buuuuuut that's just me. Guess I'm in the minority. After all, I am the *only* scholarship student in the entire school.

Between these families, there's literally billions of dollars floating around, and they can't be bothered to search out a dozen qualified students to lift out of poverty. Fantastic.

"Shit," Miranda mumbles as we file into the elevator, our bookbags held in front of our short skirts. I'm starting to learn that when the wind blows, and a Marilyn Monroe moment is imminent, the bookbag's to be used as a shield. Oh, and also, I need to seriously invest in better panties. The ones I'm wearing currently are plain cotton, and an embarrassing shade of baby pink. From what I've seen—and I've seen a lot on the walk between the chapel building and what the students call Tower One—everyone else is wearing lacy thongs and silky scraps. "Tristan's coming this way."

"Out of the elevator, Charity," he tells me, a smirk curving his lips as he slams a palm against the closing doors and halts them in their tracks. "You're new, so I won't have you flogged for the infraction, but get the fuck out."

"First off, the name is *Marnye*. Second, there's plenty of

room in here for all of us," I start, but Miranda's already grabbing me by the arm and dragging me back out into the lobby. Tristan's gray eyes track my movements like a predator just waiting for his prey to slip up. I can imagine that if I fell, he'd be at my throat in an instant.

"Idols ride first, and they ride alone," Miranda says, but that's just before Tristan herds the trio of smirking girls behind him into the elevator. He watches me as the doors closed, but his expression is far from pleasant. It's like he's trying to drink in my suffering, no droplet too small to lap up. "Unless, you know, they want company. Day one and he's already gathered himself a harem. Typical."

"How is he already an Idol if he's a first year?" I ask, and Miranda sighs, waiting for the elevator to tick up to the top floor before it starts to come down again. "Is there a legacy bonus for that, too?" I do my best not to eye roll, but the scores I needed to get into this school had to be *forty percent* higher than some of the other students because of their 'legacy bonus', i.e. points on their application granted to them simply for having family members who attended the school before them.

"Well, not technically, but reputations do carry. Tristan Vanderbilt's been a big deal since he started going to preschool on the junior campus." The doors to the elevator open, and Miranda waves me on. We stand side by side, our shiny black loafers identical from heel to toe.

Pursing my lips, I decide to keep the rest of my commentary to myself. My day hasn't even officially *started* yet, and I'm already in a world of trouble.

Filthy Rich Boys

The elevator dings and the doors slide open, revealing a classroom beyond the likes of anything I ever could've imagined. Even the website and the brochures didn't prepare me for this.

"Holy crap," I whisper, looking up at the chandelier above our heads. It's clearly new, but designed with the time period of the building in mind, little flame-shaped bulbs where candles would've stood once upon a time. Instead of desks, there are three tables set in a U-shape, their mahogany surfaces gleaming.

Ms. Felton sits in the center at a small, but ornate desk of her own. Most of the chairs are already filled, and I realize that everyone's looking our way, waiting for us to sit. Miranda and I take hasty seats in the last two available spots, and I'm relieved that *she* is sitting next to that Gregory guy, and I'm not.

"Good morning everyone," Ms. Felton says, standing up and smoothing her hands down the front of her skirt suit. Politician. That's what I get when I look at her. That, or maybe lawyer. Lobbyist. Something of that sort. She looks far too smart, and far too cunning to be holed away at a private university in the middle of nowhere. "My name is Carrie-Anne Felton, and I'll be your homeroom teacher for the rest of the year." Plastering a smile on her face, she makes her way around the room. "This is your safe space, so to speak, in the world of academics, a place to feel grounded, to discuss problems—"

Ms. Felton pauses, and the entire room turns to look as the elevator opens, and a guy with razored mint green hair appears, the sleeves of his crisp, white shirt pushed up, his muscular forearms covered in tattoos. My eyes widen and my heart skips several beats as he steps into the room like he owns the place.

"Sorry I'm late, Carrie-Anne," he says, green eyes sweeping the room and coming to rest on me. Pretty sure I'm the only person in this room he doesn't recognize. He surveys me for a moment, and then flicks his attention back to our teacher. "No seat for me?"

"It seems we're short one chair," Ms. Felton says, checking the iPad in her arms. "We have one more student than originally planned …"

"Get up, Charity," Tristan whispers, leaning over and focusing quite clearly on me. "You're the one who's attending for free. Zayd's family actually pays for him to go here. Don't you think he deserves a chair?"

My cheeks heat up with anger, but I don't move from where I'm sitting. I'd rather die. Little do I know in that moment, the Idols will try their hardest to achieve that end.

"I think if Burberry Prep can afford elevators, it can afford an extra chair." My voice is quiet, but firm. Miranda makes a small, helpless sound from beside me, and Tristan sits up, lifting his chin like I've just seriously pissed him off.

"It's not a matter of affording chairs," Ms. Felton interrupts, misreading the situation and waving her hand dismissively. "This is a small room, and we didn't want more furniture than necessary. I'll have the maintenance staff bring another up. Mr. Kaiser, seeing as you're the only person who refused to show up on time, you can stand for the time being."

Filthy Rich Boys

"My *pleasure*, Ms. Felton," he purrs, swaggering over to the window and propping himself on one of the wide, stone sills. His eyes go half-lidded, and he looks the teacher up and down appreciatively. "Anything for you." Most of the students chuckle, but I can't seem to stop studying this guy. Colored hair is expressly prohibited in the student dress code, and here this guy is with mint green hair, piercings in his lips and brow, and arms covered in tattoos.

"Zayd's agent got him some special working contract," Miranda whispers, reading my mind. "Like, he has to maintain a certain look for his career. That, and it's rumored this his agent, Bob Rosenberg, is fucking Vice Principal Castor." My mouth twitches at the corner, but I'm not surprised. Nothing at this school could surprise me at this point.

"And what's his career?" I ask, casting another glance in Zayd's direction. He's easy on the eyes, that's for sure. My stomach twists into a little knot, and I bite my lower lip.

"Rock star." Miranda grins when I give her a questioning look. "Lead singer of the band Afterglow. They're kind of a big deal; they had over a hundred thousand downloads of their debut album last year, and like a hundred million streams."

Ms. Felton gives Zayd a narrow-eyed look, like she's used to this sort of bullshit from entitled teens, and goes back to her speech, telling us all how we should be able to speak freely in here, how there are no limits to the discussions we can have, and so on and so forth. Pretty sure I'm the only person listening, and when the bell in the chapel sounds, I'm also the last one out.

Except for Zayd Kaiser.

"You," he says, like he expects me to leap at his beck and call. "You're new here?"

"This is Marnye Reed," Miranda says, beaming happily and gesturing at me like I'm her newest, greatest find. I think she senses a possible Idol ally for me, but ... I don't think so. The way Zayd's looking at me, like I'm a piece of meat he might use and throw away, I'm pretty sure she's dead-wrong. I have a way of reading people. Been doing it my whole life. Back at LBH, it could literally be the difference between life and death. At the end of last year, one of the freshmen was *murdered* by two seniors.

"Marnye Reed," Zayd starts, his voice this husky purr that gets under your skin in the best possible way. He taps an inked finger against his mouth for a moment, and then snaps his fingers. "Right. A few of the others texted me about you this morning, before the great phone purge." He crinkles his brow and then flicks at one of his silver lip rings with a tattooed finger. "What they're saying about you, it's just not right." My mouth pops open, and I feel the briefest inkling of relief. Maybe I don't have to be in a feud with every popular kid on campus. "They're calling you the Working Girl, but they're also saying you're not fuckable."

"Excuse me?" I choke, but Zayd's already smiling at me with sharp, sharp lips, like a razorblade threatening to cut. His hair is spiked up, his shirt mussed, and half his buttons are undone. I can see another tattoo lingering on the fine planes of his chest.

"What I'm saying is, you can't be a Working Girl *and* an

Filthy Rich Boys

unfuckable virgin all at once." Zayd leans in close to me, close enough that I can smell cloves and tobacco on his skin. Maybe he thinks smoking clove cigarettes makes him a badass. It doesn't. All it does is make him look like a douche. "And really," he reaches out to tease some of the loose hair hanging by my face. "I'd fuck you, if you were game." Zayd grins at me, but it's not a kind expression. It's derisive, mocking, demeaning. "That's the best offer you'll get all year, so I suggest you take it."

"Why don't you go to hell?" I blurt back, my cheeks flushed, my head swimming. How is this happening? I haven't even had my first class yet, and I've already been put through the wringer. I'm *exhausted*. I wonder how long it'll take them to get tired of picking on me. Maybe never. In middle school, they didn't get tired until … Zack changed things.

"Last chance, Working Girl." Zayd leans in even closer and puts his mouth near my ear. "I'll even pay you for your services: whatever the fee is, I can afford it."

Without thinking, I lift a hand, intending to slap him in the face. Zayd intercepts the motion, giving my wrist a squeeze before smirking and stepping back. He releases me, but not before looking me up and down with a dark glimmer in his green eyes.

"You're going to regret that move," he tells me, and I'm so flustered that I can't seem to come up with a response.

Me? Regret this moment? The only person who's going to regret anything today is Zayd Kaiser when I report him to the school administration.

"It's not worth it," Miranda whispers, putting her arm

through mine. "Come on, let's go to class and hopefully by the end of the day, they'll forget about tormenting you."

With a nod, I follow along behind her. My eyes are stinging with tears, but I won't shed them.

I refuse to give these guys the satisfaction.

By the time lunch rolls around, Miranda's done some recon, sliding into the seat across from me and picking up the menu from her plate. And yes, I said it: menu. The 'cafeteria' is set up like a restaurant with servers and busboys, tables set with plates and cloth napkins, small menus printed on cardstock that make me think of two birthdays ago when Dad splurged and took me to a fancy restaurant for dinner.

My mind is racing, and I feel cold all over, like I'm so far out of my element I may never get warm again.

"It's bad, Marnye," she says, sighing and then pausing to place her order with our waiter. Me, I've already got a plate of *souvlaki chicken with roasted lemon potatoes topped with feta.* Frankly, I don't know what half of those things are. Back home, we have sloppy joes, burgers, and hot dogs. That's dinner at the Train Car with Dad. "It's really, really bad."

"What's bad?" I ask, wondering how my day can get any worse. I came into Burberry Prep this morning with high hopes, ready to take on the world. Right now, I feel like I'm living a social apocalypse.

Filthy Rich Boys

"The Idols, they've declared war on you." My mouth pops open, but I'm not really sure what to say to that. How do you respond when someone tells you the richest, most popular kids at your school want you socially killed?

"All of them?" I ask, glancing over at the large table in the corner where Tristan, Creed, and Zayd sit next to Harper, Becky, and a girl who I can only assume is Gena Whitley. They aren't looking at me. Instead, they're laughing and eating, drawing all of the energy out of the room. I have to admit, they've got charisma, all six of them. Then again, Hitler had charisma, too, and look how that turned out.

"All of them," Miranda confirms, lifting her glass of ice water to her lips and glancing at the round table and all of its royalty. "They don't want you here."

"Why?" I ask, but I needn't have bothered. Miranda glances at me, but her face says it all: they don't want me here because I grew up in a neighborhood of trailers and mobile homes, because I lived in an old train car most of my life, because I don't have a net worth or a family legacy. "What am I supposed to do about that? I was thinking about reporting Tristan and Zayd to the administration. There's an anti-bullying policy that I read about in the student handbook—"

Miranda's look stops me dead in my tracks.

"What?" I ask, picking up my fork and poking at my fancy Greek-inspired chicken dish. It tastes ... strange. Maybe my palette just isn't as refined as everyone else's? I wonder if I could ask the kitchen to make me a peanut butter and jelly sandwich? "Am I supposed to just let them get away with their bullshit?" My eyes wander back to the table again and I catch Creed staring at me. His blue eyes narrow, and he reaches up to brush some blond hair back from his forehead. If it's possible to arrogantly brush hair from one's face, he manages it. Zayd and Tristan notice him looking my way, and soon all three Idols are glaring at me.

Fantastic.

At my old school, I saw the effects of bullying firsthand; I felt them. I felt them in ways I can never forget, never erase. My heart begins to thunder in my chest, and my palms grow so sweaty I have to put down my fork.

I glance back at Miranda.

"If you report them, that's it," she says, exhaling sharply. Her eyes stray over to the Idols' table again, watching as Andrew approaches and starts up a conversation with Tristan. "They will end you."

My mouth flattens into a thin line, but I don't doubt that what Miranda's telling me is true. These kids, they have more money than the GDP of a small country. Shit, than several small countries *combined.* If I think that has no influence over the administration and staff, then I haven't learned as many hard life lessons as I think.

Closing my eyes, I sit stone-still for a moment, thinking. There has to be a way out of this; there's always a way out if you know how to be patient and look. For the moment, I'm drawing a blank, but give me time, and I'll work it out.

There's a reason I got chosen for this scholarship, and it wasn't my ability to roll over and take it.

No, I'm a fighter, always have been.

Filthy Rich Boys

I just think I'm going to have to fight harder than I ever have before.

CHAPTER

4

As my first week at Burberry Prep progresses, it seems like the Idols have forgotten about me.

I know in my gut that's not true.

Bullies don't quit until circumstances force them to. It's the nature of the beast, and humans are the worst animal of all. Smart enough to manipulate, stupid enough to care. My mind flickers with images best left forgotten: ribbons of silken red, the smell of wet pennies, peaceful blackness closing in.

Running my tongue across my lower lip, I double check my schedule. The first and third Friday of the month I have my Monday schedule; the second and fourth Friday I have my Tuesday schedule. The last Friday—if there is one—is a day

Filthy Rich Boys

off.

Period 3: Government, History, and Civics, Room CH3

The *CH* in *CH3* stands for chapel, meaning the classrooms located in the building attached to the old chapel. Miranda disappeared during the second half of lunch, but I think I know my way around now. Following the maze of hallways, I slip unnoticed by the other students—the *Plebs*, as they're supposedly called—enjoying my anonymity. Only the Idols and their Inner Circle look at me sideways. Nobody else cares.

I pass unscathed into the classroom, breathing a sigh of relief as I slide into the chair in the back corner. Tristan Vanderbilt is the only member of the Bluebloods—their term, not mine—that shares this class with me and Miranda. He glances up when I walk in, his blade gray eyes slicing through me before he returns his attention to the short, raven-haired girl in front of him.

In the past week, I've seen him with a good dozen different girls, flirting and smiling and leaning in close. Even when the guy's trying to get laid, that arrogance of his sits like a mask over his handsome face. He never seems to let his guard down, or show any emotion that isn't tainted with superiority and entitlement.

Just looking at the jerk makes me sick to my stomach.

"Sorry I'm late," Miranda breathes, sliding into the chair next to me. Her eyes flick up to Tristan, and he meets her gaze dead-on before returning his attention back to his newest conquest. Miranda's cheeks burn pink, and I raise an eyebrow.

"Don't apologize. You've sat with me during every class

and every lunch period for the entire week. You're not going to get, like, put on probation by the Bluebloods for that, are you?"

Miranda pulls her iPad out of her bag and sets it on the desk. The tech policy here is crazy strict, so all the laptops and tablets are school-issued and locked down on a private network. It's insane. I miss my phone like crazy, but today after school, I get it back for the weekend.

Even a digital escape from Burberry Prep sounds like heaven right about now.

"No. I mean, I don't think so since Creed is my brother …" Miranda trails off, and exhales, swiping her hand across her forehead before tossing a genuine smile my way. "I know he's been a royal prick to you, but he's pretty overprotective when it comes to me. Once, back in middle school, this guy stood me up for a date, and Creed held me while I cried. After I fell asleep though, he went over to the boy's house and punched him." Her smile gets a little wider, and I smile back.

That is, until I realize that Tristan's standing directly in front of my desk, this enormous shadow collapsing the good-natured humor of the moment. I glare up at him in challenge. I'm not afraid of anyone, not even billionaire boys like Tristan Vanderbilt.

"Party tonight, Mandy," he says, his face a cold, cruel mask. "You gonna be there?"

"Is Marnye invited?" Miranda echoes, and although I appreciate her trying to stand up for me, I cringe on the inside. Tristan lets his eyes swing over to me, his gaze darkening with distaste. He really and truly seems to hate me,

Filthy Rich Boys

and I can't seem to figure out why.

"There'll be enough willing girls at the party; we don't need Working Girls there, too." His delivery is ice-cold, and somehow, that makes his hatred of me even worse. It's a cold, empty loathing that settles across my skin like salty fog off a quiet sea.

"She's my friend, Tristan," Miranda says, but he's already turning away, dismissing the conversation before it's even begun. With a sigh, she turns back to me. "If you want to go to the party, Marnye, we'll find a way to make it work."

"I don't think I want to," I say, watching Tristan's back as he makes his way over to the dark-haired girl again. "Go, I mean. I don't want to go." My eyes flick over to Miranda, watching as she settles into her seat with her iPad on her lap. "Watching that guy hit on every available girl at the party, not my thing."

"The parties here are epic though," Miranda says, lifting her eyes up from the screen as our professor calls for the class' attention. She's talking to me, but she's distracted. I may not have known her for long, but I can already tell. "You can't go through your entire high school career without going to any. I'll talk to Creed after class."

I open my mouth to tell her not to bother, but class has already started, and if there's one thing I do know about my career at Burberry Prep, it's that my grades are more important than any party, any bullshit from entitled rich boys. But if Miranda wants to try to get me in, I'll go, if only for the experience.

And what an experience it turns out to be.

C.M. Stunich

My new apartment is located on the bottom floor of the chapel building, as opposed to Tower Three like all the rest of the students. While they enjoy penthouses and sprawling studios with views of the ocean, I'm placed in the old janitor's quarters. Doesn't bother me. Honestly, the one bedroom, one bath space is twice as large as the Train Car back home.

"Spoiled rich brats," I mumble, flopping onto the edge of my bed and putting my face in my hands. Walking these halls is like running a gauntlet; I've never been so exhausted in all my life. "I would've been fine with a regular sized dorm." Throwing my arm across my eyes, I take a breather before sitting up and turning my phone on.

Every Friday after third period, the entire student body gets their phones backs. Until then, phones are banned on campus. If anyone needs to make a call, they're required to check in with the vice principal. Burberry Prep is hardcore. Supposedly, taking away technology helps students focus on their studies and cuts down on bullying. I'd say sure on the first premise ... and most definitely not on the second.

Sitting up, I cast a glance around my new apartment. All the furniture, including the bed, was purchased via the scholarship fund, and while I'm sure it's a far cry from what my fellow students have in their rooms, it looks like luxury to me.

Filthy Rich Boys

My headboard's almost as tall as the ceiling, this lavishly tufted white velvet arch with crystal sconces on either side. It sets the tone for the whole room, this effortless elegance in creams and grays, draped across the ancient stone floors and walls with an expert's touch.

"Okay, Dad, let's see how much trouble you've managed to get yourself into during the week." Powering my phone on, I do a brief check of my email, texts, and social media, but there's not much to see. A few goodbyes, and greetings from casual acquaintances, but nothing substantial. I haven't had any real friends since …

No. Banish that thought. I'm not interested in entertaining shadows of the past, not when I have a fairly grim present to deal with.

I dial up my voicemail and wait, smiling when my dad's voice comes over the line.

"Hey Marnye, it's Dad"—as if I didn't know—*"I just wanted to see how things were going at your new school."* He pauses, and I tense up, wondering if his voice sounds warbled, wondering if he's drunk again. *"I bet you're making all sorts of friends. I just hope you don't have a boyfriend yet, though I'm sure you've already gotten offers."* He chuckles, but I frown. Offers? Not so much. Being called a Working Girl and offered money for sex? Yeah, there's that. *"I'm already looking forward to Parents' Weekend. Until then, keep me in your thoughts. Love you, bye."*

I'm feeling pretty good about leaving Dad alone until I realize that's the only message he's left me. Just one voicemail, no texts, no social media tags. My mouth purses into a thin line as I dial our home number and wait. Nothing.

If he's fallen back into old habits, Dad'll be at the bar on Chambers. But that's worst-case scenario. I shoot a text over to our old neighbor, Mrs. Fleming, to see if his car's in the driveway. She's practically deaf, so she's the only ninety-seven year old I know of that exclusively uses text messages for communication. She's also an incorrigible gossip, a Supernatural superfan, and the head of the local neighborhood watch.

When she doesn't text back right away, I figure she's probably on one of her Sam and Dean binge sessions, and head over to my new wardrobe in the corner, this towering antique piece with fleur-de-lis designs carved into the decorative arch on the top. Opening it, I get a sharp stab from the blade of reality.

During school hours, everyone wears their uniforms.

At a weekend party, nobody will be wearing them, and my twenty dollar Target dress will stand out like a sore thumb. That is, if Miranda even finds a way to get me an invite.

As I'm thumbing through my meager collection of thrift store, Walmart, and garage sale finds, there's a knock at the door. With no small amount of caution, I move over to open it. If it's anyone but Miranda, I'm leaving it bolted.

But when I peek through the peephole, I find Miranda grinning and waving, holding a dress in one arm and a shoebox in the other. I open it, and she bounces in, grinning from ear to ear.

"I got them to agree," she says, breathless from sprinting over here from her shared apartment with Creed. They have a two bedroom with a balcony that Miranda promises I can see

Filthy Rich Boys

someday, but which I don't think I ever will seeing as her brother hates my guts. "Well, I got Creed to agree, and that's all we need."

"Wow," I say as she tosses the dress on the bed, and I see that it's an expensive, tight-fitting little black number that I wouldn't be caught dead in. I'm sure Miranda will have no trouble pulling it off though. "Your brother really does have a soft spot for you, doesn't he?"

"He'll have a soft spot for you, too, when he sees you in this dress," she says, smirking and popping out a hip. For a moment, the expression reminds me of her twin, and I get goose bumps. "And these shoes." Miranda points a long, shiny fingernail at the box.

I can't miss the label printed on the top.

"Manolo Blahnik?" I choke out, and then my eyes flick to the dress again. "And I don't care what designer made that dress; I won't fit into it."

Miranda rolls her eyes like I'm a crazy person, and then slides a bottle of champagne out from under the dress that I didn't see before. "You're being too hard on yourself. Let me dress you up while we pre-drink, and we'll have an epic party. This is the first weekend of our freshmen year; we have to live this up." She pops the champagne, and the cork flies up and hits the ceiling, making us both laugh. Me, with nervousness. Her, with her usual good cheer.

"So is Creed like the Yang to your Yin?" I ask as Miranda opens the clear plastic of the garment bag, revealing two little black dresses instead of one. And I'd thought there was little fabric to be had to begin with. Now there's even less.

"He's ... complicated," she starts as she moves into the

kitchenette, opening the frosted glass cabinet door and pulling out two crystal cups. There aren't any champagne flutes, but that's not particularly surprising considering we're several years off from being able to legally drink. "You can't let him get to you. He's just ... he's so concerned at being 'new money' that he overcompensates." Miranda pours a generous glass of champagne for each of us, handing one over to me.

If I get caught drinking, I could be kicked out of the academy—permanently.

At the same time, I don't want to spit on Miranda's goodwill. I wait for her to move into the bathroom and flick on the lights before I quickly empty my glass into the sink.

"They redid this whole place, huh?" she asks as I step in behind her, taking in the deep tub, the stand-up shower, and the windows overlooking the park-like courtyard behind the church. They each have a set of handy wooden blinds that block out all the light, but they're open now, showing off the dusky evening sky.

"This is basically a palace to me," I say with a smile, a flitter of nervous energy taking over my belly when I see the amount of makeup that Miranda's stuffed into her purse. She unloads it onto the burnished gold stone of the countertop, and then turns to look at me with a critical eye. "What?" I ask, suddenly wary, and Miranda grins at me.

"How do you feel about curls?" she asks, reaching out to play with my hair. I look past her and into the mirror, locked into my own brown-eyed gaze. My lips are too thin, my chin too pointed, my nose too big. At least those judgements are my own. The things they used to say to me back home rarely had anything to do with my appearance. Mostly, they attacked my character.

"Curls are great," I say, trying to force a smile. On the inside, I'm wondering if there's anything I could wear or do that would make a difference tonight. I imagine not. Because on the inside, I'll still be poor. At the end of the night, I still won't own a private jet or a series of islands in the fucking Caribbean. "Do whatever you want; I'm no good at hair or makeup."

Miranda lets out a small sound of excitement, downs her champagne, and pours us both another round.

I wish I could drink it.

I have a feeling I'm going to need it to get through tonight.

The walk down to the beach is easy, lined with solar-powered lanterns that give the winding, pebbled walkway a warm yellow glow. Picking my way down in the stilettos that Miranda brought me is no easy feat, and I'm sure I look like I'm already drunk by the time we get to the bonfire.

Doesn't matter, I suppose, since it looks like everyone else here already is.

"Mandy!" this redheaded girl calls out, waving her arms like she's on crack. At my old school, she might have been. Here ... she still could be. Instead, she stumbles over to Miranda with her heels hanging from one hand, the distinctive red bottoms of the Louboutins obvious even in the flickering orange light from the bonfire. The bottoms are scuffed and the shoes are wet and covered in sand. Without a second thought, the girl chucks them into a pile of other expensive designer shoes, like they're Walmart flip-flops or something. "I'm so glad you're here. Tristan was asking about you."

"Right," Miranda says, biting her bottom lip and glancing over at me. She seems nervous about something, but I'm not about to ask what it is with the redhead standing next to us. I know I'm supposed to know her name, but even though I've memorized the entire list of Bluebloods, I can't remember exactly which one she is. Inner Circle, for sure. Anna, maybe? Or Abigail? "I'll talk to him later. For now, point us in the direction of the drinks?"

The redhead is too drunk to care about me, or maybe she just doesn't recognize me with a headful of big, chocolate curls, and a designer dress. She points us over to a table that's been hastily piled with glass bottles and cups. There isn't any hired help here tonight, and it's starting to look like a rich teen party is much the same as a poor teen party, just with much better alcohol.

"I'll make us some drinks," Miranda says, dragging me toward the table by my wrist. She lets go and starts to put together some concoction while I stand there and fidget, my eyes searching the beach for potential predators. After all, I'm used to being hunted.

My borrowed outfit is far too tight and too short to be comfortable, and I find myself tugging the fabric down in the

Filthy Rich Boys

front. I don't feel right in it, like I'm playing the part of somebody else, somebody who wears bodycon dresses and Manolo Blahniks, and parties with the children of the ultra-wealthy.

"Wow. Looks like you've already taken my advice," a voice drawls from behind me, raspy and husky and sexy. The sound of it gives me chills in the best way possible, but when I turn around, I find Zayd Kaiser standing there in a pair of black swim shorts, sans shirt and shoes, his body ripped and muscular, all of those hard planes catching the red and orange light from the bonfire.

"I'm sorry, what?" I ask, my heart hammering as I take in his sea green hair and emerald eyes. He's got more tattoos than I thought, including that chest piece I glimpsed on Monday. It's hard to tell what it is in the half-light, but I'm not about to take a step closer and find out. Already, I'm on edge and waiting for an attack. If I were the Marnye Reed from middle school, I would probably crumble at just the sight of Zayd. His eyes are narrowed to slits, and his mouth is just a cruel slash on his face.

"You're dressed like a Working Girl now. Good for you. But I'd still like to get a price. How much for a fuck?" My cheeks heat, and my nostrils flare, but I'm not going to lose my cool, not over something so pointless. Still, I can't help the twisting anxiety in my stomach, the embarrassment creeping its way up the back of my neck.

"Having sports cars and private jets and mansions isn't enough? You have to add a little cruelty into the mix, too?" I ask, but Zayd's already circling me, his eyes taking in my every curve. My dress feels too short, too tight, the neckline too low, but I stand there with my back straight, waiting for him to lose interest and go the hell away. I'm stronger now, because of what I've been through, but I'm not invincible. I still want to believe there's good in the world. Zayd is working really damn hard to make sure that I change my mind about that.

He smiles at me, stepping so close that I can smell the salt on his skin, see the hickeys on his neck.

"Why are you still here? We've been nice this week, but it won't last. Starting Monday, you're going to be really sorry you haven't gone crawling back to whatever shithole suburb you crawled out of."

"Zayd, screw off," Miranda says, appearing at my side before I can respond. I'm so mad, maybe that's for the best. Who knows what might escape my mouth right now. "Creed invited her tonight."

"Did he, really?" Zayd asks, and if possible, his scowl gets even more intense. His green eyes lock with mine, but I refuse to look away. At the very least, I can do this, hold his gaze. "Idiot. He's going to get himself in trouble trying to appease your every whim." Zayd pauses as several busty brunettes hop up to him, grabbing him by his surprisingly muscular arms. "Fine. Keep your pet peasant for the night. Just remember: there's a class system for a reason. Some people belong on the bottom."

Zayd turns away with his two new girlfriends, smiling at them in a way that's not entirely different from the way he was smiling at me. He's just not a very good person.

"Forget him," Miranda says, shoving a Solo cup at me.

FILTHY RICH BOYS

Wow. Solo cups, the universal key to getting drunk, no matter what socio-economic class. "Have a drink, and let's go dip our feet in the water." She slips her designer heels off and chucks them next to the table, much the same way as that redheaded girl. Even Miranda, as nice as she is, has no idea the level of privilege she exists in. The price of those shoes could feed and house a family in Lower Banks for an entire month. Maybe more. No, no, definitely more.

Forcing a smile to my face, I follow after her, noticing that Creed is lounging in the sand near the bonfire with a captive audience. His eyes meet mine from across the beach, but there's no hatred there. There's not even *acknowledgement.* Like, I'm so far below him, he doesn't even feel the need to admit to my existence.

At least I don't see Tristan anywhere, I think, exhaling a small sigh of relief. Unfortunately, that relief doesn't last long because Harper, Becky, and Gena are watching us, *topless.* Yep. Standing topless in the waves and studying us with eyes that glitter like obsidian in the dark. I pretend to lift my drink to my lips, so I can have a moment of staring into the cup instead of their eyes.

"Try to enjoy yourself tonight," Miranda says, giving me a friendly elbow bump as we walk along the wet sand and away from the Idol girls. Idols. What a pretentious title. Who started *that* tradition, I wonder. "Creed said you could be here; they'll leave you alone for now."

Miranda's really trying, so I force myself to stay positive.

"Thank you, and you're right. This is the first party of the year. And really, it's beautiful out here." I wait for her to turn away and then pour my drink out in the water, enjoying the surprisingly warm waves and the moonlight on the horizon.

We spend most of the night chatting and walking along the shore, a little bit of it dancing next to the bonfire. After a little while, Andrew joins us, and even though he's in the Inner Circle and supposed to treat me like I've got the plague, he dances with Miranda and me both, until we're sweaty and laughing, and I've forgotten that my dress keeps riding up my ass crack.

Close to midnight we make our way back to the school, and Miranda and I part with a hug outside the chapel. It's easier for her to get back to Tower Three by taking the path that winds between the buildings. So, with my borrowed shoes in hand, I make my way barefoot down the stone halls, only to pause when I see Ms. Felton and the Vice Principal, Mr. Castor, standing in front of my door.

"Marnye," he says, voice and face grim. "We need to have a serious talk with you."

"What? Why?" I ask, seeing my dreams at Burberry Prep go up in smoke before they've even really begun. I can't go back to Lower Banks High with its crumbling gymnasium, dinosaur-age computers, and outdated textbooks. Not after I worked so freaking hard to be here.

"We had several people call the emergency line saying they'd seen you drinking heavily." My mouth pops open, and this wave of injustice surges through me. What the hell?! Me, drinking? I was the only person *not* drunk at that party.

Wow.

So ... it's not cool for me to report Zayd and Tristan to the administration, but they can report me all they want?

Filthy Rich Boys

"I ..." Words escape me. I'm so blown away by the accusation that I have no idea how to respond. Crude laugher sounds at the end of the hall, and I turn to see a group of students watching me, still dressed in their bathing suits. Creed is among them, leaning against the wall in a deceptively casual pose, but it's all there in his eyes: the reflection of my doom.

I turn back to Ms. Felton and Mr. Castor. In the vice principal's hand, I see a device that I well recognize: it's a breathalyzer. Because of my dad's issues, I know them well. He used to have to breathe into one to start his car. There were a lot of mornings when I was in elementary school where it didn't start at all. I love my dad, but he spent a lot of my life fucking things up for both of us.

"I'm going to have to ask you to breathe into this," Mr. Castor says, his voice hard but not unkind. Ms. Felton doesn't say anything, arms crossed over her suit. I'm surprised to see her all dressed up still, considering the hour. Mr. Castor's wearing gray sweats and a clean but oversized white tee.

My eyes water so bad that I have to close them to keep the tears from falling. It may not seem like that big of a deal. I mean, just breathe in and show the world that I'm not drunk. But ... I'm doing everything I can to *not* end up like my mom and dad. There was this one time when I was seven that both my parents were so drunk that I thought they were dead, lying comatose on the carpet in the Train Car. We didn't have a phone at the time, so I walked almost two miles to the convenience store to ask the clerk to call 911.

Being accused like this ... it's devastating.

I nod, and Mr. Castor hands over the breathalyzer, waiting

for me to exhale into it.

When I'm done, I hand it back to him and he watches the lights on the front side. Zero. My blood alcohol level is zero. Mr. Castor's face flushes, and he hands the breathalyzer over to Ms. Felton.

"I'm sorry, Marnye, but with as many accusations as we received, we had to look into it." I nod and glance back down the hallway to see Creed staring at me with slightly widened eyes. The other students are whispering behind their hands, eyes narrowed to slits, venom in their glares. But Creed, he looks *pissed*, like I've committed a grievous personal attack against him.

I turn back to the teachers and force a smile.

"It's no problem," I say, and then I use my key to let myself into the apartment … and cry.

CHAPTER 5

By the time Monday rolls around again, I'm thoroughly exhausted. I spent all weekend trying to get a hold of my dad, and fending off Miranda's attempts to get me to go out again. Instead, I convinced her to stay in on Saturday and watch movies. Sunday, she texted to let me know that she wasn't feeling well and wanted to sleep in.

But even as I'm looking for trouble around every corner, nothing comes.

That's a form of mental torture right there, expecting all these horrible things, a low-grade anxiety humming through me. The classes, at least, are challenging, more so than I expected. I end up spending most every night that week in the five story library, studying my ass off. The librarians are pretty much book Nazis, so I feel safe in there. Even the Idols can't touch me in their domain.

Thursday, I scoot into my seat in art class, right next to

Miranda, feeling my heart thunder in my chest. Our assignment from last week was to create an abstract piece of media that represented our favorite painting, song, book, poem, or dance. Thinking creatively doesn't come easily to me. You'd think growing up the way I did that I would've wanted to escape into a made-up world. While I was an avid reader, I was also overly practical. As much as I enjoy a good novel or movie or game, I also knew that the only way to change my situation was to fight in the real world. Banishing dragons with magic blades is great, but it wouldn't get me out of Lower Banks. It wouldn't get me into a good college. It wouldn't get me a high-paying job.

So I really struggled with the assignment, settling on J.K. Rowling's *The Tales of Beedle the Bard* as my inspiration. One of my favorite childhood memories is of sitting on my bed with both Mom and Dad, neither of them drunk, taking turns reading that book to me. No matter how horrible things got, I had that moment to hold onto.

We don't just have one art teacher at Burberry Prep, we have *three*. They each have their own specialties, and their impressive lists of accomplishments and awards. I've decided I like Mrs. Amberton best. The way her eyes sparkle when she talks about creative writing makes me wish I could find my own passion. I mean, I did okay with my scholarship essay, but that was all real pain pouring out of me, my entire life story in similes and metaphors. It was so personal that when I wrote it, I cried the whole time. Knowing Miranda's read it, too, is a weird feeling, but even though we haven't known each other long, I trust her.

Filthy Rich Boys

Maybe that's a mistake, but … it's mine to make, I guess.

"Public speaking can be an art, in and of itself," Ms. Highland says, her dark hair pulled back in a severe bun. Her clothes are playful, but her glasses, makeup, and hairdos are anything but. It makes me wonder what's going on inside of her, that she should be so controlled and so open all at the same time. "And it's important in most anything you might think to do with your future. So for today, you'll be presenting your projects in front of the class—in random order."

There's a chorus of groans, and I feel my heart start to pound. Presenting to an audience, I'm okay with. Presenting to Harper, Becky, Zayd, and Tristan … not so much. The four of them sit in the back of the class, not quite together but not far apart either. I'm getting the idea that the three Idol boys don't much like each other.

Mr. Carter uses his iPad to select a student from the class to go first.

And, because I have the worst luck known to man, that student ends up being me.

"Marnye Reed," he calls, and I let out a sharp breath. I can feel the eyes of every student in that room swing toward me. It's not a good feeling.

"Let's go Working Girl!" one of the girls shouts, and cruel laughter breaks out around the room. I ignore it, taking my art up to the front of the multi-tiered lecture hall. I decided on resin and acrylic, creating this mirror like surface of rainbow colors on the square canvas.

"Miss Fanning, that's quite enough, thank you," Mrs. Amberton says, her voice hardening. It's the first time I've ever heard her snap quite like that, and I hold back a small smile. It's nice to feel like I have a member of staff on my side. "Beautiful piece," she adds, moving to the side to give me the stage. I return her genuine smile and prop the art on the waiting easel.

"You fucking suck!" some guy shouts, but I ignore him. If there's anything I'm good at, it's school. This is where I shine. If I could, I'd be a professional student for the rest of my life. Taking a deep breath, I turn and face the class. My eyes catch on Tristan's gray glare and sharp frown before sliding over to Zayd's emerald green irises and derisive smirk. *I won't let anyone beat me down, not ever again.*

"My inspiration for this piece comes from J.K. Rowling's *The Tales of Beedle the Bard*," I start, projecting my voice toward the audience. I had to do this to win the Cabot Scholarship Award, too, give a speech. What makes this any different? The thing is, I'm definitely not going to be spilling my guts to the Burberry Prep students. No way in hell. "As a child, it was not only my favorite book, but it also gave me my favorite memory. That's something I'll forever be grateful for." Pausing, I run my fingers over the shiny surface of the canvas, marveling at the colors. It wasn't easy to get the effect I was looking for, this rainbow balayage that fades from violet at the top to red at the bottom.

"Isn't that a faggot flag?" the asshole guy asks, the one who shouted at me. "Did you make a frigging Pride flag for art?" The laughter that follows his statement is dark and threaded with violence, a sound that's echoed in the chuckles of those around him. Zayd and Tristan aren't laughing, but

Filthy Rich Boys

they seem to be enjoying my pain, letting their followers do the dirty work for them.

"Mr. Hannibal, would you like to go to the office with me and discuss your treatment of LGBTQ individuals?" Mrs. Amberton's lips are pursed, and the way she looks at John Hannibal is less than pleasant. He's in the Inner Circle, that much I have memorized. Know thy enemies and all that.

"Go ahead and take me in. You know my father's stance on that stuff." Mrs. Amberton frowns, but she doesn't say anything else. I decide then that even if I do like her, she isn't strong enough to protect me in here. John Hannibal's father is a conservative senator from Tennessee, and built his platform on keeping gay marriage off the books in his state. Of course, that's null and void now with the Supreme Court ruling, but I'd bet my life that his views have remained much the same.

"The warm memories from that time in my life have filtered through a child's mind and turned into a prism of color," I continue, feeling my palms start to get sweaty. I can feel the eyes of the Idols on me, especially Tristan and Zayd. The latter has one brow raised, his tattooed fingers tapping a rhythm out on the arm of his seat. The former ... he's got a slight quirk to one edge of his mouth now, like he's just thought of something horrible to do to me. "Turning the words of that book, and the memories of that time, into a piece of dynamic art was a cathartic experience. I lived my best childhood memories with each and every stroke."

"That's what she said," Harper purrs, and the class erupts with laughter.

Mrs. Amberton sighs heavily, but none of the teachers does a damn thing.

Classism holds sway in every corner of the world, I guess. Not even art and academics are safe.

"Thank you," I say, leaving my piece on the stage and heading back to my seat. Nobody claps for me except Miranda and the teachers, all the more humiliating for the way it echoes in the giant lecture hall. Mr. Carter moves my piece aside, and calls the next name on his list.

On my way back up the steps to my seat, someone puts their foot in the aisle and trips me. I go down so hard that my chin slams on the floor and my mouth fills with blood.

I spend the rest of the day in the nurse's office with a migraine.

When I get back to my dorm later on that afternoon, there's a bunch of rainbow flags taped to my door, and a lesbian porno Blu-ray on the floor. I pick it up with a sigh, and pull all but the biggest flag down, leaving it to hang proudly on my door. I'm as straight as they come, but I'm also a fierce ally. I have no problem letting my Pride flag fly.

The rest of the flags, I tuck into my nightstand drawer for safe keeping.

If the students at Burberry Prep want to break me, they'll have to try much, much harder than that.

"This week wasn't so bad, right?" Miranda asks, sitting on the edge of the table in the library and kicking her legs. Her skirt is so short today that I can see that she's wearing a garter

Filthy Rich Boys

belt and thigh-highs instead of just tights like I'd thought. I wonder about that, but I don't feel like we're good enough friends to ask. A part of me thinks she might be dating Tristan Vanderbilt, but it's such a horrible thought that I don't want to put words to it.

"If you call opening my locker and having rainbow condoms spill out not that bad, then you're right: it wasn't." I lean in close to my laptop, and squint at the screen, like I'm super focused on the essay I'm writing for government. Really, I'm distracted as can be. While everyone else is excited that it's Friday again, I'm dreading getting an invite from Miranda to attend whatever party happens to be on.

She doesn't say anything, sipping an iced coffee that she swiped from the teacher's lounge.

"Evening ladies," Andrew says, pausing next to our table. His eyes land on mine and hold there, a smile taking over his mouth. I swallow hard and pretend to be so engrossed in my work that I can barely look away. *Lie.* I like the way he's staring at me, like he might actually be interested. "What are you two up to tonight?"

Miranda adjusts her skirt to cover the straps of her garter belt, raising an eyebrow at his question.

"If you're fishing and trying to find out whether we're attending Tristan's party, the answer is … it's up to Marnye." Ah. So it's Tristan's party tonight. Based on the gossip Miranda's been feeding me, the bonfire thing was Zayd's idea. Guess it's true that the three Idol boys don't get along all that well. They take turns entertaining their loyal subjects.

"It's on his father's yacht," Andrew adds with a shrug of his shoulders, like having a weekend party on a yacht is no big thing. "Since it's parked in the harbor behind the school, we don't even need off-campus permits to go." I lift my eyes to meet his again, a sparkling blue that matches his smile. When he lifts his fingers up and runs them through his chestnut hair, I almost smile for real. Andrew Payson really is pretty cute. "If you don't have a date already, Marnye, I'd love to take you. If you're with me, the others won't bother you."

"As much as I appreciate the offer, I don't think my presence there would be appreciated." Just the *idea* of lounging on Tristan's yacht makes me sick to my stomach. I gather up my books, and rise to my feet. I'd rather walk back to my room with Miranda than risk going alone. Zayd promised me pain this week, and I have yet to see much of it.

I imagine he's just waiting for the right time.

"If you're with me and Miranda," Andrew starts, but I give him a look and he raises his hands in surrender. "Promise: by the time we get there, Zayd will be too drunk to mess with you. Tristan will be on the top deck, surrounded by girls. And Creed ..." He glances over at Miranda and she gives me a sympathetic look. She knows what he did to me; everyone does. "We'll just stick to drinking soda, and dancing. What do you say?" Andrew grins with those pearly whites of his, but all I really want to do is go back to my room and see if I can get ahold of my dad. I'm starting to get worried.

"Oh, come on, Marnye," Miranda pleads, putting her hands into a prayer position. "I'm not saying throw caution to the wind, but you're not going to let them win either, right?"

Filthy Rich Boys

Crap, she has a point. Sighing and nodding my head slightly sends Miranda into a squeal, and she wraps her arms around me, giving me a squeeze. "You won't regret this," she promises me, but I'm already certain that I will.

Tristan's yacht is like nothing I've ever seen before. It has several tiers of decks, some with furniture, one with a hot tub, another where students are already in the midst of drunken dancing. Miranda tells me that *The Idol* cost over a hundred million dollars to build custom, and my stomach feels sick with the level of excess. A hundred million dollars for a boat? It's like a floating freaking palace.

"And naming it *The Idol*?" I start as we walk across the grass toward the dock. "Is that because of Tristan?"

"Nah," Miranda says, giving me a sympathetic half-smile, "that's because his great-grandfather started the Idol tradition here at Burberry Prep. All the Vanderbilts have been Idols since."

Great.

So even Tristan's bullying has a legacy. That does not bode well for me.

There are so many people already on the boat and the dock that I wonder if there's going to be anything more than standing room. My palms are sweaty as I swipe them down the front of my jeans. Wearing a fancy dress to the last party didn't do me any good, so this time I'm dressed in my own clothes. At least when I'm dressed like this, I know how to act, how to respond.

"This is not a good idea," I groan as Andrew puts his arm through my left, and Miranda does the same on my right. They drag me through the crowd and onto the boat, locating a couch in the downstairs cabin that we can sit on. Drinks are passed around, but I don't touch a thing. Not that I'd planned to, but this time, I don't even pretend.

I was trying to fit in, and all it did was make me stand out. I think I'll stick to being myself for now.

Miranda's already on her second glass of champagne, but it looks like Andrew is willing to go total teetotaler with me. He sees me looking his way and smiles; I smile back and take a sip of my cherry Coke.

"So, are Idols supposed to date each other?" I ask as I see Harper du Pont leaning on some guy in a black t-shirt and ripped jeans that I'm damn near positive he bought pre-torn. I could recognize a pair of well-worn denim jeans anywhere, and those starched monstrosities are not it. "Because I sort of see them ... all over the place."

"Everybody knows year one is, like, the time to experiment," Miranda says, her eyes wandering around the room and lingering on Tristan for a minute. There it is again, her strange obsession with him. They have to be dating, or at least sleeping together. Something. "But everyone also knows that Harper and Tristan will get together at the end of the year."

"And why's that?" I ask, as Andrew adjusts himself on the cushions and leans back. He's still wearing his academy

Filthy Rich Boys

uniform, like several of the other guys. Most every girl in there is wearing a designer dress and heels of some sort. I think I might be the only one in jeans and sneakers.

"His family is old money, good breeding, flawless reputation." Miranda turns her ice-blue eyes over to me. For a moment there, I'm reminded of Creed, staring at me down the length of the hallway, and I get the chills. "Harper's grandfather is the one who brought the du Ponts into money, so relatively speaking, they're new on the scene." She smiles and answers the question I'm about to ask before I get a chance to voice it. "If we weren't the richest family in this school, Creed and I would be Plebs for sure." She waves her hand around dismissively, sloshing champagne onto her rhinestone studded nude dress. "Harper's family wants the prestige of the Vanderbilts, and the Vanderbilts want the du Ponts' money. It's just simple economics."

"How ... romantic," I hedge as my eyes wander back to Tristan, standing in the corner with his arms crossed over his chest. He's listening to some play-by-play from one of his friends, the edge of his lips curving up in a cocksure smile. His gray eyes turn my way, and I meet his gaze. It only lasts a second because a group of drunk girls stumbles between us, but it was enough. He knows I'm here.

"I'm going to get more champagne," Miranda declares, rising to her feet and stumbling a bit in her heels. I get the feeling she hasn't worn many pairs in the past. She flicks her blond hair over one shoulder, succeeding only in tangling it around her long nails, and I grin. Like I said, she's too nice to be able to hair flip properly.

"I'll grab some more soda, before Greg uses it all for his

rum and cokes," I mumble with a roll of my eyes. "You need anything?" Andrew shows off his nearly full cup, and I take off, weaving through the crowd and heading for the kitchenette in the back half of the room.

Creed is there, unfortunately, and his eyes narrow when he sees me.

"If it isn't the Working Girl," he drawls, his fingers curved around the top of his cup. He swishes the alcohol around inside as he watches me. "Come to work the party? There's a lot of money to be made here for a girl like you."

"Your sister brought me," I deadpan, grabbing a handful of ice from the bucket on the counter, and pouring soda over it. "If you have a problem with that, take it up with her."

"Miranda's always liked having pets," Creed says, pushing off the fridge with his shoulder and dislodging the blonde on his arm. She pouts at him and gives me a death glare, but I raise my eyebrows. *I assure you, you have nothing to worry about, sweetheart.* "She's too nice, always willing to overlook other people's flaws."

"Being poor is a flaw?" I ask, and Creed shrugs his shoulders. He's wearing his academy uniform, too, and in that same lazy, elegant style I recognized on day one. His entire persona is based around not caring, even though it's obvious to me that he cares. Oh, he cares a whole hell of a lot.

"I hear Tristan brought a special gift tonight," he continues, circling me like a predator would. I can feel it, too, the restrained violence in him. Creed Cabot really and truly hates me. I stay where I am, sipping my soda and watching him. My first instinct is to run, but where would I go? The

Filthy Rich Boys

crowd is thick around us, the heat from so many bodies cloying. He gets close to me, so close that his breath feathers against the back of my neck, and I stiffen up. "A gift, just for you, Working Girl."

"Are you okay?" Andrew appears on my left, pushing through the well-dressed crowd. Creed looks him up and down, gives an arrogant little smirk, and turns away. The students move out of his way, giving him a clear path to the door. "I was thinking maybe we could go, just me and you." I look over at Andrew and find him with a strained smile on his handsome face. One of my brows goes up. "We could walk on the beach instead."

"Are you trying to get me off this boat, after working so hard to get me here?" I ask, this knot in my stomach tightening. Dread washes over me, and I know for a fact that I'm about to get all the week's bullying in one, big dollop. At my old school, that would've meant getting my ass kicked behind the science building.

At Burberry Prep Academy, I have no idea what it means. And that scares the crap out of me.

"Let's just go for a walk or something," Andrew says, almost pleadingly, but then I notice the crowd is funneling out of the door and up the steps to the top deck. Even though I know I shouldn't, even though I know I'm going to regret this … I follow after. "Marnye, wait!"

Andrew chases after me, but I'm too far ahead, weaving between girls in Alexander McQueen and boys in Givenchy. It's like the crowd is parting for me, too, but for all the wrong reasons. Miranda's up top when I get there, red-faced and disheveled. She's looking at Tristan Vanderbilt with narrowed eyes.

"What's going on?" I choke out, and she startles, turning to look at me with wide eyes.

"Oh, look, Charity's here, everyone," Tristan says, and he doesn't bother to raise his voice. It's low, and dark, as cool as the fog rolling in across the bay. "I'm glad you could make it to the party tonight." His smile, when he gives it, is about as warm as the ice in my cup. His dark hair is smooth and shiny, falling across his forehead in a way that makes my stomach clench, but his silver eyes are about as inviting as his smile.

Zayd crows with laughter from the corner, a brunette snuggling up against his left side. He doesn't look at me, just tilts a bottle of what looks to be rum to his mouth and makes a joke about pirates that I can barely hear.

Tristan, meanwhile, is busy unwrapping something from a cloth bundle that's sitting on the edge of the railing. The breath of the crowd is hushed, their excitement subdued. Every now and again, a pair of eyes flicks my way, and I feel them burning into my skin like flames. When Tristan gets the wrappings undone, I see that he's got a book in his hand.

"Just don't ever say we don't listen when you talk," he continues, flipping the book around, so I can get a look at the cover. My heartrate picks up speed, and it's suddenly hard to breathe. Even without touching it, I can see what title he has in his hand. And even without asking, I know it's the real deal. "Do you know what this is, Charity?"

"One of the seven hand-written copies of *The Tales of Beedle the Bard* by J.K. Rowling," I whisper. I know I'm playing right into their hands right now, but I can't seem to

Filthy Rich Boys

help myself. There are only seven total copies of that book in the world. Six were given to friends and family, and one was auctioned off for a charity benefit.

Oh.

Oh no.

No, no, no.

"That's right: a rare edition of your *favorite* book, the one that inspired you to make such ... interesting art." Tristan cracks the book open and peers inside, licking a finger before turning the page. "We wanted to honor the working class, and by proxy *you*, so we all chipped in our weekly allowances and bought it." He lifts his gaze to mine and smirks, cruelty dripping from every pore. "Three hundred and sixty thousand pounds—roughly four hundred and seventy-five US dollars—and it was ours." He snaps the book closed and turns fully to face me, balancing it in one hand while he gets a lighter out with the other.

I'm shaking now, sweat pouring down the sides of my face. My cup falls to the deck, and I start to move forward. Someone holds me back, and at first I think it's Miranda trying to prevent a fight, but then I realize it's actually a pair of Harper's closest cronies. They twist their arms around mine as the king of the Idols lifts the lighter to the first open page. My eyes dart around looking for allies, but both Miranda and Andrew are being held back. Creed stands near them, looking as if this is a boring but necessary little chore.

"Please don't. That book is a modern classic. That's history in the making right there." My words are choked; I sound strangled. What else am I supposed to say? Please don't destroy a priceless artifact to torment me? There are other, less destructive ways. Trust me: I've been privy to a lot of them.

Tristan ignores me, letting the flames lick the edge of the page until it starts to smoke and burn. He sets the book on the edge of the railing, watching as it's slowly consumed, twisted into flakes of gray ash that scatter with the wind. Zayd saunters up beside it and lifts a white bottle of lighter fluid, making eye contact with me before he gives it a squeeze and sets the rest of the book up in a gush of heat.

Tears trail down my cheeks, but I've stopped struggling. It's too late now. The book is ruined.

The crowd cheers as Tristan shoves the flaming book over the edge and into the bay.

When he moves up close to me, it takes every ounce of strength I have not to scream.

"I told you, Charity. This isn't the school for you. Consider this your final warning."

He stalks off, and finally, the two girls relax their grips enough for me to tear away.

"Marnye, wait!" Miranda calls out as I shove my way through the snickering crowd, down the steps, and across the dock. I start running, and I don't stop until I'm safely back in my dorm.

Guess this is where I'll be spending the rest of the year, miserable and alone.

It's not a good feeling.

CHAPTER 6

For the next several weeks, it seems the Idols are content to watch and wait. But if they think they've beaten me that easily, they've got another thing coming. At Lower Banks Middle School, a stunt like that would've been met with closed fists and blood spatter. I'm not saying I'm going to start a full-on brawl with the Idols (surely the cowards would gang up on me, and I'd lose), but watching that book burn, while upsetting, was not the final nail in my coffin.

"Parents' Week starts on Monday," Miranda says, settling beside me in the 'cafeteria'. Not exactly the best descriptor for this place. That word denotes red plastic trays, pizza on paper plates, and long lines. This is … nicer than the nicest restaurant I've ever been to. The sign outside says *'Dining Area'*, but the students here just call it The Mess. "Are yours coming?"

I take a bite of my pasta, and try not to wonder how much this plate cost the scholarship fund.

"My dad should be here," I hedge, trying to decide how best to describe my mom. The full truth is too hard to say aloud; it cuts like a knife, and I'm already bleeding from the scene on the yacht. "My mom ... remarried and moved." *Yeah, across town. From the trailer park to a mansion.* "She lives in Grenadine Heights actually, with my sister."

"You have a sister?" Miranda asks, her glossy pink lips parting in surprise. "Would I know her?" I shrug my shoulders in response because the last thing I want to say is: *maybe, but I don't.* "And how did I not know you had a sister?" she continues when I stuff my mouth with more pasta.

As Miranda frowns at me, Andrew stops by our table and pulls up an extra chair. Pretty sure he and Miranda have been getting into trouble for hanging around with me, and yet, they still do. I'm starting to wonder if I might actually be making real friends with the pair of them.

"You have a sister?" he repeats as I sigh and swallow my food, picking up my water glass and staring at the clinking ice cubes.

"Her name's Isabella. But she's three years younger than us. She just started sixth grade at Grenadine Heights Middle School." I take a drink of my water and hope this story ends here. Now I'm kicking myself for bringing my mom up at all. See what I mean? I've already got that tight, sick feeling in my stomach.

"Isabella Carmichael?" Miranda asks, and I feel that tight feeling get even tighter, like a knot with a chokehold around my stomach. "Yeah, I remember her. I think I had her in one of my art groups, like when they pair older kids up with younger ones." She shrugs and raises a perfectly arched blond brow at me. "I still don't know how I've been friends with you for weeks and haven't heard about your sister."

"Maybe because I've never met her?" I blurt out, and both Andrew and Miranda share a look. Standing abruptly, I turn and slam into the firm body of Creed Cabot. He puts his hands on my shoulders, and my skin burns, even through the fabric of my black academy jacket. He scoots me back a space, and turns his attention to his sister.

My gaze lifts to his cold, cruel face, his porcelain skin and angelic hair. And those eyes of his, like chips of ice, blue but cold as winter. His heavy lidded expression makes him look bored and tired, like at any moment he might just lie down and take a nap like a cat.

"Tristan wanted me to talk to you about something," he says, his voice cocksure and drawling, like it'd be too much to speak up or enunciate. For a split-second, I think he's talking to me which is just stupid because, like, why would he be? He's staring at his sister, but he hasn't bothered to take a step back from me. We're so close that if I were to breathe in deep, my breasts would brush up against the slightly rumpled fabric of his white shirt. "Do you have a second? Or are you too busy giving charity to the working class?"

"I don't have anything to talk about with you," Miranda says, flicking a glance in Andrew's direction. He pretends not to notice, but I swear, there's something going on here that I'm not getting. It's bugging the crap out of me, but I'm afraid to ask. These two are the only ones in the whole school that I feel comfortable with, and I refuse to mess that up. "Not when you're treating Marnye like she doesn't exist."

"Oh, I'm aware she exists," he says, still looking at his sister, and lifting long fingers up to tousle his white-blonde hair. "Trust me: we're all very aware she's here." He turns his attention over to me, and I'm forced to take a step back. Just the weight of his stare is enough, like a physical push to the chest. "What I don't understand is *why* she's still here."

"*She* is standing right in front of you," I grind out, remembering Creed's face on the yacht, his bored, almost put-out expression as Tristan torched the book. "You can throw whatever you want at me. I might bend, but I won't break."

In a flash, Creed's long fingers are on my chin, lifting my face to look at him. My skin, where his fingertips touch it, tingles and burns. Swallowing down a lump, I force myself to look him straight in the face.

"Made of stronger stuff, hmm?" he asks, tilting my head from side to side like he's studying me. I slap his hand away, and take another step back. The way his mouth twists to the side in an arrogant smile is disturbing, so self-assured and cocky. I'd love to see it wiped right off of his face.

"You should've read her scholarship essay," Miranda interjects, rising to her feet. I'm aware that the entire room is focused on our confrontation. "Marnye is a class-act, unlike you. I know Mom and Dad have given up on you, but I expected better." She moves around the table and grabs my arm, dragging me away as her brother tucks his fingers into his slacks pockets, watching us with narrowed eyes.

But if I cowered every time one of the Idols looked at me

like a bug to be crushed under their expensive loafers, I'd already be enrolled in Lower Banks High and long-gone from Burberry Prep Academy.

My dad's been purposely avoiding my calls. I haven't been able to talk to him once since I got here. Instead, I get missed calls and vague voicemails. Pretty sure he's been drinking again, but there's nothing I can do from here, a day's drive away and trapped in a hell of my own.

Parents' Week is supposed to start off with a special breakfast, and a speech from both the dean and the infamous Kathleen Cabot. My dad—and by proxy, me—has already missed that. I'm the last student sitting in the front courtyard, waiting for her parents to show up.

Well, second to last, really.

Zayd Kaiser leans against the stone wall of Tower Two, arms crossed over his chest, green eyes focused on the horizon. They're devoid of expectation as he watches the winding road and taps his inked fingers against the leg of his slacks.

When he sees me looking at him, he scowls and turns away.

"My dad's on tour right now. What the fuck is your parents' excuse? Too busy working at the factory?"

"There's nothing wrong with working at a factory," I grind out, my jaw clenched tight, "but no, my dad will be here."

I'm not about to explain to Zayd that I'm worried he's too drunk, that he passed out somewhere, that he forgot. That'd just give him more ammo to throw at me, and even without a whole lot, the Idols are doing a damn good job gunning for me. "He'll be here," I repeat, crossing my arms over my chest and shivering at the cool breeze. I've always disliked October and the cold chill of fall. While everybody else was going to the pumpkin patch with their families, trick-or-treating, having big Thanksgiving get-togethers, it was just me and Dad struggling to get by.

Zayd ignores me, humming some song under his breath that I vaguely recognize. I'm more of a classical music person, so I'm not super familiar with rock, but I'm pretty sure Zayd's dad is Billy Kaiser, the lead singer for Battered Wings, a popular rock band from my parents' days. I bet that's hard, having a parent who's on the road all the time.

Then Zayd mumbles something like *poor little Working Girl* under his breath, and all my sympathy fades away.

We both perk up a bit at the sound of a car coming down the winding road. It's impossible to tell who's in it because the windows are tinted, and it's got the academy's logo on the side. Parents aren't allowed to drive up to the school and instead have to park in the visitors' lot five miles away. Everyone—even the working class—gets a ride to the front entrance in the same vehicle.

When the door opens, and I see my dad climb out, I have to hold back a small shriek of joy, my cheeks lighting up. As I stand up and smooth my skirt out, I notice Zayd watching me, and try not to feel smug. *My dad is here, so where is yours?*

Filthy Rich Boys

Even if the guy's a jerk, the thought's just too mean. I'm not that kind of person. Or ... at least I try not to be.

I start down the stairs with a perky bounce in my steps, grinning from ear to ear when Dad smiles at me and opens his arms for a hug. He's clearly sober, and his hair looks freshly-washed and styled, his face clean-shaven.

"Baby girl!" he calls out, wrapping me up in his strong arms and spinning me around. We haven't been separated for this long since ... forever ago. When Mom first left and tried to take me with her. Shaking my head, I decide not to think about that. Those memories are best left forgotten. "I've missed you so much, honey."

I open my mouth to tell him the same when a second figure climbs out of the car, and my heart turns to ice in my chest.

"Zack," I choke out, eyes widening.

"Hey Marnye," he says, his voice still that same dark bass it was in eighth grade. Zack matured faster than the rest of the boys, shooting up to an impressive six foot three, with big hands and muscles from football and track. But over the summer, he's just gotten ... *ripped.* My mouth goes dry, and my palms start to sweat.

"What ..." I start to ask my ex-boyfriend what he's doing here, but Dad answers for me.

"The school gave me two tickets for today, and your mother ..." He doesn't have to finish that thought; we both know what Mom's up to, taking care of her replacement husband and daughter and leaving the two of us to rot. "Well, I called and asked, and they said it was okay if I wanted to bring a family friend."

"A family friend," I whisper, tucking a loose strand of brown hair behind one ear. It's basically down to my ass now, and difficult to control in a strong wind. "That's one way to put it." My eyes sweep Zack's large, muscular form, wondering when his chest and stomach got so flat, his arm muscles so big that the sleeves of his leather jacket look strained. His dark hair is gelled up on the top, and as I stare at him, he reaches up and smooths it flat with his palm.

"Zack's been helping out around the house," Dad says as I glance back and find that Zayd's disappeared. Good. The last thing I need is him eavesdropping on our conversation. God knows what sort of crap the Idols would pull out after hearing his. "He's been helping me stay sober, too."

Biting my lower lip, I nod, looking Dad's outfit over. He didn't pick those black slacks and white button-up on his own. Zack's family owns a series of shops catering to wedding attire, a few bridal shops, some tailors, a tuxedo rental place. I used to think the Brooks family was rich. Compared to the students here, he's as poor as I am.

"Well, I'm glad you're both here," I say hesitantly, trying to ignore the way Zack's brown eyes take in my uniform. He's clearly appreciative, and I don't know how to feel about that. We dated for six months, but that was in middle school. That means less than nothing in the scheme of things. "Come on, we can make the morning tour."

I take my dad's arm and lead him up the steps, Zack trailing behind us. He whistles as we walk past the fountain and down the path toward the chapel.

"Nice place you got here," Zack says, his voice sending

Filthy Rich Boys

ripples of goose bumps across my skin. Dad holds open the stained glass doors for us both and our arms brush, making me swallow hard.

"Nice to look at," I mumble, and while Dad misses that statement, Zack definitely hears. The way he looks at me, I know he's thinking about the pranks, the fights, the constant torture. At first, he was the one that started it all, but then we started dating and ...

No. *No, Marnye, we're not reliving old memories.* Burberry Prep is supposed to be a fresh start.

"The teachers are posting grades today," I say with a small sigh. "I know I've done well, but the competition here is fierce. I've never been a part of anything like it."

"They post grades publicly?" Zack asks, his dark eyebrows rising up in surprise. "Sounds like a recipe for disaster." I shrug my shoulders, but I know he's right. Whatever my ranking, I'm going to be destroyed for it. I've already tried to prepare myself.

"Marnye!" Miranda shouts, waving her arms wildly. I'm happy to see her, but my chest gets tight when I notice Creed close behind. Fortunately, his mother, Kathleen Cabot, the founder of the Cabot Scholarship Award program is right there with him. She smiles at me, too, and the knot loosens up a bit. "Marnye," Miranda gasps out, panting as she wraps her fingers around my upper arm. She starts to open her mouth to say something and pauses, looking past my dad and straight to Zack. "Oh. Who's this?" She blinks those long lashes of hers as I chew on my lip in nervousness.

"Miranda, this is my dad, Charlie, and my ... our family friend, Zack Brooks."

"Well hello, Zack Brooks," she says, flashing that winning smile. "And Mr. Reed, lovely to meet you." She holds out her hand and shakes with both men as her mother and brother make their way over to us. Creed hangs back, but I notice his eyes taking in Zack with disdain. When I glance over my shoulder, I find my ex staring with narrowed eyes. I've seen Zack destroy stronger people than Creed Cabot with nothing but words. I used to think he was a monster.

"What were you going to say?" I whisper after I greet Kathleen with a hug, and her and my dad start up a conversation about the Burberry Prep campus. "You were practically panting when you ran over here." Miranda's blue eyes light up, turning them into sapphires. There's so much warmth there; I can hardly imagine Creed's eyes doing the same. Nope. Hell's more likely to freeze over.

"Right," she says, grinning at me. I notice her skirt's not rolled up at the hem today, hitting her at the knees instead of mid-thigh. "Grades were posted just after breakfast." I raise an eyebrow, waiting for the other shoe to drop. "And Marnye, you won't believe it."

"Believe what?" I ask as Creed and Zack continue to stare each other down. Honestly, they're both assholes. They'd probably make great friends. Then again, I get the feeling that Creed, Zayd, and Tristan don't much like each other. Birds of a feather flock together until the cat comes, huh? "Stop being cryptic and just tell me."

"Dude," she gushes, and it's the first time she's ever called me that, so I grin, "you're number one." My mouth drops open, and all the blood rushes from my face to my feet.

Filthy Rich Boys

"What?"

"You're number one, out of the whole first year class."

"You're kidding me," I choke out, feeling the first wave of dread hit me. Creed's just switched his attention to me, and I can see hatred burning deep in his gaze.

"First?" Dad echoes, putting a hand on my shoulder and making me jump. "Marnye, that's incredible."

"I knew we picked the right girl," Kathleen says, her red hair curling and falling in a graceful wave over her shoulders. She has the same blue eyes as her kids, the same warm smile as Miranda. "Congratulations, Marnye, you're off to an incredible start."

An incredible start that's going to get me killed, I think, looking back at Creed again. But he's already turned away to flirt with some girl in a second-year uniform. There's no better way to light a fire under a bully's ass than to outdo them at their own game. Me being first in academics only spells trouble.

"Thanks everyone," I force out with a smile. Zack catches my eye, and I look away. We didn't exactly part as friends, although Dad doesn't know that. I'm not about to spill my fears to either of them. "Should we get going?"

I notice the tour starting down the hall, and wave our little group along to join it.

Because I'm lost in my thoughts, I lag just slightly behind, and feel a shiver overtake me just before a palm slams into the wall in front of my face. I glance over and find Tristan with his blade gray eyes starting me down.

"You little bitch," he growls out, the vehemence in his voice thick and unmistakable. "What'd you do? Fuck your way to straight As?" My cheeks flush, and I curl my hands into fists.

"I studied, Tristan. Maybe if you spent less time drinking and sleeping with random girls, you could succeed, too." He hits the wall with his palm again, and I jump. There's so much tension in his body that even in a hall full of people, I'm afraid.

"This little Mary Sue act of yours is getting old," he snarls, pushing off of the wall and looking me up and down with a sneer that, unfortunately, does nothing to mar the handsome features of his face. "If you've got skeletons in your closet, you might want to make sure they're buried. Because I'm going to destroy you."

"Marnye, are you okay?" Zack asks, appearing on my left side. The way he looks at Tristan makes me wonder if they've met each other before. Something flashes across Tristan's face before he smirks.

"Brooks. I'm surprised to see you here. Didn't you get rejected? Even your family's money wasn't enough to get Burberry Prep to take your loser ass." Tristan's anger subsides slightly, replaced with haughty arrogance. He lifts his chin and smiles, reaching up to brush dark hair from his brow. "Or are you sleeping with Charity, too? Even with her looks, it seems she has plenty of customers."

"Charity?" Zack laughs, that dry, dark, scary sound that used to make me tremble. "Do you think you're clever, Vanderbilt? Don't forget that I've kicked your ass more than once, and I'm happy to do it again."

"So you are fucking her?" Tristan continues, his silver

Filthy Rich Boys

gaze sliding back to me. He seems excited to have unearthed this scandalous bit of news. Too bad for him that I'm a virgin. There's no skeleton to dig up here. I'm not sure what Zack means about kicking Tristan's ass, but it's clear these two do know each other. Still, Tristan doesn't fazed by Zack's presence, not at all. "Where did the two of you meet? At that ghetto school of yours?"

"Save it for fall break, dickhead," Zack snaps, and my brows wrinkle up. When he reaches down for my wrist, I jerk from his grasp, and we end up staring at each other. Family friend my dad might call him, but he was never a friend of mine. Zack's eyes narrow, but he turns and heads down the hallway where Miranda's waiting, watching and listening to the verbal scuffle between the boys with her mouth hanging open.

"Enjoy your tour, Charity," Tristan schmoozes, lifting a cocky brow. "Because you won't be around much longer."

The next morning, we have class as usual. The only difference is that the families are allowed to hang around and observe. Most do, but I notice that Zayd's dad still isn't here. I guess he's not coming at all. The asshole acts like it doesn't bother him, hitting on girls, and letting out that raucous laugh of his, as usual. I wonder though if it's all a front to cover up the pain. I know all about that.

Zack sits beside me during the morning announcements,

but Charlie's nowhere to be seen. I know the parents were being housed in the cabins (think glamping style cabins) out by the lake, and being driven in at their leisure. But when I ask Zack where my dad is, he just shrugs his big shoulders and refuses to look at me.

By the time we get to our mixed media class, I'm already starting to sweat. Not only is Dad still missing, but today we're focusing on music, getting a feel for everyone's talents, and starting the auditions for the school orchestra. I figure I probably don't have much competition considering I play the harp. It's kind of a rare instrument. Good thing, too, since there's usually only one spot for a harpist.

"Everyone take a seat," Mr. Carter says, taking control of the class for the day. He's the conductor for the Burberry Preparatory Academy Orchestra, and the one I need to impress most this week. "Today we'll be getting a feel for the type of music and instruments each student is interested in."

An email pops up on my academy-issued iPad from Mr. Carter, and I tap on it, glancing down the length of the form as he explains how to fill it out.

"You think any of these uptight assholes can outplay you?" Zack asks, and I shrug. Harper du Pont is sitting right behind me, and the last thing I want to do is draw attention to my instrument of choice. The way she looks at me, it wouldn't be surprising if she picked the harp just to spite me.

"Guess we'll find out," I murmur as I submit the form, and then sit back to wait for everyone else, listening to Mr. Carter drone on about the choir program, the orchestra, and the music industry internship opportunities. The door to the

Filthy Rich Boys

lecture hall opens, and I glance lazily over my shoulder to see who it is.

It's Charlie.

And he's drunk off his ass.

He stumbles into the classroom, tripping over his own feet, one hand landing on Anna Kirkpatrick's shoulder. She twists her face in disgust and pulls away from him as I stand up, dropping my iPad to the ground.

"Marnye, baby?" Dad calls out, and a bevy of dark snickers takes over the room. "Where are you?"

My whole body's frozen over, and I feel rooted to the spot. Zack is quicker to react than me, bulldozing his way out of the aisle and grabbing Charlie by the shoulders.

"No, I want to see Marnye," Dad slurs, trying to throw Zack off. But despite their age difference, Zack is about a million times stronger. He gets my father under control, hustling him toward the door as the entire class looks on in silence.

"Guess the apple doesn't fall far from the tree," Becky Platter sneers, and the room lights up with laughter.

"If you need a minute, you can excuse yourself, Miss Reed," Mr. Carter says, but he doesn't correct Becky for her comment. Why should he? Most of these kids have the staff wrapped around their fingers. Cheeks flaming, I pick my way down the aisle, and head up the steps, holding back tears.

Shoving my way out of the mixed media room, I find my dad slumped against a wall, Zack's hold just barely keeping him upright. I'm torn between being worried and upset, my emotions a wild turmoil inside of me. I love my dad, but his behavior, it's … it's fucking unacceptable.

"Do you know what you've just done?" I whisper, choking back the tears. "You've given them the ammo they really need to take shots at me."

"They?" Zack asks as Dad groans. The man's barely conscious. My yelling at him isn't going to do a thing. So much as I want to voice my anger, I take up his other side and help Zack lead him toward the front where the cars are waiting to ferry parents back and forth from the cabins.

"Don't worry about it," I murmur, feeling Zack's dark eyes still on me. He says nothing as we move down the hall and out the door, along the corridor, and into the courtyard.

"Your dad got some news last night," Zack tells me, but when I ask what it is, he clamps all the way up. Jerk.

I'm soaked in sweat by the time I get my dad into the back of the car. Zack pauses, like he's not sure whether he should stay or go.

"He needs you," I say lamely, holding up a palm. "He can barely walk let alone change his clothes and get into bed. Just make sure he sleeps facedown." My eyes lift up to meet Zack's, those dark pits that are completely and utterly unreadable. "I don't know why you're helping me, but … thank you."

"Don't bother," Zack says, sliding into the backseat next to my dad. He slams the door, and the car starts off down the side road that leads to the lake. I watch it until it disappears, closing my eyes and doing my best to gather myself before going back to class. It isn't easy, not with my hands shaking, my shirt sticking to my back with sweat, but I manage.

As soon as I walk in the door, I can feel it, the weight of

their judgement, the depth of their hatred.

I settle myself into my seat and manage to hold back my tears for the rest of the day.

Next week, I might not be so lucky.

CHAPTER 7

"Please tell me more about Zack," Miranda begs, lounging on my bed and watching as I examine my borrowed costume in the mirror. We still have two weeks until Halloween, but apparently, the party here at Burberry is a huge deal. Not that I'm surprised. I'm pretty sure *all* the parties here are big deals.

"What's there to tell?" I ask, turning to the side and wondering why every costume Miranda's brought over for me to try on is so short and low-cut. Oh wait. Remember that scene in *Mean Girls* when Lindsay Lohan has the voiceover about Halloween, explaining that it's a day for girls to dress slutty without actually being called sluts? Not that I agree with slut-shaming, but that statement is still, unfortunately, true.

"He was so dark and mysterious," she mumbles, burying the lower half of her face in my pillow. "Pretty sure he has a thing for you." I snort and decide that wearing a red bodycon dress with horns and Prada heels isn't going to work for me. Miranda sees the expression on my face and slaps the bed with her palm. "How clever is that outfit?! It's a conceptual thing, like *The Devil Wears Prada,* you know?"

"I got it," I tell her with a small laugh. "I just don't think it's going to help my reputation as the Working Girl, you know?" Grabbing the next outfit off the stack, I head into the bathroom and start to change into another nearly identical costume. "And Zack does not have a thing for me. He's always hated me."

"Hated you? He was practically drooling." I hear the bed creak as Miranda gets up, covering her eyes with her hand and leaning in the doorway of the bathroom. "Come on, don't tell me you don't think he's hot."

"He's ... Zack Brooks." My lips purse as I slip into an angel costume that's even shorter and tighter than the devil one I just tried on. Nope. If I do go to this Halloween party, then I'm wearing jeans and a t-shirt. "He treated me like crap for all three years of middle school. I've hated him since I was twelve." *Except for those last few months when we dated.* Ugh. I haven't told Miranda about that part yet.

"Yeah, but, people change ..." Miranda hedges, peeking out from behind her hand, her eyes lighting up. "You look so freaking cute in that," she says, but I'm not even going to put the halo on. It's just not happening. "Although the devil costume was my favorite." She steps into the bathroom and scoops the massive fall of my hair into an artful chignon. "Maybe with an updo? You have fabulous hair, by the way. Combine it with that costume, and you'll be the hottest girl at the party."

I smile, she's sweet, she really is, but there's just no way.

"You should wear it," I tell Miranda, shooing her out of the bathroom, so I can change again. She goes, grabbing the red Prada heels and dress on the way. When I hear her rummaging around in my wardrobe, I roll my eyes, yanking a gray tank top and shorts on before I go out to confront her with a hand on my hip. "What are you doing?"

"I'm going as Farrah Moan, I told you that." She peeks out at me from behind the wardrobe door. "The drag queen? From *RuPaul's Drag Race*. Oh, come on, Marnye."

I cross my arms over my chest and gesture at her with my chin.

"I know what *RuPaul's Drag Race* is. What I'm asking is why you're shoving that outfit into my closet?"

"If I leave it here, maybe the subtle suggestion will take over you in your sleep, and you'll wear this to the party." Miranda shuts the doors and raises her eyebrows at me. "Now stop avoiding the subject, and tell me about Zack."

"There's nothing to talk about. He … his family used to know my dad. Sometimes he comes around and helps out. That's all I know." Miranda sighs at me and grabs her bag, giving me a hard look.

"You better not be holding out on me." She pauses and her expression softens. When she reaches out to tuck some hair behind my ear, I smile. Everything she does comes from a

Filthy Rich Boys

good place. It's hard to be angry with her. "Remember, I read your essay. You put your heart and soul into that, and there was no mention of Zack. I smell a mystery."

"Zack wasn't in there because he's not a part of my heart and soul," I tell her, grabbing her arm and steering her to the door. "Now go home and go to sleep."

"Love you, night!" she calls out as I close the door and lock it.

Miranda's nowhere to be found the next morning, so I muddle through morning classes without her. I catch a glimpse of Andrew with his friends, but only in passing. He raises a hand to wave, and I wave back, but that's about it. My day is a social desert, and surprisingly, I'm grateful for it. It's nice to have a break from being bullied and asked if I'd like a drink. Come on guys, the first few times it's clever, but really, as an alcoholic's daughter, I've heard it all. They'll have to come up with some new material if they want to mess with me.

Flopping into my seat in mixed media, I take out my iPad and, as per the instructions on the screen at the front of the class, check my email for my instrument assignment. Instead of being assigned the harp, the *only* instrument I checked on the form, I've been put into choir.

My mouth pops open, and I glance up, noticing a pedal harp on the stage up front.

A squeal breaks out behind me, and Becky is up and

moving down the steps in a blur, her skirt at least two or three inches shorter than mine and Miranda's. I see flashes of her panties as she scrambles down to Mr. Carter. I can't hear what they're saying, but she's gesturing wildly, and then ... sitting down at the harp.

"What the ever-loving hell?" I grumble, my hands tightening on the edges of my tablet. The smell of vanillas and peaches wafts over me as Harper leans forward, her brunette hair fluttering forward and tickling my right cheek. Slowly, I slide my eyes her direction.

"What do you think, Working Girl? My mother's on the schoolboard, and she *really* likes Becky. After all, we've been friends for years." She taps a sharp nailed pink fingernail on my tablet screen. "I noticed you checked off choir in the *No Thank You* section of the form. But girls like you need to expand their horizons, don't you think?"

I'm shaking, but I don't say anything to her, not right now. What good would it do to cause a scene? Instead, I look forward and pretend I don't notice Tristan making his way over to sit behind me.

Okay, so, I've been assigned to choir. Fine. That doesn't mean I can't try out for the academy orchestra. Without skipping a beat, I click the link to the sign-up form and start to fill it out when a hand clasps onto my shoulder. Glancing back, I see that it's Harper again.

"Don't you dare," she hisses, but I jerk from her grip and continue what I'm doing. "You try out for the orchestra, and I'll kill you myself." This time I do turn around, meeting the harsh blue of her glare. Tristan sits stoically beside her, his

Filthy Rich Boys

face locked into a mask of arrogance that seems impossible to break. But I saw it, during Parents' Week, his perfect façade shattering into anger.

"Instead of threatening me, maybe you should ask why you're so afraid of me?" I raise both brows, and then hit the submit button. Harper's pink painted lips curl up in a snarl, but she doesn't say anything, choosing instead to ingratiate herself to Tristan.

On the plus side, as class continues, and Becky plays her first piece, I realize it right away: I'm a lot better than her.

Good for me. I'll have to be if I want to win that seat.

After classes are done for the day, I spend a few minutes looking for Miranda, and then give up, heading to The Mess without her. As soon as I walk in, I know something's wrong.

Creed is lounging on top of a table like a lazy prince, all coiffed elegance, one leg straight out in front of him, the other bent at the knee. He's resting on his left elbow, and in his right hand, he's holding a stack of paper. His icy blue eyes lift to mine as soon as I walk in the door.

"*There wasn't a moment in middle school that I didn't feel like I was under attack. The siege came from all sides: an alcoholic father at home, a mother who didn't want me, and classmates who'd made it their personal mission to destroy me.*" He pauses, the edge of his mouth curling up in a smile. His captive audience turns to look at me, a knowing gleam in their collective gazes.

Without realizing it, I drop my bookbag to the floor. My knees feel weak, and my head swims. *No, this isn't happening. This can't be happening.*

Creed clears his throat again, and peers back down at his

phone.

"For the longest time, I couldn't figure out why they hated me so much. When I did, it nearly broke me. One day, when I was at my lowest, I sat down on the floor of the girls' bathroom and I swallowed a bottle of prescription pills I'd stolen from my mother's purse. Ironically, the first and only time she'd visited me in years was going to be the last time she'd see me: that was my plan. Use her pills, end it all, let the pain fade away."

My heart is thundering so fast, I can barely hear Creed reading my scholarship essay aloud to the room. Blood pounds in my ears, as loud as the ocean waves against the rocks outside. As Miranda said, I put my heart and soul into that essay. It was everything to me, the whole story of my life, and my ticket out of poverty, into Burberry Prep, into a future that didn't involve train cars converted to houses or relying on my dad's on-again, off-again welding work for food and clothing.

I felt like I'd been gutted, like pieces of me were lying on the floor at the feet of the Idols and their wicked Inner Circle.

Memories flickered in my head, memories of Zack bursting into the room and kneeling beside me, putting his fingers down my throat, making me throw up. If he hadn't gone in there after me, I might very well be dead. And yet, he was one of the instigators, one of my worst critics. I'd never understood that, how he changed after that moment.

"Stop," I choke out, but Creed just smiles bigger, Zayd grinning from ear to ear on one side, Tristan standing stoic and silent on the other. "Just stop."

Filthy Rich Boys

"*Bullying nearly broke me, so much so that I tried again, just two months later. I tried to slit my wrists, and I failed at that, too.*" Creed pauses as Zayd roars with laughter and Tristan crosses his arms over his chest. *Game set and match,* his face tells me. I can barely see Harper, Becky, and Gena standing beside him. They're getting blurry. The whole room is swimming.

The door opens beside me and Andrew and Miranda walk in. Andrew catches me right before I fall, and I hear Miranda screaming at her brother. The last thing I see before Andrew scoops me up in his arms and carries me out is Miranda yanking the papers from Creed's hand.

The others boo at her and throw napkins, but we're already out the door, and Andrew is carrying me straight to my room.

"I can't believe Creed would go that far!" Miranda chokes out, her face flushed as she paces in front of my bed. Andrew lays me down and gets me a cold rag, and a glass of water, sitting beside me and putting his hand on my leg. I cover his fingers with my own and squeeze. *There's no spark there,* I think absently as I try not to throw up. What a random thought to have at such a horrible moment. Maybe I'm in some form of emotional shock?

"How did he get access to that?" Andrew asks, his voice quiet and dark. He glances back at Miranda, and she shakes her head.

"I have no idea. My mom, probably. But how he got that from her, I don't know. She's fiercely protective of those essays."

Leaning back into my pillows, I cover my face with my

hands.

From sixth grade through the first half of eighth, I was bullied so badly that I wanted to die. So badly that I tried to end it not once but twice. After that, things got better. People let up, and I realized I had to embrace the positive or the negative would drown me. When I came to Burberry Prep, I came with that idea in mind: embrace my new life, make a fresh start.

And now I'm drowning in it.

"I think I'm going to be sick," I whisper, shoving up from the bed. I just barely make it into the bathroom before what little I had for lunch makes its way back up. Miranda moves into the bathroom and helps me hold my hair back, stroking my forehead for comfort. "I'll never be able to go to class again."

"Don't let them win, Marnye," she whispers, voice warbly, like maybe she might cry, too. "Creed is … he's the worst kind of bully there is. Him, and Zayd, Tristan and Harper and Becky. Don't give into them."

Without meaning to, I end up crying and hating myself for it. I can take a lot of crap, but that essay was my soul on a page. Now the Idols have everything they need to make my life a living hell. They know all about my father's alcoholism, his struggle to make ends meet, the things my mother did to me.

After I finish throwing up, I kick Miranda out and climb in the shower, letting the water scald away my humiliation. It's just never-ending with these people. And all because I'm poor. That's it. I thought the reasons for my bullying at Lower

Filthy Rich Boys

Banks were bullshit. This is even more arbitrary.

Climbing out of the shower, I find that Miranda's snuck a stack of pjs into the room, so I change into them and head back out to find that Andrew's already left.

"I had to beg him not to beat Creed up," she says, wringing her hands. I raise an eyebrow, but I'm too tired to ask why Andrew would even bother. We're friends, sure, but just barely. I can't imagine him beating up an Idol for me. "Do you want me to stay with you for a while?"

I shake my head.

"No, I just … I want to be alone for tonight."

"Yeah, okay," she says, giving me a hug before she lets herself out.

Sitting down on the edge of the bed, I seriously consider walking to the principal's office and asking to go home. If I left, maybe I could breathe again. It feels like I haven't taken a single breath since I got here.

All I want is to study and graduate, that's it. Why does that have to be so hard?

Lying back on the bed, I close my eyes, and within minutes I'm asleep.

Navigating the school without running into the Idols or their cronies is impossible. They're everywhere, and they've amped up their game. Even homeroom with Ms. Felton isn't safe. When her back is turned, I get pills thrown at me. Most everyone's drawn on their wrists with red Sharpie, lifting up the sleeves of their academy jackets and flashing me in the halls.

The only person who doesn't seem thrilled by my destruction is Tristan. He's always moody and frowning, and just barely makes it to class. The Thursday before Halloween, I slip out of third period to go to the bathroom.

As soon as I step inside, I hear the moans.

Tristan has a girl bent over the sink, and he's fucking her.

He glances over at me when I come in, but he doesn't stop. His eyes narrow, glittering with some unreadable motion.

Me, I just stand there gaping, completely and utterly shocked by the sight in front of me.

"You gonna stand there and watch?" he snaps at me after a minute. Backing away, I turn and run from the bathroom, turning the corner and leaning my back against the stone wall. I'd thought Tristan was dating Miranda behind the scenes, but … that most definitely wasn't Miranda. Pretty sure that was Kiara Xiao, another first-year student.

For some reason, my body feels hot with frustration, and I want to punch something. Mostly I want to punch Tristan. He doesn't care about that girl. He doesn't care about anyone.

When I tell Miranda about it later, she chokes on her iced tea and raises huge eyes to me.

"Right there in the girls' bathroom?" she asks, blinking rapidly. "He's usually more discreet about it."

"More discreet?" I whisper back, face flaming. All those times he touched me or got close to me and I felt sparks …

make me sick. What a creep. "So ... all the girls know he'll sleep with whoever he can get his hands on, and they don't care?"

Miranda shrugs her shoulders and takes a sip of her drink. We're the only ones in The Mess, taking advantage of the early dinner service. I've tried to come in here while everyone else is eating, but it's just too much. I've been relegated to slinking around the halls. Believe it or not, for someone who tried to hurt themselves, the constant flashes of red-lined wrists, and the bottles of pills are pretty triggering.

"He's handsome, popular, and rich. Of course they all want to sleep with him." Not for the first time, I wonder if *she* is also sleeping with him. I hate to think that of my friend, but she disappears randomly and doesn't tell me where she's been. She sometimes shows up places with him, and he's always giving her looks.

Honestly, I don't want to know.

I focus on my food, but I don't feel like eating. My stomach feels like it's been encased in ice.

"Well, *I* don't want to sleep with him," I murmur, putting my fork down as anxiety prickles across my skin. I'd like to get out of here before anyone else shows up for dinner. Frankly, I feel like I've been wrung dry, my last reserves of strength bled out along with the words to my essay. I'm dreading getting my phone back tomorrow. What if Creed posts my essay online? That'd really be the end of me.

Besides, I'm afraid to hear what my dad has to say to me. There's no apology in the world that can make up for what he did. I'm desperate to know what this 'news' is that he received that supposedly upset him so much, and damn Zack for not telling me what it was.

"Is there anyone you *do* want to sleep with?" Miranda asks, putting her fork aside and scrambling to stand up and follow me out the door. "Like … maybe Zack?"

"Would you let the Zack thing go?" I turn a glare on her, but Miranda just smiles back at me. "He used to bully me, you know? That, and he said some weird stuff to Tristan when he confronted me about my grades."

"What sort of weird stuff?" Miranda asks, her shoulders stiffening up. Yet again, a single mention of Tristan and she gets all cryptic.

"It was pretty clear the two of them have met before. Zack challenged Tristan to come at him during fall break, and Tristan insinuated that Zack applied to Burberry Prep and didn't get in." Miranda's chewing on her lower lip, a habit that's usually left to me. She doesn't look at me, just attempts a half-hearted hair flip.

"Well, I've never seen Zack before," she adds with a shrug of her shoulders. She twirls around to face me, her red-pleated skirt spinning. "Maybe they met during summer break or something? Tristan's family always goes to the Hamptons."

I have no idea where Zack goes for summer breaks, only that he's rich enough to go to a private school like this one, but had gotten kicked out of so many before he was relegated to Lower Banks Middle School. No clue where he's going to school this year. If he were here now, I wonder if we'd be friends?

"Your family doesn't go to the Hamptons, too?" I ask, and

Miranda flushes, like she's been caught in a lie.

"Sometimes, but not for the whole summer like some people. We have a cabin in Lake Tahoe ..." she trails off, and then switches up our conversation with a rapid change of subject. "Are you sure you're not going to the Halloween party on Saturday?"

"Positively not," I tell her, shivering as we pass the smiling faces of Harper and Becky, their arms linked, their eyes on me. Harper purposely elbows me in the side, and I stumble. Anger fills me up, white-hot and pulsing, but there's no point in acknowledging it. If I punch Harper, then I guarantee I'm the one who will be in trouble. "But I want you to go and have fun. Take pics for me, okay?"

Miranda gives me a look, but lets me go at the chapel, veering off with a wave.

I don't even remember getting back to my room or falling asleep.

Actually, the next thing I remember is waking up with a hangover.

My eyes are sticky, lids heavy, as I struggle to sit up in my bed. I've got a serious case of dry mouth, and a massive migraine.

"What the ... hell?" I groan as I reach up and run my fingers through my hair.

My hair.

Scrambling out of bed, I skid across the floor and into the bathroom, gaping at myself in the mirror above the sink. When I touched my hair, something felt wrong. But oh my god. Something is really, really wrong.

My long, brunette waves are gone, replaced with a red pixie cut. And when I say red, I mean as red as blood. A scream lodges in my throat, but I choke it back, leaning forward and staring at the ragged ends of my hair. It's so short, I'm not even sure that I could style it.

For several long moments, I just stand there and stare, my brown eyes wide, my lips parted, my hair … a hot freaking mess. Stumbling back into my room, I check my bedroom door, and find the bottom lock in place. The chain lock however is undone, and I always, *always* hook it—because I was scared of something like this happening.

In a daze, I sit down hard on the edge of my bed, mind whirling with possibilities.

"I slept through it," I murmur, running a palm over my new do. But then my head throbs and I cringe. No, no, I was *drugged*. Fucking drugged. There's no other explanation. A normal person doesn't sleep through a full bleach, dye, and cut job. That's just not possible.

I'm still wearing my uniform from the day before, but when I pinch the white shirt and glance down at it, I can see red stains that look like blood.

This is the work of women, for sure. No way one of those asshole Idol dudes would realize how much this would hurt me. My hair, my hair, my freaking hair … I've been growing it out since before I can even remember. It was damn near to

Filthy Rich Boys

my ass, and now it's all gone, and it's not something I can get back.

My bones feel like jelly, so I flop down on the edge of my bed and stare at the floor. I'd cry, but my eyes are so sticky, and I feel so drained. The length of my hair, the slight wave, the fullness ... it was one of the few things I truly liked about myself. Years and years of work, of brushing out tangles, braiding it before bed, spending a hundred dollars I didn't have to get some gum removed during my middle school bullying years ...

An exhale escapes me that sounds like a cry, and I put my hands over my face.

My first instinct is to run. Combined with the pain of having my essay read aloud, this is almost too much. I'm shaking; my defenses are crumbling.

What good would running do? I ask myself instead. Mom thought her life with dad and a young daughter was too hard, and she took off. The last person in the world I want to be like is her. Dropping my hands to my lap, I force myself up and into the bathroom, splashing my cheeks and forehead with cool water.

I can't run.

And I'm never going to let myself slip into that dark place again. The first time, with the pills, I was so out of it, all I remember is throwing up and then crying into Zack's chest. The second time, it was agonizing, sitting there and bleeding and hurting, wondering what was waiting in the incoming darkness. I don't want to see that darkness again, not until I'm old and wrinkled and have lived a good life. Not yet. Not yet.

And my best chance at a good life is this school, stellar grades, orchestra.

I can do this.

Pushing up from the sink, I change out of my stained uniform and shower. The red dye runs out of my hair, staining the bottom of the shower as red as my blood did that day I cut my wrists. It's bad. It's so bad. My stomach churns, and I almost break down again.

Instead, I somehow find the strength to dress in a clean uniform, and head down the hall to where Miranda waits for me every morning. She's there with Andrew, and the two of them gape at me as I step into the crowd.

All eyes are on me.

"Marnye," she whispers, putting her hand over her mouth. Andrew just stares at me in shock, his mouth in a thin line. The laughter starts slowly, but spreads like wildfire, until everyone's looking at me, pointing, cracking Working Girl jibes. "What did you do to your hair?"

I give her a look, and whatever she sees in my expression makes her tear up. She throws her arms around me in a hug, but it doesn't escape my notice that she was the only person with me at dinner last night. She could've easily drugged me. I might've only known her for a few months, but I trust her. Was that my mistake?

"Are you going to report this?" Andrew asks, tucking his hands into his jacket pockets. His tie is crooked, and I see the distinct print of a hickey on his neck. Oh. I sort of ... well, I thought maybe he liked me. Not that I care. There was no spark between us, but ... it's just another small blow to add to

FILTHY RICH BOYS

the overwhelming load on my shoulders.

"What am I going to say? That some master plan was executed involving drugs and beauty supplies? Who's going to believe me?"

"Hey Hester!" Harper calls out, her face lighting up with supercilious joy. "Nice *scarlet letter*!" She chortles, and Becky follows suit. But the way they're looking at me ... I have no doubt in my mind who the main perpetrators are. Zayd strolls up a few seconds later, glances my direction, and his eyes widen. He flashes a grin that would be charming if it wasn't being used to destroy me, and laughter roars from his throat as he throws an arm around the two Idol girls.

"Let's go," I grind out, leading Miranda away, and heading for Tower One, and homeroom with Ms. Felton. She's pretty straight-laced, and colored hair is most decidedly against the school dress code—with the exception of Zayd Kaiser because, you know, his agent's screwing the vice principal.

We hit the top floor and head into the classroom. As soon as Ms. Felton's eyes fall on me, they widen, and I see her cheeks redden.

"Miss Reed," she says, and the class bursts into sneers and giggles. Tristan watches me carefully, but it's impossible to read that stony expression of his. "Can I speak to you in private a moment?" I nod and follow her into the adjoining room that makes up her office. She's barely got the door closed before she's turning to me. "Miss Reed, what's going on here?"

"What do you mean?" I ask, choking as I struggle to hold back the tears. From her office window, Ms. Felton has a spectacular view of the beach, and the harbor with its bobbing boats. Burberry Prep has a *splendid* student-run yacht club, didn't you know? I hope all their boats capsize, and they drown in drunken stupors. My hands curl into fists.

"Did you cut and dye your hair last night, Miss Reed?" she asks, phrasing her question very, very carefully. I have no idea what to say, so I just stand there and stare at her. There must be something in my face that makes her take pity on me because she sighs. "You know that unnatural hair colors are against the academy's charter?" I nod my head, pursing my lips tight. "But, considering your academic excellence, I'm willing to send you back to your dorm with a warning. You won't be attending class today, but I'll have Miranda Cabot bring by notes and make-up work." Ms. Felton looks me over and sighs. "Just make sure you correct the problem by Monday?"

I nod again because I'm just too wound up to talk.

I'm so wound up that … I feel like I might do something rash.

Pushing through her office door, I make eye contact with Tristan, but he doesn't smile or smirk. He gives me nothing to direct my anger. Without looking at anyone else, I head back to my room and I yank the devil costume from my wardrobe.

CHAPTER 8

The next day is Halloween, and I've made my decision about the party.

"You …" Miranda stares at me, dressed in the red bodycon dress, red Prada heels, horns, and clip-on tail. I've even done my makeup, putting on a smoky cat eye and vibrant lips. Red glitter adorns both cheeks, and I've taken a razor to what was left of my hair. It's now gelled up into a stylish but soft crest down the middle, gentle waves curving around my ears. "Look so freaking hot." She clamps her mouth closed and just stares at me like she's never seen me before.

I'm still fuming, but I'm also going stir crazy. Creeping around the halls and hiding in my room isn't doing it for me.

I smile.

"So do you." I gesture at Miranda's tight, pink dress and

coiffed blonde hair. Her makeup is flawless, long white gloves on her arms, gold rings glittering on her fingers. I haven't completely forgotten that I was drugged at some point on Thursday, but I also don't think I can survive Burberry Prep without her. Besides, it's easier for me to hold onto trust than believe deceit from my friends.

"I'm kind of … in shock," she continues, circling me and looking me up and down. "You look so freaking fierce." She snaps her fingers in my general direction. "*Devil Wears Prada-Scarlet Letter* realness, hunty." A genuine laugh escapes my throat as I smooth my palms down the front of my dress. It's too tight, too short, and I'm pretty sure it would look better on Miranda's thin form than my, uh, less than thin form, but I'm determined.

I'm going out tonight, and nothing's going to stop me.

I've been banned from getting my phone back this weekend, so I don't worry about Dad or whatever messages he may or may not have sent me. No, I'm going to focus on survival instead. I'm still leading the school in grades, and I'm already preparing for the orchestra auditions this Friday. If I can excel in my own ways, then I'll keep my head down and endure whatever the Idols throw at me.

"Wait until Andrew sees you," Miranda giggles, lifting my hand up and making me twirl for her. "He's going to lose his mind." She leads me out into the hall where Andrew's waiting, dressed in a ridiculously expensive looking Zoot suit. I've seen cheap versions at the Halloween store in Lower Banks, but this is … holy crap. His hair is slicked back from his face and hiding under a wide-brimmed fedora. His shoes are black and white, as shiny as the chain hanging from his pocket. He twirls it as he gapes at me. "Does she not look totally and completely *gorg*?"

Andrew's brows go up, and he reaches to adjust his pinstriped hat.

"You seriously turned this hair thing into a miracle," he tells me, and I grin, doing a little twirl before letting him take both Miranda and me by the arms. The party tonight is actually an academy sponsored event, so it's being held in the gym with a DJ, gaudy streamers, and plenty of chaperones. From what Miranda tells me, the real party starts afterwards, over by the lake.

"I'm trying to stay positive." I exhale as we approach the ridiculous arch over the gym door. It might be expensive—I'm pretty sure those are real roses woven into the trellis—but it looks much the same as every other school dance I've been to. "Tristan called me a nervous, eager charity case. And I'm okay with that. I am eager, and I am nervous, and I am here on charity, so I'm going to embrace that tonight."

"You're going to *slay*," Miranda drawls as she drags us in and over to the photo booth. People are staring at me. No, not just people, *everyone* is staring at me, but I ignore them, snatching props and taking ridiculous, over-the-top photos with my friends. We settle at a table next, and Andrew leaves to grab refreshments.

Glancing over my shoulder, I see that the dance floor is completely packed, mostly with Idols and their Inner Circle goons, but there are Plebs, too. Honestly, I've stopped even bothering to differentiate. Whatever the Idols want to happen spreads through the school like wildfire. I've been treated just as poorly by the regular students as the self-appointed elite ones.

"Look who it is," Zayd purrs, coming over to the table and leaning his forearms against it. I'm not sure what he's supposed to be, but it looks like he's taking advantage of the lax dress code to go topless. His entire upper body and both arms are covered in tattoos, and the muscles underneath are rock-hard. Something tightens in my lower belly, but I'm pretty sure it's hatred so I ignore it. "Look at you, Working Girl. Don't you look fuckable tonight."

His grin is infectious, but it's not meant to be kind, so I steel myself against the smile that tries to steal over my lips. For fuck's sake, he just called me Working Girl again. Of the three Idol boys though, he's been the least cruel. I try to give him *some* credit for that.

"Don't dick with the devil, Kaiser," I deadpan, and even when he roars with laughter, I don't react.

"Wow," he starts, standing up and raking his fingers through his sea green hair. Those emerald eyes of his sparkle as he takes me in. "Vicious." He gestures at me with fingers covered in rings, and uses the other to tug up his very low-slung black skinny jeans. "I'm digging the hair. Becky did a nice job." He pauses and pretends to grimace, like he let information slip on accident. From what I figure, Zayd Kaiser doesn't do anything on accident. As I stare at him, I try to remember the hurt on his face when the car pulled up, and it was my dad inside and not his. Then he opens his mouth again. "Ah, but you already knew she did it, huh, Charity? Her mother runs some famous beauty line." He rolls his eyes like this is information hardly worth repeating.

"Who drugged me?" I ask, because if he's already half-drunk and loose-tongued then I may as well get something out of him. "Because clearly someone did."

"I don't know, why don't you ask your friend over here?" he points to Miranda with a black-painted nail, and teases one of the lip rings pierced through either side of his mouth. When I flick my attention her way, the hurt is evident in her expression.

"I would never do something like that," she spits, and the vehemence in her voice makes me want to believe her. "I don't know how you guys did it, but you're lucky Marnye didn't press charges." Zayd shrugs his shoulders like he couldn't care less, and moves past, giving me a patronizing pat on the head before he grabs Anna Kirkpatrick around the waist and hauls her into his arms as she squeals. "Marnye?"

I turn back to find Miranda watching me, and I make myself smile.

"Don't worry. I know it wasn't you." I sit back down as Andrew approaches the table, setting out three glasses of red punch and a plate piled with hors d'oeuvres. Miranda's still staring at me like she thinks I'm mad at her, but tonight is not about what Becky and whoever else did to me. No, we're supposed to have fun tonight.

I take a sip of the punch and then raise my eyebrows. It's clearly spiked. Setting it aside, I rise to my feet, palms on the table.

"Do either of you want to dance with me?"

"I'm not drunk enough yet!" Miranda moans, and Andrew laughs as I yank her to her feet and drag her to the dance floor. Zayd's already out there, grinding up against Anna. On the opposite side of the room, I see Tristan with his hands all over some third-year wearing a yellow dress. Creed is just lounging at one of the tables, but he's got a captive audience all to himself.

I ignore them and try to have a good time with Miranda, even when Harper du Pont purposely moves over beside us so she can elbow me and whip me with her hair. Petty crap like that doesn't bother me anymore. Between the essay and the butchering of my hair, I almost crumbled, but instead I stood tall. Something as silly as this means nothing.

After a while, I trade places with Andrew and grab a bottle of water from the cooler near the front door. That's when I notice that Zayd, Tristan, Creed, Harper, Becky and Gena are all leaving with an entourage.

They must be off to the lake.

"We should go," Miranda says, breathless as she comes to stand beside me, her glitter-covered skin soaked with sweat, hand clasped around Andrew's. She grabs mine, too, and pulls me out into the cool October air before I get a chance to respond.

There are cars everywhere, and students are just piling into them at random. Miranda looks around carefully, and then selects one driven by a fourth-year girl that I don't know. Smart choice. The girl looks at me and shrugs her shoulders, too close to graduation to care maybe. Either way, we get a ride up to the lake in her blue convertible, winding down the dirt road to a picnic area that's already strung with lights, littered with kegs, and pounding with a strong bass beat.

Filthy Rich Boys

Who set this up, I have no idea.

Tonight's party is so much more colorful than usual, but it's a little creepy too, with so many students in masks. There's a graveyard nearby that I can just vaguely see through the trees. I know from the brochure that it's a family plot for Lucas Burberry, the founder of Burberry Prep, and his descendants. Nobody's been buried in there since the fifties, but it's still eerie as hell, dressed in a blanket of salty fog off the bay.

Students are hanging out in there, too, balancing on graves, making out against the sides of mausoleums. Not my thing—though I can appreciate some of the architecture. My eyes wander away from the gothic eeriness of the graveyard, and over to the row of jack-o-lanterns burning on the shore of the lake. It looks dark and endless right now, like one wrong move and you'd go tumbling through the ice-cold depths forever.

A shiver takes over me just seconds before an arm wraps around my waist and yanks me close to a warm, sweaty body.

"You showed up at the after-party," Zayd crows, clearly already on his way to being drunk. "You've got bigger balls than I thought."

"I hope you didn't actually think I had balls at all," I counter, reaching up with a hand to push against his chest. It's a mistake, putting my bare palm against those hard, inked muscles. My throat gets so tight it's suddenly hard to breathe. "I have big ovaries, maybe."

Zayd pauses for a minute, and I can feel his heartbeat underneath the wing tattoos that cover his chest. In the center, there's a crest of some sort that reminds me vaguely of the

Burberry Prep crest with the griffins on either side. And then he howls with laughter and scoops me up in his arms, like he did with Anna back in the gym.

Miranda's eyes mirror my shock as Zayd carries me over to one of the kegs where Tristan and Creed are watching some of their Inner Circle buddies face off in chugging contests. When they see him holding me, they exchange a quick glance.

"Look who has big ass ovaries!" he shouts, hefting me up in his arms like I weigh nothing. I'm shocked, actually. I know I'm short, but I'm not exactly the thinnest girl in school. "Working Girl came to party." He spins me around and I automatically reach up to put my arms around his neck, feeling the fine hairs at the base of his scalp tickle against my skin. "Do you dance, Working Girl?"

"Not really," I reply, but I'm now surrounded by the Idols and their Inner Circle. I feel like I've just walked into a trap. Of course, it's hard to be upset with Zayd's strong, inked arms under my thighs and around my waist. His body is rock-solid and piping hot. In all the places our bare skin touches, I burn. "I try, for fun, but it's not pretty."

"Kind of like you," Harper interjects, dressed as a—and I don't use this word lightly because there's really nothing wrong with being a slut—slutty princess. She has a crown, a scepter, and a puffy skirt that just barely covers her underwear. The top is pink with a plunging neckline, and she's covered head to toe in sparkles. I hate to admit it, but she looks good in the outfit.

Tristan stands beside her, dressed in a sharp as hell suit, all

Filthy Rich Boys

tailored lines and creases that could cut. I'm not sure what he's supposed to be until he sees me looking at him and smiles, a slow awful parting of his lips that reveals two expertly placed fangs in his mouth. Vampire, how creative. Only ... the sight actually makes my heart palpate just a little.

Creed is dressed in a blood-red shirt, tight black pants, boots, and an eye patch. Pirate. I think the sword at his side might actually be real. He studies me like an insect that needs to be pinned, wings forever stilled, encased behind glass. Scary.

"I don't remember you being invited to this party," Becky spits out, dressed in a matching outfit to Gena Whitley. I think they're both supposed to be genies, but all they're wearing are see-through flowy pants, top knots, and bras covered in sequins, so I'm not sure. "Was she invited, Harper?"

"Everyone's invited to this party," Zayd shouts with a hoot, and half the crowd cheers along with him. I think most of the people here tonight are too drunk to hate me. Miranda and Andrew hover nearby, a part of the Inner Circle but *this* freaking close to being pushed out of it. "Everyone's invited," Zayd repeats, spinning me around, and then carrying me through the crowd, toward the bonfire and the dance party happening at its edges.

He sets me down and then stumbles a little, using my shoulder for leverage.

Zayd blinks green eyes up at me, and then squints.

"Do you want to go swimming?" he asks, but he doesn't wait for me to answer, raising his fist in the air with a shout that draws the other students in. He grabs my hand and takes off for the dock, but I pull away at the last second, watching in disbelief as he jumps in with a dozen other partygoers. My heart skips a few beats as I wait for them all to surface from the inky blackness, but they do, bobbing up like apples in a barrel.

Zayd pulls himself out of the water, soaking wet, his green hair plastered to either side of his face. He's grinning as he stands up, towering over me with water dripping everywhere.

"You really are pretty with that red hair," he says, and then he cups my face in two wet, cold hands and leans in, pressing his lips against mine. There's the initial shock from the cold water, and then the strange realization that I'm kissing some guy I barely know, a guy that hasn't been all that nice to me to begin with. But then his lips turn to ardent heat against mine, stirring up strange feelings in my belly.

For the briefest of instances, his tongue sweeps mine, and I feel like I'm melting.

But then someone pulls Zayd back and shoves him back into the water. He comes up laughing as I stand there with my lips parted, cheeks burning. I turn and make my retreat while Zayd's friends splash him and pretend to push him under. Probably not the safest game drunk and in the dark, but there's not a chance in hell that any one of them will listen to me.

"Did I just ..." Miranda starts, and I grimace, noticing that Andrew's also staring at me like I've grown a second head. "Did you just kiss Zayd Kaiser?"

"I ... have no idea," I whisper, but of course, I do. I can still feel the tip of his tongue, scalding as it slid against my own. "He's drunk off his ass," I add, but Miranda's still

Filthy Rich Boys

staring at me like I've lost my mind.

"True," she hedges, shrugging her thin shoulders. "Whatever. He does that to everyone when he's plastered. I once saw him kiss John Hannibal on the lips after too many beers. Then they got into a fistfight and Tristan had to break them up."

My heart sinks a bit, but I push the feeling away. Zayd didn't kiss me because he has any feelings toward me. It's just something he does when he's drunk. Obviously. I mean, we don't even get along. I didn't even *want* to kiss him.

Miranda, Andrew, and I get sodas from the cooler next to the parking lot and carry them into the cemetery. Someone's lit candles, and there's a group gathered around the base of one of the graves. Tristan Vanderbilt sits on top of it with a girl in his lap, one arm around her waist, the other stroking her knee.

He's telling a ghost story of some sort, his voice so low that I can't quite make it out. We avoid their little group, which includes Harper and Becky, and meander through the rest of the graveyard, fingers brushing across the worn tops of headstones as we read off names and dates.

"Boo," Creed drawls when we come around a corner and find him sitting with a few other students, a joint in his hand. He doesn't even bother to hide it as I stare at him, lifting it to his lips and taking a drag. His blue eyes are narrowed to slits as he frowns at me before switching his attention to Miranda. "You aren't getting into any trouble, are you?" he asks, and she gapes at him.

"Asks he who has a beer in one hand and a joint in the other? Are you kidding me?" Miranda puffs out her chest as her brother comes to stand beside her, glancing first at Andrew and then back at me again. "Don't get all preachy on me, Creed. You're my *twin*, not my older brother."

"So that means I can't protect you?" he asks, still looking at me. "Why are you even hanging out with this girl? Nobody likes it. If it weren't for me, you'd be committing social suicide." He hands the joint over to Andrew, and after a split-second of hesitation, he takes it, moving away from Miranda and me to sit with his friends. He gives me an apologetic sort of look, but it's okay, I understand.

"She's a good person, unlike some of the other people in this school." Miranda turns to leave and Creed grabs her arm. When she snaps a look over her shoulder, his face hardens but he lets go. "I bet Mom would agree with me. If she had a choice, she'd swap Marnye for you in a heartbeat." The edge of Creed's mouth lifts up in a snarl, but he doesn't say anything. "Do your new friends know you used to be bullied when we lived in Grenadine Heights? I'd think you, at least, would know better."

My eyes widen as Creed grits his teeth, but then Miranda's grabbing my arm and dragging me away from their little group.

"Andrew, fucking traitor," she grumbles as we head for the exit. I know I shouldn't look back as we leave, but I do, catching Tristan's gray gaze on me. He tracks me as I go, even as he's got a girl straddling his lap, his hands cupping her ass.

Gross.

In their natural element, these guys are even worse than

Filthy Rich Boys

they are at school.

The rest of the night, I make it a priority to avoid them. Miranda helps, showing me where to find extra pumpkins, knives, and candles. We carve jack-o-lanterns, sip apple cider, and eat miniature candy bars from an orange bowl. As long as I steer clear of the Idols, everything is fine.

Reaching up to touch what's left of my hair, I cringe.

Too bad that's not an option most days.

If I want to stay here, I'm going to have to fight for my own space.

I just hope it's a fight I can actually win.

The next day, I take the off-campus pass Ms. Felton gave me, have one of the academy's cars take me into town, and buy a box of rose gold hair dye. Since the shower I took this morning washed most of the blood-red out, it takes just fine, and I find that when I look in the mirror ... I actually like it.

Take that, Becky Platter, I think, flicking off the bathroom light and heading for the mixed media room to play the academy's pedal harp. Bet I'm the only student practicing their instrument tonight.

And that's how it's going to be from now on: I'm going to go above and beyond for *myself*. What other people do or say, I'm going to let roll off of me like water off a duck's back.

Easier said than done, right?

C.M. STUNICH

The Friday after Halloween is the day I make my real stand against Becky.

Revenge can be sweet, especially when it's only my success that inflicts it.

Orchestra auditions are after class, held in the school theater. Everyone is welcome to come and watch. Back at Lower Banks, nobody would. Okay, so maybe an anxious parent or two, a best friend wanting to lend support, but for the most part, nobody cared.

Here ... everyone does.

The room is packed so full that some students are standing up in the back, watching as Mr. Carter makes his way through each student on the audition roster. According to the number pinned on my shirt, I'm dead-last, right after Becky. We're the only two students in the school gunning for first chair in harp. Good thing, too, because there *is* only one chair.

Harper is here for support, but she's not trying out. Instead, she's focused on the choir, satisfied that at least in some respect, I'll be under her thumb. Singing for the junior choir for class credit, and trying out for the academy's performance choir group are two totally different things, but she's content to rule them both.

"Tristan is starting to come around," she tells Becky as I stand there, leaning against a column and watching a petite brunette girl fumble around with her flute. She's so nervous, her hands are sweating and she can barely keep hold of the instrument. "I told him I was done sleeping around and asked if he wanted to make it official this summer."

Becky chuckles and adjusts the number pinned to her blouse.

"Well, I'm not sure I'm done playing around with the boys, but to snag Tristan, I'd do it, too." Becky pauses, and the two girls glance over at me like they've just realized I'm standing there. "Getting engaged to someone like him this early and locking him down is probably a good idea." My mouth tightens, but I don't turn to look at them. What do I care if one female monster wants to get engaged to another male monster? They can make little monster babies and go on to terrorize the world together. They deserve each other.

My lips twitch as I think about Tristan, bending Kiara over the sink. Harper can have her man-whore fiancé. And yet … my stomach twists, and my good humor is short-lived.

There are some incredibly talented students in this school, and watching them play onstage is awe-inspiring. So much so that I soon forget that weird twinge of jealousy, my mind numbing to the constant chatter of the two Idol girls. Zayd is front and center in the auditorium, sitting right next to Mr. Carter. He's a student 'helper', along with a half-dozen fourth-years who are all in the advanced orchestra. How that jerk got to be on the panel is beyond me. He's a rock star, not a concert pianist.

I don't think about that kiss. Bet he was too drunk to remember it anyway.

Once Becky's turn rolls around, she shoves her way past me, nearly knocking me over. I let it go, gritting my teeth, and wait as she sits down to play. A hush falls over the crowd because there's not a student at this school—first-year or fourth-year alike—that doesn't know what's going on with me.

Becky inhales, tossing her blond hair over one shoulder, and flashes a winning smile to the crowd. She starts to play, and I recognize it as the one and only piece Mozart ever wrote for the harp: *Concerto for Flute, Harp, and Orchestra*. It's a good choice, and one of my personal favorites. Becky, however, just doesn't have the skills to pull it off, not even with her friends from the Inner Circle accompanying her.

She's pretty when she plays, her eyes half-lidded, that evil smirk of hers wiped clean for a brief moment in time. Makes me love the harp all that much more, knowing it has the power to ward off hate. Her expression is clear and open, as if she wasn't the daughter of Satan. Well ... I glance over at Harper, running her fingers through her long, brunette hair and completely ignoring her friend's performance in favor of her phone. Maybe Harper is the daughter of Satan, and Becky's just her bestie.

Becky finishes to a standing ovation, bowing and blushing, touching a hand to her chest. When she turns to look at me, her eyes flash with darkness, and I make sure to give her a wide berth as she passes, moving onstage to the sound of booing and hissing.

"Alright, alright," Mr. Carter shouts, standing up and lifting his palms until there's silence. "Next sound I hear out of someone's mouth that's anything but encouraging, and you're out." He sits back down and nods for me to continue.

Filthy Rich Boys

A smile lights my face, and I take a seat.

I've chosen a more contemporary piece, at my own risk, but it speaks to me, and I need to feel that joy to sit up here and play in front of such a hostile audience. My eyes wander the crowd and catch on Zayd's emerald gaze, sparkling as he leans forward and rests his chin on his folded hands. Tristan and Creed are easy to spot, sitting on opposite ends of the auditorium. Their pull is equally strong, and I flick my gaze between them before refocusing on the Lyon & Healy harp in front of me. It's a beautiful instrument, easily worth more than my father's house … err, Train Car.

Closing my eyes, I center myself and take a deep breath.

My fingers begin to move, playing *How Hill* by Patrick Hawes, written for royal harpist Claire Jones. The tune starts off nice and light, like sunshine through clouds, and I do my best to convey that feeling in my playing, a smile curving across my lips. Pedal harps are no joke, one of the most expensive instruments out there. To rent even a shitty one, Dad had to work a second job. He brought me here, to this place, and even if I'm upset with him for Parents' Weekend, I love him to bits.

That, too, I try to put into my music, feeling the vibrations on my skin, like I'm bathing in sound. The song slows, stops, and picks its way back to life, the upbeat tune reminiscent of rain on a warm summer day, feeding the parched earth. I lean into that feeling, forgetting for a moment where I am, and who's watching me.

The song finishes with a little flourish that fades out, softens, and says good-bye with a kiss.

Exhaling, I drop my arms to my sides and look out at the

audience.

Zayd's mouth has dropped open, and before I even get a chance to stand up, he's on his feet and clapping. I'm a little ... shocked, to say the least. He's been nothing but rude to me, and now he's clapping? Mr. Carter stands up, too, and then everyone else follows suit.

Tristan doesn't clap, and neither does Creed, but they watch me with a certain level of appreciation that's impossible to hide. My cheeks flush, and I take a small bow before scurrying offstage.

Later that night, when the results are posted online ... I get first chair.

CHAPTER 9

After the Halloween party, and the orchestra auditions, I'm left with two weeks of jibes, elbows, and crappy notes taped to my door, but that's pretty much it. I swear, I can feel the three Idol guys watching me, but mostly, I'm ignored. Becky and Harper are the worst, carving the words *Working Girl* into my locker. When I walk up and catch them doing it, they don't even look sorry.

Zack's been messaging me on and off, just random things, but I'm so puzzled over *why* he's bothering to text me that I don't respond much. About a week after the auditions, Miranda is hanging out in my room and happens to see a series of texts come in. She digs her claws into me and refuses to let go until I tell her everything, about Zack being the ringleader of the bullying I suffered in sixth, seventh, and eighth grade. How he was the one that found me after I took the pills. How we briefly dated.

She leaves the subject alone for about ... three days before she brings it up again. I'm able to avoid her questioning for the most part by pretending I'm embroiled in schoolwork. It's mostly true, too. With the workload pushed on us before our first official break of the year, I'm worked to the bone. It's a relief when I turn in the final assignment of November.

The first day of fall break is a blur of activity, students saying their goodbyes, packing trunks up and leaving in the shiny black academy cars. I watch them go from the cozy penthouse where Miranda lives with Creed. The first time she invited me up here, I refused because I didn't want to end up running into that jerk. She promised he was barely here, and so far, she's been right. I haven't had a single run-in with Creed in or around the apartment.

"So you're leaving Monday?" I ask, and Miranda nods, stuffing her volleyball uniform into a duffel bag. The Cabots are out of the country for the rest of the month, so Miranda's going on an academy-sponsored athletics giveaway. I'm not exactly the sporty type, and Dad is out of town on a job, so ... I'm stuck here. "I feel like Harry in book one," I groan, putting my face in one of the decorative pillows lining the window seat. "Left alone at Hogwarts for break."

Miranda grins, putting her shiny blonde hair up in a high pony.

"Creed will be here," she jokes, and I shudder. I don't even have to fake it; my disgust for him is involuntary. "But I already warned him to stay away from you. He'll probably be busy with ... you know, whatever it is that he does." Miranda chucks her bag next to the front door just before we both hear

Filthy Rich Boys

the click of a lock. We exchange a look as it swings open and Creed enters, freezing when he spots me in his living room.

"Hey." There's a dark note in that syllable, those blue eyes of his sliding over to me. He takes in my rose gold hair and flat facial expression, and then looks back at Miranda, closing the door behind him and then reaching up to unbutton his shirt. Unbidden, my gaze falls to his long fingers, watching as the fabric of his shirt parts and reveals smooth, hard muscles underneath. "I'll be in and out. Don't worry about excusing the help."

"You can go to hell," Miranda snaps, putting her hands on her hips as her brother breezes by, slamming his bedroom door behind him. Just before it closes, I catch a glimpse of his back, all sinuous muscle over a lean frame. *Shit.* When I look back at Miranda, she's gaping at me. "Are you checking him out?" she chokes, and I'm such a terrible liar that my mouth just opens and closes a couple of times. "You *were* checking him out! And after he's been so mean to you."

"I ... he's ... I'm not blind," I grumble, crossing my arms over my chest. My cheeks are flaming as I glance back out the window and see Tristan walking Harper and Becky out to a car. He doesn't get in though, just helps them in and closes the door before stepping back. Huh. Is he not leaving for the week either? If I end up getting stuck here with more than one Idol, this could be a worse Thanksgiving than the time Dad passed out from one too many beers, and the raw turkey rotted on the counter. I was only five at the time or I would've tried to cook it myself.

"Gross," Miranda mutters, shivering and shaking her head, ponytail flying. "I still think you should message Zack back." My mouth purses, but my phone is burning a hole in my pocket. From Zack: *I'm sorry about what happened with your dad. I'll be in town for Thanksgiving if you want me to pick you up.* I mean, what the hell is *that* invite about? My brain scrambles for an explanation, but comes up blank. Zack's words to Tristan echo around in my head: *save it for fall break, dickhead.* Save what? This whole situation is weird. "Why not?"

"Because he treated me like total crap for *years*, and then dated me behind the scenes for six months. Like, he never told a single person we were together." Looking down at my hands, I pick at the edges of my nails. I could really use a new paint job. The red I lacquered on for Halloween is coming off in ragged pieces.

"And what exactly did you do when you were together?" Miranda asks, plopping down next to me on the window seat. She leans in conspiratorially, eyes shining. I'm sorry to disappoint her, but there's not much to tell. Besides that, Creed's just one door away, and I'm not about to spill any secrets.

"Went to the movies. Walked in the park. Kissed." I shrug, and run my fingers through my hair. I'm still getting used to the length, but I like the new color. The rose gold looks good on me, and the lightener that Miranda put on my brows actually turned out okay. "What else?"

"So you're just going to ghost him then?" she prods, sighing and leaning back against the window. Her eyes scan the apartment, its simple but elegant white couches, the chandelier above the dining table, the kitchenette. Even in

Filthy Rich Boys

Grenadine Heights, an apartment like this would cost ten times my dad's usual monthly salary. As a student dorm, it's just ... excessive. Everything at Burberry Prep is excessive. I like my classes, but I'm not sure how I feel about everything else.

The door to Creed's bedroom opens before I get a chance to respond, and I gape as he walks out in a pair of gray sweats, slung low on his hips, those gorgeous V lines of his glaringly obvious in the low light. They're so prominent they cast shadows. He's tugging on a wifebeater as he walks in, and I catch sight of a broad, flat chest and stomach before he finally pulls it down. Pretty sure I see a tattoo, too, but it's hard to be sure.

"If you have any sense at all, you'll steer clear of Zack Brooks," Creed drawls, his words effortlessly flowing past those perfect lips of his. He opens the fridge and bends low, his long form folding in half, muscles in his upper back and shoulders tensing as he rummages around for something to drink. "He's no good."

"Like you are?" I snap, feeling a hot warmth rush through me. It's an unfamiliar burn, one that makes me shift in discomfort.

Creed stands back up, pushing white-blonde hair from his forehead, eyes heavy and half-lidded. He has a can of soda in one hand, a blank, bored look on his face.

"Did I ever say I was? Make no mistake, Charity: I don't like you. I've been pretty clear about my feelings, *and* my agenda. So take what I'm saying into consideration: Zack Brooks is bad news." He moves into the middle of the room, and cracks the top on the can, looking at me over the rim as he takes a drink.

"Fuck off, Creed," Miranda snaps, but he ignores her, standing there and staring at me. Things have felt different since the Halloween party; I can feel it now as he looks at me, and sweat begins to bead on the back of my neck. When she gets no response from her brother, Miranda sighs and pushes a few strands of hair off her forehead. "Is Tristan staying for the week?"

"Yeah, why?" Creed asks, and I realize with a start that I actually like the sound of his voice. You know, when he's not reading my most private thoughts aloud to the world. "You two have something you want to talk to me about?" The way his voice cools as he speaks is impressive, conveying about a million different emotions that are invisible in that bored princely face of his. The only noticeable change in his expression is the narrowing of his eyes.

"Just … when you and Zayd and Tristan are left alone together, bad things happen." The way Creed smiles at his sister's words makes that statement so much more terrifying. All three of the guys are going to be here this week? Fantastic.

"Mm." Creed looks to me again, and I try not to notice that his nipples are slightly hard beneath his white wifebeater. I can see the shadow of them beneath the thin fabric, too. Swallowing the lump in my throat, I force my attention back to his face. "Zack might be around, you know, whether you ghost him or not." He takes another sip of his soda, staring at me from those ice-blue eyes of his.

"What would Zack be doing here?" I ask, and Creed

scoffs, shaking his head at me.

"Tell him to go to hell, transfer out of this school, and I'll make sure you get into Grenadine Heights High. What do you think about that?" My mouth pops open, but he holds up a hand before I can respond. I'm shaking, and there's this weird twisty feeling in my stomach again, but I don't have time to analyze it. "I'm not doing any of this for you. This is for Miranda."

"Sending my one and only girlfriend away because you don't like her net worth is somehow a boon to me?" Miranda snaps, but Creed's already turning away, pausing in his doorway with those long, elegant fingers of his resting against the doorjamb. The way he's staring at me makes me want to fidget, but I force myself to sit still and stare back.

"This offer lasts until Monday. You have two days to figure out what you're going to do." Creed smiles at me, a slow curving twist of lips that makes my stomach burst into butterflies. I know he's cruel, and I'm no masochist, but I can't help the strange flutters of excitement I get when he looks at me. "This is my final offer."

"Or what?" I ask, lifting my chin in defiance. Creed ignores me, slipping into his room like a shadow and slamming the door. After a few moments, we both hear the slow, sensual sounds of a man pleasuring himself.

"Oh gross!" Miranda yells, slamming her palms over her ears. "We might be twins, but that's serious TMI, you asshole!" She stands up, grabbing me by the arm and dragging me into the hall.

But I can't deny that those sounds are going to stick with me for a long, long time.

Damn. Maybe I really am a masochist?

On Monday, I finally get up the courage to text Zack. The very fact that Creed's trying to put me off of him makes me want to keep going. Stupid, I know, but anything that pisses the Idols off makes me happy.

I don't have any plans on Thanksgiving, I type out, considering my words for a moment. *I wouldn't mind having someone around to eat turkey and pumpkin pie with.* Shooting the text off before I can question myself, I fall back on my bed with a sigh. Miranda's gone, but Andrew's here … somewhere. I consider going to find him and decide that I may as well hit The Mess for lunch.

As far as I can tell, there are maybe a dozen students on campus, possibly less. There's a skeleton staff of cooks, cleaners, and teachers. Ms. Felton and Mr. Carter are on duty, and I figure it couldn't hurt to get in some extra harp practice over the week. I mean, what else am I going to do? Sit on my phone and scroll Instagram all day?

Slipping into a pair of holey jeans, a pink tank, and a leather jacket, I head out into the hall and make my way around the corner, past the chapel entrance, and down towards The Mess. I don't see Andrew, but I do shoot him a quick text to see if he wants to eat with me.

Just before I head into the restaurant, I catch the faintest blur of green, and do a double take. Zayd is making his way

Filthy Rich Boys

down the hallway like he's on a mission. Even though I know I'm being stupid, I decide to peek around the corner and see what he's up to. I mean, without girls to hit on, me to bully, or schoolwork to focus on, what do these guys even do?

Zayd heads straight down the hall and out the back door that leads to the outdoor amphitheater, and the small staff parking lot. Against my better judgement, I head the same way. I figure if he catches me following him, I'll just say I'm going for a walk to the pond to read. I've got my phone, and a Kindle app, so who's to say I'm not?

The back doors are covered in stained glass, images of weeping angels etched with bright colors and lined with lead. They let light in, but block the view from outside. So I wait a good minute or so to be safe, and then slip out, heading down the graveled path until I'm in sight of the parking lot.

"Well, shit, Vanderbilt, I'm impressed," Zayd whistles, tucking his inked fingers in the pockets of his skintight black jeans. He circles a black vintage car with his brows raised, sliding a look over to Tristan Vanderbilt as he leans against the hood.

"I suppose you needed a new car after you wrapped the last one around a tree," Creed drawls, already lounging in the car with his arms spread open across the seatbacks. "How much did this set daddy back?"

"Do you really care?" Tristan asks as Zayd lights up a cigarette, pausing near the front of the sleek little sportscar. "It's a 1961 Ferrari Spider. Price is irrelevant. Besides, my dad has enough cars. He can spare one for the week."

"And if he finds out you took it?" Creed asks, but the look Tristan levels on him proves to me without a doubt that the three of them might be passably friendly, but they're not exactly *friends*. "I mean, he can't be thrilled with you, considering your grades." Creed smiles, but it's a nasty expression when turned on Tristan. "Second place just means first place loser, right? And to some chick who went to public school? How humiliating."

"Why don't you let me worry about my dad?" Tristan says, his voice like dark poison. It makes my skin tingle, and my brain goes to places I'd really rather it didn't. *Tristan's hands wrapped around that Kiara girl's hips, his cock thrusting between her legs.* Shaking my head, I throw the image off, putting my palm flat against the stone wall in the alcove. "You have more important things to think about: like how I'm going to win Harper for sophomore year. After all, she's practically begged an engagement ring off of me."

"Well, I guess your family needs the money, huh?" Creed replies, his blond hair fluttering in the wind. His smile is wicked. "We'll see how the week goes though, won't we? Don't count your bitches before they hatch."

"Clever," Zayd whistles, and then he throws his head back with laughter.

The door to the amphitheater opens behind me, and one of the janitors—I think his name is Mark—steps out with a push broom. All three guys swing their gazes his way, locking onto me.

Shit.

Well, now that I've been spotted, I can't just stand here, and turning around to go back inside feels like running, so ... I make myself start off down the path, veering off at the last

Filthy Rich Boys

second to stand between Tristan and Zayd.

They just stare at me while Zayd smokes, Creed lounges, and Tristan's eyes narrow.

"Nice car," I say, exhaling sharply and tucking my hands into my pockets. For the life of me, I can't figure out why I walked over here. I must be crazy. It's like there's this string inside of me, tugging me toward these crazy assholes.

"Why don't you climb in?" Tristan asks, managing to keep his usual hatred and disdain from his voice. He towers over me, wearing a black wool coat, black button-up, and slacks. He looks thirty, not fifteen. But in a good way, mature, mysterious. His raven-dark hair swirls in the wind, and he brushes it back. "It's the nicest car you'll ever sit in. May as well take advantage."

"You're a jerk," I spit out, feeling that hot anger surge up in me. "What on earth makes you think I'd ever get into your car?"

"Because you're curious about what we're doing," Zayd says, his voice husky, his green eyes shimmering with mischief. He's wearing a leather jacket, but it's much edgier than mine, with a dozen random zippers, patches, and pins. He finishes his cigarette, tosses it aside, and crushes it with his boot before climbing onto the trunk and putting his boots in between the two front seats. "It's why you followed me, right?"

"I ..."

"You can sit on my lap," Creed says, completely deadpan. He stares at me, searching my expression as I look between the three of them and weigh my choices. I can turn around and go back inside which is probably the smart decision. Or I can risk going with three guys that hate me just to satisfy my curiosity. My tongue runs over my lower lip in thought.

"Get in," Tristan repeats, stepping close to me. He smells like cinnamon and peppermint, and I feel those little butterflies in my stomach take flight. They're idiots, those insects of emotions, reacting to the beauty in Tristan's face instead of the anger in his soul.

After a moment, I give in and head over to the passenger side door, opening it and looking at Creed's lap with a wary eye. *This is weird, Marnye,* I think, but I shove the feeling aside and take a seat before I can think too hard about it.

Creed's arm curls around my waist, and that familiar knot in my chest tightens up. My heart is pounding, pulse racing, as he closes the door, and I sit perched on his lap, facing toward Tristan as he climbs into the driver's seat. When I shift slightly on his lap, Creed's fingers dig into my side.

"Don't wiggle like that; you'll give me a hard-on," he drawls, like his words are no big deal. Me, I gape and I wonder if I've just lived a sheltered life, or if these guys are just hedonistic as fuck.

"Seriously? I thought I was just a useless charity case?" Creed shrugs and leans in close, putting his lips near that sensitive spot between my neck and shoulder. His breath is warm, but I shiver when it feathers across my skin.

"Even whores have their purpose." I raise my hand to slap him, but he grabs my wrist, squeezing just hard enough to make me cry out. As soon as he releases me, I finish what I started and crack my palm against his cheek. Tristan laughs, this low, cruel sound, as he starts up the sweet purr of the engine and takes off at such a rapid speed I'm worried Zayd's going to tumble off the back into the gravel.

He just hollers in excitement and lifts his arms in the air like he's on a rollercoaster.

Tristan does a few wild donuts on the gravel, making my stomach lurch and causing Creed's arm to tighten even further around me as we're thrown around inside the little sports car.

"I'm not a whore," I grind out finally, when we stop spinning and take off down one of the dirt roads that lead deeper into the campus. Most of the third and fourth year classes are held in outbuildings spread throughout the vast acreage of Burberry Prep, but as a first year, there's hardly any reason to come back here, so it's all new to me.

"That's right: you're a virgin," Creed amends, but he doesn't sound any less disdainful. "My mistake."

"How …" I start, and then realize I should've denied the accusation. My mouth flattens into a tight line as Tristan smirks from the driver's seat.

"How fucking cliché. You really are pathetic, aren't you."

"Pathetic? Because I don't screw everything that walks? If you ask me, *you're* the one who's pathetic. Have you ever cared about a single girl you've slept with?" Tristan's hands tighten on the wheel, but he doesn't respond, acting like I'm invisible again. I can't decide what's worse, being mocked or being ignored.

"Some guys have a thing for popping cherries," Zayd remarks absently, like we're discussing the weather. "Never been my thing. Sorry, but it's so not attractive. I like a girl who knows what she's doing."

"Guess I'm not your type then," I snap back, and he howls with laughter. Pig. Turning away, I try to focus on the changing leaves of the trees, the gorgeous yellow, orange, and red that dots the landscape, broken up by green lawns, and small brick buildings with gold-letter signage.

"Guess not," Zayd murmurs, leaning forward and putting his elbows on his knees.

We rumble down the road, past the classrooms, taking a sharp left just before we hit the athletic fields, courts, and stadiums. There's one for every sport: baseball, lacrosse, golf, track and field, tennis, football, soccer, cross country, hockey, basketball, squash, wrestling, swimming, and riflery. It'd be impressive, if I cared at all about sports.

After a while, Tristan turns on the stereo in the car, and a semi-familiar voice purrs out.

It's Zayd's band.

"Turn that shit off," Creed snaps, and Zayd scowls from behind him.

"Really? Screw you, dude."

"It's better than your dad's crappy music, but it still sucks," Tristan adds, and Zayd's face darkens several shades. He runs a tattooed hand over his face as Tristan changes over to a different song, some hip hop track that I don't recognize.

We end up pulling into a small parking lot behind the main lodge at Lucas Lake, and my brows crinkle as Tristan parks next to the rear entrance.

"Why did we drive the back way if we were just coming up here?" I ask, and I get looked at like I'm an idiot.

"Because we're doing horrible, horrible things to you

Filthy Rich Boys

here, and we don't want anyone to know where we're at." Tristan looks at me with those dark eyes, his full lips in a flat line, and even though my heart leaps in my chest, and a rush of discomfort comes over me, I get the idea that maybe this is his idea of a joke. As a young woman, I don't really find it all that funny.

"Don't joke like that," I snap, my skin breaking out in goose bumps as I start to wonder whether this was a good idea or not. Zayd laughs at me again, hopping out of the car and then reaching in to pull me from Creed's arms. He tosses me over his shoulder and smacks me in the ass.

"Chill out, Working Girl. We're just here to party and gamble, that's it." He carries me over to the steps and sets me down while I debate punching him in the face.

"Did you seriously just touch my ass?" My face is flaming, and I don't know whether to hit him or verbally ream him or what. Before I get a chance to do either, the sound of cars coming from the academy's south entrance cracks the still air, and I raise my eyebrows as a good two dozen cars rumble into the parking lot, filling up every available space and then some. It's like Tetris, but with million dollar cars. The cheapest thing here is a Cadillac Escalade with the sports package.

The door to an orange McLaren opens, and out steps Zack.

My mouth drops open at the sight of him, his dark eyes sweeping me and narrowing. He flicks his gaze from Zayd to Creed to Tristan, and then back to me again. He doesn't look very happy to see me here, or with them.

"Marnye," he says, his voice like cool shadows as he steps

closer, his huge frame blocking out the rest of the crowd. I'm relieved to see other girls, and I realize how freaking lucky I am that these guys aren't rapists. After my time living in Lower Banks, I should know better than to take chances like this. "What are you doing here?"

"I could ask you the same thing," I start, looking him up and down in his letterman jacket, jeans, and black t-shirt. The cotton fabric stretches across his broad chest, emphasizing how toned he got over the summer. The boy I'm looking at now is more like a man than the kid I last saw at LBMS. "I texted you back to confirm Thanksgiving plans." He tucks his hands in his pockets, and I meet his gaze again, realizing absently that Tristan, Creed, and Zayd are all staring at me.

"I haven't had a chance to look at my phone," I hedge as Tristan slips out of his jacket and tosses it into the backseat of his car before heading up the steps toward the lodge. He unlocks the doors with a pair of keys from his pocket, and the crowd starts hauling in duffel bags and suitcases.

Um, what?

"Your hair," he starts, but he doesn't exactly finish his sentence, and I'm left wondering if he likes it or not. I mean, it doesn't matter *what* he thinks, but it'd be kind of nice if he did, right? Zack turns back to his car, yanks out a duffel bag, and carries it toward the steps, pausing briefly next to me. Our eyes meet, and a crackle of electricity snaps in the air between us.

I'm having trouble remembering to breathe.

"Looks nice," Zack finally adds, and then he's on his way past me, and I'm left gaping behind him.

Filthy Rich Boys

"I bet you Lizzie shows up tonight," Zayd tells Creed as Zack takes his bag up the steps, glancing back at me one last time before disappearing inside.

"Bet me what?" Creed asks, leaning casually against the exterior wall of the lodge with his arms crossed over his chest. "If you say those cowboy boots your dad got you at auction, then you're on."

Zayd gapes for a moment, and then snaps his mouth shut, letting the edge of his lips curl up in a small grin.

"You want to be a cowboy, baby?" he drawls, laughing and tugging at his lip ring for a moment.

"I want to fuck a cowgirl, that's what," Creed amends, as I look between the two of them with scrunched brows.

"It's a deal, but if I win, you lay off Becky Platter for the rest of the year. She's mine." Creed shrugs, and then holds out a hand. Both boys shake, and then I hear Zayd mumble *idiot* under his breath.

"Could someone please tell me what's going on?" I ask as Zayd throws an arm over my shoulder and turns me around to head inside. Even though I'm not particularly thrilled about him touching me, he seems to do it to everyone, so I let it go. "Are we even allowed in here?"

"Allowed, that's an interesting word." Zayd pulls me into the cool darkness of the lodge, and I can see that someone's already started a fire. To be fair, it's pretty chilly out here, and it'll take the heater a while to get to all the rooms. This place is massive. "I wouldn't worry so much about that, Charity."

"My name is fucking Marnye," I grind out, but I know it's useless. Doesn't mean I have to accept them calling me that, though it's preferable to Working Girl. "Who are all these people?"

"Friends." Zayd winks at a dark-haired girl who's glaring at me from the direction of the sliding doors. Her eyes track our movements as Zayd leads me into the kitchen, and finally drops his arm, unpacking a couple bottles of alcohol from one of the paper bags on the counter. "From other schools." He unscrews the top on a bottle of rum, tips it to his lips, and then offers it over to me. I raise an eyebrow and politely decline. "Suit yourself," he grumbles, shrugging his shoulders and then grinning as a pair of guys in letterman jackets appear and start handing out high fives and some of those awkward man hugs where they slap each other in the back.

"Marnye." It's Zack again. I don't even have to turn around to know who's talking to me. His voice is far too distinct, cutting through the murmur of the other students. When I spin to look at him, he's shed his jacket, showing off the thick, hard muscles in his arms, the wide breadth of his shoulders. Those brown eyes of his snag mine, and my heart shudders in my chest. "Are you staying the night?"

"We're not sleeping here," Tristan scoffs, coming out of the back hallway, his silver eyes focused on Zack's face. He's rolled his sleeves to the elbow, and as I watch, he untucks his shirt, flashing a bit of the skin above his waistband. I catch the briefest glimpse of a tattoo there, but then he covers it up and I'm left wondering if I imagined it. "We'll go back to the main campus." The smile he gives Zack reminds me of a black widow spider, calculating and self-serving. There's no room for emotion in that expression. "Why? Were you hoping to get Charity to stay in your room?"

Filthy Rich Boys

Zack doesn't say anything, but his eyes move from Tristan to me, like he thinks there's something going on between us. Nothing could be further from the truth. Honestly, just the idea makes my stomach hurt. Tristan is, well, for lack of a better word, he's *mean*.

"I'm confused," I start as Tristan looks me over and smirks. "What festivities? Isn't this just a party?"

"You brought her here, and she doesn't even know what's going on?" Zack snaps, his voice angry and thick with emotion. "What the hell, Vanderbilt?"

"We were getting to that, *Brooks*," Tristan snaps back, his voice like whiplash, striking through the room like lightning. He could probably command armies, this guy. Considering his penchant for cruelty, that scares me. I rub my sweaty palms down the front of my jeans. There's clearly a lot going on here that I'm not understanding, and I get the feeling I won't understand it until one of these cryptic assholes sits down and explains it to me.

That's not likely to happen either, I gather.

"Bet she hates you by the end of the week," Tristan purrs, smiling like the cat who's licked—and maybe also fucked—the cream. "Once she finds out what you did, that girl you killed …"

"Jesus Christ, man," Zack snarls, and I raise my eyebrows. Even in the years he picked on me, he was never angry, just cold and matter-of-fact. Seeing him get angry is pretty terrifying. And … wait, what did Tristan just say?

"You killed somebody?" I choke, and Zack shakes his head, running his fingers through his chocolate hair. He looks like he's about to kill Tristan, that's for sure.

"It's not like that," Zack continues as Tristan makes himself a rum and coke, and then heads outside, leaving more questions than answers in his wake. I stare at Zack for a moment, waiting for him to explain further, but instead, he just turns and walks away, slamming the door to one of the bedrooms.

Wow.

I'm really out of the loop, aren't I?

Zayd's busy setting up kegs in the corner, and Creed is nowhere to be seen. So even though I'm most definitely *not* friends with any of these guys, I seek Tristan out on the deck, his gray eyes the same color as the sky above the lake.

"I owe you an explanation," he says, his voice as smooth as silk. Just the sound of it makes me shiver. I try really hard not to notice the swell of muscle in his forearms, just a peek at how much strength must be in that tight body of his. *He has a nice ass, too, for a psychopath.* I mean, he must be one, right, considering the way he acts?

"You really do," I start, softening slightly. How stupid am I? I forgive too easily, I know that. Dad once told me that when he was super drunk, that I forgave my mom too easily for leaving us. She found her way to greener pastures, but I always tried to keep it in my mind that she tried to take me with her. Tried. And then ... dumped me at a rest stop at age three because her newest boyfriend didn't like kids. My eyes close against the pain, and when I open them, Tristan is staring down at me with that stony expression of his.

"I said if you lasted the first week, I'd tell you about that girl I fucked." My mouth drops open, but I'm seriously speechless. Every time I think these guys have hit a new low, they plummet even further down my list of respectability. They've been so horrible to me, that even if they started farting rainbows, wearing halos, and gifting me the world, I don't think we could ever truly be friends.

"Believe it or not, I don't care what you did with that girl or any other." I cross my arms over my chest and take a step away from his chilly peppermint scent. The wind teases his hair around his cruel face, but there's not much left of mine to tease. Sadly, I lift my fingers to the back of my neck. No more tumbling brunette waves.

"You were the one that asked," Tristan continues, turning to face me, like he's scented a challenge and now can't bear to let go. His eyes glimmer like flint, hard but ready to spark and start flames. "I assumed you were curious because you wanted to know what I could do for you."

"Dude, are you talking about your conquests again?" Zayd asks, dragging a keg out to the deck and standing up to wipe some sweat off of his face with his shirt. After a moment, he just shrugs and takes it off completely, flashing all those colorful tattoos of his. When he turns around, I look again, and I'm sure I see it this time: there's an infinity tattoo on his right hip.

So … Zayd definitely has one. Pretty sure I saw one on Creed. Tristan, too.

What the hell?

"Why don't you just tell her about the girls you *aren't* banging? It'd be a shorter list." Tristan smirks, but the way he looks at Zayd isn't pleasant. There's some rivalry there for sure. Zayd looks between me and him for a moment, and then shakes his head. "Creed's up to something, and I have a feeling it's nothing good." He pauses as Andrew comes out onto the deck.

Right away, I can feel it, a tension between Andrew and Tristan. The latter man's fists curl tight, knuckles whitening. With the other hand, he sips his drink.

"Marnye?" Andrew asks, blue eyes wide with surprise. "What are you doing here?"

"We invited her," Tristan says, stone-cold. He looks down at me, and his expression morphs into something savage, but ardent, too. When he leans close and his lips brush my cheek, warmth blooms in my chest. "Try to survive the party, and we'll see what you're really made of." He stalks off into the house, leaving me alone to the wolves.

I swear, everyone's staring at me.

"You keep saying you don't drink, but maybe tonight, you should give it a try." Zayd holds out a red Solo cup, green eyes focused on me. "You might need it. Don't worry: Creed never tries the same trick twice. No breathalyzers tonight."

He drops the cup in my hand, and then turns away to focus on his friends.

I pour the liquid out in the bushes next to the deck and steel myself for a long, long night.

CHAPTER 10

Luckily, not everyone at the party is a maniacal psycho, and I end up sitting around a table with a bunch of drunk football players, kicking their asses at various boardgames. I'm laughing so hard, my stomach hurts, and for the first time since I got to this school, I almost feel normal again.

Inside though, I know it won't last long.

And I'm right about that. Around eleven o'clock is when the shit starts, and Creed comes sweeping through the lodge and onto the deck. He turns the surround sound system off, and the entire crowd goes quiet.

"Derrick Barr," I hear him say as I scramble to my feet and push through the crowd until I'm standing on the deck, finding Creed facing off against this huge guy in a red football jersey. I move around the circle that's formed until I can see his face. He's not smiling.

"Shit, here we go," Zayd murmurs, clearly drunk. His eyes though are still sharp. He takes another drink from his plastic cup, and then lifts it up in a salute. "Good riddance, Derrick, it was nice knowing you."

"What's going on?" I ask, but Zayd just shrugs, standing so close to me that I can feel the heat from his body. Underneath the slight smell of alcohol and tobacco, I get a whiff of geranium and sage, this sweet-and-savory scent that makes my nose tingle.

"Creed's about to destroy someone," he says, and then pauses, like he's just thought of something. Zayd turns fully to look at me, cocking one dark brow. His hair might be sea green, but his brows are still black. "When Creed decides it's time to end someone, he does it with one, clean cut. Tristan, he likes to play with his food. I've never seen the pair of them fail before ... except with you." Zayd cocks his head to one side. "Holy shit. Except for you, huh, Working Girl?"

I purse my lips at the nickname, but turn my attention back to the scene on the deck.

Creed is barefoot, but still dressed in the shirt and slacks that make up the academy uniform. His white-blond hair gets tousled by the wind, but the rest of him is still, unmoving.

"You've been texting my sister?" he asks, and I see both Andrew and Tristan perk up on the opposite side of the circle. Andrew's friends with Miranda and me, so that makes sense. But Tristan? I still can't figure out his intentions toward her. He clearly dislikes her brother with a passion.

"So what about it? She's a big girl," Derrick says, tossing back his cup and then crushing the plastic. He chucks it off the edge of the deck and into the darkness which bothers the crap out of me—I can't stand littering—but I'm rooted to the spot, looking between the two men.

"Did she give you permission to share her photos with your friends?" Creed continues, his blue eyes narrowing to slits. Damn. I thought he hated me, but the ice in his voice is about as warm as deep space. Derrick runs his fingers through his frost-tipped hair, his face tight, like he knows he messed-up big time, but isn't sure how to fix it. "Well, I asked you a question, you fucking Neanderthal. Yes or no?"

"What do you care what I do with your sister?" Derrick starts to move away when Creed's hand lashes out and grabs him around the shoulder.

"You don't leave until I'm finished with you," he says, and he's no longer drawling in that lazy, royal way of his. Instead, he sounds like he's about to lose his shit. "I've made it very clear: my sister is off-limits."

"Yeah, well, your sister's a whore," Derrick says with a brutish laugh, shaking Creed's hand off. He starts toward the sliding doors, and I think for a brief moment there that Creed's actually going to let him walk off. Silly me.

"Your brother, Darryn Barr, how's he been doing lately?" Creed asks, and the ice in his voice seriously gives me goose bumps. It's an awful, awful sound. Derrick pauses, but he doesn't turn around. "Because from what I've seen, he's been enjoying his new team members more than usual." Creed slides his phone from his pocket, and sends out a mass text that pings every phone at that party—including mine. I wonder how he got my number, but then, I figure he could've easily stolen it from Miranda's phone.

Oh Miranda, I think, feeling my stomach clench. It doesn't take a genius to figure out what sort of pictures might have been shared around. *Why didn't she tell me?* A niggle of hurt worms its way into my chest, but I do my best to ignore it. We've only been friends for three months. It makes sense that there'd be things she hasn't shared with me. After all, I haven't told her about my mother and the rest stop. Or how she only lives thirty minutes from me, but I've only seen her a handful of times in the last twelve years.

We all have secrets we can't or won't share. It's human nature.

I don't look at my phone, but I can see Zayd holding his. There's a picture of some guy in a football jersey sucking another guy's dick. My brows go up in surprise as Derrick snarls and spins on Creed.

"Where the fuck did you get this?" Derrick demands, getting up in Creed's face. Creed is a few inches shorter, and not quite as wide as Derrick, but to be fair, Derrick is built like a pickup truck, and he's got a bit of a belly. If it came down to a fistfight, it'd be a pretty even match.

"You don't have to watch this, you know," Zack says, making me jump when his voice sounds from beside me. I glance over, but his dark gaze is focused solely on Creed and Derrick. "If you want me to take you back to campus, I can do that."

"No, I'm ... I'm fine." I cross my arms over my chest to ward off the late evening chill, and find that I'm short of breath, an anxious energy taking over the crowd that's quickly becoming infectious.

Filthy Rich Boys

"I have plenty more where that came from, if you'd like to see," Creed says, lifting his phone again. Derrick snatches it from his hand, chucks it onto the floor, and crushes the screen with his sneaker before he gets back in Creed's face again.

"You're going to regret that shit," he snarls, but Creed doesn't seem concerned, not in the least.

"Mm, I don't think so." He tucks his fingers into the pockets of his red slacks, and lifts his chin. "Somehow, I'm pretty sure it's you that's going to regret this moment for years to come." His face hardens up, mouth a thin slash of ice, and then he smiles. I have to say, between Tristan and Creed … well, if I saw either of them in a dark alley, I'd run like hell. "You're out of the Infinity Club."

"You can't make that decision!" Derrick roars, but Creed just shakes his head.

"But I can, and I did, so get in your car and fuck all the way off." Derrick launches himself at Creed, but Miranda's twin is a lot craftier than he looks. He sidesteps the attack, letting Derrick stumble, and then prepares himself for the big man to swing around. When Derrick throws a punch, Creed is there to catch it. He uses Derrick's own weight and momentum against him, ducking low and then launching the other man into the air with his back.

Derrick flips over the side of the deck and lands in the bushes with a curse, Creed standing over him, limned in porchlight.

"Myron, get the gun," Creed says, and a dark-haired boy in the crowd nods before moving off. Gun? What gun? Oh my god, he isn't going to shoot him, is he? My throat gets tight, and my hands curl into fists. There's no way in hell I'm going to stand here and watch some kid—no matter how big an asshole he is—get shot.

But when Myron comes back, he's got a tattoo machine in his hand, a box of gloves under his arm, and a small plastic bin with bandages and other various first-aid supplies in it.

"Remove his mark," Creed says, moving away from the edge of the deck as the crowd ripples, and the whispers start up. On his way back inside, those blue eyes land on mine and stick there. Something strange travels through me, but I don't know how to identify it, so I ignore it. I've been doing that a lot lately. "Come upstairs with me," he says, and my eyes widen to marbles. Come upstairs?! Is this asshole propositioning me? "We're going to start a game."

The crowd mumbles appreciatively, but then Derrick is back up and coming for Creed again.

"You're just as much of a bitch as your whore sister," he growls, spittle and blood from his fall flecking his lips. "Next time I get a hold of her, it'll be more than just a few pictures I'll be taking."

Creed turns around oh-so slowly, but he doesn't get a chance to step in before Tristan's there, just inches from Derrick's face.

"You're finished with the Club, Derrick." Tristan's blade gray eyes narrow, and I almost—*almost*—feel sorry for Derrick. Being on the receiving end of that stare is not a pleasant experience. "Your father's already being investigated by the FBI for money laundering." Tristan smiles like a shark, all teeth and primal, driving hunger.

"You ..." Derrick stutters, eyes widening. "You set this

Filthy Rich Boys

up."

One of those perfectly arched dark brows goes up, and Tristan's smile morphs into a sneer.

"You think I forced your father to divert the interest from his clients' accounts into a trust in the Cayman Islands? Mm, that's a little beyond my paygrade I'm afraid. Unfortunately for you, Derrick, you're about to be friendless, moneyless, and outcast, and I didn't have to do a thing."

Myron steps forward, a pair of black latex gloves on his hands, and nods toward a chair that's been placed in the center of the deck.

"Sit down and comply willingly, or see how easily it is for you to be overwhelmed by a mob." Tristan just stands there, waiting, as a muscle works in Derrick's jaw, and his eyes dart back and forth across the crowd. Nobody's smiling anymore, and a distinct icy chill sweeps over the group.

For a minute there, I think Derrick's really going to do it, that he's going to make a run for it. But eventually he sits down and tears his jersey over his head, scowling and shaking, his teeth clenched so hard they look like they might crack.

Myron kneels down, and starts to swab at the area above Derrick's right hip with a disinfectant wipe. That's when I see it: the infinity tattoo. A tingling starts in the base of my neck, and I shiver, wrapping my arms around myself as I watch the scene unfold. Myron cleans the area, and then positions the tattoo machine near the infinity symbol, turning it on and filling the sudden silence with the mechanical buzzing.

I stand up on my tiptoes, straining to see what design he might be inking into Derrick's skin. It only takes a few minutes, and then Myron's wiping the excess ink off with a clean paper towel. He stands up and hands his tattoo machine over to someone else before bandaging up the spot.

A dark black line runs horizontally down the center of the infinity symbol, slicing it in half. As simple as it is, there's something violent about it, severing the original design like that.

"Get up and get out." Tristan stands stone-still as Derrick replaces his jersey and heads inside, an entourage following behind him to make sure he grabs his duffel bag and leaves. I beat the crowd by running around the side of the lodge, so I can get a sneak peek at the parking lot.

Derrick climbs into a yellow Aston Martin and peels out of the driveway with the shriek of his horn, and a middle finger. I stand there in the shadows as the dust settles, and then jump when I feel a hand on my shoulder.

Spinning around, I find Tristan standing far too close to me.

"What ... was that all about?" I manage to choke, trying to understand why I feel equal parts terrified and excited at being alone in the dark with him. He just stares at me, silent and cold and unreadable. It makes me want to crack his façade and see what's lying underneath, if anything.

"Come upstairs and play a little game with us, and maybe we'll tell you." He runs his palm over my shoulder and down my bare arm. I shed my leather jacket a long time ago, but now I'm wishing I had it on. His skin is too hot where it touches me, sending this violent little thrill through me that has nothing to do with fear. *"I assumed you were curious*

Filthy Rich Boys

because you wanted to know what I could do for you." His words thunder in my skull, but I push them away.

My mother lost her virginity at age fourteen, and just before I left home to come here, she stopped by for her first visit in years. *"You won't last long at that school. You're too much like me, Marnye. You'll be sniffing around those filthy rich boys like a dog in heat."* I've made it a whole year past her mark, and I plan to make it a few more at that.

Not … that I'd be interested in losing my virginity to Tristan Vanderbilt anyway. He's beautiful, I can't deny that, but he's too cold on the inside, too cruel. *Even though his hands are wicked hot.*

"What sort of game?" I ask, and he smirks, looking me over with a flicker of heat in his eyes that surprises me.

"Poker."

The way he sneers as he says that tells me definitively that I'm witnessing a very big mistake.

Poker, huh? The way he says it makes me think he's a damned good player. I bet they all are.

The thing is, I grew up in Lower Banks, the poorest neighborhood in Cruz Bay. There's nobody that can outdo me at a round of Texas hold 'em.

Holding back a smile, I follow him back inside and up the stairs.

There's a second lounge area on the top floor with its own

wet bar and series of round tables. Creed and Zayd sit at one, each with an empty chair beside them, while the other partygoers take up the rest. Zack is already there, seated at a different table, but his dark eyes follow me as I move across the room.

Cards and chips are already set out, but I get a feeling we're going to be betting more than money here. The Idols don't give a crap about money. Well, I mean, in all reality, they care a lot, they just have so much of it that playing for cash probably doesn't excite them much.

And that ... scares me a little.

"Take a seat, Working Girl," Zayd says with a smirk, reaching up to smooth his palm over the gelled spikes of his hair. I sit next to him, watching as he downs another full cup of beer. After how much he's had tonight, I'm surprised he's still standing. Then again, practice makes perfect, and I'm guessing he's built his tolerance up over many, many parties.

Creed deals a hand, and then distributes the chips evenly amongst us.

"Texas hold 'em?" I ask, and he flicks his eyes my direction, barely acknowledging me with a slight tilt of his chin. He's still clinging to that anger from outside, his rage toward Derrick only partially satisfied. Tristan sits across from me, and folds his forearms on the table, leaning in close.

"We'll start with a warm-up round," Tristan begins, and I have to hold back a smile. They think they're going to smoke me here. I'm happy to prove them wrong. Zayd lights up a cigarette and Creed wrinkles his nose, but I'm used to it. Everyone in the Cruz Bay Mobile Home Village smokes, including my own dad. "Buy in is ten grand; I'll cover for the charity case. You shouldn't have any problem with that, right, Working Girl, taking other peoples' money?" He stares at me with zero emotion in his eyes, and I shrug.

"I can't afford a ten thousand dollar buy in, so if you want me to play with you, then yeah, I accept." I stare him down, but he just smirks at me. He probably thinks he'll win it all back anyway. On the inside, my heart is pounding and I'm having trouble not thinking about how much ten thousand dollars could help my dad. He could fix the moldy walls in our bathroom, buy a truck that actually starts up on a reliable basis, maybe even take a vacation …

"Figures." Tristan leans back in his chair and looks between the three of us. "You ready?"

"I was born ready," Zayd says, flashing a bright grin, and then the round starts. I'm sitting on Creed's left, so I start with a small blind, trying to see the chips as just chips and not actual dollars. If I do, I'll get distracted.

Everyone knows what they're doing so the rounds move quickly. Zayd is so outgoing and expressive that I pick up his tells within minutes. If he's confident in his cards, he reaches up to play with his hair. If he's not, he scratches at his tattooed chest with inked fingers. He's the first to fold.

"Man, fuck this game," he groans, putting his hands over his face as I smile. Creed is as unreadable as ever, but he's cautious, and eventually, he folds too.

Tristan is the one to beat. He bets high every time, and when it comes time to show our cards, I've got a royal flush, and he has a straight.

He scowls at me as I collect the pile of chips, and find it

impossible to hold back the smirk on my face.

"Did we just get wiped by the Working Girl?" Zayd asks, blinking wide, green eyes in my direction. "Holy shit."

"Where the fuck did you learn to play?" Tristan snaps, as Creed studies me with his bored, too-rich-to-care look.

"I grew up in the Lower Banks neighborhood," I explain, my hands shaking as I stack the chips. *Did I just win forty-grand?* Impossible. Literally impossible. I fully don't expect the guys to actually pay up. Why should they? What could I possibly do, complain to the staff that we used the student lodge during break to play illegal rounds of poker, and I didn't get my payout? "You think you're good at poker? I know kids who could wipe the floor with all of us."

Tristan's mouth tightens, but it doesn't stop him from passing me the dealer button and demanding we start a new round.

"Text us your account information, and we'll wire the money," he says, the anger fading from his face and voice. Back to being stone-cold again.

"I don't have a bank account," I say, and all three boys turn to look at me. Zayd cocks a disbelieving brow, and Tristan sighs.

"Of *course* you don't," he says, as I stare skeptically back at him. No way are they really going to wire me any money. No freaking way. "I'll have my dad's assistant set one up for you."

"You don't have to pretend," I tell him as I shuffle the cards. "I don't expect you guys to actually pay me."

"Why wouldn't we?" Creed drawls, putting his curled

Filthy Rich Boys

fingers up against the side of his cheek. "Those are the rules of the Infinity Club: you make a bet, you pay out."

"You're going to give me forty thousand dollars?" I choke out with a scoff. Well, technically half of my winnings belong to Tristan for loaning me the buy-in, but that's a moot point if money never exchanges hands.

"No, you *won* forty thousand dollars, fair and square," Creed says, dropping his hand into his lap. His blue eyes are so intense, I want to look away, but I feel like I'm losing something if I do. We end up just staring at each other. "Besides, my mother wipes her ass with that amount of money. It's not exactly going to break our banks."

He pulls his phone from his pocket and frowns at a text message.

I'm too caught up on the idea of having that much money to even notice. My dad could use the money to put down on a house. Or, selfishly, I think about keeping it for college. How amazing would that be? I'd always assumed scholarships and loans would be there to help me make ends meet, but this money could really be life-changing.

"Excuse me," Creed says, standing up and giving Zayd a look.

Tristan watches with narrowed eyes as Zayd follows after, heading down the stairs. A few seconds later, and there's the sound of a car coming up the driveway.

"Guess we're taking a break?" I start, but Tristan isn't looking at me, or even listening. Instead, he's staring out the window like he's seen a ghost, his face going white, hands curling into fists. He shoves up from his chair, nearly knocking it over in the process, and makes his way downstairs.

"What's going on?" I ask as Zack moves over to look out the window. Whatever he sees there makes his face tighten up. "Zack?"

"Tristan's ex is here." He glances back at me, his mouth turned down in a sharp frown. "Lizzie Walton."

"You know her?" I ask, and Zack shrugs his massive shoulders.

"We're going to Coventry Prep together." My brows go up. I'd just sort of assumed Zack would be moving onto LBH.

"You got into Coventry?" I ask, and he shrugs again, moving away from the window and heading downstairs. Since I don't know anybody else here, I end up tagging along yet again. What I come down to is a tense, uncomfortable scene. Nothing's being said, but there's a palpable tension in the air.

Tristan is staring at Lizzie, eyes narrowed, while she stands next to some tall guy with light brown hair and eyes to match. He's got a cocky swagger that immediately puts me on edge. Unsurprising since every other cocky guy here is a nightmare to deal with.

"Lizzie," Tristan says, and she smiles. She's got a soft, sweet smile, too. For some reason, I get this jittery feeling in my stomach, and clamp a hand over my belly. Zack notices and raises his brows, but I'm not really sure what's bothering me, so I drop my hand to my side.

"Tristan," Lizzie replies, her amber eyes crinkling. She separates from the tall guy with the brown hair, and I notice

Filthy Rich Boys

his eyes following her across the room. To my chagrin, she makes her way right to me. "You're not a member of the Infinity Club, are you?" she asks, but not like it's a bad thing, more like she's hopeful. *Infinity Club.* What the hell is it anyway?

"Definitely not," I reply, and her chest deflates as she exhales. Lizzie hooks her arm through mine, her bouncy black curls falling around her face as she smiles.

"Get a drink with me?" And then she drags me toward the kitchen, and the tension breaks. I can feel Tristan watching us though, his silver gaze cutting across the room and boring into me. Lizzie ignores him, filling a glass with ice and soda, and then offering it to me. I take it gratefully, feeling a small smile bloom on my face. "Lizzie Walton." She points to her chest.

"Marnye Reed," I reply, pausing as one of the guys brings over a stack of fresh pizzas and stacks the white cardboard boxes on the counter. There's a rush for food, but I notice that a small bubble of space is left around Lizzie and me. Considering I'm a nobody here, I have to wonder who this girl really is.

"Are you here with Tristan?" she asks, but not like she's being judgmental, just curious.

"Not really," I say, snatching a piece of cheese pizza and dropping it onto a paper plate. I hold this out to Lizzie, and she takes it with a bright grin. As soon as there's a break in the pizza hungry hands of the boys, I snatch another. "I mean, he drove me up here with Zayd and Creed but—"

"Zayd Kaiser and Creed Cabot?" Lizzie asks, eyes gleaming with interest. "So you go to Burberry Prep?"

"I won a scholarship," I start, waiting for her expression to change. It doesn't. Actually, she seems more interested in me now. She's wearing a peach-colored t-shirt and jeans, a totally unassuming outfit, but I can tell every piece on this girl is expensive.

"The Cabot Scholarship Award, right? I had a friend try for that one, too. You must've been good to beat her out." Lizzie pauses to take a bite of her pizza, but she's still smiling at me. Once she swallows, she continues. "She got the Coventry Award of Excellence which is almost as good, and to be quite honest, I'm glad she's going to school with me."

"Coventry Prep is … what, three hours from Cruz Bay?" I ask as Lizzie starts to move for the sliding doors, and I trail behind her, finding a pair of seats outside. Tristan is still staring at us. I can feel his gaze like a ray of ice, burning me with frigid cold as I flop down into a wooden Adirondack chair. Zayd and Creed are arguing in low voices in the corner opposite the front door, and Zack's disappeared again.

What a night.

I won forty thousand dollars, I remind myself, but I won't believe it until I see it. I've learned some pretty hard lessons in life, and not counting your chickens before they hatch is a big one. Still, I can't shake the bubble of excitement in my lower belly.

"Coventry Prep is about … thirteen hours north of here," Lizzie says, "so yeah, that sounds about right." So, closer to home than Burberry Prep. I guess that's how Zack's been able to help my dad out. "Northern California, near the redwoods."

"I'm from Cruz Bay, so I know exactly what you mean," I

Filthy Rich Boys

say with a grin. "So how do you know Tristan?" Zack had said she was Tristan's ex, but I'd rather hear the story from the horse's mouth, so to speak. Lizzie pauses, the crust from her pizza halfway to her lips.

"We've known each other forever," she says, setting the crust down on her plate and sighing. "We started dating in seventh grade, but this summer my dad—"

"I thought my ears were burning," Tristan says, pausing next to us with his hands tucked into the pockets of his slacks.

"Your friend here was curious about how we know each other. I was just saying we met in ... what, third grade?" Tristan smiles, and although it's slightly less venomous than usual, it's still not a very happy expression. "And that we dated for over two years." She pauses, and the tension returns to the air. Tristan's face softens, and he opens his mouth like he's going to say something. But then it's like he remembers that I'm still sitting there and starts scowling again.

"We're getting ready to head back to campus." He practically barks that at me, like it's an order or something. Checking my phone, I see that's it damn near midnight. Technically there's no curfew during break, but couples are starting to break off into dark corners, and I imagine the party's only going to get more ... sordid from here on out. "Lizzie, do you need somewhere to stay? You can sleep in my dorm tonight."

My eyes go so wide, I swear they're about to tumble out of my face.

Wow. Is Tristan ... being nice to this Lizzie chick? I'm finding it really hard to believe, but when he looks at her, he wears a completely different expression than when he's looking at me. That knot in my belly twists tight, but I ignore it.

"Marnye," Zack says, appearing in the doorway. Tristan lifts his head to look at him with narrowed eyes. "Do you want to stay here tonight? I've got an extra bed in my room."

The tension rachets up to unbearable levels. Both Lizzie and I are darting glances between the two men, but it's impossible to tell what's going on behind the masks they wear. Tristan, hiding behind a sheet of ice. Zack, crouching inside a sea of shadows.

"I'll take that extra bed," Lizzie says, looking down at me. "That is, if you're okay with that?" She glances back at Zack again, blinking rapidly. "Or … I guess that's presumptuous of me. Are you two together?"

"No," Zack and I both blurt at the same time. "That's perfect," I add, giving Zack an apologetic smile. "I think I'd be comfier in my own bed." He nods, sighs, and then turns away, disappearing into the crowd. I watch him go before I look back at Tristan. His pissed-off meter has cranked to an all new high.

"I don't want you sleeping in a room with Zack Brooks," Tristan grinds out, and Lizzie jerks back like she's been slapped. Her eyes darken, and she looks away sharply.

"I don't care what you want, Tristan. My dad doesn't even want me talking to you, much less taking your advice."

"And his word is law, huh?" Tristan breathes, lifting his chin up in defiance. Lizzie puts her plate aside and stands up, brushing dark hair back from her face.

"Excuse me, Marnye." She starts to go and then pauses,

glancing back at me. "I'll see you tomorrow night at the casino?" My mouth pops open, but Tristan answers for me.

"She'll be there," he says, and I spin around in my seat to glare at him.

"You don't speak for me." I'm indignant, a bright coal of anger burning in my chest. Tristan leans forward, putting his palms on either side of me, effectively pinning me to the chair.

"If you come tomorrow, I'll play you again." He pauses and moves his head, so that his lips tease my earlobe. "I'll bet you an entire month of freedom: no bullshit from me or any other Idol." My whole body's on fire right now, and I'm frozen in place. It feels impossible to move. Tristan turns his head so that his lips are pressed to my cheek. "No bullshit from *anybody* at Burberry Prep. It'll just be you and Miranda doing your own thing." *That feels like heaven,* I think, a small sound escaping my mouth as I correct my own thought, *that sounds like heaven.* "What do you say, Charity?"

"Tristan," Lizzie snaps, and he pauses for a moment, brushing a kiss to my cheek before he stands back up, his cruel mask sliding firmly back into place. "Leave her alone. I won't let you bother my new friend."

"Friend?" he scoffs, looking back at me like I'm scum. And I feel so sick inside because I *liked* his touch. Actually, even as I'm sitting here, I want more. There's a strange, warm feeling between my thighs that's new, and I don't know how to put it into words. "You just met her."

"I know good people when I see them," Lizzie declares, starting to turn away from us. She pauses again and looks back. "If you're mean to her, I'll know, Tristan. And I'll be sick about it." Lizzie takes off, heading for the bathroom and disappearing inside.

Tristan stares at the closed door for several minutes before he takes out his keys and narrows his gray eyes on me.

"Get up, and let's go."

He takes off around the side of the house, and I follow, my emotions a jumbled knot that I don't see myself undoing anytime soon.

CHAPTER 11

There's a knock on my door bright and early, and I groan, rolling out of bed and padding over to open it. As soon as I've got the lock undone, the door flies open and there's Zayd waiting for me, one forearm leaning against the doorjamb. He's dressed in a torn, black tank top with a zipper sewn diagonally across the side. Paired with white skinny jeans and boots, he looks like a punk rocker from the 90s—but in a good way.

"Morning Working Girl," he says, whistling as he pushes his way into my apartment and looks around. "Didn't expect the Brothel to look this nice."

"The Brothel?" I ask, rubbing sleep from my eyes. I'm too tired to be angry about it. Too tired to be concerned about Zayd tromping around my room. He reaches up and touches the crystals on the chandelier, letting them clink together with a soft tinkling sound. "Really?"

"It's what everyone calls your dorm," he says with a shrug of his shoulders, like it's no big deal. "You ready or what?"

"Ready?" I ask, checking my phone. There's a text from Zack: *Let me know you made it back okay? I worry about you with Tristan Vanderbilt.* Oops. I was so tired last night that I forgot to check my phone. Plopping down on the edge of my bed, I send a quick response to let him know that I'm fine. "It's seven thirty in the morning."

"Long drive to the casino," Zayd says, turning to look at me. I keep my eyes on my phone, but I can feel his gaze burning into me like fire. When I lift my attention to his face, I see him studying my legs and realize with a start that I'm not wearing anything but panties and a tank top.

"Jesus Christ," I blurt as Zayd laughs, the sound following me into the bathroom as I slam the door closed and yank on the jeans from last night. When I open the door again, he's still howling with laughter. "How long of a drive?" I ask, hoping to distract him. It almost works, but I notice his eyes are still lingering on my denim-clad legs.

"Dunno. Never been there before." He pulls his phone out, glances at the screen, and then taps out a text with his thumb before glancing back up again. As I browse through my other messages, I feel a pang inside my chest at one from my dad. *I'm really sorry, honey. Please call me.* My anger's long-faded, and even though his words ring in my head—*you forgive too easily*—I decide I'll give him a call today, see how his out of town gig is going.

"Are you sure the casino's going to be okay with a bunch of kids showing up on their doorstep? I mean, it's illegal for

Filthy Rich Boys

us to even set foot in there, right?" Zayd lifts his dark brows at me, running his tattooed left palm down his equally inked up right arm. There are so many designs twisted together on his skin, it's hard to make them out without getting a little closer. I'm just fine across the room from him, thank you very much.

"The casino's been out of business for, like, years." He shrugs his shoulders again, and I get chills down my spine. "But it's all set up for gaming." He flashes a grin at me, and I imagine how easy it must be for him to woo crowds. *Note to self: look up some videos of Zayd Kaiser later.* I've never actually listened to or seen any of his work. "They even have a racetrack."

"Like, for racing cars?"

"No, dummy, for racing greyhounds." He rolls his green eyes at me, and I frown. "Yeah, duh, of course it's for cars."

"Why would a casino have a racing track?" I ask, and Zayd groans, reaching up to twist his gelled hair into spikes.

"Seriously, you ask a lot of stupid questions. Get dressed, and let's go."

"I'm not riding on Creed's lap for hours." I'm serious about that, too. I don't care if a whole month of freedom's on the line here. It's not happening. Just those few scant minutes were enough to be ... confusing.

"Yeah, no worries then because I'm driving you." Zayd moves over to the wardrobe in the corner and throws the doors open. My mouth gapes open, shocked at his forward behavior, but he's not looking at me. Instead, he's tossing the Manolo Blahniks that Miranda got me onto the bed. He adds the black dress to the pile, and then goes for my underwear drawer.

"Hey!" I shout, scrambling off my bed and over to him. I try to yank him back, but it's like tugging on cement. "Hands off, asshole." Zayd fingers a pair of the red lacy panties I wore on Halloween. It's the only nice pair I have, and I got them as a last minute gift from my mom. Yeah. That's the kind of gifts my mother gets me: slinky dresses, high heels, and lacy lingerie. Pretty sure her exact words were: *snag yourself a rich one, Marnye, you'll be glad you did. Look how that turned out for me!*

Part of me wonders if I hate her, but then I feel guilty for even thinking that, and I banish the thought.

"Wear these," Zayd continues, adding the matching red bra to the mix. "You'll look fly as fuck."

"Right. And then you'll all call me Working Girl and tell me to fuck you and then crawl back to my Brothel. Sorry, but it's not happening." I reach around him to grab a t-shirt from the stack, my breasts brushing up against his back. Zayd stiffens and flicks his gaze down to me, but I'm already blushing and pulling away, clutching a white t-shirt in my hand. It says *Lower Banks High* on the front, and honestly is probably the ugliest thing I own. I only ever intended to wear it as a pajama top.

"You want to wear like, Goodwill shit instead? How is that better?" The scowl forming on his face infuriates me, and I shove past him to get access to the drawer on the bottom of the wardrobe, pulling out a pair of raggedy black jeans, a worn leather belt I inherited from my dad, and some sneakers.

"Be right back," I say cheerily, snagging the red bra and

panties when he's not looking. I'm not squeezing past him again to grab a different set. Slipping into the bathroom, I change into my new outfit, realizing as I pull the shirt over my head that it's literally covered in holes. The red of my bra shows through, and I sigh.

When I open the door to grab a new shirt, Zayd's waiting for me, leaning against the wall near the kitchenette. He gives me a wicked-slow onceover, running his tongue over his lower lip and flipping one of his rings around.

"I figured you'd look like a charity case in that, but it's actually pretty edgy." He steps forward and fingers one of the rips near my shoulder. I slap his hand away, but it only makes him grin. "Hey," he purrs, lifting his eyes from my chest to my face. "We're all alone right now, whole school to ourselves."

"So?" My voice comes out a bit shakier than I intended. Great. I have no problem standing up to these jerks when they're being cruel, but when they start with the flirting, a different sort of heat mixes with the anger.

"So ..." Zayd runs his finger along my shoulder and then tickles his fingertips across the back of my neck, making me shiver with pleasure. It feels good to be touched there, even by someone I hate as much as this asshole. "We could christen the school, take our time in each and every room. I've never fucked in the chapel, you know. You could be the first."

Revulsion mixes with lust inside of me, and I smack Zayd's hand away. He narrows his green eyes at me, but he's still smiling. It's an infectious sort of smile, nothing at all like Tristan's cruel twist of lips, but I know it's not anymore genuine. Zayd is a performer. He woos people for a living. Frankly, I'd be better off throwing my hat in the ring with Creed.

"I'm not sleeping with you," I tell him, and this time, my voice doesn't waver at all.

Zayd scowls at me and reaches up to play with his hair. I catch sight of the tattoo on the back of his left hand, a stylized bluebird over a black and white guitar. The rings on his fingers glitter in the light from the chandelier, and for a second there, I can't help but think how handsome he looks. Then, of course, he opens his mouth.

"Who are you sleeping with then? Andrew? Because Creed and Tristan might get off on the virgin thing, but I have a hard time believing it. A girl like you, from Lower Banks, there's just no way."

"Because everyone who's poor is automatically promiscuous?" I ask, trying not to think of my mom. She's the exception, not the rule. "And even if I were, it's none of your business, and it has nothing to do with the character of a person. Look at you and Tristan and Creed, sleeping with anyone you can get your hands on. And that's not what makes you bad people. There are plenty of other things, but that's not it."

"Well, look at you, standing up for yourself. I bet your drunk daddy would be real proud." Zayd steps away from me before I can figure out how to react and tugs a pack of cigarettes from his pocket.

"At least my dad showed up," I whisper, and as soon as the words leave my mouth, I regret them. It's okay to defend

Filthy Rich Boys

myself, but I don't ever want to make someone feel the way I did in junior high. Nobody deserves to feel that low. Zayd's jaw clenches, and his nostrils flare, but then he smirks and lights up his cigarette with sharp, jerky motions.

"Nice one, Charity. Guess even girls like you can come up with a clever retort every now and then." He smokes his cigarette and stares at me, still scowling. "If you're done dicking around, we gotta go. I don't like being late to Club shit."

"I'm sorry about your dad," I say instead, and he pauses, like I've just slapped him. Zayd turns away and kicks open the door to my dorm, stepping out into the hallway. I can only pray there's not enough of a cigarette smell in here to get me busted. That'd be just my luck. "What is the Infinity Club anyway?" I ask as I hold the door open and toe my sneakers on.

Zayd keeps his back to me, but there's a band of steel in his voice when he glances over his shoulder.

"You're a guest, Marnye Reed. Don't fuck it up."

"First rule of Infinity Club, don't talk about Infinity Club?" I joke, but Zayd doesn't laugh. Instead, he starts off down the hallway, a trail of cigarette smoke wafting behind him. With a sigh, I follow after, taking the same path as yesterday out to a gravel parking lot.

There's a crimson colored sports coupe with dark rims and tinted windows.

"Maserati GranTurismo," Zayd says, gesturing lamely in the direction of the car. "I borrowed it from Sheldon Barnes." He finishes smoking his cigarette and then just chucks the butt like he expects somebody else to clean up after him. I bet for most—if not all—of his life, people have. "He's allowed to have a car on campus because he's eighteen, and his grandma's like, sick or something, and she only lives fifteen minutes from here. He gets to come and go as he pleases."

"Well, for his grandma ..." I start, but Zayd's already tossing a smirk over his shoulder at me, sea green hair flopping into his face. He reaches up and twists it into a gelled spike.

"He never actually visits the old bat. She's got an entire nursing staff on-hand at home anyway. He just uses her as an excuse to go pick up hookers in the city." My brows go up at that, but I can't decide if Zayd actually means this Sheldon guy pays prostitutes for sex, or if he's being a judgmental, slut-shaming prick again.

"It's a nice car," I hedge instead, and Zayd howls with laughter.

"You could buy a hundred for these for the price of that Ferrari Spider." Zayd cracks the driver's side door and climbs in. I notice he doesn't bother to open my door for me. Not that I'd expect him to, but still.

The inside has that new car smell, this mixture of leather and oil that makes my nose tingle. There's a torn scrap of paper with a lipstick smudge and a phone number on it stuck to the dash, but that's really the only sign that anyone's ever used this vehicle before. There aren't any old coffee cups or fast food wrappers or muddy boot smudges like in my dad's truck.

Zayd starts the car, and then cranks up the stereo, blasting a stream of rock music from his own band. That husky voice

Filthy Rich Boys

of his is just too recognizable. As he pulls out of the parking lot, I slide my phone from my pocket and surreptitiously do a search for Zayd Kaiser.

He comes up right away, with over ten million results. *Zayd Kaiser, lead singer of the American band Afterglow, a contemporary rock group with several number one hits. Their latest summer tour was a huge success, opening for headliners and superstars Indecency. Also on the roster were Amatory Riot, Beauty in Lies, Caged Impulse, and Pistols and Violets.*

"If you want to know something about me, you could just ask," Zayd says, turning the music down slightly. He's got rubber bracelets trailing up his right arm, and I notice that the names of the bands listed on the tour roster match up. Interesting. Too bad I don't follow popular music much. Instead, I'm the weirdo in the corner listening to obscure Carlos Salzedo pieces.

"My dad listens to some of your dad's songs," I start, "but personally, I spend most of my time listening to classical music. Honestly—and don't take this the wrong way—I have no idea who you are, other than some jerk who goes to my school."

"Some jerk, huh?" Zayd asks, but he sounds slightly pleased by the sentiment. "I'm the fourth generation in my family to have a number one hit. My personal net worth is larger than the family net worth of some of these other assholes. I play four different kinds of instruments, and my manager is fucking the vice principal."

I blink at him and then cock an eyebrow.

"That doesn't tell me a whole lot about *you* as a person. I mean, do you have any hobbies other than music and bullying?" Zayd smirks at me, green eyes sparkling, but he doesn't take his attention off the road. Good thing, too, because now that we've exited the academy gates, he's edging close to a hundred miles an hour.

"I like fast cars, pretty girls, and wicked ink. What else is there to know?"

"Do you ever sit down and just lose yourself in a good book? Are you overly emotional, or do you clamp down on your feelings? What's your greatest fear and your biggest pleasure?" Now Zayd does look over at me, eyes wide and brows raised. He's staring at me like I'm some sort of alien creature.

"What the hell is wrong with you?" he asks, shaking his head and turning back to the road. "You're seriously fucking strange, you know that? Most girls would either be trying to suck me off, or cursing me out right now. You let us beat up on you, but you barely fight back, just enough to stay standing. And yet, you could've fucked all three of us by now if you'd wanted. Why haven't you?"

I could've slept with them? I think, and then even though the only person I'm talking to is myself, I add, *not that I care because I definitely don't want to. Definitely not. No way.*

"You seriously need to ask?" I lean back against the door and look Zayd over. "Because maybe I don't want to have sex with men who treat me like shit. Is that somehow surprising to you?"

"Honestly, yeah, it sort of is. I've never had a girl tell me no before, not when I've blatantly offered myself up. Most of

Filthy Rich Boys

the girls at Burberry Prep drool and hang all over me."

"That's their prerogative," I say, exhaling and closing my eyes. "Everyone is looking for something different."

"What are you looking for, Working Girl? Romance? Affection? Love?"

"A good education, a promising career, and some outlet for me to play the harp for an audience. That's it." I open my eyes again, but Zayd doesn't look like he's listening. Instead of answering me, he just cranks the music up and sings along with the lyrics, harmonizing perfectly with his own voice. I'm guessing he doesn't use auto-tuner.

"Basking in the glory of my followers, bathing in the blood of my enemies, drowning in the waves of my own lies. That's what it means, that's how it feels, that's what it's like to be me."

I listen to Zayd sing his own lyrics and I wonder if any of them are true.

If they are, then I feel really sorry for him.

Money can't buy everything.

I must be exhausted because I end up falling asleep on the drive, waking to an empty car. Zayd is nowhere to be seen, and I'm left wondering where the hell I'm supposed to go. The building in front of me is very clearly abandoned with boarded up windows and doors, overgrown brush crowding the pathways.

A knock on the window startles me, and I scream, turning to find Zack waiting for me with his brows drawn together. I open the door, and he helps me out, his hand cool and dry against mine.

"I was wondering where you were when Kaiser sauntered into the party without you." Zack runs his fingers through his chocolate hair and sighs. "I still don't understand why you're hanging out with those guys."

"They warned me away from you, too, you know," I tell him, and watch as his eyes darken. "And you're warning me away from them. Frankly, I'm inclined to stay away from all of you."

"Why did you come out here, Marnye? You're not a part of the club; you never will be." My mouth tightens, and my nostrils flare. If I have to hear Zack rip on me for being poor, then I'm going to lose my shit tonight.

"Tristan made me an offer I couldn't refuse," I say, chewing on my lower lip and looking up at the multi-level casino. The name on the sign is hard to read, but I'm pretty sure this used to be a Native American run place. That would explain the remote location. I think we might be on a reservation. My skin prickles, and I feel disrespectful for even standing here. Clearly, the casino's closed. Maybe they'd rather not have annoying white people traipsing all over their land?

"What did he offer you?" Zack asks, putting his hands into the pockets of his letterman jacket. It's blue and gold, and I figure those must be the colors of Coventry Prep. Burberry Prep is all about red and black although the jocks most definitely don't rule our school: money does.

"A month without anyone bothering me about my scholarship status—or anything else for that matter." I glance over at him, but he's as unreadable as ever. "He wants to play me at poker. You know I can kick his ass." The faintest brush of a smile touches Zack's lips before it disappears again.

"Just be careful with those guys. They're Idols for a reason. They demand sacrifice." He starts off down the path without bothering to explain that cryptic little nugget of information. With a sigh, I follow after, around to the back of the house where white lights are strung, kegs are set up, and people are already dancing. There's a bevy of gorgeous sports cars lined up back there, too, with girls lounging on the hoods or making out with guys inside them.

Zack leads me in the back door, past counters fitted with dark screens where customers used to drink and play slots. Some of the machines are plugged in, glowing brightly, and raucous laughter fills the room as students tug on the handles and watch the screens light up.

"Those don't actually give out money, I'm guessing?" Zack shakes his head at my question.

"Any bets made are private bets. The machine just makes it all random." He shows me to an area enclosed by a half-wall. It looks like it used to be a restaurant or something. The plants lining it, and hanging from the ceiling are all fake, so it looks weirdly current, even amongst the strange urban decay of the rest of the place.

Tristan, Creed, and Zayd are seated around a table with three girls, all of them topless.

My nose wrinkles, as the girls giggle and pretend not to

know what to do with their cards. Either that, or they really have no idea how to play poker.

"Strip poker," Zayd explains to me, flashing a bright grin. "You should get in on this, Working Girl."

"No thank you." I cross my arms over my chest. "If I played strip poker with you, I'd win, and then I'd be forced to stare at the three of you naked. Sorry, not interested."

"You've gotten brave," Creed drawls, looking like he's half-asleep with boredom. Not even three bare-chested girls have aroused his attention. No, the only time I've seen him look alive is when he was destroying that Derrick guy. "We've been pretty lax in reminding you of your status, haven't we?" Tristan and Zayd give him a pair of cryptic looks that he doesn't bother returning. "You three, get up. We're done here."

The girls all gape at each other, snatching up their shirts and leveling dark glares on me, as if it's my fault the game's over.

"Guess you're going to entertain all four of them," she starts, jerking her thumb in the direction of Tristan, Zayd, Creed, and Zack, "all by yourself. No wonder they call you the Working Girl." The redhead shoves me out of the way with her hip, and I grit my teeth. Truth be told, I feel sorry for her. It must be awful to be so angry all the time.

"Take a seat, Charity, so I can wipe the floor with your ass." Tristan shuffles the cards, and then deals out a new hand, pausing as he glances up at Zack. "What the fuck do you want? I don't remember inviting you."

The two of them glare at each other for so long that Creed

Filthy Rich Boys

actually rolls his eyes, the first signs of life on his bored, princely face. He flicks some of that white-blonde hair of his off his forehead with long, elegant fingers. I wish Miranda were here, but since she's on an academy-sponsored trip, no phones allowed. I can't even text her.

"Let him play, Tristan. Who cares? I'm not scared of this asshole."

"Mind if I jump in, too?" Andrew asks, coming from the direction of the slot machines. He's wearing his academy uniform, and his chestnut hair is smooth and shiny. He smiles at me, and I grin back at him. Tristan, on the other hand, goes completely stiff and his eyes turn into silver slits.

"Whatever." Creed gestures absently at the three empty chairs the girls left, and then turns his blue eyes to me. "You understand that by playing here, you're committing to the Infinity Club rules."

"I don't even know what the Infinity Club is," I say as I sit down and pretend I don't notice Creed and Tristan studying my outfit. They seem ... perplexed. Like they've never seen a girl in a ratty t-shirt and old jeans before.

Tristan chucks something at me, and it smacks me in the chest before falling to the floor. He barely looks up, divvying up the chips. I narrow my eyes at him as I pick it up, finding a debit card with my name on it. There's a paper statement wrapped around it that slipped off, so I grab that, too.

My eyes bug out of my head as I stare at the statement balance.

"Forty-thousand dollars?!" I choke, flicking my eyes up to Tristan. "How ... shouldn't ..." I take a moment to clear my throat as Zayd laughs at me in a very mocking, derisive sort of way. Taking a deep breath, I steady myself and gather my thoughts. "You gave me the buy-in, so we're supposed to split the earnings, right?"

"Keep it. It's not worth my time," Tristan says, and I don't think he's in any way trying to be nice. He just literally doesn't care.

"How did you get all my information to open an account anyway?" I ask, my eyes sliding over to Creed. He just stares back at me with a half-lidded gaze.

"My mom has all your info from the scholarship thing. She checked in with your dad, and he agreed to letting you have your own account."

Andrew takes the spot on my left while Zack sits on my right, and I'm just staring down at the paper with tears budding in my eyes. *Don't let them fall,* I think. *If you let these guys see any weakness, they'll pounce.* Crumpling the paper up, I shove it and the debit card into my jeans pocket. Later, I'll lie back in bed and fantasize about forty grand. But not right now.

"So are you going to tell me anything about the Infinity Club? Or just assume I understand all the rules?"

"Once you make a bet," Zack supplies, slipping out his jacket and glancing over at me, "you're bound to it. Whatever you promise, you're mandated to deliver. Otherwise, you lose your place in the club, and you're subject to mob justice."

"Like Derrick?" I ask, and Creed stiffens while Tristan shrugs.

"Who?" he asks, and when he looks up at me with that cold face of his, I actually wonder if he's already forgotten.

Filthy Rich Boys

"Just don't bet what you can't deliver, Charity." I frown as he leans back and nods his chin at the group. "If she wins, she wants immunity for a whole month. No shit talk, no pranks, no haircuts." Tristan's mouth curves in a lordly little smile. "Isn't that right, Charity?"

"And if you win?" I ask, staring into his eyes and finding it suddenly hard to breathe. He shouldn't be so pretty, so carved and sculpted, so full of himself. It's impossible to look away. "What do you want?"

"If I win this round, I want a personal favor from each and every one of you."

"That's ... really vague," I hedge, feeling my heart thunder in my chest.

"Nothing damning or life-altering. Something simple you'd do for a friend." The way Tristan says that last word, I'm not exactly sure he knows what a friend is.

"Like ... pick up their clothes from the dry cleaner?" I ask, and I'm pretty sure every guy at that table looks at me like I'm stupid.

"Like, tell Creed to fuck all the way off of Harper. The flirting is starting to get annoying." Tristan looks pointedly at Creed, but he waves him off. This is the second time I've heard these guys laying claim to girls, like they actually have a right to do that. It's disturbing.

"Fine. But if you win and you fuck us with these favors, I'll destroy you." Creed glances over at Andrew, and a visible line of tension forms between him and Tristan. "And you?"

"I'll play for Marnye's immunity, too," he says, and I turn to look at him in surprise. He smiles and shrugs his shoulders like it's no big deal. "It's doubtful I'll win, but I'm at least here to support you."

"What a crock of shit," Tristan murmurs, shoving raven-dark hair away from his face and running his tongue ever so slowly along his lower lip. His gray eyes find Zack. "How about you? You playing for Marnye, too?"

Zack stares back at him, and then crosses his bulky arms over his chest.

Tristan scowls, and turns to Zayd.

"I want the keys to your dad's Spider for the rest of the week, no questions asked." Zayd's face takes on a suggestive leer. "I have plans."

"Fine. Creed?" Tristan turns to his friend, and I watch as those blue eyes slide over to me.

"I want to know who my sister's fucking."

"What?" I ask, the word just falling out of my mouth unbidden. My cheeks redden because even if I *did* have that information, I wouldn't give it to him. "What makes you think she's sleeping with someone?"

"Well, the naked pictures that Derrick had for starters," Creed drawls, waving his hand at me. "You're her only friend. Surely she's told you something." He stares me down, like if he looks hard enough, maybe I'll spill the truth onto the poker table. I just look back at him.

"I won't make that deal. Miranda trusts me." Creed clenches his jaw, the hardness in his face such a stark contrast against his usual lackadaisical nature. "I'm not playing if that's all you want."

"She cried herself to sleep the other night," he counters, blue eyes narrowing on me. "And she won't tell me what's wrong." My heart stutters over a beat, and I find myself sucking on my lower lip. I'm aware he's playing with me, but I'm also pretty damn sure he's telling the truth, too. The only thing Creed seems to actually care about is his twin. "She doesn't have to know the information's coming from you."

"Fine," I choke out, but I've already decided that as soon as we're done here, I'm going to text Miranda and tell her about this. Creed asked for information; he never said I couldn't tell Miranda he was gunning for it. Besides, secrets breed distrust. Without them, there aren't any skeletons to be pulled out of the proverbial closet. "It's a deal—*if* you win."

"Are we done with the chitchat?" Tristan asks as a small sea of people forms around us, curious to see what the Idols are up to. The girls all left on various family getaways, but I can't help but wondering if they're a part of the Infinity Club, too. Maybe all the Bluebloods are? Anyway, I'm still not entirely sure *what* the club is, but it doesn't matter. I'm here for one reason, and one reason only: to win that month of freedom. And maybe a little respect, too? "Because if you assholes want to gossip, you can do it somewhere else. I have an appointment with Ebony Peterson tonight."

"Isn't she dating Jalen?" Creed asks, an insouciant smirk on his face.

"So?" is Tristan's reply. My cheeks flush red as he deals out a fresh hand, and gestures for the game to start. We still use chips for betting, but it's all just a show. There's no money at stake, just personal gains to be had.

It goes much the same as before, with Zayd folding quickly, Andrew following suit, and Zack, Tristan, and Creed watching my every move. Eventually, they all fold, and I'm the last one left standing.

With a grin, I flip my cards over and drop them on the table.

It's all bullshit.

"You have quite the poker face," Andrew says with a smile, putting a hand on my knee. My grin turns into a moue of surprise, and his cheeks flame. He pulls his hand back like he didn't quite realize what he was doing. Our eyes meet, and he gives me that winning grin I saw on my first day here. Andrew Payson was the first person to be nice to me, and he hasn't stopped. "Could I give you a ride back to the academy? There's a twenty-four diner on the way."

"Seriously, Payson?" Zayd spits, leaning in and putting his forearms on the table. He didn't seem to care about folding, but he looks pissed now. "I brought her here tonight. She's mine. You know the rules."

"I'm what?" I ask, and Zack stiffens up beside me. "You don't even *like* me."

"When an Idol brings a date to a party, they're off-limits. Everyone knows that, even the fucking Plebs. Do you like being in the Circle, Andrew? Or do you want to join the working class?" Zayd flicks one of his lip rings with his tongue, his inked fingers tightening on the edge of the table.

"I'm sorry, man, Jesus." Andrew runs his hand over his shiny chestnut hair, and shoots me an apologetic look. "Sorry, Marnye."

"Let's go another round," Tristan says, looking directly at me. When I lift my eyes and find his silver gaze on me, I feel weighted down, like I couldn't stand if I tried. My kneels feel

Filthy Rich Boys

weak, and I'm glad I'm sitting down already.

"What about Ebony?" Zayd asks, switching from angry to excited in a split-second. He's got a huge grin on his face. "If you cancel with her, kiss that ass goodbye. She'll never leave Jalen."

"Her fucking loss." Tristan keeps his attention on me. "You win again, and I'll offer this: the rest of the year, no shit from the Bluebloods." My eyes widen.

"That's a pretty big boon," Creed drawls, leaning forward and putting his elbow on the edge of the table. He puts his chin in his hand, eyes half-lidded and devoid of any interest whatsoever. It must be tough to feign disinterest all the time. I imagine all my emotions clogging up and getting stuck inside with not outlet, and almost feel momentarily sorry for Creed. "Are you sure you want to offer that up? Where would you get your kicks for the rest of the year?"

"The Bluebloods are gonna be mad enough about the freebie month. Harper will lose her *shit* over this." Zayd sits back in his chair and crosses his arms over his chest. "Becky, too. They won't like it."

"Assuming her winning streak holds," Tristan continues, still staring at me.

"You should cut and run while you have the chance," Zack tells me, standing up from the table. His dark gaze captures my attention, and his fingers hover over my shoulder for a moment before he pulls them away. "I'm not a part of the Burberry Bluebloods, so I don't give a shit about their rules. Let me take you home."

"If you stay and play, I'll add another five grand into that account of yours." Tristan sets the stack of cards down, and pulls out his phone. He shoots off a text and then sets it screen side down on the table. "What do you say? Five grand for nothing. I bet that sounds like a lot to someone like you."

"It *is* a lot," I correct, feeling anger overtake me again. When I got bullied in junior high, it made me sad. All I did was cry. These guys just piss me off. "But if you want to pay me five-k to get your ass kicked again then fine."

"This is a terrible fucking idea," Zack growls. "They might be smiling now, but these guys are monsters." He tosses a hand out to indicate the three Idol boys on the far side of the table.

"We're the monsters? Didn't you get some girl killed last year as part of a bet?" Tristan looks up at Zack and smiles. "You lost a race against me in your grandpa's fancy dragster, and—"

"Shut your mouth, Vanderbilt, or I'll shut it for you." Zack takes a step forward, and Tristan rises to his feet. The two of them look like they're about to fall to blows when I stand up, too. Fortunately—or maybe unfortunately considering the circumstances—they're interrupted by a large group emerging from the crowd.

Abigail Fanning and Valentina Pitt are at the front of the posse, but I can see Ebony red-faced and flushed behind them, Jalen Donner clinging to her hand. He doesn't seem to realize that his date was all set up to sleep with Tristan tonight.

"We didn't say anything last night," Abigail starts, her green eyes sliding over to me, "but now I feel like we need to. Why is she here, Tristan?"

Filthy Rich Boys

"She's here because I asked her to be," he says, voice smooth and dark. He turns away from Zack to look at the small cluster of Bluebloods behind him. I've never seen such a large grouping of the Inner Circle in one place before. It's intimidating, to say the least.

"Well, Harper didn't know about it, and she's pissed." Abigail pops a hip out, puts her fist on it, and then swings a mane of aubrn hair over her shoulder. She's a *really* good hair-tosser. My stomach knots up, and I feel a bead of sweat work its way down my spine. Zack might back me up if a confrontation were to ensue. Andrew ... I have no idea. But I'm suddenly nervous, like a sheep who's just realized she's playing poker in a den of wolves. "She doesn't want her here."

"I don't answer to Harper," Tristan says, narrowing his eyes.

"Working Girl came with me," Zayd adds, not bothering to stand up. He's leaning back in his chair, ankles crossed and feet resting on the table. He's balancing on two chair legs, and I'm starting to wonder if he's going to topple over. "And I also don't answer to Harper. I don't answer to Tristan either. Don't talk to him like he's the fucking king of the academy."

"Harper and Becky are coming back early, thanks to you," Abigail continues, lifting her chin. She doesn't acknowledge me whatsoever. Valentina stands by her side, eyes narrowed, attention focused on my face. She wrinkles her nose like I'm the scum of the earth. "They'll be here on Friday instead of Sunday."

"Tell them not to bother," Creed drawls, waving a hand around. "Charity here has earned herself a get out of jail free card. Until January first, she's off-limits." He also doesn't bother to stand up, leaning back and lounging like he's on a chaise instead of a hard, wooden chair.

Abigail's mouth opens, but Ebony's already grabbed Jalen's hand and pulled him away before it gets ugly. Abigail's boyfriend, Gregory Van Horn (yes, the same asswad who called me out on my first day) steps up to take his place beside her.

"We all agreed on this: she's trash. She doesn't belong at Burberry Prep. The other students are already talking about it, how the academy's losing its prestige. With every peasant we let in the door, there are a dozen more clambering to get in." Gregory ruffles up his shoulder-length brown hair and puts his arm around Abigail's waist. "We all worked hard to be here. Our families worked hard for their money to send us here. And just because we have resources and she doesn't, we're automatically required to share? That's fucking communist-fascist shit right there."

I'm pretty sure Gregory Van Horn doesn't know the meaning of all the words he's just used.

"I worked hard to be here, too," I blurt, and everyone turns to look at me, including the senator's son, John Hannibal, who's just waltzed up with a second-year girl on his arm. She's in uniform … sort of. Her top's unbuttoned, a lacy bra showing underneath. And her white skirt is rolled up so short that I'm surprised I can't see her panties.

"Did we give you permission to talk, Working Girl?" Abigail snaps, and Tristan holds up a hand.

"I said, she's *off-limits*," he repeats, voice growing even colder and darker. There's an unspoken threat there, too. *Keep talking, and I will end you.* I can practically hear him say it.

"So she gets to cheat her way to the top of the class, fuck Mr. Carter for first chair in harp, and suck up to Kathleen Cabot's daughter looking for more free lunches? I know you enjoy having pets, Tristan, but you're taking this one a little too far, don't you think?" Abigail turns to me, her eyes flaring with heat. I remember her at the Halloween party, glaring at me while Zayd held me in his arms. "You might be fucking the Idols, but it won't last. You're called the Working Girl for a reason, right?"

"Abigail," Tristan says, his voice softening. He's a good actor, this one, and if I hadn't seen him talking to Lizzie before then I might've believed his tone was genuine. "Come here." She blinks at him, and Zayd chuckles. He knows something I don't. Creed, too, based on the almost-smirk resting on his lips. "I said come here."

She hesitates again, glancing at her boyfriend for comfort. He crinkles his brows, but doesn't say anything.

"What's wrong?" Tristan continues, smiling. It's such an awful expression on him. I thought before that maybe it was because there was no joy in it. Now that I'm really looking, now that he's focusing it on someone else so I actually have a moment to think, I realize that it's scary because he *does* find joy in tormenting others. "You didn't have any problem coming for me before."

Abigail's mouth drops open, and Gregory lifts himself to his full height.

"More Burberry Prep bullshit," Zack mutters under his

breath. He reaches down and takes my hand, burning a trail of fire up my arm. Creed notices and narrows his eyes, same with Andrew. Well, he doesn't narrow his eyes but he does raise his brows. I pull my hand from Zack's grip and cradle it against my chest.

"What's he talking about?" Greg asks as Abigail's eyes lock on Tristan's face. She looks scared … but hopeful, too. Greg's brown gaze darts between the two of them. "Abi?"

"Aren't you going to tell him?" Tristan asks, raising an eyebrow. "I can't exactly ask you to the winter formal if he doesn't know."

"Know what?" Greg asks, and Abigail's eyes go dark.

"Stop it, Tristan. Save your lies and your bullshit for the Working Girl."

"Abigail and I slept together the night before the Halloween party. Didn't you know that? I figured you two had an open relationship." Tristan tucks his fingers into the pockets of his slacks, his smile growing as Greg's eyes widen with rage. He takes a step closer to her, and Greg rushes him. With an effortless sidestep, he moves out of the guy's way, and Greg ends up crashing into Zack.

Zack shoves him to the floor, and watches the drama unfold with impassive distaste.

Tristan moves up to Abi, cupping the side of her face in his hand. Her angry expression softens, and her eyes go half-lidded. When he leans in close to whisper to her, her cheeks redden with pleasure. But as he continues talking, her eyes begin to widen and her mouth turns down in a terrified frown. Tristan pulls back and runs his thumb over her lower lip.

Filthy Rich Boys

"When I said that Charity was off-limits, I meant it." He releases her, and Abigail spins away, taking off across the casino with Valentina chasing after her. John helps Gregory to his feet, holding him back when Greg tries to rush Tristan again.

"You son of a bitch!" he snarls, tearing from John's grip as Zayd howls with laughter. Creed watches the entire thing like one might watch raindrops fall outside a foggy window. He's bored, couldn't care less. This time, I'm pretty sure he's not pretending. He truly just doesn't care about Abigail and Greg. "I'm going to—"

"Going to what, Gregory?" Tristan asks, smiling at him. He's so wicked, spinning his little webs. I wonder how he ever managed to snag a girl like Lizzie Walton. Her demeanor is essentially the opposite of his. "Defy me? Start a social war? Go ahead. We both know who'll win." Tristan puts his hand on Greg's shoulder, and he shoves him off. The move doesn't seem to bother Tristan; he just smiles wider. "You have two choices: fall in line and go find your philandering girlfriend, or declare war on me. Go ahead, I'm waiting."

Gregory stares at Tristan for so long that I actually wonder if he's going to do it, throw a bomb in the social scene of Burberry Prep Academy. If he hadn't treated me so horribly before, I might feel sorry for him. Tristan's a formidable opponent. My skin prickles, and a sheet of ice settles over my soul. Holy shit. I don't think I'd quite grasped the kind of man I was up against.

"Fucking asshole," Greg groans, sounding like he's on the verge of tears. He shoves John away when he steps forward to help, and then stalks off through the gathered crowd. Nobody says a word, and soon the laughing and the drinking and the gambling starts up again.

Tristan sits back down at the table like he's just popped over to the bathroom for a moment and come back.

"Shall we start another round?" he asks as Andrew rises to his feet.

"I'm going to take off. Marnye, I'm free tomorrow if you want to have lunch?" I nod and he smiles, a genuine sort of expression that's almost jarring after looking at Tristan for so long. "I'll text you." He reaches out like he's going to touch my arm and stops short when he sees Zayd staring at him.

After he leaves, I take my seat again.

"You hanging around, too, asshole?" Zayd asks, grinning. He just eats up the drama with a spoon. "Because if you're panting around Charity here looking for an easy fuck, you'll be sorely disappointed. I already asked this morning, and it was a no-go."

"You're beyond rude," I grumble, watching and waiting to see what Zack's going to do. He doesn't say anything, just sits back down and levels his dark eyes on Zayd.

"I don't play by your rules, Kaiser. Remember that." He nods his chin at Tristan. "Deal the cards, and let's go. I'm playing for Marnye again."

"Same stakes?" Creed asks, turning his eyes to me. "Only … I want to add in a caveat that Charity won't tell Miranda a damn thing. Seems fair to me, considering what's on the table."

"Agreed. If Working Girl's going for such a huge pot, then I want something better than a borrowed car." Zayd pauses and taps his tattooed fingers on the table. "I want a kiss. A real one. Tongue and all." He smirks at me, and I glower back at him. "What? I'm not asking for much. It's just a kiss."

"Fine." I don't intend to lose, so I don't care. "Deal the cards."

He pauses as Lizzie strides up to the table, the tall guy from last night trailing behind her.

"Hey Marnye," she says, her dark hair twisted up into a fancy knot on the back of her head, makeup dark but appropriate for the evening. She's wearing a lavender dress that's the perfect compliment to her amber eyes. "Zack, thanks for letting me stay in your room last night." Zack nods, but nothing more passes between them, so I figure it was a pretty tame night. A coolness settles inside of me, and I realize that I was actually nervous, jealous maybe.

Over Zack? Seriously?

"Nice to see you, too, Lizzie," Tristan quips, practically tossing the cards out. "Thanks for the greeting."

"I was getting there," she says, looking taken aback. There's something more between them than a simple friendship and an amicable breakup. I'm pretty sure Tristan's still into her. Lizzie steps back and hooks her arm through her friend's. "This is Marcel Stone, my date for the evening." She touches the back of his hand, but I notice Marcel is more interested in smirking at Tristan than paying attention to his date.

Lizzie adjusts her hand and the lights catch on a ring on her finger.

Tristan notices it right away, and goes completely stiff.

"Did she mention we just got engaged?" Marcel asks, his

brown eyes locked on Tristan's gray ones. I remember Andrew saying a lot of the students at Burberry Prep were engaged, but to hear Miranda tell it, these are more like tentative business arrangements. Students still do what—and whom—they want.

"We're sort of testing the waters," Lizzie adds as Tristan's face goes from blank to red to an ashen sort of gray. "We're not actually getting married until after we graduate college, but our parents ..."

"The Waltons and the Stones, a medieval match to join two great families." Tristan narrows his eyes and glares at Zack. "Well, put your blind down."

Zack glares right back at him, but pushes forward a stack of chips. Lizzie, meanwhile, just stands there, looking lost. I actually feel sorry for her. No fifteen year old wants to get engaged, especially not to some random guy her parents picked for money or prestige. I thought that stuff stopped happening in the middle ages.

"Tristan," she begins, but he's so furious right now, his hands are shaking as he holds them in his lap, waiting for play to pass around the table. "Can we talk? You know I still want to be friends."

"Get fucked, Lizzie," he says, but there's a sadness in his voice that isn't faked. He misses her. I start to wonder if this is the reason they broke up, the reason her dad doesn't want her talking to him. Her face falls, and she lets go of Marcel's arm to come around the table, taking up a chair behind me.

She watches us play, her presence bringing up so much noticeable tension in Tristan that he's impossible to read. He

Filthy Rich Boys

bets everything, and I can't decide if it's because he's really got a good hand, or if it's because he's angry. I take a risk.

At the end, it comes down to the two of us, and when he slams his cards face up on the table, I feel my stomach knot painfully. He's got three of a kind; I've got two pair. We're both full of shit, but that still means I lose.

"Guess we all you owe blow jobs, huh?" Zayd asks, but Tristan isn't in the mood to laugh, and my eyes are bugging out of my skull. If he asks for that to satisfy the favor he's just won, I'll kill him.

"Marnye," Zack begins, but my skin is all hot, and I can practically taste the freedom that's being promised me. A whole year without being bothered. I could focus on my studies, have fun with Miranda, walk the halls without worrying …

"Again," I say, and I hear a small gasp from Lizzie. "Same stakes?"

But Tristan is already pushing up from the table, his eyes dark, lips pursed.

"I'm done here," he says, and then he storms off. Lizzie rises from her seat like she might go after him, but then stops cold. After a moment, she turns to me, eyes shimmering with unshed tears. Marcel watches the whole thing with a scowl, and I decide then that even though I don't like Tristan, I like this guy even less..

"Do you think we could trade numbers?" Lizzie asks me after a moment, and my mouth pops open in surprise. "I felt a connection last night, I dunno." She smiles and then pulls her phone from her purse, offering it up to me. "I mean, it never hurts to make new friends, right?"

"Definitely not," I reply, plugging my phone number into her contacts list and then texting myself, so I'll have her number on hand, too. "I haven't exactly made a lot of friends at Burberry …"

"No shit," Zayd snorts, but we both ignore him. Lizzie takes her phone, and her obnoxious fiancé, and disappears into the crowd. "Well, Tristan won't be back tonight. He's been carrying a torch for Lizzie Walton since elementary school. When her Dad forbid them from seeing each other, he was gutted." Zayd picks up a bottle of beer from the case on the ground next to him, and pops the top, downing most of it in one go. "He's probably off to find some Pleb to lick his wounds."

My face scrunches up at that, but I don't say anything. I'm not surprised.

"If you still want to play," Creed says, ignoring Zayd and the incident completely. His eyes are locked on me, and my heart races wildly in my chest. "I'm in. There's another five grand in it for you, too."

"We should go," Zack growls at me, but when I pick up the cards to deal, he just sighs and stays right where he is.

Unfortunately, I'm too full of myself, too desperate to show these guys who's boss. Creed's been watching me all night, picking up my tells. He takes the next round, and even though I know I should stop, that I'm pushing too hard, and too far, I raise my chin up.

"Again."

The looks on Zayd's and Creed's faces should've been my first warning. Zack puts his hand on my knee and squeezes,

Filthy Rich Boys

but I ignore him, determined to win this, desperate for it.

Zayd deals, we play … and I lose. Again.

CHAPTER 12

Lunch with Andrew the next day is pleasant, easy, no hidden threads of intent in his voice. We talk about his family's beach home in Hawaii, about the winter formal next month, and I briefly tell him about my home in the old train car. There's no judgement in his face, and when he asks me if we can go out sometime, it's a yes. That spark of interest I thought I saw the first day of school is still there; I can see it when he looks at me.

Andrew invites me to spend Thanksgiving with a family friend of his who has a country home near the academy, but I've already made plans with Zack. Dinner at his family's lake house ends up involving just the two of us, and a huge catered meal with all the usual fixings. It's delicious, but kind

Filthy Rich Boys

of lonely, especially since I can sense that Zack's frustrated about something. I figure it's about his parents and their friends cancelling over a last-minute business meeting, but he's impossible to read and I don't ask.

I still don't quite get why he invited me over in the first place, or why he's suddenly so interested in me and my dad again.

"Who cares *why* he showed up?" Miranda groans, putting her hands over her face and then dropping them into her lap. She's definitely shipping me and Zack. When I told her what happened while she was gone, she was strangely close-lipped about everything. She didn't even weigh in on my date with Andrew. But right now, I can't seem to shut her up. "He clearly likes you. Besides that, he has an amazing body, he could go pro in football if he wanted, and he's got that overprotective quality that I like."

"Are you dating him or am I?" I ask, smiling as we walk down the halls to the sound of sweet, sweet anonymity. It's been two weeks since the party at the casino, and nobody's bothered me. No rude notes shoved into my locker, or condoms pushed under my door. They've briefly stopped calling me the Working Girl, and I've been left alone to practice the harp in peace, eat in The Mess, or even go for a swim in the academy pool.

"I'm just saying, Zack's a good guy. I like him." Miranda swings her leather bookbag as we walk, heading for the gym. Harper, Becky, Abigail, and Valentina have made this class a living hell for me, snickering about my body behind raised hands, shouting at me when I'm on the diving board, stealing my towel when I'm in the showers. But not since casino night. I'm actually starting to enjoy learning how to swim properly. Before coming to Burberry Prep, all I could manage was a shaky dog paddle.

Of course, in the back of my mind, I know this peace is on a time-limit, and I'm counting down the days until the first of the new year with dread. That, and … there's all the rest of it. I didn't just play the guys once and lose. I played three times, and lost three times. How that happened, I have no idea. I should've just let it go after the first loss.

At least I now have fifty-five thousand dollars in my account—forty for the first game we played, and an additional five for each of the three rounds I lost. I feel like I let my greed get the best of me, and my cheeks flush just remembering it.

I've decided that for now, I'm going to save it for college.

On the plus side, Lizzie and I have been texting since the casino, and I feel like we're actually starting to become friends. Miranda seems guarded whenever I mention her, but I'm guessing that has more to do with Tristan than Lizzie herself.

I try not to think about what I owe the Idols.

A favor. A kiss. A secret.

Miranda holds open the door to the gym, and I step inside, slamming into a chest so hard that it hurts my nose.

Creed is standing there, and he narrows his eyes as I reach up to rub at my face.

"Your pecs are painful," I grumble, but he's already ignoring me, focusing on his sister instead.

"You haven't spoken to me in weeks. I'm sick of it."

Filthy Rich Boys

"So you'll follow me into the girls' locker room?" Miranda asks, pursing her lips. Her eyes brim with sudden tears. "Why don't you just control my entire life?" She turns to leave, and I'm so shocked that I just stand there. Creed, however, reaches out and grabs hold of her upper arm, keeping her in place. "Tristan told me you were sniffing around, asking everyone at the party about me." She tries to pull from her brother's grip, but his fingers tighten until she winces. He sees, and an almost imperceptible muscle in his jaw twitches before he lets go. "If you want to know something, *Creed,* then ask me yourself." She glares at her brother, nostrils flaring, left hand curled in the pleats of her skirt.

"Who are you dating, and how did Derrick fuck-face get a hold of nude photos?"

"Derrick ..." Miranda starts, cheeks flushing. I told her what happened at the lodge, but she laughed it off, saying that Derrick Barr was just a texting fling. She showed me the images that Creed was referring to, rationalizing that she was wearing a bra so they 'weren't really nudes'. I didn't know what to say to that. Doesn't matter how naked she was in those pics, that didn't give Derrick and his friends a right to pass them around and make vulgar commentary. I'm almost glad he got his ass handed to him by Creed and Tristan. "He's nothing."

"Are you screwing Tristan?" Creed asks, blue eyes sparking with rage. My mouth drops open. He came to the same conclusion as I did ... I remember Abigail's face when Tristan whispered in her ear. He's a monster, no doubt about that. Just before Zayd and I left the casino, I found him and asked what he'd said, and he smiled at me. *"I told her she could never have me. Nobody can. And if by some miracle, I were going to choose a girl, it sure as hell wouldn't be her."* Tristan smirked at me then, leaning close and putting his cheek against mine. *"I said I'd rather date the eager little charity case."* And then he'd pulled back and left in his father's car.

"Tristan?" Miranda chokes out, sounding nervous. She flicks her gaze in my direction, and then shakes her head. "I'm sorry, Marnye, just ... tell coach I'm having period cramps." She turns and takes off down the hall, her bookbag and ponytail bobbing.

Creed and I turn and look at each other, almost in unison. He frowns at me.

"You've had two weeks, and I haven't heard shit."

"Whoa," I start, as he reaches up and shoves some of that white-blonde hair of his from his face. He's scowling now, and I'm reminded of his expression when he challenged Derrick on the back deck. When it comes to family, Creed is dead serious. "She hasn't told me anything, Creed. We talk about everything *except* for her love life. Literally, I could tell you your sister's favorite brand of tampons, but not who she's dating."

"Please don't," Creed says, closing his eyes. He looks tired for real right now, leaning up against the wall with his shoulder. The bored princely routine is put on hold for the briefest of instances, and I find my cheeks heating up. I imagine this doesn't happen often. "I'd rather not know that about Miranda."

Filthy Rich Boys

"She *is* your twin, after all," I joke, trying to force a smile. Too much. Creed's eyes snap open and he stands up straight, locking his insouciant expression back into place. "But I'm worried about her, too. She's being kind of ... distant. She barely talks to me, she got mad at me for texting Lizzie, and when Tristan comes around, she bolts. The only other person she seems to talk to besides me is Andrew."

"Andrew, huh?" Creed starts, thinking for a moment.

"Creed!" Harper calls out, waving enthusiastically from the other side of the gym. "Hurry up and get changed. We've got a bet going on which boy can get the best lap times." She drops her hand and turns to go, but not before giving me an angry little scowl and a supremely bitchy hair-toss.

"You think Miranda's dating Andrew?" I ask. "But what about Tristan?" At the sound of his fellow Idol's name, Creed starts scowling again.

"If I find out he's banging my sister, I'll kill him." Creed pauses, like he's just realized who he's talking to. His face shuts down, like he's got that arrogant heir look on speed dial. "Don't forget our bet."

I roll my eyes.

"Like I could if I tried. I don't know anything."

He looks me up and down, narrows his eyes, and then turns to head in the direction of the boys' locker room. The tardy bell in the chapel sounds, and I groan.

I am now officially late to class.

Thanks, Creed.

Our chemistry teacher, Mrs. Zimmerman, is ancient, like eighty-something years old. She moves slow, but her mind is like a whip. I've seen her silence Tristan with a single command. On Friday, she has us meet in the lecture hall instead of the lab room.

"What the hell is this for?" Harper asks, popping her hip out. She seems to hate Mrs. Zimmerman with a fiery passion. Maybe because she's one of the only teachers on campus that doesn't bow to the Bluebloods?

"We're switching lab partners," Mrs. Z croaks, glaring at Harper through the thick lenses of her glasses. Her white hair is gathered into a bun on the top of her head, and she looks elegant in a white button-down blouse and floral skirt. She may be the only teacher at Burberry Prep besides Mrs. Amberton and Ms. Highland that doesn't dress like a politician.

"Switching?" Harper shrieks, and I cringe. She sounds like a dinosaur sometimes. Every time she shouts like that, I imagine that gif with the screaming guy and the words *pterodactyl screech* written across the bottom. "Why?" She immediately looks to me, like I've somehow orchestrated this whole thing.

"Familiarity breeds laziness." Mrs. Z turns on the screen at the front of the classroom, and shows off a list of grades with names next to them. Shame, never underestimate its effect on student motivation. Before I was even allowed to sign up for classes at Burberry Prep, Dad and I had to sign a waiver that allowed the school to publish student grades. "Take a good look at this list."

I bite my lower lip. Miranda (who still isn't here yet) and I take the number three spot while Tristan and Harper are in first place. Even though I hate to admit it, keeping up with Tristan on an academic level is tough. Guess he's smarter than he looks.

"Tristan and I are doing well together. What right do you have to separate us?" Harper runs her tongue along her lower lip as she scowls.

"A right that was earned with three doctorates and time spent tutoring royalty in Europe. You are not the most special person in this class, Miss du Pont. You're relying on Mr. Vanderbilt to carry your partnership. Same with Miss Reed and Miss Cabot, who I see has chosen not to join us today." I cringe a little when Miranda stumbles into the class late, tripping as she struggles to make her way down the steps and slide into the seat next to mine. "Ah, you've decided to grace us with your presence I see."

"I'm sorry," Miranda whispers as Mrs. Z points from her to Harper.

"Pair up."

"What?!" Harper's got her pterodactyl screech thing going on again.

"Mr. Vanderbilt, Miss Reed, you're paired up." She continues down the line, directing students together. Harper's still gaping when Miranda gets up to sit beside her. Tristan slides onto the stool next to me, his arms crossed over his chest. He doesn't seem nearly as bothered as Harper.

"This must be your worst nightmare, huh?" I ask, and he slides those gray eyes of his in my direction. A smile grabs the edge of that wicked mouth of his.

"My worst nightmare? Hardly. More like yours." Tristan turns to look at me, reaching out to straighten my tie. His fingers brush across the tops of my breasts, and my breath leaves me in a rush. Harper is staring at us, eyes flaming, like I'm the girl standing between her and her intended future fiancé. Ironically, I might be the only girl in the class that Tristan hasn't slept with. "If we didn't have our little bet, I'd destroy you." He pauses, considering. "Although I suppose that somehow, even with your piss poor public school education, you excel academically. I figured you were fucking some of the professors, but I don't imagine you run to Mrs. Z's tastes." He glances toward the front of the room where Harper is now standing, arguing with Mrs. Z in hushed, angry tones.

"That's such an ignorant, misogynistic thing to say, I'm not even going to comment." I open my laptop and download next week's lab materials, opening the documents up and scanning the experiment as Tristan watches me.

"How do you do so well? If you're not screwing anyone, then what is it? Pity? Affirmative action?"

"Try hard work and determination," I snap, slamming the top on my computer closed. My eyes meet Tristan's, but it's hard to hold his stare. He's just so … ugh. He's got this cavalier attitude toward me that started on day one. Also, he's too pretty for his own good. The worst part is that he's fully aware of his looks. "Getting into this school was one of the hardest things I've ever done. I spent my entire eighth grade year gunning for this scholarship and this position."

"I've spent my entire life working to get into this school." Tristan stares down at me from eyes that are the color of the stormy sky above the sea, a flat gray with incoming clouds, thick with thunder and flickering with lightning. "For four generations, the Vanderbilts have taken valedictorian at Burberry Prep. If that's your goal, I suggest you move to a different school."

"Last I checked, I was still number one in the first year class," I quip, and his face tightens. But Harper's finally stomped up to sit next to Miranda, seething, her fingers digging into her pale thighs so tightly that I can see red marks. Mrs. Z starts her lecture, and I pull out my tablet to take notes.

Tristan doesn't speak to me the rest of the day, but I know he heard me.

And I know he means to fight back.

Come January, I am so screwed.

CHAPTER 13

On Friday, Zayd appears at my door, slipping in before Miranda and Andrew get a chance to close it.

"You were not invited in here," I say, but he ignores me, green eyes taking in my friends without interest, and then flicking over to me.

"No, but I have something I want from you." He pauses and raises both eyebrows, his uniform completely unbuttoned, tie loose and lopsided. He's stuck a pin through the lapel on the jacket, obscuring the Burberry Prep crest. "I'm collecting on our little bet. And I want to do it at Becky Platter's party tonight."

My cheeks flame, and Andrew frowns. Miranda crosses her arms under her breasts and glares at Zayd. She's in the

Filthy Rich Boys

Inner Circle, a member of the prestigious Burberry Bluebloods, she's allowed to do that. Her connection to Creed makes her invincible. As long as he's in power, so is she.

"Where is Becky having her party? Because I wasn't invited." Miranda glances over at Andrew, and he sighs.

"She didn't tell me about it either."

"Naw, because you two are always up here in the Brothel." Zayd scoops a handful of peanuts from the bowl on my counter. "She's telling everyone you three are in some sort of fucked-up ménage relationship, and that you've all got chlamydia or something. Or was it gonorrhea?" He pauses to pop the peanuts into his mouth, eyes darkening. "Here's the thing: I want to bang Becky Platter. She responds well to jealousy, and you know, she freaking hates you, Charity. Come to the party, dance with me a little, and then kiss me."

My mouth opens and then snaps closed.

"These bets are stupid," Miranda snaps, pushing blond hair back from her face. She looks just like Creed when she does that. "This is why I've never joined the Infinity Club. It's not worth it."

"The Club is so much more than that, and you know it." Zayd smiles at me, and then lifts his shirt, showing off his infinity tattoo. "So fucking mysterious, right? Girls always ask me about it when they're going down on me." He drops the fabric, and I frown. I'm not impressed.

"Aren't you worried that I know too much?" I ask dryly, my heart pounding. The last thing I want to do tonight is party—especially not with Zayd. And kiss him? I mean, it wouldn't be our first kiss. The one on Halloween might've been though if Zack and I hadn't had exactly one incredible make out session before we broke up.

"Uh, why? My dad pays over a million for security a year. If you started running your mouth, he could just, like, send his goons after you." Zayd reaches up and musses with his hair. He wears a lot of eyeliner which bothers the hell out of Miranda. I haven't admitted it to her yet, but I think he looks really good with it. Makes his emerald eyes pop. "Party's at Becky's parents' place, about an hour from here. Her folks only use that house when they've got a horse competition or what the hell ever. She says it'll be dead, no teachers, no police, in the middle of nowhere."

"Guessing the dress code is per the usual: slutty, short, and tight?" Miranda asks.

"Preferably," Zayd says, chuckling. He sits down on my bed like he intends to wait for me. He crosses his feet at the ankles, and I realize he's wearing boots instead of loafers. So this *is* his change of clothes for the party. He notices me looking and gestures with his chin. "Couple of other schools might show up tonight. I want to represent." That's when I notice what his pin says: *Idol.* Wow, how subtle.

"I'll wear my uniform with some sneakers then," I say and Zayd groans, pushing up from my bed and going straight for my wardrobe again. "Excuse you, we are not friends. Get your hands out of my freaking clothes." Zayd tosses a tight black tank top at me, grabs my leather jacket next, and then steals my red Prada heels from Halloween.

"Put this shit on with your skirt."

"I'm not wearing heels to a party. I can barely walk in them." I dump the pile on the bed, but maybe I will wear the

Filthy Rich Boys

tank and jacket. The crisp white academy blouses can be stifling, and they're expensive as hell. When I picked up my uniforms from the tailor, I had to sign a zeroed out bill. It was for over five thousand dollars. "And besides, our bet was for a kiss, not a party."

"Tell you what," Zayd says, coming over to stand in front of me. I keep thinking of him as shorter than Creed and Tristan because he's always slouching. Standing straight in front of me like he is now, I can see that that's not true at all. I crane my neck to look up at him. "You come to the party, dance with me, and I'll consider that payment for the kiss."

"You're really interested in Becky Platter, huh?" I ask, but all Zayd does is laugh.

"Interested?" Miranda echoes, shaking her head. "He just wants to check her name off his bingo list." Zayd doesn't deny her accusations, sliding his phone from his pocket and tapping out a text message.

"Yeah, so? Becky's a bitch anyway. What do you care if I bag her?" he lifts his green eyes up from the screen and cocks a brow. "You should hear the crap she talks behind your back, Working Girl."

"What other people think about me is none of my business," I say, and Miranda grins. That's a RuPaul quote right there. "But fine. I'll go to the party, dance for a few songs, and my obligation is cleared?"

Zayd gives me a thumbs-up, and a smirk, glancing over at Andrew. He hasn't said much, just leaned against the wall, watching our exchange. Maybe ... he's jealous that I'm going out with Zayd tonight? I don't know. I mean, not that I encourage fragile masculinity and over-the-top jealousy, but a little proof that someone cares is never a bad thing, right?

"What about you, Payson? Take Miranda and make it a double date?" Zayd leers at him and reaches up to twist tufts of his sea green hair into spikes.

"I think I'd rather stay home tonight, if that's okay with you?" Miranda asks, answering for Andrew. "If you need my support, I'll come, but nobody in the Inner Circle will defy Tristan's orders."

"They're not just Tristan's orders," Zayd snaps, and I get the idea that both he and Creed resent the fact that everyone acts like Tristan's the king of the school. "And she's right: you'll be safe tonight. If anyone rags on you, they're socially fucked. Even Harper knows that if she messes with you, she'll lose her chances with Tristan."

"Stay home," I tell Miranda, thinking about her expression when Creed confronted her in the gym. My eyes flick to Andrew but only for a second. I don't want Zayd to know what I'm thinking, not yet. If I get confirmation that she's dating Andrew or Tristan or whoever else, I have to tell Creed. But I don't have to share that information with Zayd. "I've got this."

"Love you," she says, kissing me on the cheek. I think she means it, too, and I smile.

"I'm going to take off, too, but maybe I'll come to the party later?" Andrew gives me a quick hug, and whispers in my ear. "Don't let the Idols bulldoze you." He stands back up, waving as he heads into the hall with Miranda.

"They are so fucking," Zayd says as soon as the door slams closed.

Filthy Rich Boys

"They are not," I blurt automatically, thinking about my date with Andrew. "Why do you say that?"

"Anyone who hasn't figured that out yet is either blind, or named Creed Cabot." Zayd gestures at the stack of clothes on my bed and then taps the fancy watch on his inked wrist. "Hurry up, Charity, I've got a one Becky Platter to incense with your presence."

"Why would Creed not know?" I ask, gathering the clothes into my arms. Zayd rolls his emerald eyes at me.

"He knows everything about everything except when it comes to his sister. She shuts him out, and he hates it."

"Could she be dating Tristan?" I ask, and Zayd howls with laughter.

"Tristan? Fuck no. He'd be an idiot to tap Miranda. Maybe in a long, drawn-out fight Tristan would win, but Creed would make his life a living hell. They'd both tear each other down so far that neither of them would be Idols again. Maybe he suspects Tristan, but there's no way."

Filing that information away for later, I slip into the bathroom to change.

But I definitely don't wear the heels.

∞

Zayd drives us to the party in the same Maserati as before, taking the turns so fast that I end up white-knuckled and clinging to the seat. I most definitely don't fall asleep this time.

The house we pull up to is several stories tall, and as wide as the academy's main building. There are floor-to-ceiling windows along the entire length of the ground floor, and all of them are open, people spilling out into the front courtyard.

Zayd pushes his way through them with the car, rolling down the window and hooting as he slams on the horn. Nobody seems to care that he parks half on the front step, leaving the vehicle at an awkward angle.

"Come on, Charity," Zayd says, holding out his hand for me. I have no choice but to take it, scooting across the driver's seat to get out. Because of the way we're parked, I can't open my door; it's blocked by a giant square of cement with a statue perched on the top. Zayd pulls me out and I stumble, falling into him. My heart pounds so loud that it drowns out the crowd around us. When he leans down and puts his mouth a hairsbreadth from mine, I stop breathing. If I inhaled, our mouths would meet. "You're mine for the night, 'kay? And I can be a very possessive asshole."

I move to take a step back, and end up pressed against the side of the Maserati. Zayd puts his palms on either side of my shoulders, his smile a smoldering ember that threatens to fall and burn me.

"Fine, whatever," I snap, feeling sweat trickle down my spine. "For the bet. Just make sure nobody bothers me tonight." Zayd chuckles, and puts his face up against mine, murmuring against my skin.

"You got it, Working Girl." He pushes up from the car and turns to head up the stairs, slapping palms with some of the other guys. Several girls glare at me, but none of them are in

Filthy Rich Boys

the Inner Circle, so I don't know their names. Nobody's been nice to me, and the Idols and Inner Circle have been the cruelest. Know thy enemies, right?

"Slut," one of the girls spits as I walk up the steps. I turn to look at her, but she's got on a pale blue Beverly Hills Prep jacket. The girl next to her, who I vaguely recognize from gym, is grinning maniacally. Using a student from another school to attack me. It's sort of a brilliant move. "We've *all* heard about your exploits."

"I'm not sure what exploits those are," I tell her, a light breeze teasing my rose gold hair around my face. "But regardless, what right does that give you to harass me? You should probably take a women's studies class or something, and read up on internalized misogyny."

"The hell are you even talking about, you bitch dyke?" the Beverly Hills girl snaps, taking a step toward me.

"She's telling you to fuck off, and I'm strongly encouraging it," Zayd snaps, appearing at the top of the steps. Beverly Hills girl looks taken aback, but apparently even she knows who the Burberry Prep Idols are. "And Clarissa, you think you can work through a puppet and not get caught? You're off the swim team for the season."

"Zayd!" she cries out, but he's hooking his arm through mine and pulling me up the steps. He pauses, once, at the top to look back at her. His face is as dark as Creed's, but white-hot instead of ice-cold.

"Bother Charity again before the first, and risk your own neck. If I hear you've been at swim practice, you can forget going to the winter formal with Sai." Zayd turns back around, and the anger disappears from his face. He escorts me through the massive front doors, and I do my best not to gape at the beauty of the house. Because, I mean, it *does* belong to Becky Platter, and she's a horrible person, but ...

"This house," I start, blinking in shock, "looks just like the Magnolia Plantation in Charleston. It was built in 1676, and burned during the—"

The look Zayd throws me is nine parts confusion and one part peaked interest.

"You actually give a crap about that stuff? A house is a house, right? Who cares?" I roll my eyes, but he's already dragging me past a curving staircase, original wood moldings, and across floors that I suspect might actually be cypress. Damn. Cypress is protected now, but back in the day, it was commonly used for building in the south. To see it in California is really weird, and speaks of great wealth. Either Becky's family has always been rich, or else they bought this house from someone else with an affluent family legacy. "Dance floor's this way."

We move down a long hallway, filled with pictures of a smiling Becky and her family. Every single one of them is blonde and blue-eyed, all of them tall and thin. They stare at us as we pass through the shadowy hall with couples making out, and emerge into a giant ballroom of sorts.

There's a DJ in the corner, tables littered with glass alcohol bottles, and the distinct smell of weed.

Different location, same party I've seen a dozen times.

Zayd gets himself a drink and hands me an unopened can of soda, tossing his shots of rum back faster than I can sip my own drink. How we're going to get back to campus with him drunk off his ass is beyond me. I won't get in a car with a drunk guy, regardless of any bets.

"Becky's in the corner," he tells me, pointing her blond head out. She's twerking on John Hannibal, his hands all over her hips. To be honest, they both look ridiculous. "Let's make our way to the middle." Zayd reaches down and takes my hand, his fingers burning a brand into my skin. My throat feels suddenly dry, and I throw back the rest of my soda before Zayd pulls the can from my fingers and hands it to some random guy. "Pleb," he explains, like the other students at Burberry Prep are his personal slaves.

"I'm not really a good—" I start as Zayd spins and then pulls me into his arms. A pop-rock song starts up all of a sudden, and I realize as he grins that this is his music.

"Just mold your body to mine, and I'll take care of you." Zayd pulls me close to him, and I quickly find out that the way he moves his body is as infectious as his smile. He's a born performer, bouncing to the tune and mouthing along to the words as he grabs my hand and gives me a spin. He even dips me, and I find my heartrate picking up as the crowd moves back from our spot in the center of the room, directly beneath the crystal chandelier above our heads.

Nobody else seems to know how to dance to this sort of music, so they just watch. Becky Platter is front and center, her face burning. Harper stands beside her with her hands on her hips, eyes narrowed on us.

"Show off!" she calls out, and the group gathered around her titters.

"Kissing you is like kissing the stars. Fucking you is like sleeping with sirens. Your touch is a hot iron that burns, and I

love you and all of your scars." Zayd's voice coos out of the speakers, this husky purr that gives me goose bumps. If he weren't such a jerk, I might actually look him up on Spotify or iTunes or something.

The song ends, but another starts up right away, some dark, sweaty hip hop beat that Zayd embodies with his dance moves. His pelvis is pressed against me, his hands on my waist. The way he looks at me as we move is ... I have to shake my head to clear it. I feel drowsy from the heat, and the dancing, and the way he's holding me.

His hands slide up my waist, and my breath comes in rapid pants. I'm seriously close to passing out, and I can't decide if it's the press of the crowd, the heat, the fact that I haven't eaten since lunch ... Zayd is full of wild chemistry, I can't deny that. He's been a jerk to me, but my body doesn't know that. Without even meaning to, I find myself leaning into his touch, my arms going around his neck.

He presses his sweaty forehead to mine, and we grind together, working our way through three more songs. At this point, I think I can feel his hardness pressing up against me through the red fabric of his academy slacks. It's super distracting.

"Zayd ..." I start as his mouth brushes up against mine. *This is a bad idea,* I think, but then it's happening and my breath is leaving in a rush. Zayd's lip rings tease my skin just before he closes that distance between us, his tongue sweeping my lower lip before he drives into my mouth. His inked hands tighten on my hips, and our bodies slow their motion, lips taking over the rhythm.

Filthy Rich Boys

I've only ever kissed one guy before Zayd, and that was Zack. Zayd's kisses are completely different, white-hot and sure of himself, like he knows he can get most any girl he wants. When Zack kissed me, it was with a dark possessiveness that scared me so bad that I stopped talking to him for a week after. Then he broke up with me, and I ... maybe he was adverse to my kiss as much as I was to his?

My arms tighten around Zayd's neck, and he presses deeper into me, melding our bodies into one. His tongue sweeps my own, controlling the kiss, but not overpowering me. It feels so good that it's hard to remember that he hates me, that he probably kisses all the other girls just like this.

With a gasp, I find my rational brain hiding in there somewhere and push away from him, his grin sharpening, eyes locking onto mine. Wiping my arm across my mouth, I realize that I'm shaking, that there's a warmth between my thighs that I'm not used to.

Zayd chuckles, low and seductive and suggestive, but at least most of the other students have gone back to dancing. The only ones still watching us are Harper, Becky, Valentina, and Abigail. Uh-oh. Their eyes track me as I turn and flee towards the door. Zayd had said my debt to him would be resolved by just dancing, and yet ... I kissed him anyway.

At least I don't have to worry about there being any doubt as to whether or not I played by the Infinity Club rules.

"Whoa, Working Girl, where are you going?" Zayd comes out behind me, but I've stopped cold. Tristan's at the bottom of the steps with a girl pressed up against the statue on the opposite side from where Zayd's parked the car. He's kissing her, and one of her thighs is in his hand, but I don't think they're having sex ... yet.

He glances up at me with cold, gray eyes, and then ... this sharp burst of anger and heat snaps through him, and he pushes away from the girl. She gapes after him and reaches for his arm, but he shakes her off.

"What are you doing here?" he snaps, but not at me, at Zayd. When I glance back at the rocker boy, he's got his inked fingers tucked into his pockets, an arrogant smirk stretched across his face. "We agreed you wouldn't come tonight."

"A suggestion was made, but it was never an agreement." Zayd pauses as Creed comes up behind him, his blue eyes snapping to mine and then back over to Zayd's face. "If you wanted to make sure it didn't happen, you should've bet me." He tosses me the keys to the Maserati. "Be my designated driver, Charity?"

"What about Becky?" I choke out, my brain whirling with the after effects of that kiss. I'm not even going to try to decipher the fight that's going on between the three Idol boys. They won't tell me anything, even if I ask. "I thought you were going to 'bag her tonight'." I can't keep a scowl off my own face as I squeeze the car keys in my palm.

"Nah, I think I put in enough face time with you to piss her off. Once she calms down though, she's mine."

"You're despicable," Creed drawls, but I don't think he means the Becky thing.

"Fuck you, Zayd," Tristan growls out, his eyes burning as he takes me in. "I hope you know you came to the party with a snake tonight."

Filthy Rich Boys

"As opposed to what?" I ask, because I can't shake that black widow reference. Tristan is venomous, manipulative, content to wait and plan his revenge. When he doesn't answer me, I turn and open the door to the Maserati. Zayd smirks at his friends (or are they even friends?) and then climbs into the passenger seat. I join him, start up the car, and put it in reverse. Even though I don't have my license, I've been driving my dad around since I was thirteen. Sometimes he was just too drunk to do it himself.

We drive back to Burberry Prep, but neither of us mentions the kiss. Zayd, because it probably doesn't mean much to him. Me, because it means a little too much.

CHAPTER 14

Winter formal—and winter break—are fast approaching, but I don't know how I feel about that. I'm enjoying a quiet life of studying and hanging out with Miranda and Andrew. Zack and I have been texting, but not as often as Lizzie and me. She seems really nice, and I'm starting to look forward to her messages.

"I'm dreading the New Year," I groan, because it feels like time is slipping through my fingers. Not being bullied has put my year into hyper speed, and now I've got anxious butterflies in my belly when I think of going back to that, this low grade anxiety buzzing through me, always wondering if I'm being hunted. "And I'm not sure how I feel about going home either."

Filthy Rich Boys

Miranda looks at me sympathetically, but her family's going to Paris for winter break. Staying in the big, cold academy with a skeleton staff was fine for fall break, but not over winter. I want to celebrate Christmas, decorate a tree, have a ham and sweet potatoes with marshmallows. Besides, I can't stay mad at my dad forever; I miss him.

"You seem to be getting along with the guys okay," Miranda offers, her mouth twitching at one corner. I roll my eyes, but I know we're going to talk about this again. "Those videos of you kissing Zayd—"

"Please don't," I groan, pausing outside the elevator in Tower One on our way to homeroom. "I already told you, that was just part of a bet."

"Whatever you say," Miranda whistles, pausing as Tristan approaches us, sans his usual gaggle of girls. The elevator doors open, and he holds out a hand, gray eyes sharp and focused. He looks like he wants something. Oddly enough, he looks like he wants *me*. I've had that thought many times over the past week, ever since the party at Becky's. I try to figure out when this shift happened, when the Idol guys started being marginally nicer to me, and I can pinpoint it to just after the Halloween party.

Makes a girl wonder.

"Ladies first," Tristan says, but it's said with such intense feeling, that a shiver runs down my spine. I'm not about to argue, and I think the Idol/elevator rule is stupid, so I walk in and lean against the back wall with my bookbag held tightly in front of me. Tristan presses the button for floor twelve, and we all sit in silence. "Miranda," he says finally, but the doors are opening and she's scoffing, bolting out and into the classroom without even waiting for me.

"What's going on between you two?" I ask him, and he drops a dark gaze on me. His raven-black hair shines in the sunlight as we step into the classroom. It's blue-black, and feathered in the front so that it falls softly across his brow. *I wonder what it'd be like to run my fingers through it?* The thought crosses my mind, and I feel a hot blush fill my cheeks.

"Going on between us?" he asks, like he's considering the question. "Mm. Why don't you talk to your friend and fulfill your end of Creed's bet?" He moves into the classroom ahead of me, but when his usual flock of girls bounces up to him, he brushes them aside and takes a seat, cracking open his laptop.

Interesting.

Something is definitely going on with the Idol guys. Harper watches Tristan for a moment before turning her narrow-eyed gaze to me, mouth tightening. She flips me off when he's not looking, and then turns away to take her seat next to him. Before she can pull out the chair, Tristan's grabbing the back of it and turning a dark glare on his fellow Idol.

An angry, whispered conversation passes between them before her eyes go wide and she storms off, nostrils flaring with rage. After a minute, Tristan turns around and makes eye contact with me.

"This is your new seat," he says, pulling the chair out, and then going back to his laptop.

I'm so shocked that I don't even argue, sliding into the chair as Harper sits next to Miranda. My best friend and I

Filthy Rich Boys

exchange a look across the room, but I can't decide if mine should be relief, excitement, or confusion.

The guys are being nice to me, but why? And for how long?

Some part of me knows it won't last. The rest of me ... wishes that it would.

Because Burberry Prep is a boarding school with strict on/off campus privileges, most of the students have had their winter formal gowns all along. Me, I couldn't afford one, so Miranda brings over some extra dresses for me to try on. It's like a repeat of Halloween all over again, me trying on things that are too tight, too short, not remotely my style.

"You can't wear holey jeans to the dance," she tells me, eyeing my expression of distaste in the full-length mirror on the back of my wardrobe door. "Just pick one. You look gorgeous in every single one." Miranda leans back on my bed, dressed in a sparkling blue gown that shows off how stunning her natural eye color is. She's a goddess in pale blue, with her blond hair coiffed and decorated with pearls. And this isn't even her trying, just a practice run. On the day of, she'll be irresistible. "Besides, I'm pretty sure Andrew's going to ask you to go with him."

"Andrew?" I ask, because after our one date, and that one time he put his hand on my knee, I haven't gotten any vibes off of him that he's interested in me. "Really? I don't think he's into me like that." I snap a photo of myself, and send it to Lizzie. I see the dancing dots that shows she's typing, and then I'm inundated with screaming emoji faces.

You look freaking amazing! she sends, and I smile. That's all Miranda's said, too, but I don't feel pretty. Maybe it's just my nerves getting to me, but I'm not as excited about the dance as I should be. On a whim, I also send the photo to Zack.

He doesn't answer right away, and I put my phone on the bed. My hands run down the silver sequined front of the dress, but I shake my head. It doesn't look right with my new, edgy haircut. A pang of agony goes through me when I imagine how nice my brunette waves would've looked with this outfit. Miranda could've used some of her magic on me, twisting my unruly locks up into a fancy do.

"He told me he was thinking of asking you," she says, sitting up and pushing around the sea of glittering dresses. "You should go with him, even if it's just as a friend."

"Why don't you go with him?" I ask, and there's a tenseness in her shoulders that's impossible to miss. Hmm. "Or maybe with Tristan? He seems to like you?" Miranda lifts her eyes up to me, brows raised, and then she laughs.

"Tristan's a jerk. No way in hell would I go with him. I'll probably just go with Creed, do the twin thing or whatever." She pulls out the gold dress with the long sleeves, and the disturbingly low-cut back. It's super short, hitting me at mid-thigh, but it does look nice with my rose gold hair, and the skirt is flowy, like a fairy princess. The little girl in me is super attracted to it. "I'll call my mom and ask her to get us an off-campus pass. We can take ask someone for a ride, and shop for new shoes. My treat."

"I can't ask you to do that," I start, but Miranda waves her hand, cutting me off.

"I want to do it. Besides, who doesn't love shoe shopping? I could use a new pair, too." She lifts her foot up and wiggles around the shiny silver Cinderella slipper. Pretty sure those are Louboutins. And they look basically unworn. Getting out of Burberry Prep for a while on a girl's day out sounds pretty awesome though …

"Okay," I say, lifting up the gold dress for another inspection. "Let's do it."

Kathleen gets us an off-campus pass with no trouble, and even arranges for a driver to take us into the city. Unfortunately, Creed also decides to go with us.

He sits on the opposite side of Miranda in the car's backseat, but his smell tickles my nostrils, like fresh laundry and soap. It's annoyingly addictive. Miranda fills the silence, but it's a mostly one-sided conversation, and I'm beyond relieved when we pull up to the shoe boutique. It's situated in the small but exclusive little town of Lujo. It literally means luxury in Spanish, and it reminds me a little of the Coachella Valley near LA.

The street we're on is brick, lined with historical buildings, and designer shops. It's the first time I've been back in town since leaving for Burberry Prep, and I feel a little dizzy with excitement when we climb out.

"Café first, then shoes. As important as high heels are, coffee is god." Miranda hooks her arm through mine and pulls us into a sweet little café with high-backed leather chairs, a fireplace, and plush faux fur rugs on the brick floors. We study the chalkboard menu, and I decide on a latte and a cheese danish while Miranda goes for full chocolate overload and grabs a chocolate brownie and a mocha.

Creed pays for us, and then looks me over before turning his attention to his sister.

"Go find a table, and I'll bring our stuff over."

"He's being awfully mild-mannered today," I say as we head through a small doorway and into a second seating area. It's much less crowded on this side, and we snag a spot on a small cream-colored sofa with silver-painted wood accents. I'd so take it home with me if I could. I'd take this whole street with me if possible. The inner architecture geek inside of me is squealing.

"Yeah, well, he's bound to his own rules, you know? He can't pick on you either." Miranda leans back in the sofa and looks up at the antique chandelier above us.

"Are you guys … okay now?" I hedge, and she drops her eyes to mine. There's a pleading there, like she wants to talk to me about something, but there's no time for it. Creed appears, balancing two coffees and two plates. He deposits them in front of us and disappears again to grab his own food.

"We're always on shaky ground, Creed and me. I mean, we used to be super close as kids, but not since maybe sixth

Filthy Rich Boys

or seventh grade. He tries too hard to control me, and he never listens to our parents. They've sort of given up on him a little. They know he'll get good grades, graduate, whatever, but he's done some really messed-up stuff. I think he might be jealous of my relationship with Mom." Miranda pauses as Creed comes back and drapes himself over the leather chair across from us. He never just sits. No, it's always a production.

"You're buying shoes for the formal on Friday?" he asks, this small thread of interest in his normally bored voice.

"Marnye needs shoes," Miranda starts, and then her eyes narrow like she's just thought of something. "She also needs a date."

Creed stares his twin down, and it's like some secret hidden messages pass between them. Eventually, he licks his lips and then turns his full attention to me.

"Come to the winter formal with me." Not a question, a statement. I raise an eyebrow.

"Really?" I ask, and I hate the way my voice sounds, a little too eager for my tastes. "Why? You hate me."

"I did. Not anymore." Just that. Wow, the guy sure is loquacious. He puts his elbow on the arm of the chair and rests his chin in his palm. The pale blue of his eyes is picked up by the color of his shirt, the top two buttons undone, his black jeans an edgy contrast against such a proper looking shirt. Creed's wearing men's dress shoes with a skull and crossbones on the toe, a little gothic for his tastes. When he sees me looking, his mouth curves up into a sharp smile. "Paxton Blackwell, have you heard of him?"

"Not exactly," I start, wondering where this is going. I

pick up my latte while Miranda inhales her brownie. "Why?"

"He's the lead singer of Beauty in Lies. They went on tour with Zayd's band, Afterglow. These shoes, Barker Blacks, are his favorite. He wears them to every concert."

I blink stupidly, taking a sip of my drink to cover up the silence. This is the longest and most normal conversation Creed and I have ever had. I'm not even sure what to say.

"Sorry, I don't listen to rock or pop or really any mainstream music for that matter. Mostly, I'm focused on Sophia Dussek or Catrin Finch." I switch my coffee out for the Danish, and Creed watches me, like he's studying my every movement. I realize I haven't given him an answer to his question: should I go to the winter formal with this guy?

"Harpists," Creed says, but not like he's at all unsure, more like he would expect any cultured person to recognize those names. "Becky wants to kill you for taking her spot in the orchestra."

"I didn't take her spot; I'm just a better player. Besides, she's the understudy. That's a big deal, too."

Creed leans forward, his lashes long and curled, paler than his sisters, but not as fine as his hair. They've got more of a golden-brown color, bringing more attention to those gorgeous eyes of his.

"You sweep into our school, and you destroy students who've had every advantage in life. You play better, you study harder. People feel like you're taking the luxuries of their birthright away from them."

"For all I've heard them complain that I'm a charity case, taking other people's hard-earned money, nobody seems to be

Filthy Rich Boys

willing to actually work harder to beat me. They just want me to disappear." Creed reaches out and touches the corner of my mouth with his knuckle.

"Crumb," he explains, but my face is on fire, and Miranda is looking between the two of us like she's never seen us before. Creed proceeds to lick said crumb off which can only really be interpreted one way: he's hitting on me. "So yes or no, will you go to the winter formal with me?"

"You haven't given me any reason to say yes," I tell him, and his lazy lips curl into an insouciant smile. He picks up his coffee—black, no sugar, no cream—and sips it, watching me over the rim of the mug. I guess he's not going to argue that point. He probably just thinks I'll give in.

I make a point to ignore him while we finish our food and drinks, turning to Miranda and discussing her plans for the upcoming trip to Paris instead. She's been there so many times it's not that big of a deal to her, but my heart aches at the thought of seeing the Eiffel Tower or the Louvre or the Catacombs. One day, if I stay on track, I'll be able to pay my own way across the world.

Once we get inside the boutique—some place called *Chaussures du Monde*—I'm completely gob smacked. Glass shelves line every wall and go all the way up to the twenty foot ceiling with its vintage tin ceiling tiles and chandeliers.

"Impressive, right?" Miranda asks, breathless and excited. She pulls me over to a display in the corner and starts pointing out things she thinks I should wear. Fortunately, after pointing out a good thirty or so pairs she wants me to try on, she gets distracted by shoes for her own outfit.

I feel rather than hear Creed step up behind me.

He reaches around me, his body brushing up against my back and giving me chills as he snags a pair of heels decorated with gold moons and silver stars. They're honestly perfect for the dress I'm borrowing, but I can only imagine how expensive they are.

"Try these ones," he whispers, voice so close to my ear that I have to close my eyes and take a deep breath to ward off the strange fluttering feeling in my stomach. I turn around, expecting him to move back, but it doesn't quite work that way. My chest brushes up against his, and my breath escapes in a rush. Creed looks down at me for a long moment before reaching up to push a loose strand of rose gold hair away from my eyes. "Can we see these in a thirty-seven?" he asks, and the associate helping us scurries off to comply.

"That's creepy," I tell him as he finally steps back, and I move over to sit on the curving gold couch that winds its way through the center of the store. It's just one continuous piece, and I have to wonder where they got it, and how they managed to squeeze it in the doors. "How do you know my size?"

"Because Miranda's my twin, and you share shoes with her." He waits for the associate to come back, and then takes the box from her hands. "I'll do it." His voice brooks no argument, and his clothes and stance clearly speak to money, so the woman moves to the side and watches as Creed kneels in front of me.

Oh.

Wow.

My heart is pounding as he looks up at me through strands

Filthy Rich Boys

of that silky white-blonde hair of his, and I wonder if this is what a peasant girl might feel like if a prince were to bow to her. My throat is tight, and I'm having trouble remembering the English language.

Slowly, almost agonizingly slowly, Creed pulls off the white lace flats I borrowed from Miranda, teasing the arch of my foot with his long fingers. My skin prickles with pleasure, and I have to close my eyes for a second to keep from moaning. When I open them, I see Creed pulling one of the heels from the box, reverently slipping my right foot into it. He ties the suede ankle clasp, and then moves onto the other.

When he's done, he stands up and holds out a hand for me.

I'm quivering a little, but I reach up and take it, feeling a small shock of electricity at his touch. He walks me the length of the store and back, our footsteps softened by the plush rug that covers the floor.

"What do you think?" he asks as we pause in front of a mirror. I've only tried on one pair, but I think I'm in love. With the shoes, I mean. In love with the shoes.

"They're beautiful, but far too expensive," I start, but he cuts me off by turning to the sales associate. When I look up, I see his eyes burning with something that looks like desire.

"We'll take them," he tells me, pulling out his wallet. He hands his card over to her, and she disappears behind the counter. Those ice-blue eyes fall on me, and it feels suddenly hard to breathe. Miranda has paused in her shopping spree to stare at us.

"This doesn't mean I'm going to winter formal with you," I whisper, and Creed reaches out to touch my chin, lifting my gaze to his. His stare burns straight through my defenses and into the swirling depths of my emotions.

"Yes it does."

Creed leans down, and before I can even figure out how to react, he's brushing his lips over mine, and then pulling back. I'm still reeling from the electric shock of his mouth on mine when he turns, grabs his card from the associate with two fingers, and walks right out the door.

CHAPTER 15

"Maybe this was a mistake?" I whisper as Miranda finishes my makeup and combs her fingers through my hair. We've styled it similarly to how it was on Halloween, but with a little extra length, and Miranda's superior skills, it looks a hundred times better.

I turn in my seat to look at her.

"What's a mistake? Going with Creed?" she blinks at me and steps back, her pale blue dress catching the light and sending shimmery sparkles across the walls of her bathroom. We've never gotten ready in her apartment before, but seeing as Creed's not only stopped picking on me, but is also taking me to the dance, it seemed safe enough.

But now, I'm starting to worry that I'm setting myself up for failure.

"What if this is, like, every teen movie ever made, where the popular guy asks the loser girl out and then throws eggs at her or takes something else to the dance …" I trail off as

Miranda stares me down like I've lost my mind. She puts her hands on her hips and takes on a seriously scary facial expression.

"If Creed did that to you, he would lose me forever. He knows that."

"He's well-aware of that," Creed drawls, appearing in the doorway, one shoulder leaning against the doorjamb, the rest of his tall, muscular form dressed in a white-on-white-on-white suit. The pants, jacket, shirt, and shoes are all the same color. The only thing that's not is the tie, a bright gold to match my dress.

My cheeks flush, and my hands curl into the sequined fabric.

"Your presence tonight is too valuable for me to fuck up," he continues, moving into the room and holding out a corsage. It's made up of white roses, with one solid gold one in the center. Part of me wonders if it's real gold. Creed opens the box and puts it on my wrist, his fingers trailing across my sensitive skin and giving me chills all over.

"Valuable?" I ask, and he smirks, taking my hand and pulling me to my feet.

"Zayd and Tristan, they're pissed off because they wanted to ask you first." My brows go up at that. Not once did I ever get an indication that they were interested. I mean, they've been nice enough to me, but only comparatively to how shitty they treated me before. My palms get sweaty as Creed's eyes go heavy and half-lidded, drinking me in like my appearance is something to savor.

Zack was not happy about the news that I was attending

Filthy Rich Boys

winter formal with Creed. I'm not even sure why I told him in the first place, but my stomach is all in knots now, and I'm starting to second-guess myself. Maybe because I want this to work out so bad? I want to go with Creed and dance the night away, see him watching me across the room the way he's watching me now.

"Gross, get a room," Miranda snorts, pushing past us and heading into the living room. After some encouragement from me, she and Andrew finally decided to go together. There's a warmth to her cheeks, too, that I don't miss. She's as excited as I am, and I'm starting to think that I've been staring this puzzle in the face all alone.

Zayd was sure that Miranda and Andrew were together. I'm starting to think that, too, although I can't figure out why he'd ask me on a date, or why she'd push *me* to go to tonight's dance with him. Something's off, especially in regards to Tristan. Maybe he knows? Maybe there's a reason none of them want Creed to know?

He leads me out and over to elevator where Tristan, Zayd, and Andrew are already standing. Tristan and Andrew are glaring at each other, but Miranda pretends not to notice, taking Andrew's arm and giving Creed a small sideways glance that only I seem to notice.

"Where are your dates?" I ask the other two Idol boys. Creed stiffens up beside me, and he levels that icy glare of his on his friends. Well, maybe peers is a better word choice. "I assumed you two would be going with Harper and Becky?"

Zayd grins and shrugs his shoulders, his suit jacket red and covered in pins, his pants tight and tucked into boots. His hair's slicked back nicely, and his tie is straight, but he's very much the picture of a rock star.

"Goin' stag, checkin' out my prospects," he says, eyeing me up and down and then letting out a whistle. "Although if this frigid fuck drives you off tonight, I'll be nice and warm and waiting. Lookin' hot there, Working Girl." I narrow my eyes on him, but some small part of me warms at his words. Creed notices and slips an arm around my waist, pulling me close.

"Don't you two look pretty," Tristan drawls, his gray eyes taking us in. I wonder if maybe he's holding out on taking a date because of Lizzie or something, but she assures me they haven't talked since the night at the casino. Still, I think he's in love with her. "What an enchanting couple you'll make." His words are dry and sarcastic, and he seems salty as hell, but for the life of me I can't figure out why.

"No date?" I ask again, but Tristan ignores me, stepping into the elevator as soon as the doors are open. We head down to the first floor and join the crowd in the courtyard. Everyone's waiting to get into one of the limos lined up outside, so we can be ferried over to the harbor.

The dance is taking place on an old-fashioned steam boat called the L.B. Burberry, after the school's original founder, Lucas Benjamin Burberry.

"You guys know the story behind the steamboat, right?" I ask as the crowd parts for us. Tristan leads the way and people just move aside instinctually, leaving a clear path from the elevator to the steps. The next limo in line is quickly vacated by the students that were climbing in, and left for us.

Half of me is thrilled by the attention, and the other half is

Filthy Rich Boys

… disturbed. What a life these guys lead.

"Some guy built it for his mistress, right?" Zayd asks, scooting into the limo and then folding his hands together behind his neck like he owns the place. Knowing him, he probably owns a limo that's even nicer than this.

"Not his mistress," I choke out as Creed takes a seat and then pulls me onto his lap, just like he did in the car that day. My whole body goes white-hot and then dulls to an agonizing simmer. I do my very best not to shift around on top of him. If I feel him harden up beneath me right now, I might die. "For his *wife*. He had the boat designed just so he could take her to dinner on the top deck. She'd always wanted to go to New Orleans and do a steamboat cruise on the Mississippi, but she got sick and couldn't travel." My heart clenches, and I know my inner history buff is showing, but I can't help myself.

"That's so romantic," Miranda says, squeezing Andrew's arm. He gives her a look, and the two of them pause to stare at each other before scooting apart. Creed is watching, and his eyes narrow.

"Are they fucking?" he whispers, and his breath tickles my ear, making me squirm. He grunts, and then we end up staring at each other. Too late. I can feel his body responding to me, his arms curling tighter around my waist. My heart is beating so loud right now that it's giving me a headache.

"I don't … I don't know …" I whisper back as he leans in further, hand traveling up my side.

Another person slides into the limo, and we all turn to see Harper, followed by Becky, Abigail, and Valentina. Fantastic. Their dates come next, and I recognize the scowling face of Gregory followed by John. The last Idol, Gena Whitley, is nowhere to be seen. I've noticed she has her own circle of friends she gravitates to sometimes.

"What are you doing in here, Harper?" Tristan snaps, and he sounds like he wants to kick her butt right out onto the pavement. The door closes, someone taps the roof, and off we go. Harper is smiling, but the expression reminds me of a shark.

"I'm your date to the dance, what else, silly?" she says, her pink dress riding up her thighs as she scoots to Tristan and latches onto his arm. He shakes her off with a dark scowl, but it doesn't seem to faze her. She's made of strong stuff, that one. His expression would scare the shit out of me. He looks like a man who's just run into an obstacle that's blocking something he really, *really* wants.

"You asked me, and I told you *no*," Tristan says as my eyes flick between the two of them. Whoa. During our game at the casino, he inferred he was going to use his favor with Creed to keep him away from Harper. And now …

"Tristan," Harper snaps back, sitting up straight. Her eyes cut right through him, and I see then that all the lip biting and hair flipping and giggling is an act. There's a rod of steel making up her backbone. "Don't you think your future is more—"

He turns and puts a finger against her lips, leaning in with a growl.

"If you keep talking, I'll toss you right out of this limo, and we'll find out if the Plebs enjoy their queen better … or their king. Don't test me, Harper." She rears back like he's slapped her, eyes flashing with hurt.

Filthy Rich Boys

"You always get like this when Lizzie—"

The look on Tristan's face right then is venomous.

"Don't you dare mention her name." His words are an order, snapped off a whip-like tongue. "Mention Lizzie again, I swear, and Harper du Pont you'll be sorry."

The limo rolls to a stop, and Harper practically throws herself out, tears brimming in her eyes. Becky follows, Abigail, Valentina, and the boys behind her.

Zayd whistles.

"That was mad harsh," Zayd breathes, but then he's grinning like it's all fun and games. Torturing people doesn't bother the Idol boys. "She's in love with you, you know."

"She's in love with my last name, and the Vanderbilt reputation." Tristan steps out of the limo and takes off down the dock. Zayd helps me off of Creed's lap, and onto the pavement outside. It's actually somewhat painful for me to wear these shoes outside. They cost *two thousand dollars*. For one pair of shoes. It's just ... I can hardly even imagine spending that kind of money on footwear.

"I've got an awful boner," Creed drawls, and Miranda wrinkles her nose up.

"You're gross. Nobody wants to know that," she says, steering clear of her twin and guiding Andrew up the gangplank and onto the ship. Zayd grins and turns around, walking backwards as Creed takes my arm again.

"Sorry?" I start, and then I can't help but laugh. Creed narrows his eyes, but the slightest hint of a smile rests on his lips. He doesn't give two craps that everyone can see the proof of his arousal in his slacks. In fact, he seems to enjoy the attention.

The tension that brewed between us in the limo is still there, dampened only slightly by the drama between Harper and Tristan. When Creed guides me inside and over to our assigned table at the rear of the ship, he puts his hand on the small of my back, and my bones turn to jelly. He pulls my chair out for me, pushes me in, and then lays his hands on my shoulders, leaning down to put his mouth to my ear.

"I'll be right back." He presses a kiss to the side of my jaw, and my eyes go wide.

"So ... are you really into him then?" Miranda asks, staring at me from across the table like she's never seen me before. "He ... read your essay *aloud.*" My cheeks flush. I hadn't forgotten that, but I also can't deny that when he's not being a total and complete prick, I enjoy Creed Cabot's company. Like I said, it's easier for me to trust than to believe deceit. And I want to believe I can be friends with these guys.

"I don't know," I whisper, putting my napkin on my lap as Zayd, and then Tristan, joins our table. The table next to us has the Idol girls, including Gena and her date, as well as Ebony Peterson and Jalen Donner. The rest of the Bluebloods are split between the two tables at the base of the dais on which we're sitting. I think the design was meant to house a wedding party or something. The stage is positioned diagonally across from us, dimly lit and waiting for the band.

According to the program that's on the back side of my menu, the music doesn't start until after we eat. As of right now, there's the faintest whisper of classical music coming from the speakers.

Creed rejoins us just before dinner service starts, and Zayd

Filthy Rich Boys

gives him a knowing smirk.

"What the hell were you doing in there? Taking a shit?"

"Oh stop," Miranda groans as Creed smirks, and scoots his chair closer to me, putting his arm around my shoulders.

"I was taking care of a little problem," he says, his blond hair obscuring his eyes. He leans in close and turns so that his lips are against my cheek. "And I thought of you while I did it."

"Did you just infer you jerked off in the bathroom?" I choke, and Creed leans back in his seat, all lazy and happy as a sated cat. He doesn't answer, but Zayd's howling laughter and Miranda's red face tell me all I need to know. I catch her leaning in to whisper to Andrew a few times and decide that if they are dating, they haven't been very discreet about it. They're always together, and they do weird things, but ... maybe I didn't see it before is because there's no spark? Zero. They look like friends, and that's it.

The spark I'm feeling with Creed is a hundred times theirs, and I don't even like the guy.

"It's them, isn't it?" Creed whispers, just before warm bread and butter is served, drink orders taken. I don't respond, but I really don't think so. At some point, I'm just going to have to ask.

Dinner is extravagant, as usual, but everything is good, even foods I've never tried before.

The eyes of every person in that room are on us, observing what the Idols eat, how they sit, what they're laughing about. I'm now sitting at the table I spotted that first day of school, the one brimming with energy and charisma. A smile curves my lips, and a warmth bubbles in my chest.

I feel like ... I belong.

After dessert is served—a fantastic chocolate torte with fresh fruit and edible silver beads—Creed stands up and offers me his hand, making us the first couple on the dance floor in the middle of all the tables. There are silver streamers made of stars above our heads, vases stuffed with fresh flowers, and little white Christmas trees decorated with twinkling lights.

The band that takes up the stage is young, hot, and clearly very recognizable. Every student in that room goes nuts when they start playing, and I feel like the gap in my pop culture knowledge is showing. Creed doesn't seem bothered, helping me through the bouncier songs and holding me during the slow ones. He's got this permanent half-smile on his face that I think might actually be real.

Dancing with him is not like dancing with Zayd. Zayd Kaiser is a force in and of himself, pulling me into orbit, making my body move with his. Creed is a patient teacher, showing me where to go but expecting I'll get there on my own. I like both approaches. *I wonder how Tristan would dance?* The thought pops into my head, and my eyes flick back to the table to find him watching me.

He doesn't seem interested in dancing tonight. But his gaze is dark, inquisitive. It gives me the chills—in a good way.

I focus back on Creed, his blue eyes staring into mine, his hands drifting lower. He cups my ass briefly before readjusting his hands. My mouth drops open, and his smile gets a bit wider, his eyes still half-lidded. Bedroom eyes,

Filthy Rich Boys

that's what he has. I hadn't figured out how to describe them before, but that's the expression he's always got on, like he's about to have sex.

"You should tutor me," he says after a while. "You'd make a sexy teacher, and I could use the boost to my grades." My brows go up, but that's not a bad idea. Burberry Prep has an official tutoring program I could enroll in, and get credit for. And then I'd get to spend some one-on-one time with Creed …

When the band takes a break, Creed leads me up to the top deck. Even though it's freezing outside, we huddle up on one of the benches and look out across the water at the glittering lights of the academy campus. Creed takes off his white jacket and covers my shoulders with it, pulling me into his lap again. It's ice-cold out here, and my thighs were sticking to the bench, so I'm more than happy with the arrangement.

My right arm is around is neck, fingers teasing the fine blond hairs there.

We don't talk, just watch the horizon as the boat makes it way along the shore and then turns around to head back toward the harbor. Between the food and the dancing and … whatever this is that's happening between me and Creed, I find that my eyelids are starting to droop. I end up resting my head on his shoulder, nestled in the crook of his neck.

"Thank you for the shoes," I whisper, and then Creed's turning and lifting my chin with his fingers.

Slowly, almost slowly enough that it feels like we're not moving at all, Creed and I lean in. His fingers slide to the back of my neck, and our mouths meet. There's no tongue at first, just lips, but then Creed pulls me closer, adjusting my body so that I'm straddling him.

I've never done anything like this before, and my body throbs like crazy. It feels so damn good, I want to keep going. My hands curl together behind Creed's neck and we kiss until I feel him stir beneath me again.

No.

Shit, no.

I've known this guy for four months, and he's treated me like crap for most of them.

"I ... have to go," I whisper, tearing away from him and racing down the length of the boat to the bathroom.

Before I can slip in the door, Tristan is stepping in front of me and blocking my way.

"What—" I start, and then he grabs me by the hips, pulling me forward and crushing me against his body. Creed's jacket slides off my shoulders and flutters to the ground as Tristan digs his fingers into my hair and claims my mouth with his own.

My entire body collapses in his arms.

My own fingers dig into the front of his sharp black tux, clawing for more. It's like I've been shot with Cupid's arrow, slowly drowning in need and want. *Wake up, Marnye!* I shout at myself, but I can barely move, barely breathe. The only thing that matters in that moment is that Tristan's tongue is sweeping against my own, his hands squeezing my hips.

He takes me to the edge of what I can handle, and then steps back abruptly, releasing me.

His gray eyes glimmer with lust, and even though he's now scowling at me, it's quite clear that he's interested.

Filthy Rich Boys

"What ... was that for?" I pant, bending down to pick up Creed's jacket. My heart is pounding. I'm going to have to tell him about this kiss. I have to.

"Just remember that Creed isn't the only one that's interested." Tristan turns and stalks down the length of the boat. My lips are swollen, my heart pounding, and I know I'm going to need a moment before I can face any of the guys again.

I slip into the bathroom and push in the door to the first stall without checking to see if it's occupied.

It is. And it's not locked.

It swings open and reveals Miranda, sitting on the toilet with her lipstick smeared and tears running down her face. She snaps her gaze up to me, eyes wide, and then shoves the door closed again.

When she comes out a few minutes later, we don't mention it.

"I'm going to grab another torte," she says finally, disappearing and taking the awkwardness with her.

After going to the bathroom and washing my hands in the coldest water I can manage, I head back to Creed, and I blurt it out.

"Tristan kissed me," I whisper, feeling my cheeks flush as he turns his half-lidded eyes on me. "And I think ... I kissed him back."

"Do you like him?" Creed asks, lounging on the bench, the only noticeable sign of his discomfort the way his hand curls into the white fabric of his slacks.

"I don't know," I whisper, sitting down beside him.

I'm so confused.

Thank god winter break starts tomorrow.

I'm not sure how much of this I can handle without a breather.

CHAPTER 16

Dad's waiting for me in the visitor parking lot, standing next to his rusted-out Ford with his hands in his jeans pockets. He smiles at me, but I'm having a hard time smiling back. Climbing out of the air-conditioned leather palace of the academy car, my pleated skirt billowing gently in the wind, I feel like I'm straddling two realities.

"Hey," I whisper as his eyes take in my hair. I hadn't thought to mention it. I was too pissed about Parents' Week, and honestly, it didn't seem like he had the emotional capacity to handle any of my crap. He's struggling enough on his own. The driver gets out and shuts the car door behind me before taking off.

Then it's just me and Dad, standing alone in an empty parking lot.

"Your hair looks nice," he says, and at least I think he actually means it. He's dressed in a plaid button-down and new jeans, and it seems like he's actually trying. Charlie seems sober, too, which is a relief. Last night was fun, if a little confusing, and I'm a bit too tired to drive us both the whole way home. "When did you decide to cut it?"

"I ... my friend Miranda cut it for me," I decide to say instead. "Remember the girl you met? Kathleen Cabot's daughter?" Dad nods as he opens my door for me and takes my bag. He chucks it into the bed of the truck, next to his toolboxes, and gets in the driver's side. The urge to add *but maybe you were too drunk to remember* flickers in my mind, but I keep my mouth shut.

We drive in silence for a little while, and I try not to get my feelings hurt that he's not asking me any questions. We barely talk when I'm at school, and now that I'm going home, I thought he'd want to know everything. We've always had a good relationship.

"Your mother wants to see you for Christmas," he blurts, and that's when it all starts to make sense. Great. He's never fallen out of love with that woman, even after all the crap she's put us through. Sometimes, I just wish she'd go away and leave us completely alone. Popping in and out of our lives only makes things harder.

"Why?" I ask, my heart pounding. My phone buzzes in my pocket, and I pull it out to find a text from Zack, replying to a pic of me in my dress last night. *You're a fucking vision.* I run my tongue along my lower lip, my heart pounding as he continues to type. *On my way home. You?*

Filthy Rich Boys

"She's your mother, Marnye," Dad says, but he doesn't sound anymore excited about this than I am. "She wants to have a relationship with you." I tap out a response to Zack. *Yep. For the whole two weeks.*

"Maybe she should've thought about that before she left me at a rest stop and drove off?" I ask, lifting my face up to study Dad's. He's staring at the road with unwarranted intensity. His brown hair is tousled and flecked with hints of gray. The man's only forty years old, and he's already got gray. That worries me.

"People make mistakes, Marnye," he says, and I roll my eyes, slumping against the door of the truck.

"You're always making excuses for her, even now. She *left* me at a rest stop because her boyfriend was bothered by my crying. I was three, Dad. I could've been kidnapped or …" There's no point putting to words all the horrible things that might've happened. He knows. He drove over to her fancy new house in Grenadine Heights, and punched her new boyfriend—now husband—in the face. Dad ended up in jail for two weeks, and I stayed with Mrs. Fleming.

Hang out with me sometime? Zack sends, and then a minute later. *Please. We haven't gotten to the house yet, and I'm desperate to escape already.*

"I know it's been tough, Marnye, but wouldn't you rather have your mother in your life some than not at all?" I'm not entirely sure how to respond to that, so I don't say anything at all. Instead, I just lean back in the torn old seat and text Zack again.

Same. When can you meet?

There's a brief pause and then I can see him typing.

Tonight.

I smile tightly, turn my phone screen off, and lie back, closing my eyes against the curving country road.

At least now I have something to look forward to ... although I'm already wondering if trusting Zack again is a mistake.

The Train Car is, quite literally, a pair of passenger cars from an old steam train that have been converted into a trailer of sorts. Each is shorter and narrower than some of the other trailers in the park, but at least they've got some character. When I was little, I loved living here.

Standing on the sagging front porch, I'm not so sure how I feel.

"What? A few months at that prep school and you've got champagne tastes?" Dad asks, smiling at me as he unlocks the door and lets us in. I'm nervous at first, but as I step inside, I see that it's clean, and there aren't any alcohol bottles anywhere.

"Definitely not." I carry my bags into my room, tossing the ratty old duffel onto my floral bedspread. It's a nice one, too, a present from Dad for my middle school graduation. He thought I could take it with me to Burberry Prep, but the packing list expressly asked students not to bring linens from home.

My room is in the second train car, right next to Dad's,

Filthy Rich Boys

with nothing but a narrow hallway between them. The two train cars are connected by a makeshift hall of their own, metal welded together to keep out the elements, insulated, and covered in dry wall. It's pretty cool, actually.

As I sit there, I get this surreal sense of belonging but not belonging, like maybe Dad's right. Maybe my time at the academy has changed me a little. The person who lived here last summer isn't quite the same person who's sitting on this bed now. Putting both hands over my face, I lie back and just sit for a minute, taking it all in.

"What do you want for dinner tonight?" Dad asks as I drop my hands and prop up on my elbows to look at him. His brown eyes are crinkled with kindness at the edges, and his smile is clear and genuine. "We could barbeque? Or just order in pizza or Chinese?"

"Simple, normal food, that's my only request." I grin as I sit the rest of the way up. "At Burberry Prep, the food's good—amazing, actually—but sometimes I can't even pronounce it." Dad laughs and whips out his cell.

"Pizza it is then." He moves into the living room to make the call, and I check my phone again.

I've got messages from Lizzie, Miranda, Zack ... and Creed.

Miranda misses you so much, she won't stop talking about you. It's annoying as hell. I smile and try to figure out how I'm supposed to respond back. Part of me wants to ask about January, if he's really going to go back to treating me like garbage. Same with Tristan and Zayd. They've been sort of ... nice? And those kisses ... I'd just assumed that for their portion of the agreement, they'd simply leave me alone. Not the case. If anything, I've been getting *more* attention from the three of them.

Tell her I'm having pizza with Dad and thinking about her, is my response.

An instant later, *Are you thinking about me, too?*

My heart hammers in my chest, but I'm not ready to respond to that message, so I turn my screen off again, change out of my uniform, and join Dad in the living room for pizza. He worked late the day before, and then basically left right after to come pick me up, so he's asleep before our movie even ends. I cover him with a blanket, turn the volume on the TV to a whisper, and then grab a jacket.

Zack's waiting outside when I step onto the porch.

He's got on a black jacket, dark blue jeans, and a beanie. It's surprisingly cold out here, even for December, and when we exhale, little clouds puff into the darkness.

There's his orange McLaren sitting next to Dad's truck, and worth as much as this entire trailer park. It's a nicer car than I remember Zack's family having before. He glances over his shoulder in the direction of my gaze and shrugs his shoulders.

"Grandpa unblocked both my and Dad's trust funds," he says, and then shrugs again. "I guess he wrote us back into the will, too, but there are all these stupid fucking stipulations. I'm trying to enjoy the money while I have it."

"Your grandpa cut you guys off?" I ask. I hadn't known that. Would probably explain why I hadn't realized he was quite so wealthy before. I mean, he's part of the Infinity Club, so he has to be a lot more loaded than I originally thought. All of a sudden, I feel tired.

"Yep." Zack moves over to the driver's side door and opens it. His dark eyes lift to mine. "Get in," he says, and after a split-second's hesitation, I do.

We drive to some weird little twenty-four hour diner on the coast. It smells like seafood in there, and all the tables are covered in sticky plastic, but when our orders come out, I swear it's the best thing I've eaten in years.

"This clam chowder is ..." There aren't even any words. Zack just stares at me with those dark, unreadable eyes of his, and I have to wonder how he even managed to stumble on a dive like this in the first place. Imagining any of the Idols sitting in here is damn near impossible. Even Miranda would be hesitant to walk in.

"My dad owns half the fishing vessels on this dock." He points out the window behind me, and I turn. "He'd own them all if the town didn't hate him so much." Zack leans back in his seat and crosses his arms over his broad chest. He's finished his fish and chips, and I've barely eaten half my bowl of chowder.

Even though Trini Bay is close to Cruz Bay, it's always functioned on its own set of rules, more like a small town than the pseudo-suburb of a city. There are *Buy Local* signs all over the diner. That explains why they don't want anything to do with the Brooks family.

"How's life at Coventry Prep?" I ask, when I can't decide how to respond to his statement. He shrugs, his arm muscles bunching with the movement. My eyes lock on and can't seem to pull away. He was by no means skinny in eighth grade, but … he definitely went through a maturity boost over the summer.

"It's fine." Just that. His dark eyes bore into mine, and I feel my cheeks heating. Zack and I are a world apart, and we have so much history, but I like hanging out with him. *"Once she finds out what you did, that girl you killed …"* Tristan's words ring in my head, but I push them away. I don't know what he's talking about, and I don't care to. I'm sure whatever *actually* happened isn't as grisly as he's making it out to be. Clearly, Zack didn't kill anyone or he'd be sitting in jail.

Right?

My phone lights up, and I glance over, seeing another text from Creed.

Is that a no? he asks, and I glance at his previous message: *Are you thinking about me, too?*

I tuck my lower lip under my teeth and tap out a message. *Maybe. Why?*

My heart thunders and I tuck the phone into my coat pocket, too nervous to read whatever he responds with. After break, things might go back to being bad at school. He might start bullying me again. Nothing's changed, right? Not even a glorious dance under silver sparkle streamers and crystal chandeliers can fix the injustices in the world.

"Is that one of the Idol guys?" Zack asks finally, and I look up from my food. He's just staring at me, that darkness

Filthy Rich Boys

making his face unreadable.

"Yeah, why?" There's an imperceptible tightening around Zack's mouth.

"Because they're pieces of shit, all three of them. And this is coming from someone who knows he's an asshole." We stare at each other, and my cheeks heat.

"They warned me away from you, too, you know," I start, cutting a potato into pieces with my spoon. "According to them, you're even worse." Zack doesn't say anything, and we sit in silence for a while. "If it makes you feel better, they've been so cruel to me, I don't think we could ever be friends."

Not friends, but ... didn't Zayd's kiss burn on the dance floor? What about Creed's hands on your waist last night? And Tristan ... I try hard not to think about Tristan.

Exhaling, I banish the thoughts and try asking about football instead. That does the trick. Zack tells me about his team, their brutal practice sessions, how much he likes his coach. It's the longest and most continual conversation we've ever had.

After we're done eating, he takes me for a walk down the pier, and along the small stretch of beach next to the restaurant, pausing to pick up an intact sand dollar. He grabs my hand in one of his huge ones, uncurls my fingers, and then places it on my palm. When he curls my hand back over it, my heart races and I feel so lightheaded that I have to sit down in the sand for a moment. He sits beside me, and we watch the moonlight or sunlight reflect off the gentle waves.

"For all the things I did to you in middle school," he says, exhaling, "I'm sorry."

There's a long stretch of silence because I don't know

what to say. Even after we started dating, he never apologized, and we never talked about it.

Zack doesn't move, just sits there, staring at the water.

I look from him to the ocean and back again.

When he reaches over, puts an arm around my waist and pulls me closer to him, I don't resist.

The rest of the week is spent decorating for Christmas. Dad's helpless without me around, so I've got my work cut out for me, pulling cardboard boxes full of lights and ornaments from the luggage compartment on the bottom of the first train car.

We hang white lights outside, red and green ones inside, and drag a Christmas tree home from the lot up the street. Neither of us is religious, but we've got a ceramic nativity scene that Mom left when she moved out, and that goes in its usual spot on a shelf in the living room. Compared to the pictures Miranda keeps sending me from Paris, it's not much, but it feels homey, familiar, and safe. That's all I really need right now.

Since Dad has to work everyday of my vacation save the weekends and Christmas Day itself, I have a lot of free time on my hands to lie back on my bed and text. I've got an interesting back and forth going on with Creed, and, surprisingly, messages from Zayd and Tristan as well.

Zayd's a great texter. Honestly, we're having conversations now that make me feel like we're friends.

Filthy Rich Boys

Almost. But then I close my eyes and I remember him telling me he'd pay my price, and my stomach twists into knots. Tristan, on the other hand, is as dark and intimidating over text as he is in person. Our conversation centers mainly on the project we're doing for chemistry and not much else. At least his zeal for schoolwork matches my own, so there's that.

I've completely forgotten about my mother coming over until I open the door on Christmas Day and find her standing on the porch in an expensive white fur coat, diamond earrings, and strained smile. Every single cell in me vibrates with emotion, and I can't seem to stop thinking about the lingerie she got me for my birthday. *Snag yourself a rich one, Marnye, you'll be glad you did. Look how that turned out for me!* My throat goes dry, and my stomach turns to ice.

"Marnye-bear," she says, holding her arms out for a hug. She hasn't called me Marnye-bear since that one time when I was five and she called me drunk and bawling her eyes out. I don't move into her embrace, instead stepping back so she can come inside. She frowns at me, but she steps into the living room anyway, giving the scattered bits of wrapping paper a dirty look. The way she dresses now, you'd never know she lived here with her husband and daughter once upon a time. "Charlie." Mom—although I'd rather just call her Jennifer—nods her chin in my dad's direction. It's painful, the way he looks at her, like he's still desperately in love.

"Jenn," he replies softly, and then he looks away, like he can't bear the sight of her.

"So, how's that academy treating you?" she asks, her blue eyes and blond hair nothing at all like my brown eyes and brunette waves. Well … I guess I don't have brunette waves anymore, and I reach up to touch the short rose gold locks with a tentative gesture. Jennifer notices and smiles. "Love the hair, by the way, very chic." She winks at me, like we're old girlfriends or something. In reality, I barely know the woman.

"I'm top of my class," I say with a shrug. My stomach and chest have gotten so cold that I feel numb now. Looking at Jennifer, I'm not really sure what I'm supposed to think. Some little part of me, buried deep down and covered over, wants to fall into her arms and let her hold me like she did before she left. The rest of me knows that'd be a disaster waiting to happen. "And I got first chair for harp in the orchestra."

Jennifer smiles, and I think it really is a genuine expression. Only … she's happy for all the wrong reasons. She isn't proud of me; I'm just an extension of her, my accomplishments becoming her own.

"See, I knew I had good genes," she says, reaching out to touch my hair. I step back and she frowns, but that ice is melting inside of me, giving way to anger.

"Genes? This has nothing to do with DNA. It has everything to do with Dad working a second job to pay the four hundred dollar a month rental fee for a harp, so I could play at home."

"Marnye," Dad starts, rising from his spot on the couch. I haven't told him about the fifty-five thousand dollars in my new account yet, but I did use some of it to buy a few Christmas gifts when I was out with Creed and Miranda. He's

Filthy Rich Boys

got a new watch on his wrist that costs more than I've ever spent on a single item in my entire life. I'm not sure that he realizes how valuable it is. Pretty sure Dad thinks it's a knock-off. "Your mother's here to take you with her for Christmas dinner."

"We're going to Avondale," she says, beaming, so supremely proud of herself for booking a reservation at the most expensive restaurant in the city. "You'll love it there."

"Is my sister going?" I ask, and some more of that ice melts, giving away to rage. I haven't even met my sister yet. As far as I know, she isn't aware I even exist, and we're barely three years apart. Mom was already pregnant with her when she abandoned me at that rest stop.

Jennifer's mouth turns down into a frown and she glances over at my dad.

"Why are you looking at him when you're the only one that can answer my question?" I cross my arms over my chest and lean against the counter, trying not to think about how Mom was missing when I … those two times that I … My throat dries out and I almost choke on a lump when I try to swallow.

"Go get dressed in something nice," Jennifer says instead, not bothering to actually answer any of my questions. "If you don't have anything, you can wear your uniform—" She's not done talking, but I'm already pushing away from the counter and heading down the hall to my bedroom. Once inside, I slam the door, lock it, and pull my phone from the pocket of my pj pants.

Are you busy today? I text Zack, surprised when he starts typing right away.

Fuck no. This is boring as hell. You want to get out of here?

Yes, please. Pick me up at the road?

I don't wait for him to respond, dressing in jeans, a t-shirt, the Bear Paws that Dad gave me as a present this morning, and my warm red wool academy coat. There's a door behind my bed from the car's original life as a train. It would've connected the passenger car I'm in to another passenger or dining car. If I stand on my bed and unbolt the top lock, I can push it open and climb out.

Closing it softly behind me, I hop down to the muddy gravel drive and take off for the road.

Since I don't know how long it'll take Zack to get here, I hide behind a tree, wondering if Jenn and Charlie will come looking for me. After a while, I hear them calling to me, and my phone buzzes in my pocket. I turn it to silent, and then crouch low until Zack's McLaren pulls up on the side of the road.

"Where are we going?" he asks as I climb in, huddling into the seat. Seat warmers are so underrated. I glance over and find his dark eyes on mine. When we look at each other, I know he knows what he's done to me. He can never forget; I can never forget. How can we really be friends? Look how our dating life went.

"Anywhere but here," I say, and I mean it.

For the rest of the day, we just drive.

And it's the best day I've had in a long, long time.

CHAPTER 17

Arriving back at Burberry Prep after the break is bittersweet. I'm excited to see Miranda again, but I'm nervous to see what happens with the bullying ban lifted. First thing I notice when I head inside is that my locker is covered in condoms with a note taped in the center. *These are for you, Working Girl. XOXO.*

Fantastic.

I tear the note off with a sigh. Dad was not happy with me for taking off, and Mom was long-gone by the time I came back. I apologized to him, let him ground me for the rest of my vacation, and devoted myself to studying when he was at work. Whatever's going on between me and Zack, I can't figure it out right now.

"Welcome back," Tristan says, sweeping past me and heading down the hall with an entourage in tow. He doesn't look at me, but his fingers just barely brush the back of my hand, leaving this tingling sensation that lasts for hours.

Once Miranda's done bouncing around in excitement over seeing me again, she starts telling me all about her vacation, how Creed was much less combative than usual, how her mom bought her a pair of Louboutins at the flagship Paris store, and how their apartment overlooks the Eiffel Tower. Miranda Cabot is a wonderful person, but her life is so different from mine that I don't even know where to begin.

Andrew joins us for lunch, and although the snide comments and sneers in the halls are back, there aren't any life shattering moments like the breathalyzer or the essay. In fact, all three Idol guys are still being relatively normal towards me.

Since our first day back is also a Friday, the third of January, we get our phones back right after class, and I find a text from Tristan inviting me to work on our chemistry project. We end up spending most of the weekend walking the campus and taking soil samples to test in the lab, looking for various contaminants. We also take samples of paint, the insulation that's visible in the half-finished walls of the school basement, and even a piece of roof tile.

Just over a week later, we've finished our experiments and make plans to meet up in the library to finish the last bit of research, using the school's old archive files and newspaper slides to get information about the campus that's most definitely not available online.

Of course, I have to get through PE first.

It is one hundred percent, without a doubt, my least favorite class now that the bullying ban is lifted.

We dress down into our school-issued swimsuits, and the

Filthy Rich Boys

teasing starts. The Bluebloods—Harper and Becky in particular—are relentless, doing their best to make up for my brief reprieve from their cruelty. They come to class with red Sharpie lines drawn on their wrists, and whisper about how fat I look in my suit. When that doesn't faze me, one of them pushes me into the deep end with the coach isn't looking, and I end up with a huge amount of water in my nose and lungs, choking on the burning sensation as I surface and drag myself back onto the cement.

Their petty bullshit doesn't get to me. Instead, I brush it off and focus on the fact that Tristan and I are going to snag the highest grade in chemistry. There's no doubt in my mind about that. I take no small amount of pleasure when Harper starts complaining that Tristan won't hang out with her after school because he's 'too busy banging the Working Girl'.

After showering in the—thankfully—private stalls, I wrap a towel around myself and open my locker, grabbing my shirt, skirt, tie, socks, shoes … and where are my damn underwear? I dig through my stuff, but don't see the pale blue cotton panties I was wearing earlier. With a frown, I steal back into the private shower stall to change. There is no way in hell I'm getting naked in front of these girls. Knowing my luck, they'd probably sneak a phone in here and snap photos of me to share around the school.

Once I'm dressed, I head back into the locker room and start the search for my panties all over again.

After clearing my locker out completely, it dawns on me.

"Goddamn it," I grumble, rising to my feet and slamming my locker door closed. I throw my bookbag over my shoulder and make a beeline for my dorm, fully aware that this is yet another Idol prank. Knowing them, they're probably waiting around a corner somewhere to flip my skirt up and snap a pic. Using extreme caution, I go the back way—out the door where I first saw Tristan's Ferrari Spider and then all the way around the outside and in the other door nearest the chapel—before I hit my apartment door.

Free and clear.

After I slip inside, I set my bag down and start looking for a pair of clean panties so I can make my library meeting with Tristan.

The drawer on the bottom of my wardrobe is empty. All my bras are there, but my undies are gone.

With a snarl, I dump out my dirty clothes basket and search there.

Still, nothing.

How these girls keep getting into my dorm is beyond me. I'm going to have to ask for a lock change which means I'll have to make a report. Nothing will come of it, I'm sure, as there's no proof pointing to anyone in particular, but at least it'll be on file.

Fine.

I go for a pair of pj shorts to put under my skirt, but those are gone, too. As are my jeans. As is every single piece of clothing that's not a shirt, skirt, or dress.

Those bitches.

Sitting down on the edge of my bed with a sigh, I text Miranda, asking if I can borrow some shorts or leggings, but she's at volleyball practice and won't be able to get back to me for a while. While I'm at it, I use the online form to ask

Filthy Rich Boys

for an off-campus pass for tomorrow evening, and then grab my bag and head for the library.

Panties or no panties, I still have to get this project done.

I'll just be really, really careful.

As usual, the library is deserted, most of the students choosing to retire to their dorms or heading outside to one of the courtyards to study. That's one of the reasons I like it here; I can get a little time to myself. The Idols and their Inner Circle most *definitely* don't hang out here unless it's for a specific and necessary purpose.

The other reason I like it here ... the books. Five stories of invaluable knowledge, row after row of old tomes, and rooms filled with historical archives. The architecture is to die for: Gothic revival with soaring arches and intricately carved columns. The whole place smells of ink and paper, and I feel this sense of relaxation come over me as I wind my way toward the back corner where Tristan's waiting.

He's standing two shelves over from the entrance to the archive room, a table nearby littered with file folders and boxes of slides. Burberry Prep has had a student-run paper since 1970, but while the journalism club is in the process of scanning old articles into a digital archive, they've still got a long way to go. The time period Tristan and I are most interested in isn't even close to being uploaded.

His eyes snap over to me when I walk down the aisle, the silver of his irises glimmering with some unknown emotion. I can't seem to figure this guy out when he's not being a dick. He holds his face so still, with this practiced haughtiness covering up any real emotion that I have no idea how to get a read on him. I fully expected him to go back to treating me like shit, but instead he seems to be doing the opposite.

Tristan smiles at me, and while it's just as cocksure and arrogant as the day I met him, there's a smoldering undertone to it, like he'd enjoy searing my mouth with those full lips of his again.

"Sorry I'm late," I say, trying my very best not to think about the fact that I've got no panties under my skirt. It occurs to me then that I should've unrolled the waistband and dropped the hem a few, careful inches. My cheeks flame and Tristan raises a dark, questioning brow. "There was some … shit happened in gym."

His mouth turns down into a frown.

"Harper?" he asks, and I shrug my shoulders. "If it happened in the girls' locker room, then it was Harper. Not a single girl makes a move on this campus without her approval." He pauses and narrows his eyes, not at me but just in general. "Except for Miranda, of course … and you."

I'm not quite sure what to say to that, so I don't say anything, turning to examine the row of books in front of us. They're all titles penned by alumni, some of which pertain to the construction of the school or its many additions. Since our chemistry project has to do with levels of contamination in the soil and building materials, we're trying to match up the time period in which the contaminants might've occurred.

Tristan and I reach for the same book and our hands bump together, heat searing up my fingers and into my arm. My pulse races, and I have to swallow back a small sound of surprise. Do all the girls feel this way when they touch him? Is that why he's always sleeping with a new one?

Filthy Rich Boys

"I've got a list of titles on my phone that I looked up that might be helpful," I say, reaching into my bookbag and pulling it out. Tristan just stands there in his perfectly polished uniform, not a button out of place, not a single crease or stain. The way he holds his head tells me he knows he's the king, even if the other guys don't want to believe it. My eyes scan the list and then I hand it over to him, and we start pulling out books and laying them on the table.

When none of those gives us the information we're looking for, we head back into the shelves, our bodies pressed close in the tight space. I can smell him, too, this fresh, sharp peppermint and cinnamon mix that makes my nostrils tingle. He reaches around me a few times, effectively pinning me against the bookcase with his warm, hard body pressed up against my back.

Holy crap.

As he pulls away, there's this rush of cool air, like I'm free-falling when all I want is to be held close.

My eyes close and I exhale.

"Something the matter?" Tristan asks, still standing far too close to me. His lips touch the side of my head as he talks and his left hand finds my shoulder, kneading my knotted flesh with an expert's touch. A groan escapes me and I lean back into him without even meaning to.

Marnye, what are you doing?! I snap at myself, opening my eyes and pulling away. There's a book we missed before that I recognize from the list of titles I made, and I reach up to get it as Tristan steps back. Of course ... I tried so hard not to freak out over my lack of panties that I completely forgot to be cautious about not wearing any. My skirt lifts up and I swear, I can feel a cool breeze on my bare ass.

Tristan's hands fall on my hips, and I hear him exhale sharply.

"Can I ask for that favor now?" he whispers, his voice seduction incarnate, winding around me and working its way inside my chest.

"What's the favor?" I choke out, feeling the warmth of his hands through my skirt. He leans in close and puts his mouth next to my ear again.

"Let me touch you."

My heart explodes in my chest, and I find myself nodding before I even realize what I'm doing.

Tristan moves his hands over my hips and under my skirt, cupping my bare ass in his palms. I've literally never done *anything* like this before, so I find myself holding my breath until I've gone dizzy, leaning in against the bookshelf with my arms still over my head, fingers clutching the edge of the shelf.

He cups my bottom in a tight grip, his breath ragged and warm against my ear. I can barely hear him though, or anything else for that matter because my heart is beating so fast that it drowns out the world. A hot, warm throbbing takes place in my core, and I suddenly want his hands lower, searching for something else.

It feels fated, this meeting of ours, in the dark, quiet shadows of the library.

If Harper and Becky hadn't stolen my panties, if I hadn't stood on my tiptoes to grab the book, if Tristan hadn't been standing so close behind me …

Filthy Rich Boys

My breath rushes out in a gasp as his palms travel over the curve of my ass, sliding up and underneath the pleats of my skirt before trailing down the outsides of my thighs. With a sudden curse, Tristan steps back and I turn to face him, our bodies just inches apart. His slacks can't hide the bulge underneath, and his eyes are far too dark and dripping with lust to be fake.

This wasn't planned. I can feel it.

"Your debt to me is paid," he says, turning and heading for the table. He scoops up a box of slides and storms off toward the microfilm reader. I'm not sure whether to go or stay, but I feel hot and achy and confused, so I just grab my bookbag and bail.

The next time I see Tristan, he has the project finished, and we don't talk about what happened in the library.

CHAPTER 18

While the Idol boys are being, for the most part, pleasant, the girls are at their worst. And the Inner Circle isn't much better. On the last Friday of the month, just after grades are posted and I take second place behind Tristan (damn it!), I get a call that Vice Principal Castor wants to see me.

His office is located in the administration building just outside the chapel. My heart is thundering, my palms sweaty as I make my way out the door and along the windy gravel path. The gardens on either side are beautiful, carefully manicured, and filled with late winter flowers like daffodils, California golden currants, and fragrant rosemary. The sun is shining, and the air is perfumed with sweetness. I'm nervous, but not overly so.

Filthy Rich Boys

Not until I knock on the man's door and hear a gruff invitation from the other side.

Vice Principal Paul Castor is in his late fifties, early sixties with graying hair, a short beard and mustache, and arms thick from strenuous workouts. Sometimes I see him jogging around campus after school and on weekends. He lives on the Burberry Prep campus, several miles down the road in the staff housing.

"Come in and take a seat, Miss Reed," he says, his voice hard. The way his gray-blue eyes track me, I know right away I'm in trouble. He's staring at me like I've already done something wrong, and he's simply deciding on the correct form of punishment.

I do as he asks, folding my skirt underneath my thighs, and doing my best not to think about Tristan's hands roaming around down there. As soon as that thought enters my mind, a hot flush comes to my cheeks, and I have to swallow around a lump in my throat.

Last night, I had a three hour texting conversation with Lizzie about Tristan. The way she talks about him, you'd think he walked on water. She actually *likes* the guy. When I tried asking her how she felt about breaking up with him, she waited almost a half an hour before texting me back.

If I had any other choice, I'd still be with them.

And what sort of answer is that?

"Miss Reed," Mr. Castor repeats, folding his hands on the top of his desk. He stares me down like we're in an interrogation room. "Do you know why I called you here?" I shake my head, but I'm still all jumbled up with thoughts of Tristan, so it's hard to force my mouth to speak coherent thoughts. "We've received almost two dozen complaints from students across all four years here at Burberry Prep, that you've been selling your services."

My mouth drops open, and my cheeks flame red.

Services ... as in ... does Mr. Castor think I'm a Working Girl from the Brothel, too?

"Homework, essays, answers to test," he continues, and I almost breathe a sigh of relief. *Oh, those sorts of services.* But then I realize the implications present in that. *Over two dozen complaints?!* "The accusations have come from students with very credible reputations, and we need to take them seriously."

"As seriously as you took the accusations about my out of control drinking?" I snap, a high note of panic in my voice. Mr. Castor looks chagrined, and sighs.

"Look, I understand you've been having trouble fitting in, but two dozen complaints is too many. Miss Reed, you are talented and bright, but unless there's some secret coup against you then—"

"There *is* a secret coup!" I shout. I don't mean to raise my voice, but I'm starting to panic here. My hands curl into fists in the red pleats of my skirt.

"We have proof, copies of identical homework assignments with your handwriting on them."

My brows crinkle up, but I can't figure out how exactly they swung that one.

"Can I see these copies?" I ask, because I know if I take a look at them, then I'll be able to determine if it really is my handwriting. Mr. Castor gives me a tight half-smile and opens

Filthy Rich Boys

a folder on his desk, passing over a sheet of paper that most definitely has my writing on it. The only difference is that the name's been changed. Two minutes with Photoshop could fix that. I wrack my brain as I stare at the sheet of paper, and then it all clicks.

My locker, the day my panties were stolen. I had this exact assignment in there, and when I couldn't find it, I just asked our Japanese teacher, Mrs. Suzuki—*Suzuki Sensei*—for another one.

"We have four students who turned this in as proof, another dozen with identical math homework, and so on. Miss Reed, if you confess right now and give up the names of all the students involved, we'll make the punishment light. After all, buying these services is nearly as bad as selling them, and we can't exactly expel over two dozen students." He sighs and sits back in his chair. "We'll start with a two week suspension wherein you'll return home, but take your schoolwork with you. Any assignment that's been copied will have a grade of zero, and you'll lose your place in the student rankings."

My heart turns to ice and plummets into my stomach, shattering to pieces. I clamp my hand over my mouth and feel so sick that I'm not sure I've even got the strength to stand up and make it over to one of the potted plants in the corner. I've been working hard, so fucking hard.

The Idol boys, Tristan in particular, come to mind. He just surpassed me in rank, but it wouldn't surprise me if—

There's a sharp knock on the double doors, but whoever it is that's on the other side doesn't wait for confirmation. They swing inward, and Tristan Vanderbilt strolls in with Zayd

Kaiser on one side, and Creed Cabot on the other.

"Boys," Mr. Castor begins as they stroll up, Zayd on my left, Creed on my right. Tristan stands behind me and puts both of his hands on my shoulders. When he squeezes, a swarm of butterflies takes off in my belly.

"Vice Principal Castor," Tristan begins, his voice cold and arrogant and full of disdain. It's quite clear in the way he speaks to the man that he doesn't respect him. "I've just been made aware of the accusations leveled at Miss Reed."

"Mr. Vanderbilt, you know I can't discuss the business of other students—"

Tristan halts the man's words with a wave of his hand. With the other, he starts to massage my shoulder, and I almost melt in my chair. Zayd is grinning on my left, winking at me when I glance his way. Creed just looks bored and completely and utterly put out. If he were a cat, his tail would be flicking in irritation.

"I can name every student who came to you with a complaint," Tristan continues, his voice like an inky night sky, endless and black but with a few stars here and there to brighten things up. "And I can tell you exactly how they got the assignments in question." He reaches into the pocket of his academy jacket and pulls out a set of keys. "I found these on the floor in the chapel." He tosses them over to Mr. Castor.

"You expect me to believe that?" Mr. Castor asks, and when I look back at him, Tristan has one brow cocked over his steel gray eyes.

"Believe it," Creed drawls, yawning and rolling his shoulders. "We have a lot of influence in this school, or

Filthy Rich Boys

haven't you noticed?" His blue eyes sharpen, and I'm reminded of his confrontation with Derrick. Only this time, it's not Miranda he's defending, it's me.

A warmth suffuses my chest that I can't put a name to. But it feels good. Really, really good.

"A lot of the other students are jealous of Marnye," Zayd says, sliding his inked hands into the pockets of his slacks. "So they ganged up on her. We took care of it." He tilts his head to the side, and reaches up to rake his fingers through his mint green hair, turning it into a sea of sharp spikes. "It won't happen again."

Creed smiles wickedly and for a moment there, I almost forget that he was the first one to try to go to the staff to get me in trouble. Is this all a game? Did they report me so they could save me? But no, what would be the point of that?

"We'll be taking Marnye now. Punish the accusers however you want." Creed turns to leave and Tristan drops his hands from my shoulders, offering me one to help me out of the chair. I take it cautiously, glancing back at Mr. Castor, but his mouth is flattened into a thin line and it doesn't look like he's going to protest.

"Let's get out of here before he finds something else to bitch about," Zayd whispers, and the four of us sweep out the doors and into the sunshine.

"What was that all about?" I ask as Tristan pulls me down the path and then pushes me into a little alcove. His hands are on either side of the archway, and his face is so close we could kiss.

"Harper and Becky are not pleased with you," he says, reaching up to run a thumb along my lower lip. Zayd makes a growling sound from behind him, and Creed narrows his blue eyes to slits, but they don't try to intervene. "The half of the Inner Circle that's not loyal to us, they reported you, along with a handful of Plebs." Tristan smiles at me, cupping my chin in his hand. "But like Zayd said, we took care of it."

He releases me suddenly and steps back, making my head spin.

"Why are you guys helping me?" I ask, blinking through a sudden rush of emotion. "I thought …"

"Just keep those grades up," Tristan says, pausing on his way down the path so he can turn and look at me. "I only like beating worthy opponents. When I crush you academically, it'll be on my own merit." He turns away and leaves me with Zayd and Creed.

"Dinner in The Mess?" Zayd asks, tilting his head to one side and giving me a panty-melting grin. "My treat." My own lips twist up in a smile; I can't help it. I feel heady with emotion right now. "Creed?" He watches me, and I can't shake that memory of dancing with him during the winter formal. I felt like a princess swept away in a fairytale.

"I'll pass," he says, slouching against the edge of the alcove and kicking one foot up against it. His eyes meet mine, and a spark snaps between us. "I will, however, walk you to orchestra practice tomorrow. It's about as far as I can manage before I need a nap." He winks at me, slides down the wall, and kicks out one leg, keeping the other bent at the knee. I've never seen anyone luxuriate like he does, sitting in the sun with that white-gold hair sparkling, his phone in his hand.

"I'll take you up on that," I say, letting Zayd put his arm

Filthy Rich Boys

around my waist. He guides me down the path and I feel the strangest burst of emotion in my chest, like a flower blooming in the spring sunshine.

I wish this feeling could last forever.

CHAPTER 19

The entire social scene at Burberry Prep revolves around a single day in February: Valentine's Day.

"If you don't get a rose, you're worse than a Pleb," Miranda explains, and then flushes, clamping a hand over her mouth. I smile at her, but she's already rushing to explain herself. "Not like, well … I'll be sending you a rose for sure. You don't have to worry."

"I'll send you one, too," I say as we walk down the hall toward our lockers. I don't use mine as much since my dorm is actually in the chapel building, but everybody else lives in Tower Three, so they stuff them full of things. Honestly, because we use tablets and laptops in most every class, and physical textbooks have gone the way of the dinosaurs, the

Filthy Rich Boys

lockers function more as a social hub and a place to store personal items people want during the day. When we stop at Miranda's, she gets out a soda and a bag of cashews.

I once saw inside Tristan's locker and noticed a box of condoms. Zayd keeps a guitar in his. I've never seen Creed's.

"Maybe my brother will send *you* a flower?" Miranda teases, hip bumping me as she scoops a handful of cashews into her palm. "He's walked you to every practice and rehearsal for orchestra, hasn't he?" I shrug my shoulders, but I can't deny that it's true. Creed's been walking me around campus, Zayd's been eating with me in The Mess, and Tristan just flits in and makes my heart thunder at random moments.

Maybe … I'll get more than just one flower from Miranda?

And if I do, what does that mean? Are the Idols fucking with me?

I hate to admit how much I want this new friendship with them. Or more. Could be more than friendship …

Roses can be purchased all week in the student lounge, and are delivered during third period on Valentine's Day. It's a Friday, so everyone's already antsy and ready for the weekend. People shift in their seats and whisper behind cupped hands.

Ms. Felton gives up trying to actually teach us anything, and we all wait in nervous anticipation for the bouquets to arrive. Tristan is the only member of the Bluebloods, save Miranda, that's in this class, and my palms begin to sweat when I see him grab his things and move over to stand beside us.

I did something … risky this week.

I ordered five flowers: one for Miranda, one for Andrew … and three for the Idol boys.

I have no idea how they're going to react to that.

"Expecting any roses?" Tristan asks, and I shrug because I don't want to tell him the truth: I am. I really, truly am. He doesn't say anything, just waits for the door to swing in and the staff to come through with massive bouquets of roses in hand. There are buds in every color, all mixed together in a rainbow of differently shaded blossoms.

The rule is: a student can only order one rose for each recipient.

Tristan watches as the employee makes her way around the room, handing out bunches of long-stemmed roses and little stacks of cards. When she finishes passing out the flowers in her arms, she heads back out to the cart in the hall and grabs a bunch as big around as my waist. This one she presents to Tristan.

"Holy shit," Miranda chokes out, watching as he puts the flowers aside and moves over to the trash can near Ms. Felton's desk. The whole class holds its collective breath as Tristan begins to look through the cards that came with them. He tosses the top card into the trash and several of the girls gasp. The second card … also in the trash. Tristan's gray eyes study the names and dismiss them, one by one. I have no idea how many cards he has, but I'm guessing it's around a hundred. "I've … never even heard of someone getting so many roses."

"Trash, trash, trash," Tristan says, chucking one after the other. It's actually pretty fucking cruel what he's doing. There's no reason for it. My cheeks burn, and I can't help but wonder which one of those cards is mine. "Yawn. No thank you. Stupid bitch."

"Tristan," I hiss, but he's ignoring me. The employee comes back in and hands Miranda a dozen red and white roses, and a small stack of cards. Me, I get exactly five. Blinking in surprise, I look through the notes and find one from Andrew, one from Miranda, and three from the guys. Exactly the same people that I sent roses to.

My head snaps up and I find Tristan staring at me. He slaps the remaining cards against the palm of his hand, smiles at me, and then dumps all but one in the garbage.

"*To Tristan Vanderbilt,*" he reads, his voice so commanding that most everyone in class stops to listen. "*Thank you for being a good friend. I'm glad we could overcome our differences. Love, Marnye Reed.*" He snaps my name off his tongue like a curse … or a promise. My heart thunders as I stare at him and wonder if he's going to chuck my note in the trash next. "Thanks, Marnye. I *love* it." Tristan snatches a single red rose from the bouquet, tucks it behind his ear, and then hands the rest to some random first-year girl.

He comes over to stand in front of me, and pulls a gold box from his pocket.

"Enjoy." He tosses it on my desk, tucks his hands into the pockets of his jacket, and saunters out.

My mouth is basically on the fucking floor.

"Oh my god, oh my god, oh my god, *open it,*" Miranda chokes out, grabbing the box and practically shoving it into my arms. Everyone in class is definitely staring at me now, even Ms. Felton. "I mean, I pretty much hate the guy, but … Tristan Vanderbilt does not fall for girls. *Ever.* You're like, the second coming of Lizzie." I give her a *please shut up* look, and crack the box open.

There's a white gold diamond necklace inside with a pair of roses on it.

"What …" I start as Miranda gags next to me, fluttering her hands in my direction.

"I know this necklace. I saw it at Neiman Marcus. I almost bought it." When I just sit there staring at it, she takes it from me and puts it around my neck.

"How much is this worth?" I ask, feeling like I might choke.

Miranda clasps the necklace and sits back, looking at me with a sheepish expression on her face.

"Um, eighty thousand?" she says questioningly, and I choke, reaching a hand up to touch the pair of roses. I cannot keep this. There's no way I can freaking keep this. Why … what is going on?!

Before I can voice any of my concerns to Miranda, Harper du Pont comes storming into the classroom, ripping Tristan's bouquet away from the startled looking Pleb girl. Like a hurricane, she sweeps into the room and plucks one of the cards from the trash before spinning to face me. When she sees the necklace around my throat, she lets out of one of her pterodactyl screeches.

"You are so fucking done, Reed!" she snaps, moving out the door before Ms. Felton gets a chance to stop her.

I'm not sure whether to be afraid … or exhilarated.

Maybe a healthy dose of both?

On my way out of the classroom, one of the academy couriers who hands out mail and packages from home stops me and passes over a small box. As he moves on with his deliveries, I pull the small pink envelope off the top as Miranda whistles under her breath.

"You've gotten … popular," she says, but not like she's jealous or anything, just in awe.

I know chocolates aren't your thing, the note reads. *Enjoy. Zack.*

A smile lights my face as I open the box to an assorted collection of artisan caramels.

Wow.

"These are my favorite," I whisper, feeling a red flush warm my cheeks. I'm … this day just can't be real. Days like this do not happen to me.

"Girl," Miranda starts, raising her brows and biting her lip to hold back a laugh. "Creed is going to lose his mind. I think he actually likes you now."

"He does not," I retort, but then I think about the way he kissed me on the deck of the steamboat, and my stomach flutters. I touch a hand to the necklace and feel my heart beating beneath it. "I mean, how could he? I thought they all hated me?" Miranda just stares at me like she's as confused as I am.

We head down the hall to my room and find Zayd waiting for us. He's tapping a bouquet of roses against the wall in time to a beat we can't hear. He's got one ear bud in, the other hanging down his chest.

"Billie Eilish," he says, pointing at his ear, and then he pauses the music and tucks his phone in his pocket. "Looks like he got to you before I did." Zayd's eyes narrow as he reaches out and lifts the necklace off my chest, his fingers brushing my skin and sending shivers through me.

"Before you did?" I ask, and he grins, stepping aside, so I can use my keys to get into my dorm. I set my flowers and caramels on the counter and turn around to find Zayd offering me yet another box. Holy crap. Guess today is my lucky day?

"Any idiot can buy a necklace," he says proudly, nodding in the direction of the box with his chin. "But check this shit out." I give him a skeptical look and lift the thin top off the box, finding a sea of colorful truffles underneath. "Homemade, motherfucker." Zayd flops down on my bed and leans back on his palms.

"You made these?" I ask, and he shrugs.

"I'm taking *Practical Skills* this semester," he says, and Miranda interrupts him.

"Translation: home economics for rich kids who've never done a load of laundry in their life." Zayd flips her off, and then leans forward, putting his elbows on his knees.

"Yeah, whatever. But last week was a lesson on making artisan chocolates. As you can see, artisan fucking chocolate." He pauses as I reach into the box to pluck one out. "Just a warning: there's about ten milligrams of weed in each one of those." With a scoff, I drop the chocolate back in the box as he laughs. "Sativa, it'll keep you going all night long." Zayd lifts his hips up and makes a dirty undulating motion that I find I like way too much. "You are going to the garden party, right?" he asks, and I shrug. There are too many parties here to keep track of. "You have to go, seriously." He stands up comes over to stand beside me, plucking a rose from my bouquet, snapping most of the stem off, and tucking it behind my ear. "Come on, Working Girl."

I sigh, but I know I'm getting dragged into this.

There's a banquet starting outside at four-thirty with food and drinks and games.

"I'll go," I say with a sigh and both Miranda and Zayd get way too excited. Miranda hugs me, and kisses me on the cheek.

"Come back to my place and we'll get ready together?" I nod as Zayd once again opens my wardrobe and starts digging around inside of it. He emerges with the lemon-printed dress I wore to the Cabot Scholarship Award ceremony, and hands it over to me.

"Why are you always trying to dress me?" I groan as I take the dress from him. As he passes over the hanger, Zayd curls his inked fingers around my wrist and yanks me against him.

"Because you look like a fucking hobo half the time," he growls, and then he bites my ear, grabs a chocolate, and pops it in his mouth. "Later, ladies. See you in the courtyard."

Zayd slams the door behind him, and Miranda turns to me like I've grown tentacles.

"How are you going to choose?" she whispers, eyes wide, and I gape at her.

"There's nothing to choose." I grab the white flats Miranda lent me when we went into town to shop, and stand up, meeting her incredulous look with one of my own. "There's not. I'll never forget how shitty these guys treated me."

"Yeah, but …" she reaches out and taps the necklace with a sort of forlorn expression that I can't interpret. Once again, I question myself and try to decide if she's got a thing for Tristan. But no, no, it's got to be something else, something I'm not getting. "It's nice to be wanted, right?"

"There's more to life than boys," I say, and she lifts her eyes to mine, blue irises sparkling.

"Truer words were never spoken."

Now … what the hell is that about?

Creed is waiting in the courtyard when we come down, dressed in flouncy spring dresses, my necklace sparkling in the afternoon sunshine. He's leaning against the garden wall, head thrown back, eyes closed. His hands are tucked in his pockets, the top two buttons on his uniform undone, one foot flat against the wall.

Filthy Rich Boys

He opens his eyes and turns to us with slow precision, yawning and then stretching his arms over his head, completely and utterly unhurried.

"How many roses did you get?" Miranda demands, putting her hands on the hips of her bright orange dress. It's citrus themed, too, just like mine, but a good three inches shorter, and two sizes smaller. "Because I'm pretty sure Tristan got a hundred."

Creed's face tightens up and he flicks his sister in the forehead, tucking his hands back in his pocket and leaning in close to her.

"I got plenty. I didn't think to count." He stands back up and his eyes flick over to me. He doesn't say thank you, but his eyes sparkle in acknowledgement, and I flush.

"Right. Because you know you got less than he did," she taunts, but Creed's ignoring her, looking me up and down.

"I hear you got all sorts of gifts today," he drawls, and I bite my lower lip.

"Enough." I can hear people milling around in the garden, the soft sound of classical music spilling over to us along with the gentle sweetness of roses.

"Mm." Creed circles around me and then puts a hand on the wall near my head. "Fucking vultures," he says, reaching out to play with a loose strand of my hair. "Would it be apropos if I gave you another gift?"

"You better give her a gift," Miranda mumbles, her eyes scanning the crowd until she spots Andrew. She gives him a little wave, and then glances back at us. "I'll give you two a little privacy." She wanders away with her hands in her dress pockets, as I blush and watch Creed reach up to the top of the garden wall, grabbing something in his long fingers.

When he hands it over to me, I see that it's a copy of *The Tales of Beedle the Bard.*

"It's not the handwritten version," he says with a small grimace, glancing away like he's ashamed of himself. "But it's signed."

I take the book in shaking hands, but I can't stop the tears that try to fall. They prick my eyes as I turn away and try to blink them off. Creed notices and gives a small half-smile, pausing as Becky Platter marches over to us. She's like a little Harper clone. Whatever her mistress says or does, she just imitates.

"You think because Zayd made some stupid chocolates for you that you've won?" she snaps, and I raise my brows. I haven't even considered 'winning' anything, least of all him. This whole day has just been … weird. "He doesn't give a *shit* about you. He just wants to fuck you, so he can say he bagged a virgin."

I frown. Honestly, that sounds like the complete opposite of Zayd. He's very vocal on his opinions of virgins. But also … now I know the whole school is aware of my sexual status. Great.

"Becky," Creed says, nice and slow and quiet, but with a dripping menace that makes me shiver. "Go to hell." She snaps her gaze over to him, but she's still fuming. "Zayd spent every day after school in the kitchen this week perfecting those chocolates. He ruined over twenty boxes worth. It's more than just candy, sweetie. Now get."

"You don't control me, Creed Cabot," Becky snaps,

tossing her blond hair. "You're no higher on the totem pole than I am."

"Keep telling yourself that," he purrs, pushing off the wall and facing her down.

"And you keep telling yourself that Tristan Vanderbilt isn't a hundred times better than you, and maybe one day, the world will believe it as much as you do." Becky spins on her heel and storms off, stilettos clacking against the cobblestones.

When I look back at Creed, his face is tight, and I can see she actually hit a nerve with that one.

"Bitch," he growls, and then he turns back to me, looking for a split-second like he's actually confused about my presence there. I blink once, and the expression is gone. Creed holds out his arm, and I slip mine through it. "Don't worry about her," he tells me with a caustic laugh. "She won't last another year as an Idol. She's too weak."

"I'm not worried about her," I whisper, holding the book against my chest. Becky is just another bully, and I'm beyond accustomed to dealing with people like her at this point. I'm just glad I don't have to deal with Zayd, Tristan, and Creed anymore. Or Zack. Talk about challenging … Becky is nothing compared to them.

Creed leads us over to a table where Zayd and Tristan are sitting. Neither of them looks particularly happy about being together. Zayd's green eyes meet mine, and I smile. *Twenty boxes, huh?* The fact that he had the discipline to work so hard on those chocolates makes me want to cry. But in a good way. In a really, really good way.

"None of us could agree on who should escort you here

tonight, so ... we're basically stuck with each other." Zayd flicks a glance over at Tristan and scowls. The other boy ignores him, focusing on my necklace before lifting those stormy gray eyes to my face.

"Sit," he says, and I do. Creed leans against the column behind me as I grab a colorful little tea sandwich and take a bite. Cream cheese and cucumber. Interesting. "Do you like your necklace?" Tristan asks after a minute, sliding his legs underneath the table so that our limbs are tangled together. I look up at him, and my heart stutters in my chest.

"I love it," I say, and then I glance at Zayd, at Creed. "I love everything." *Including Zack's gift. I'll have to text him later.*

"Good," Tristan says, leaning back and smirking at me with that cocksure little smile of his. "Because I told you I was interested. And when I'm serious about something, I get what I want."

"Don't count on it, bro," Zayd chokes out with a laugh.

Creed doesn't say a thing, but the way he smiles and narrows his eyes, I see the challenge in them.

How are you going to choose? Miranda asked me.

Good fucking question.

CHAPTER 20

Tutoring with Creed is going well. He's actually ridiculously smart, he just chooses not to apply himself. When he buckles down and focuses, it's all easy for him. He could be top of the class, too, if he wanted.

Since we're both busy with schoolwork and orchestra and social gatherings, the only times we've been able to agree on for our sessions are early afternoons on Saturdays, and late afternoons on Sundays. Today, I'm hurrying over after orchestra rehearsals, taking the elevator to the top floor and knocking until Miranda lets me in.

"Hey," she says, stepping back. "Creed's in the shower, but just make yourself at home." I notice that she's all dressed up in a blue and white striped dress, strappy heels, and a fancy updo. My brows go up, and she blushes. "I'm just … Andrew and I are going into town today to grab a bite to eat at that little café we went to. You know the one." She gestures at me, and nervous laughter falls from her glossed lips.

"You know, if you're dating Andrew, I don't care. I don't think Creed would—"

"I'm … it's complicated," Miranda says, getting flushed. She lifts her head up and smiles at me, but there's a tightness to it. She's not going to be revealing any secrets to me today. "I have to go, but we'll hang out later tonight, watch a movie or something?" I nod, and Miranda takes off, letting the door slam behind her.

We've been watching a lot of movies lately in here with Creed, and he's started sitting right next to me on the couch or pulling me into his lap. I end up not watching a single second of whatever film is on because I'm focusing so much of my energy on where his hands are, if he's hard underneath me, on his soap and fresh cotton smell.

Settling down on the couch, I lean back to wait until I hear the shower turn off, and a door opening somewhere. The bathroom here has three doors, like a jack and jill, but with an additional entrance from the living room. Once I'm sure I've given Creed enough time to have safely exited to his room, I stand up, give a quick knock, and then try the door. I haven't had a chance to pee since I left my dorm for orchestra this morning, and I really need to go.

When the door opens however, I'm left staring at Creed, wet and hot and steaming, a white towel around his slender hips. He's combing his hair, and as he glances back at me, the towel slips and falls to the floor. My mouth gapes open at the sight of his firm ass, and that's *before* he turns around and shows me exactly what he's working with.

"I'm sorry," I blurt, but I make no move to leave, and

Creed's mouth turns up in a sharp smile.

He takes a step closer to me, leaning over and putting his mouth next to my forehead before brushing it with a light kiss.

"Were you trying to join me, Charity?" he asks, his voice a whisper against my skin. I can feel his lips moving and heat shoots through me. Creed lifts his hands and puts his warm palms on my upper arms. I do my best not to look down, but … he strikes a beautiful nude, this boy. "Because I'd happily get back in the shower if you'd join me."

He trails his fingers down my arms, and I close my eyes. I should tell him no, turn away, run as fast as I can. Instead I stand there until he sweeps an arm around my waist and pulls me against his naked body. One hand skims up my side and finds my breast, taking the full mound in a tight grip and squeezing it as he drops his mouth to mine. My nipples pebble, and even through the fabric, it's almost unbearable when Creed sweeps his thumb across it.

His tongue dives into my mouth and I lean into him, putting my palms on his chest. Heat sweeps my body, burning my inhibitions to ash. There's no inkling in my mind to stop, and I wonder how far I would've let it go if Miranda hadn't popped back in the apartment and dropped her purse in shock.

"Oh … shit."

I shove Creed back, turn, and push past Miranda into the hallway.

I don't stop panting until I'm safely back in my room with the door locked.

Later, I text Creed and let him know that I'd like to have our tutoring sessions in the library.

He sends me a picture in response that I very promptly delete.

And then spend hours looking up how to un-delete.

Ugh.

The rest of March is a blur, my time split between the guys, Miranda and Andrew, classwork and orchestra. Zack and I are texting almost everyday now, while Lizzie and I send messages almost every hour. She's actually going to the same getaway for spring break that I am, a musical intensive sponsored by the academy. It's open to all schools, but the competition is fierce. When I was in eighth grade, I used to dream about being accepted. Now, it's an automatic. If you're signed up for orchestra, you're signed up for the retreat if you want the spot.

Zayd is also going.

"At my old school," I start, realizing as I say it that I sound exactly like Phoebe Terese from *The Magic School Bus*. "We used to ride buses to school-related events. You know, those big, yellow things with the seat-belt free seats?"

He rolls his eyes at me, and then scoops me up in his arms, carrying me over to the back of the white Cadillac Escalade that's waiting with our luggage in the back. I can't remember how many Burberry Prep kids are going, but not a lot. Most people want to spend their spring break somewhere warm and tropical.

Filthy Rich Boys

Tristan is in Fiji with his dad while Miranda and Creed went home to Florida. Andrew is with his cousins in Texas, and Zack is back in Cruz Bay. He even texted to tell me that my dad had a bad day and didn't make it to work, that he lost his job and that rent and electricity didn't get paid. I offered to send some money from the account Tristan made me, but Zack said he'd already taken care of it.

Of course, then I felt guilty for not going home for spring break. But this music program, it could be life-changing for me.

"I know what a bus is, dumb dumb," Zayd says, hoisting me into the center row and then crawling up beside me. "We filmed my last music video in one." I roll my eyes, but I can't help but wonder how and why Zayd is even here.

"You already have a music career," I start as he glances over at me, "so what's this about?"

"You're never too good to learn from someone else," Zayd says, shrugging his shoulders and then tapping out several rapid text messages on his phone. He pauses to look over at me, his mouth twisting in this totally self-assured little smile. "Besides, I knew you were going, and figured you'd want company."

"Considering Harper and Becky will be there, most definitely." My smile stretches wide, and Zayd reaches out to pinch my cheek with his inked fingers. I slap him away, but he just laughs, and then grabs my face between his hands, kissing me smack on the lips.

My cheeks burn with heat, but I sink back in my chair, curl my legs up underneath me and just watch him for the majority of the drive. There are other students in the back seat, and Mr. Carter in the front, but nobody bothers me or picks on me, not with Zayd sitting right there. I have plenty of time to myself to text Zack and Lizzie, to look at a picture Miranda just sent me of her and Creed sitting on the beach. He's shirtless, his pale skin flawless and glowing under the hot sun. I bet he comes back with a tan … or a burn.

We wind our way south and east, toward this camp on the edge of a massive lake. It's probably three or four times the size of the one back at the academy. When we crest the hill and I see it, my breath slips out in a gasp.

There are over a hundred students attending, each with a different passion or specialty. Since I'm on the harp, I get paired up with Becky (gag), and one other girl from Coventry Prep who says she knows Zack, and assigned a cabin on the opposite side of the lake from Lizzie and Zayd, both of whom are here to focus on the piano.

Zayd gives me a goodbye kiss on the cheek, and a pat on the ass before he takes off across the grass and I flip him off. Lizzie is waiting on the other side of the lake, and I can just barely see her as she waves to me. I wave back, but we won't be able to actually hang out until later this evening, at dinner.

That's okay though, because even though I'm stuck with Becky, I know I have allies here. Besides, it's better than being at home with Jennifer hovering around, and dad gazing at her like she's the love of his life. Anyway, the harp is one of my passions, and I don't mind spending spring break getting better at it.

Doing what you love makes the day go by quickly, and before I realize it, the sun's already sunk beneath the surface

Filthy Rich Boys

of the lake, and I'm heading across the grass toward the mess hall.

Stepping into the giant log cabin with its picnic tables, red plastic trays, and cafeteria food makes me laugh. The students at Burberry Prep might call our restaurant The Mess, but this place is far more deserving of that name.

"Hey, Working Girl," Zayd calls out, waving me over to sit next to him and Lizzie. She rises from the table and gives me a big hug before scooting a tray in front of me and grinning.

"We got here before everybody else, so I grabbed you the good stuff." She points at the pizza on my plate, and then gestures in the direction of the line where people are complaining because the only thing that's left is meatloaf. Gross. Based on the smell, I'm pretty sure it has onions in it, too. Double gross.

"Thanks," I laugh, as I pick up a slice and bring it to my lips. "How was your guys' day?"

"Would've been better if you were in it," Zayd says, throwing me a sharp grin. The way he looks at me sends shivers through my whole body. If he really had been around me all day, I wouldn't have gotten anything done because I'd have been too busy staring at him, memorizing the full curve of his lower lip, or the long dark curves of his lashes. "Doesn't matter though," he continues, folding his tattooed forearms on the table and resting his chin on them. He looks at me from under half-lidded eyes, reminding me of Creed, and that strange situation in the bathroom.

"What doesn't matter?" Lizzie asks glancing between the two of us. She raises her eyebrows, but she knows how I feel about Zayd. That is to say, she knows that I have no idea what to do with his attention. Or Creed's. We don't really talk about Tristan. How can I, when I know that she still loves him?

"We're gonna make up for all that time spent apart," Zayd says, grinning. He nods his chin at my pizza and then reaches out and steals a slice. I pretend to slap his hand away, but really I'm grinning.

"How are we gonna do that?" I ask, exchanging a glance with Lizzie. She shrugs her thin shoulders and then steals the other piece of pizza from my plate.

"We," Zane begins, shoving the last of the pizza in his mouth and swallowing, "are going skinny dipping."

Zayd knocks on the cabin door after curfew, and I let myself out. Fortunately, Becky is sound asleep and snoring, a floral eye mask covering her face. Dressed in nothing but shorts and a tank top, I follow him down to the lake and over to a shadowy area protected by a copse of trees.

"Where's Lizzie?" I whisper, because honestly she seemed pretty excited to take a nude dip in the lake. It's the only reason I'm here. Not because I necessarily wanted her to see me naked. but because there's no way I'm stripping down when it's just me and Zayd.

"Skipped out," he says with a shrug, already in the process of tearing his shirt over his head. "She wanted to give us some privacy." He turns and flashes me a cocksure smirk that

Filthy Rich Boys

I can barely see in the moonlight.

And then his pants are down, and I can see that he even has a few tattoos on his legs. Zayd winks at me, and then turns and dives into the lake. He barely makes a splash, slicing through the water with his tattooed hands, and then reemerging a few feet out. The moonlight reflects off of his white-toothed smile, as I wrap my arms around myself and consider whether or not this is a good idea.

The old me definitely wouldn't have done something like this. There's always the chance that someone like Becky is waiting to sneak up and snap my photo, share it around the whole school. But … this is the new me. I'm taking chances, making a fresh start. And if Zayd were going to humiliate me, I imagine he could come up with a more creative way to do it. This just isn't his style.

My heart is pounding, and sweat is beading on my forehead. It might be cold outside, but when I dip a toe in the lake, it's still relatively warm. *I can't believe I'm doing this,* I think as I wait for Zayd to turn his back. And then I tear my shirt over my head. My shorts drop to the ground, and I wade into the water with my arms crossed over my chest.

Zayd turns around and watches me, his eyes tracking my movements hungrily. When he swims over to stand next to me, water dripping down the sides of his face, I don't miss the implication. It's dark, we're alone, and we're naked together. Plus, there's this palpable tension between us that I felt from day one. Even when he was being an irreconcilable jerk, I could feel it.

"Well *hello* Working Girl," he purrs, swimming in a circle around me. When he pauses, he's even closer, our bodies just inches apart. I reach out and put a hand on his chest, intending to push him away. Instead, as soon as my hand makes contact with his flesh, we both sigh.

"I'm not having sex with you," I say, pursing my lips firmly. And I mean it. I won't let myself get swept up in the Idols and their charisma. It's just not going to happen. If I decide to have sex, it'll be on my terms, and in my time. Tonight is not that time.

Zayd chuckles at me, but manages to keep his howling laughter to a minimum. The last thing I'd want is for the camp counselors to stumble on us out here. What a scandal that would be. Dad would most certainly kill me.

"Hey," Zayd says, flashing me another grin. "Don't make that decision just yet. We have a whole two weeks out here. A lot can happen two weeks." He starts swimming toward the center of the lake, gesturing for me to follow after him.

When I first started at Burberry Prep, there's no way I would've joined in. I was too unsure of myself in the water, and I could barely do a dog paddle. But even though Harper and Becky have done their best to make PE a nightmare for me, I've actually learned some valuable skills.

I swim after Zayd's ass, until we're both bobbing in the center of the lake, spinning in slow circles and taking in the majesty of the camp and the trees around us. The moonlight highlights the water, casting a silver glow, and taking the evening from mundane to spectacular.

The next time Zayd swims so close to me, his eyes are soft, but the tension between us is still white-hot.

"If I promise not to take it too far ..." He begins, reaching

Filthy Rich Boys

out and pulling me to him. I put my palms on his chest, and keep a safe distance between our bodies. But when Zayd dips his head to mine, our lips brush together, and I open my mouth to let him in.

His hands slide down my back, and cup my ass, pulling me closer. Without meaning to, I wrap my legs around him. Our bodies are sandwiched together, with nothing between us. His mouth works on mine, his tongue hot and demanding. A moan escapes my lips; it's a small, quiet sound, but it echoes across the surface of the lake, and I feel my cheeks heat with a blush. I push away from him, and he lets me go, falling behind me as I swim back to shore and climb out.

My ass is already in view before I realize I should've told him to turn around. It's a little too late now though, so I saunter up the beach like I intended to let him see, grab my clothes and get dressed.

"Thanks for the view," he says grinning as he too rises out of the water and flashes me. As soon as my shirt's pulled over my head, I slink back to my cabin, crawl in bed, and dream about rocker boys with incredible kisses.

CHAPTER 21

A few weeks later, there's another Infinity Club party at the lodge. This time, it's not quite so cold, so the party's spilled down the hill and into the water. The girls are dressed is mismatched bikini tops and bottoms, while the guys don colorful swim shorts, creating a splash of brightness against the endless blue of the lake.

When the Idol boys offer to play me at poker, I decline. I learned my lesson last time, and I'm not about to repeat that mistake. Things are going well for me right now, and I'm not about to mess that up by putting myself in debt. I have yet to fulfill my end of the deal with Creed, but I still don't know anything about Miranda and her dating habits.

Part of me hopes I never do, so I don't have to tell her

Filthy Rich Boys

brother. Maybe one day he'll just stumble onto the information on his own, then my debt will be null and void, and I won't have to share secrets.

It's worth a thought.

"I still don't quite get the Infinity Club or what it is," I confess to Lizzie as we sit in chairs on the edge of the shore, watching people splash around in the water. Her fiancé is out there, making an ass out of himself, and she frowns. I notice her eyes go to Tristan whenever he enters a room, and I have to fight back a strange mix of jealousy and pity. Lizzie should be able to date whoever she wants, regardless of her parents' wishes. But ... also, I think I kind of like Tristan now?

Lizzie turns her amber eyes over to me and smiles.

"I'm not allowed to tell you much, but ... it used to be a boys' club." She sighs and sits up, pushing her dark curls back from her face. "It wasn't until, like, ten years ago that they started letting women in."

"Is the gambling stuff ... necessary?" I ask and Lizzie shrugs.

"Infinity Club is about ... risks ... money, connections ... secrets." She exhales sharply and leans back. I can see her infinity tattoo just above her right hip. "Nations thrive and wither depending on the club's wants. We're all just, like, the junior version." She laughs softly, focusing on her blue painted toenails. "We're being molded into the future rulers of the world."

I get chills down my spine at the melancholy note in her voice and decide that maybe I'm digging too deep into something I don't want to know much about. I just want to live a normal life. I'll never be in their club anyway, so what's the point?

The less I know ... the better.

A shadow falls over me, and I look up to see Zack standing next to my chair. My heart leaps in excitement, and I rise to my feet to give him a hug. He holds me so tight and so close that I can hear his heart beating. His muscular arms give just the right amount of squeeze before he releases me.

"It's been a while," he says, and I grin as he pulls over a chair to sit next to me and Lizzie.

The Idol boys are off somewhere doing their thing, but I've already seen a race around the lake today that almost gave me a heart attack. I was sure one of those fancy sports cars was going in the water, and someone was going to die. They've moved onto other stupid games, gambling away fortunes my father's never even dreamed of, but so long as they don't start playing Russian roulette, I decide to just leave it be.

When you're as rich as they are, life starts to dull around you. They don't appreciate the little things anymore, so they create big things to entertain themselves. It's a little sad, actually. I almost feel sorry for them.

"It has been a while," I say, biting my lower lip and looking over at him. I guess I hadn't realized how much I'd missed him. Or that I'd missed him at all, really. Zack glances over at me, his brown eyes dark, face unreadable. He's a mystery to me, but he doesn't have that cruel streak in him the way the others do. My heart pitter-patters in my chest, and I glance away, catching Lizzie's amber-eyed stare. She smiles knowingly, and I flush.

Filthy Rich Boys

I'm a little jealous that they go to the same school. Or rather, I'm disappointed that Zack didn't get into Burberry Prep. I would've loved having him here with me.

"Your dad misses you," he says, glancing over at me. "I go home every weekend, and I usually stop by his place. You're the only thing he talks about." Zack glances out at the lake, and all the students splashing and laughing and screaming. "He's really proud of you, you know."

I nod, but there's too much emotion in my throat; I feel like it's choking me. There's something going on with my dad and Jennifer, that much I know for sure. It's been bothering me since winter break, but I just can't figure it out.

"Has there been a woman coming around a lot?" I ask, fishing for information. "One who drives a new white Cadillac?"

Zack shakes his head, and I sigh in relief. I was starting to worry that my parents might be seeing each other again. What a strange thing for the kid of divorcees to worry about, huh, their parents getting back together ...

"Nothing like that," Zack says, looking over at me again. The way his eyes take me in, it's like he's drinking me up, like he's thirsty and can't get enough. After a moment, he runs his tongue across his lower lip, like he's thinking hard about something. "Do you mind if I get changed? We can go swimming or something." I nod, and Zack gets up to head into the lodge.

When he comes back, he's dressed in black swim shorts, and nothing else. I can see the infinity tattoo above his right hip, and since my eyes are already down there ... Wow. Not only does he have a perfect six pack, he's also got those delicious V-lines. They draw my eyes down to the waistband of his shorts, briefly wondering what might be underneath.

Damn.

All this time spent with Creed, Zayd, and Tristan is really corrupting me. I pretend like I wasn't just checking Zack out, and take his hand when he offers it to me, letting him pull me to my feet. It's like I weigh nothing, and in a split-second, I'm up and in his muscular arms, and he's carrying me to the water.

Lizzie laughs as Zack puts me on an orange floating raft, and pulls me around the lake. Today is the complete opposite of my experience with Zayd, hanging out in the bright sun in the warm, warm water with a sea of people around us versus that solitary moonlit excursion …

I grin.

"Do you like it here?" Zack asks me after a while. "I don't just mean at the lodge, I mean at Burberry Prep in general?" He looks at me questioningly, and I shrug.

"If you'd asked me that question a few months ago," I start, reaching up to pull my shades down over my eyes. The sun really is bright today. You can tell that winter's long-gone, and spring is out in full force. "I'd have given you a different answer. But as of right now, it's a yes."

Zack nods, but he doesn't smile. He looks far away, lost in thought.

"They're not bothering you?" He asks, making eye contact with me.

"Not anymore," I admit, watching him as he gives me a ride around the lake, swimming with one arm and pulling me

Filthy Rich Boys

with the other. When we get to the opposite shore, Zack sits on the sandy beach, half in the water, and we hold hands so I don't float away.

"I don't even really like these parties," he says, glancing up at me from under a fall of dark hair. "I only came today because of you."

My mouth opens in surprise, and I feel a slight blush work its way to my cheeks. I don't think I ever properly thanked him for the caramels, but the fact that he remembered in the first place, that meant the world to me. We might not have had the best run of it when we were dating, but he seems to be trying to make up for it now.

He can never make up for what he did to you, my mind whispers, but I ignore it. I'd rather just forget about it all at this point.

"You came for me?" I repeat, and Zack nods, staring off into the distance. He's not very talkative, but when he says something, he means it. He almost destroyed me with those words of his. I imagine, if he put that strength of his to better use, he could move mountains.

"Yep."

Silence falls between us for a while, the only sound the lapping of the water against the shore and the birds singing in the trees. When the sun gets too hot, Zack swims me back over to the other side, and we get out, wrapping towels around ourselves and settling in to eat fruit at one of the tables inside the lodge.

We sit so close, our naked thighs touch. And I decide then that if he asks me to stay the night again, I will. Not for sex or anything like that, but just to talk, hang out. I miss hanging out with Zack.

After a while, the Idols show back up. Creed scowls as soon as he sees Zack and me sitting together, but Zayd ignores him completely. He flops down on my other side and pulls me right into his lap.

Zack notices, and his eyes narrow to slits.

"You're here again?" Tristan asks, pausing in the kitchen to make himself a drink. I reach up and touch the necklace. I didn't wear it swimming, but as soon as I got out, I put it back on. I like the way it feels against my skin.

"I can go to whatever goddamn Infinity Club party I want," Zack growls, his voice low and dark. He really, really doesn't like Tristan Vanderbilt.

"True," Creed says, sitting down on the opposite side of the table. "But not when all you're going to do is sit there and pant all over Marnye." Creed's blue eyes slide over to mine. When our gazes lock, a tingle goes through me and I shiver. Honestly, I don't mind Zack panting over me, but I'm guessing that none of the Idol boys likes it much.

"Why don't you worry about yourself, and I'll worry about me and Marnye?" Zack says, crossing his muscular arms over his chest.

"You didn't seem to give a shit about Marnye a few years ago," Zayd says absentmindedly, and Zack stiffens up like he's been punched.

"Don't." Zack puts his palms flat on the table, and his eyes meet Tristan's. He switches his gaze from him to Creed, to Zayd, and back again, but I have no idea what's going on, so I don't weigh in.

Filthy Rich Boys

"You told Marnye about that girl you killed yet?" Tristan asks casually, coming over to stand beside us with a drink in his hand. The way he looks down at Zack, it doesn't bode well. He wants to destroy him. I can see it written into every line of his face, in the way he holds his shoulders, and the way he taps his finger against the side of his cup. "Or, I'm sorry, that girl you *almost* killed? What happened to her again? She stuffed some pills down her throat in the school bathroom?" Tristan's gaze moves over to mine, and I feel this coldness come over me. His expression softens slightly, almost apologetically, like he doesn't want to say these things but has no choice.

"What are you talking about?" I ask, my voice so low it's practically a whisper. Zack meets my gaze as pain and regret shoots through his. He looks like he's about to throw up. "Zack?"

Zack grits his teeth and exhales, closing his eyes against a wave of emotion.

"Go on, tell her," Creed says, leaning his elbow lazily on the table and resting his chin in his palm. "Tell her what you did. At least give her the chance to know the real you." He shrugs his shoulders like he doesn't care much either way. "If she still wants to hang out with you, then good on her. She's a more forgiving person than I am."

"Marnie," Zack says, reaching up to take my hand. I let him hold it, let him weave his fingers through mine and marvel at how good it feels. I like Zack. I really do, despite all the things he put me through. "There's something I need to tell you."

When has that line ever lead to something good? Without

a doubt, I know that whatever Zack's going to tell me, I'm not going to like it.

My eyes dart from him to Tristan and then to Creed as Zayd's arms tighten around my waist, and he pulls me closer. It feels good, having him touch me like that. I use that as an anchor against the anxiety churning in my stomach.

"Marnye," Zack begins again, closing his eyes. "I'm just gonna come out and say it. It's better if I tell you than they do." He lifts his eyes again and looks right at me. "You know how I treated you in middle school, we don't have to relive that; we both know how horrible it was." He glances away and then turns back to me again, but it looks like it's taking him a concentrated effort to hold my eyes. "Did you ever wonder why I did it?"

I can't say anything. My throat is too tight, my pulse is beating too fast, and I feel like I'm going to be sick.

"I made a bet." Zack exhales sharply and then grits his teeth together. The way he looks at Creed, Zayd, and Tristan makes me think that he'd kill them if he could. When he looks back at me, his expression is much softer. "To get into the Infinity Club, I had to make a bet. The group wanted to taste blood, and they ..."

"The girls were the real masterminds behind this one," Creed says, but he doesn't sound happy about it. He's wearing a deep frown that looks etched into his face. When he lifts his blue eyes to mine, he looks apologetic. "Because he'd been cut off from his trust fund, they really wanted him to prove himself to the group. They bet him he couldn't make somebody kill themselves."

Filthy Rich Boys

My heart literally stops. I can't breathe. The room seems to tilt and spin on an axis.

Lizzie opens the sliding door and walks in, pausing when she notices Tristan. She seems to sense the tension in the room, and her shoulders tighten.

"What's going on here?" she asks, looking from me to Tristan to Zack and back again.

"Oh," Tristan says, folding his arms over his chest, his drink still clutched in a tight fist. "We were just telling Marnye about that bet you made with Zack." Tristan's face tightens up as he stares Lizzie down, and I have to wonder if he's doing this as much for revenge against her as he is to get rid of Zack. Maybe he's doing it for me, too, so I can finally know the truth, but it's hard to see it that way.

Lizzie's amber gaze slides over to me, and her mouth opens but nothing comes out.

"We were much younger then," Zack whispers, rising to his feet. His voice is pleading, begging me to look at him. I do, but when our eyes meet, all I feel is sick. "Marnye, what I did was wrong. It was ... it was fucked. It was *Lord of the Flies* type shit." He grits his teeth and glances away sharply. "Hanging around with this club, with these people ... they're fucking snakes."

"Oh please," Zayd snarls, squeezing me even closer. "Don't act like we had anything to do with this. The three of us weren't even around when you originally made this bet."

"No," Zack snarls, taking a step forward. Tristan moves between us, like he thinks he might need to protect us from him. "You might not have been here for that bet, but you've been around for worse. This is not out of line with something you'd do."

"Just tell Marnye you used her to get into the Club, and that you only saved her because Lizzie changed her mind and said that was enough." Creed stands up from his side of the table, his face lit with the same determination I saw when he attacked Derrick Barr over Miranda. Only this time, he's fighting for me. I'm not sure whether to be happy about it … or, no … I'm too sick to be happy.

"Marnye," Lizzie begins, drawing my attention around to her. It occurs to me then that she knew exactly who I was when she came to the party a few months ago. She looked across that room and she knew exactly what she'd done to me. That was the 'connection' that she'd felt between us. "I really do like you, and I meant it when I said I wanted to be friends."

I stand up, but my knees almost give out, and Tristan grabs me around the waist to keep me from falling.

"Please," Zack starts, but I'm already shaking my head.

"I just …" Tristan lets me go, and I manage to keep my feet, but my gaze keeps bouncing between Zack and Lizzie. I feel betrayed from both sides, from my past and from my future. Now it all makes sense, why Zack started picking on me for no reason. All for some stupid club. Years and years of pain …

It makes even more sense why he didn't want to tell anyone that we were dating back then. And Lizzie … I feel like my whole friendship with her is a sham.

"I just want to be left alone," I blurt, pushing past them all and heading down the hallway. I end up in the bathroom with

Filthy Rich Boys

the door closed, and I turn the hot water on in the shower, climbing in and huddling underneath it with my hands over my ears.

When someone knocks, I don't answer, I just sit there until the hot waters run cold and my teeth are chattering. Then I climb out, grab a towel, and step into the hallway where Zayd is waiting.

He doesn't say anything, just leads me into one of the guest rooms and tucks me in the bed. He gets on top of the covers, curls around me and holds me there for the rest of the night.

CHAPTER 22

Finding out that I was just a bet to Zack is ... well, it's devastating. I'm a zombie for weeks, going through the motions, focusing on my schoolwork and my harp. Nothing else matters. It hurts too much to think about what he did to me. What Lizzie did to me.

And the Idols ... they're still being nice to me, still acting like they want me, but ... they had to know how much that revelation would hurt, right? Yet, they did it anyway.

Still, it's hard to stay mad at them. Zayd is always charming, popping into my room at random times, flopping down on my bed and joining me for TV night without ever saying a word.

My tutoring sessions with Creed are tense, but in a good

way. That spark between us burns hot, whether we're doing math, or working on essays side by side. Every time he touches me, I can feel it, a rush of heat that infuses every molecule in my body.

Tristan ... he's a lot harder to get a read on. But he does sometimes sit in on my orchestra practice, watching me play the harp with those blade gray eyes of his. I always play better when he's in the room, like just knowing that he's listening is a boon to my creativity.

Miranda and Andrew definitely notice the change in my behavior, and call me out on it.

"Are you sure you know what you're doing?" Miranda asks as the three of us sit together in The Mess eating yet another meal I can't pronounce. It's good, it's just ... in a language I definitely don't speak. This week's menu is food from around the world. It's educational, at the very least.

"I don't know what you're talking about," I say as I pick at my food with my fork and then glance up to see the two of them staring at me skeptically. "What? I'm not doing anything but hanging out with them." *And wearing an eighty-thousand dollar necklace, and skinny dipping, and making out, and—*

"The Idols don't just hang out," Andrew says, sighing. "They divide and they conquer. The fact that they've all set their sights on you worries me. If you ask me, they're up to no good." He exchanges a look with Miranda that I can't read, and the mystery of what they're up to together starts to get to me. So much so that the next time they try to sneak off together, I follow them.

I don't intend on doing any true sleuthing, I don't have to. Just keeping a safe distance behind them as they walk through the rear courtyard and meet up with some friends in the trees is enough.

The first thing I notice is that Miranda and her new girlfriend take off in one direction, while Andrew and his male friend go the other way.

I decide to stick with Miranda.

What I don't expect to see when I round the corner of the hedges is the two of them lip-locked, their arms around each other, fingers grasping. They're both panting, kissing like they can't get enough of each other, and it all clicks in the place.

Miranda isn't dating Tristan, and she's not dating Andrew either.

Miranda is … gay.

I turn away and take off before they notice me spying on them, but honestly, I feel a sense of relief. I was expecting the worst, like a hidden pregnancy or something, but this is … this isn't even noteworthy. In a good way, I mean. Like I said, I'm a fierce LGBT ally.

For the next few days, I keep things cool, normal. But now that I know, the way Miranda acts makes a whole lot more sense.

Before I tell Creed, however, I decide to confront Tristan.

"You knew didn't you?" I ask him, planting my hands on my hips and staring down at him as he sits on one of the stone benches in the courtyard and scrolls on his phone. Tristan lifts his gray eyes up to mine, and I find myself licking my lower lip without even meaning to. One look from him and I melt.

"Oh? So you finally figured it out?" he asks me, scooting over and patting the spot next to him on the bench. If this was

Filthy Rich Boys

anyone else, that'd be a harmless gesture, and I'd just sit. But with Tristan, there's so much more to it. I'm afraid to sit that close to him.

"Is there a reason you didn't want Creed to know?" I ask, cocking my head to one side. "He thinks you and Miranda are sleeping together, you know that?" Tristan shrugs his shoulders, but his eyes land on the necklace that he gave me, and I reach up to touch it without thinking.

"No reason. It just wasn't any of my business." He stands up, and takes a step forward, towering over me. His fingers reach up and brush along the side of my jaw, a smirk taking over his lips when I shudder. "But it is yours. You and Creed had a bet."

Tristan cups my face and leans down. For a second there, I think he's going to kiss me again, but instead he just puts his lips right up against mine, so I can feel it when he talks.

"That girl she was making out with, that's Jessie Maker. Her parents are Evangelical Christians, they won't be happy with the news." Tristan runs his tongue across my lower lip, and then steps back. The absence of his body makes me feel cold.

"Is this going to hurt either of them, me telling Creed?" I look into Tristan's eyes, but he just shrugs. I sigh, but it looks like I'm going to be on my own with this one. It was my arrogance that got me into this mess after all. I should've stopped playing poker after I'd won the first round. Lesson learned.

Tristan brushes past me, making sure his fingers linger on the back of my hand before he moves away. I listen to his footsteps on the gravel path before I turn and head for Creed and Miranda's apartment.

Fortunately, Creed's the only one that's home. He lets me in, and the spark between us flares to life.

"You figured it out," he guesses, his words vaguely echoing Tristan's. Creed crosses his arms over his chest and waits for me to talk.

"I did," I start, and then I don't know what to say. It seems so anti-climactic. Miranda being gay isn't a problem, and it shouldn't matter to anyone. Then again, I know Creed's just worried about what it is that she's hiding. Maybe, like me, he's expecting the worst. This should be a relief for him. "Miranda is dating a girl named Jessie Maker," I say, waiting to see what his reaction is going to be. The skin around his eyes tightens imperceptibly, but that's it.

"You're sure?" he asks, and I nod. Creed exhales and drops his arms by his side, and I'm glad to see that he's not upset. "That's it?"

"You're not going to bother her about it, are you?" I ask, but he just stares at me and shrugs his shoulders. Oh, well, *that's* reassuring. I feel sick with guilt already, but when I think about violating the Infinity Club's rules ... I know that was never an option.

"I just want to make sure she doesn't get hurt," Creed says, and it's the most genuine thing he's ever said to me. There's a brief pause before he speaks again, changing the subject with effortless ease. "Would you like to go to dinner with me?" he asks, and even though I know he just means to take me to The Mess, my heart warms and I nod.

Everything seems fine ... until next week when the shit

hits the fan.

I hear the fight before I see it, the sound of grunting, the painful crack of flesh against flesh. Miranda and I exchange a look, take off down the hallway, and turn the corner to find John Hannibal beating the ever living crap out of Andrew.

"Stop it!" Miranda screams, dropping her bookbag to the floor and leaping into the fray. I follow after her, but the boys are in such a frenzy, they just knock us to the side and continue fighting. There's quite a bit of blood, and when Tristan and Zayd appear to pull them apart, I can see that most of it belongs to Andrew.

"Come on man," Gregory Van Horn says, stepping out of the crowd that's gathered to watch, "let me have a turn at him." It takes me a second to realize he doesn't mean John, he means Andrew.

"What the hell is going on here?" Miranda asks, spinning to look at her brother as he comes around the corner. She searches his face desperately, but he doesn't say anything. It's John that speaks first.

"We heard Creed confronting Andrew about being a faggot," he sneers, reaching up to wipe some blood from the corner of his mouth. I turn to look at Creed, my stomach tightening in knots, but he's already shaking his head.

"That's not even in the fucking realm of what I was doing. I wasn't confronting him. I just wanted to be sure he wasn't banging my sister." Creed runs his fingers through his hair. "I thought he was lying to me, so I followed him after our conversation. That's when I found him making out with Gary Jacobs." Creed shrugs his shoulders. "But whoever gave you the right to beat him up?" Creed's voice is as sharp as a whip, and he gives Tristan a run for the money in the asshole department. At least this time, he's using his asshole powers for good. "There will be absolutely *no* homophobic bullshit on my watch." His eyes briefly flick to his sister before he looks away again.

"Why would you confront him like that?" Miranda snaps, stepping up to her brother. Her eyes sparkle dangerously, and even though I'm terrified, I know I have to tell her about my part in all of this. If I don't, then how am I any better than Lizzie or Zack? Just thinking about them makes me want to throw up again, so I push the thoughts aside and reach out for Miranda's arm.

"Hey," I say, looking her straight in the face. I haven't even said anything and she's backing away from me. Andrew watches us both carefully.

"You said something to him, didn't you?" she whispers, and then she turns and takes off down the hall at a run. I jog after her, but she's waiting for me when I turn the corner.

"You said something!" she shouts, and I cringe, clinging to the strap of my bookbag. My guilt is written all over my face; I can feel it.

"I followed you one day, and—" Miranda reaches out and slaps me. I don't even stop her because I know I deserve it. Still, the explanation tumbles out of my mouth, and I'm

Filthy Rich Boys

frustrated to hear it sound like an excuse. There are no excuses for what I've done, getting Creed involved, and subsequently the entirety of the Bluebloods. "I made a bet with Creed during poker—"

She interrupts me again, and I let her.

"I *warned* you about that fucking Club!" she shouts, pacing the hall in front of me, raking her fingers through her hair. "And I warned you about the Idols." She stops and stares at me like she has no idea who I am anymore. "I thought you were different, but when it comes down to it, you're just like them."

"Don't say that," I choke out, already feeling the tears beginning to leak down my cheeks. "Miranda, I'm sorry."

"You spied on me, and you spilled my secrets, and now look what's happened. Not everyone is as progressive as you, Marnye, and our secrets—mine and Andrew's—they were not yours to tell." She sniffles and puts her face in her hands. When I reach out to touch her shoulder, she jerks away from and drops her arms to her sides, curling her fingers into tight fists. "Don't touch me. And don't talk to me."

"For how long?" I whisper, but I know I messed-up, and I can't expect her to give me a timeline on her forgiveness … if she even gives it at all.

"I don't know. Maybe forever?" Miranda pushes past me and my shoulder slams into the wall. I turn and watch her go before Creed appears around the corner, his eyes dark with pain. His sister is the one and only person he seems to care about, and he's just upset her to the core—with my help.

"I'm sorry, Marnye," he says, moving over to me and putting his hands on my waist. The world sways around me, but his touch keeps me upright. "I never meant for this to happen." He leans down and brushes his lips to my forehead, and even though I know I shouldn't believe him, I do. Because I want to. "Can I come in?" I nod, and use my keys to unlock the door to my apartment. Creed slips in behind me, and I let him stay the night on my couch.

CHAPTER 23

With Miranda, Andrew, Lizzie and Zack gone from my life, I'm left with this hollow, cold feeling inside my chest. Spending time with Tristan, Zayd, and Creed helps, but … they're all vying for my romantic attention, and I want friends who are there just because, that want nothing from me.

Since that's not exactly an option for me, I throw myself into my schoolwork, and then spend the rest of my time either practicing the harp, or hanging out with the boys. They let me sit with them in The Mess, at the high table in the front of the room.

It kills Harper and Becky to see me there, but even though their looks are seething, I'm almost always around at least one of the guys. Their presence acts as a shield, and keeps the bullying to a minimum.

"One day she's going to stalk me in a dark alley and cut my throat," I say as Harper makes eye contact with me from across the dining room. The way she's handling her steak knife is disturbing, to say the least.

"She can get over it," Tristan says, leaning back in his chair and watching her. He hunts her, like a wolf stalking a fox. The fox might think it's a predator, but only until the wolf's jaws clamp down on its throat. If Tristan wanted to take Harper down, I think he could.

"Any word from Miranda?" I ask Creed, but the way he stiffens in his chair tells me all I need to know. She's not talking to him either. "Do you think she'll come around?" He sighs, closing his eyes on what's looking to be a major headache.

"Maybe, maybe not. It's hard to say with her. Our relationship was already on a razor's edge. Unfortunately, I think you might go down with the ship." He taps his fingers on the table, his food left untouched in front of him. We're all tired, I think, ready for a break from the social scene, from grades, from … whatever this is that's brewing between the four of us.

"So, about the graduation gala," Zayd begins, pushing his plate away and leaning his elbows on the table. He steeples his hands together, green eyes sparking as he looks over at me. "Have you given a thought as to who you might go with?"

"Nobody's asked me," I respond crisply, but none of the boys has a reaction. Creed closes his eyes again, like he's about ready to take a nap, Tristan continues to glare at Harper from across the room, and Zayd sits back with a smirk before reaching for a roll and some butter.

FILTHY RICH BOYS

Still, he wouldn't have brought it up if he didn't have something in mind. So at the very least, I might be ending year one at Burberry Prep friendless, but I'll have a date to the gala.

There's a minute amount of comfort in that.

When I open my door the next day, I find three boxes stacked neatly and wrapped with twine. There's a note on top that I slide carefully out from underneath the knot. When I open it, I recognize Tristan's handwriting.

"Three princes want to take you to the ball, Cinderella. Make your choice."

I frown as I collect the packages and carry them inside, opening the first one to a beautiful black dress and a small piece of cardstock with Tristan's name on it. The second box has a blue dress with Creed's name. And the third is red with Zayd's name.

My cheeks flush pink, and I feel suddenly dizzy with choice.

Miranda's words echo in my head: *How are you going to choose?*

The question is: do I *want* to choose? I've come to like all three Idol boys, more than I ever thought possible. They're the only friends I have left, and more than that … I'm starting to care about them in ways I've only ever cared about one person. That was Zack, and he's gone now. I can never forgive him for turning me into a bet. I just can't.

But this …

How the fuck do I choose? And what happens when I do? Will I lose the other two guys? Will they stop talking to me?

Love is a cruel master.

Err. Love? I'm not in love with any of these guys. I quickly replace the tops on the boxes and set them in the corner to torment me. Every instinct in my body says I should go find Miranda or text Lizzie, but I've been hurt so many times before, I don't know how to approach them; I need more time. Maybe summer break will be the healing balm we all need? A little sunshine, sleeping in too late, the Train Car and its comforting familiarity.

Flicking the lights off, I climb into bed and I try not to think about the graduation gala, and everything that comes with it.

Just two more weeks, and I'll have made it. I'll have survived my first year at Burberry Prep. And maybe, just maybe, I'll have a boyfriend to enjoy the summer with.

Finally, I think, sitting down on the edge of my bed and pushing loose strands of hair back from my face. I've fought tooth-and-nail to make this year worth the pain, punching my way to the top of the first-year class, snatching my spot in the orchestra. I even managed to make friends with the bullies who were making my life a living hell.

Filthy Rich Boys

Of course, I miss my friends. I miss Andrew and Miranda, Zack and Lizzie.

"Hey," Zayd says, smoking a cigarette with both the bathroom windows cracked. "Don't look so sad. We have less than a week in this shithole, and then summer, bitches." When he's done smoking, he drops his cigarette in the toilet, flushes it, and comes over to sit beside me, pulling me close. I lean my head on his shoulder, but I've got anxiety for a different reason.

Tonight is the last dance of the year. It's called the graduation gala, and it's for all four years of students here at Burberry Prep. For me, it almost feels like a death sentence. Those three dresses ... they're all so beautiful. I tried them on one at a time in front of the mirror, desperate for some sign from above that I was making the right choice.

I got nothing.

The universe has left me completely and utterly on my own.

"You know," Zayd starts, exhaling sharply. "You should pick Creed or Tristan tonight." My eyes snap up to his, and I see this broken indecision in his green eyes. He looks pained as he turns to me. "Whichever one of those assholes you don't pick, they're going to get butt hurt and storm off. But, uh," Zayd exhales and runs his fingers through his hair, "I'll stick around. I don't care who you pick, Marnye."

A small smile teases over my lips as I fit my fingers through Zayd's. He seems surprised, that I'm touching him that way.

"Liar," I say, and I lean my head onto his shoulder. That's the first time he's ever called me Marnye. Seriously, first freaking time. And I love it. "I've already decided, Zayd." And I have. I did last night. It wasn't easy. In fact, I still feel sick about it, but it all comes down to the beginning of the year and the things they all did to me.

Zayd was bad. Creed and Tristan were worse. I'm not sure I'm ready to forgive the book burning or the essay reading. Also, Zayd was the first one to start being nice to me. It's that simple. I can't have all three guys, and I want to start something that might last. With Tristan, his family would never allow him to date me, I know that. Creed wants to be accepted into the ranks of old money. But Zayd … he might be a dick, and as elitist as the rest of them, but he's also a rock star. He walks his own path.

"Take me to the dance tonight?" I whisper, and Zayd's entire body goes stiff before he turns to look at me, reaching down to cup my face between his inked hands. He grins as he pulls my mouth to his, kissing me with a passion that I wish I could recreate every day for the rest of my life.

I mean, we're nowhere near that yet, but … maybe we could get there?

"It'd be my fucking honor," he purrs, dragging me down to the bed and kissing me like he intends to help me keep that promise. I laugh and let him hold me in his arms until it's time to get dressed.

And then I kick his ass out into the hallway to wait.

It's time to get ready for the ball.

Filthy Rich Boys

The dress Zayd picked out for me is bright red and layered with a tight underdress coupled with flowing skirts, and a lace-up back. It's nearly impossible to get into by myself, so I do my hair and makeup as best I can, and then text him, asking him to meet me at my door instead of by the chapel like we'd planned.

Tristan and Creed don't know that I've picked Zayd, not yet. Not unless he told them. But as soon as they see me walk in wearing this dress, it's all over. There's a fragile nervousness inside of me, this quaking that I don't quite understand. Maybe I realize that when they see me with him, this tentative thing between the four of us is over.

I've chosen Zayd.

It's done.

He knocks on my door, and I pull it open with my nerves on high-alert, butterflies filling my stomach. Zayd is ... holy shit, he's handsome. He's wearing a black and white pinstripe suit with a red tie, red dress shoes, and ... he's even dyed his hair to match my dress. His signature sage-and-geranium smell fills my nostrils as my lips curve into a smile, and I step back to let him in.

"You dyed your hair for me," I whisper, and he shrugs, like it's no big deal. But then his grin spreads from one side of his face to the other.

"Yeah, well." He notices the loose laces hanging off my

dress and spins me around by the shoulders, yanking them tight and breathing sensually across the back of my neck. When he pulls the laces taut, I get a jittery feeling inside my chest. It actually feels good, having him bind me into the outfit. "Green and red is too, I dunno, Christmas-y. And I knew as soon as I saw that dress that it was yours. Therefore, it only made sense to change my hair."

"You have an interesting way of looking at the world, you know that?" I tell him as he turns me back around and tugs me into his arms. I let him pull me close, enjoying the sensation of his tattooed body pressed up against mine. If I'm going to lose Tristan and Creed, I have to enjoy Zayd to the fullest extent. "Shall we go?"

He nods, brushing some hair back from my forehead, and then takes my arm to lead me into the hall. We make our way past the chapel, and into the ballroom on the second floor, the one with a balcony that overlooks the woods.

It's already packed with people, girls in glittering dresses, guys in tuxedos, as well as parents and chaperones galore.

The moment I walk in, the room goes quiet. Zayd pretends not to notice, taking my hand and leading me down the steps like I'm Cinderella or something. As I descend them in the red dress, I spot both Creed and Tristan, standing on opposite sides of the room.

Their stares are so intense, I swear, I can feel them.

Creed's blue eyes flash with pain and frustration before he turns away and stalks off into the crowd, heading straight for the balcony. He doesn't even wait to talk to me or hear me try to explain. He's just … gone. Tristan, on the other hand, waits

FILTHY RICH BOYS

at the bottom of the steps for us.

When we get close to him, the room comes back to life, and everyone starts talking again.

"Well, well," he says, voice tight and clipped. "Looks like you've got yourself a groupie, Zayd." I purse my lips and lean into my date. He howls with laughter, but I don't think Tristan's statement is particularly funny.

"What, now I'm not the Working Girl? I'm a groupie this time?" Tristan's eyes are the color of storms as he stares me down, lips pursed, hands white-knuckled and curled into fists. He doesn't like to lose, this man. That scares me a little. When he doesn't answer, I sigh. "We're still friends, right?"

He cocks a brow at that.

"Friends?" There's a long pause as Tristan lifts his gaze to Zayd, and the two of them share a silent exchange that I can't quite interpret. "Sure." He takes a sudden step back, turns, and then heads in Harper's direction. My stomach tightens as I think he's going to her, relaxing only when he sweeps past and follows Creed to the balcony.

"Hey," Zayd whispers, leaning down and nibbling my ear, "you want to grab something to eat?"

I nod, and he leads us through the throng toward the refreshments. It doesn't matter if there's one Idol or all three of them together, the crowd parts just as easily. He gets us each a drink and a plate of food, clearing a space at one of the high tables nearby and pulling out a stool for me.

Miranda is dancing with Andrew not too far from us, but she never looks at me, not even a cursory glance. My hands tighten in the folds of my skirt, but I don't even consider going over to talk to her, not tonight. I don't want to ruin her fun or make a scene. Instead, I focus my attention on Zayd. Once I've got him talking about his summer tour with Afterglow, he doesn't want to stop, even hints at possibly inviting me.

I can't even imagine that, going on tour with a rock band.

After we're done eating, Zayd holds his hand out to me and raises one, dark brow. His freshly dyed hair shimmers red in the flickering light. The chandeliers in here are all original to the building, refitted to burn gas, so that they retain some of their true character.

"Dance with me, Working Girl," he purrs, and then he sweeps me out onto the dance floor, using that magic of his to turn my awkward, fumbling dance moves into something beautiful. As we sway, Zayd reaches out and cups the side of my face with his hand. There's a bit of regret in his eyes that I can't figure out, but after a few songs, it resolves itself, and I forget all about it.

That's my mistake, my huge fucking mistake.

CHAPTER 24

The next morning, I dress in my uniform, but I add the red lacy bra and panties that Zayd likes underneath. After the ceremony today, we're going to one of the after parties to celebrate, and ... I don't know what might happen between us, but I at least want to be dressed for second base.

My bags are packed and left near the door to my room, ready for Dad to pick up after my harp solo. He's going to take them with him when he heads home, and I'm going to leave with Zayd. Tomorrow, he'll drive me home. How, exactly, I'm going to explain to my dad that I want to go spend the night with Zayd and a bunch of other horny teenagers is beyond me, but I'm going to try. I worked too hard this year to miss out on the party to end all parties.

Besides, I managed to finish top of the first year class. *Take that, Tristan!* I think, but the smug smile on my face fades when I remember the angry expression on his last night. The way he looked at me, I felt like I'd torn his heart out and crushed it under my heel. Touching my hand to my stomach, I close my eyes and try not to think about him or Creed. I can't have three boyfriends. Nobody does. Besides, even if I were to try some sort of open relationship thing, I'd have to be okay with them dating other girls, and I'm not. I'm not at all okay with that.

In my heart, I don't know if I made the right choice. I feel torn, split, confused.

But I made my choice, and Zayd is not a consolation prize. I won't treat him as such.

Checking my hair and makeup one last time, I make my way outside to where Zayd's waiting for me. He's not smiling when I first see him, but when I lay my fingers on his arm, he turns to me and flashes a grin.

"I was wondering where you were," he says, leaning down to press a kiss to my forehead. He weaves his tattooed fingers through mine and guides me through the winding garden paths and down to the indoor amphitheater where the ceremony's being held. There's a different ceremony for every year, just a series of accolades and performances to showcase the accomplishments of the students.

We head inside and move down the aisle, past the family members seated on other side.

I spot my dad right away. What I don't expect is to see Jennifer sitting beside him.

My feet stop moving of their own accord, and Zayd comes to a halt, glancing back at me with his brows raised in a

Filthy Rich Boys

questioning manner.

"You okay, Charity?" I shake my head, but I'm having trouble finding the words to explain. I've spent a lot of time with Zayd over the past year, but we've never delved into deeper issues. I've barely mentioned my mother.

"It's just ... my mom's here," I whisper, and Zayd follows my eyes, locating her in the crowd. She looks ridiculous, dressed up in a white fur coat with a hat, like an extra from a made-for-TV movie. With a sigh, I grab Zayd's hand and pull him down the aisle, pretending I don't notice her. She waves at me, but I just hope nobody I know sees.

"You're not cool with your mom?" Zayd asks, but his tone is detached, far away. He's in another place and another time. Or maybe he's just tired? We danced until two in the morning last night, and then made out for another hour after that. I have to say, that last hour was my favorite part.

"It's complicated," I explain as we take our seats in the front row. Tristan is right next to me, his mouth pressed into a flat line, his skin pale. I knew he was upset last night, but the look on his face now is in a whole other league. Maybe he's upset because he's second place to my first? I have no idea.

The ceremony starts, and the teachers take turns making speeches, praising our accomplishments, gently reminding us where we can do better. Awards are given out for sports, clubs, and community service first, lines of students filing onstage to collect their paper certificates. A huge screen behind them showcases the same awards in digital format.

Academics are last, and when Tristan's name is called, he grinds his teeth so hard that I'm afraid one's going to pop right out. He practically storms onstage, bites off a pathetic thank you, and then heads right back to his spot. Across the aisle, I can feel Creed watching me, so I make sure that when I'm called, my chin is high, and my shoulders are back.

My speech is short, but not overly so, and I recite it without even having to read what I wrote. I make eye contact with Dad, Mrs. Amberton, Ms. Felton, anyone but my mother. At the end, she stands up to clap, but I turn away and head back to my seat before I have to see much more of that.

She can't just abandon me, and then hop back into my life when it's convenient. No way, not happening.

After the initial ceremony, the choir and orchestra are herded backstage to get ready for our performances.

Zayd kisses me goodbye on the cheek, and then returns to his seat in the audience.

That's when I first run into trouble.

Harper, Becky, Valentina, Abigail, and a handful of other girls are waiting for me when I head up the steps that lead backstage. Right away, I look around for backup, either one of the boys or a teacher, anyone. But it's just us.

"We've tried to be patient with you," Harper says, stepping forward. Her makeup and hair are flawless, but the sneer on her perfect lips ruins the practiced pretty she's trying so hard for. "We gave you a whole year to figure it out, but I guess you're just too damn stupid."

"Figure what out?" I ask, but they're not here to talk. This time, they don't just verbally assault me. Two girls come up from behind and grab me by the arms while Harper steps forward and backhands me across the face as hard as she can. I taste blood in my mouth, and I see stars as I look back at

Filthy Rich Boys

her. She grins and moves aside for Becky who's so gung-ho for violence that she's practically drooling. She hits me closed-fist in the stomach, and I double over, held up only by the girls on either arm. I'm struggling, kicking and flailing as hard as I can, but I'm not going anywhere. When I do finally break one arm free, there are two more girls to come and help pin it back.

They take turns hitting me until I'm so dizzy and out of breath that when they let go, I fall to my knees. The beating doesn't stop there. They kick me, pull my hair, tear the seams from my blouse. The girls keep at it until a round of applause sounds from the stage. That's their cue to step back and leave me there, panting and bleeding on the floor.

For several minutes, nobody comes, so I force myself up and stumble to the nearest bathroom, using a wad of paper towels from the dispenser to clean myself up as best as I can. I'm panting, soaked in sweat, and ready to cry, but the pain is … it's damn near unbearable. My first thought is that maybe I should go find someone and report this, but then I remember my dad, and the harp, and my first solo …

No.

After.

After I play, I'll deal with this.

They can't take that away from me.

Marnye, you're in shock. I realize that, but it doesn't stop me from doing what I'm doing.

So I splash my face with cold water, clean up as much blood as I can, and then button my jacket over my torn blouse. By the time I make it backstage, Harper's finishing up a piano solo, and bowing gracefully, no sign of the violence she just inflicted anywhere on her face or hands. Her eyes widen as she passes by me, but by then the harp is already being wheeled out, and I'm announced to the stage by Ms. Felton.

A deep hush comes over the room when I walk out, but I don't think it's because of the beating I just took. I cleaned up most of the blood, and the majority of the bruises won't show until later. Maybe the room is just silent because everyone knows who I am, the scholarship winner, the charity case.

I sit down at the harp and close my eyes. My hands are shaking, and my body's gone numb with shock. Later, I'm going to be hurting pretty badly. For right now, I'm okay. My love for music covers up any jitters I might have, and I throw myself into my performance, playing the best I've ever played. My eyes find Dad's briefly, then Mom's.

Most important, I seek out Miranda, but she won't look at me.

The guys are next: Creed then Tristan then Zayd.

They're all watching me.

I've just finished one song and started on the next when I start to hear whispers and laughter, people pointing. I pause briefly and glance behind me to see that the giant screen has come down again, the one that showcased the student awards. It flickers and then comes to laugh, and my jaw drops open as I see myself, my naked ass in Tristan's hands in the library. The video is shaky, and clearly taken from the other side of the bookcase, but it's distinctly me, and distinctly him.

I want to fucking die.

This cannot be happening, I think, hating that my dad is in

Filthy Rich Boys

that audience. Worse, my mom.

I stand up, but the video doesn't stop there. Images of me pressed against Creed in the bathroom pop up, even my make out session with Zayd from last night is there.

"No," I whisper, but I hardly get the chance to move before I feel the first drops of liquid on my head. I look up just in time for a can of red paint to spatter on my hair and clothes, splashing across the harp and the screen. I've just had a *Carrie* pulled on me.

My mind quite literally goes blank, and I fall to my knees without even realizing it.

Zayd stands up in the audience, but he doesn't move to help me. Creed follows next, then Tristan. At a nod from the latter, the Idols and a good dozen other boys, all pull out pairs of panties from their pockets.

My panties. The ones that were stolen from my room.

They're all thrown at me, littering the stage as the audience fades into a roaring silence.

Dad stands up, but I can't bear to look at him. My heart is pounding, my mind is racing, and then I'm just scrambling to my feet and taking off. I don't know where I'm going, but when I blink, I end up back at my room.

One of the staff is there, my overnight bag in hand, as they lock up the door and then turn, getting ready to deliver it to the office for me to pick up later. I don't even think, I just run by and grab it, stumbling as I head outside to the courtyard and the front steps.

I only make it down the first few before I'm surrounded, by Bluebloods and Plebs alike.

Tristan Vanderbilt is front and center, with Creed on one

side and Zayd on the other.

My heart breaks, cuts me up, reforms.

The hardest hearts are forged in fire; I'll need to be made of steel to survive this one.

"Hello Charity," Tristan says, taking a few steps forward. He's got a trophy in his hand, a gold one with a white marble base. "Do you know what this is?" I don't say anything, not a word. He moves even closer, his gray eyes sparkling with the thrill of the hunt. The way he looked at Harper in The Mess the other day is the way he's looking at me now, like I'm prey. "This is a trophy." Tristan turns and hands it over to Zayd.

He takes it in his tattooed fingers, and then meets my eyes. There's nothing there, none of the fun-loving, playful asshole I hung out with on spring break or danced with last night. He's just … blank.

Kind of like my emotions.

Inside my head, it's all white noise. Marnye Reed isn't even here anymore; she's checked out completely.

"Do you want to know what it's for?" Creed drawls, tucking his fingers into his pockets. His blue eyes are half-lidded and focused on me as I stand there, dripping and shaking.

Zack's words echo in my mind: *You might not have been here for that bet, but you've been around for worse. This is not out of line with something you'd do.*

Something they'd do.

Make a bet.

"We wanted to see who could make you fall in love first,"

Filthy Rich Boys

Zayd supplies, hefting the trophy in his hand. He looks up at me and then drops it by his side. "Whoever got you to the graduation gala was the winner. Honestly, I thought it'd be a bit harder than that."

I open my mouth to speak, but no words will come out. There's nothing to say, is there?

"And you know what?" Tristan continues, cocking his head to one side. "The only prize ... was that trophy. We did it for fun."

My uniform—and my dignity—are in tatters.

I can still taste blood in my mouth, this hot copper tang that makes me want to gag.

Tristan's silver gaze is narrowed on me, and his mouth is just beginning to curve up into a smirk. He thinks he's won, that he's beaten me. Every single person in this crowd wholeheartedly believes that; I can read it on every single face here. They tricked me, lulled me into complacency, and then set out to destroy me.

But they're dead-wrong. Dead-fucking-wrong. I'm not the same girl I was when I first started at the academy.

I lift an arm up and wipe some of the blood from my mouth, still smarting from the beating the Idol girls and their goons gave me. My lacy red bra, the one I picked out just for Zayd, is showing through the torn fabric of my white blouse. He won that bet, fair and square. He made me think he cared about me. I did care about him. The look on his face now is almost alien, foreign, like looking at a stranger. For once, he isn't smiling, but the message in his face is clear: *you don't belong here.*

"Had enough yet?" Harper du Pont asks, her dark

presence like a cloud behind me. There's no point in turning to look at her, not when she matters so little to me. She's nothing. It's the guys, the Idols, the three people at this school that made my heart hurt, brought the sleeping emotions inside of me to roaring, vibrant life. Creed is frowning, but he has a very matter-of-fact expression on his handsome face, like this was all in the cards from the beginning.

A breeze tears through the courtyard, blowing the ragged pleats of my skirt around my thighs. Beyond the walls of Burberry Prep, the sea sings its melancholy song, the same song picked up in the irregular beat of my damaged heart.

Tristan moves toward me, slow and cool, with the hint of violence tainting the air around him. I try not to think of that first day, when he presented me with this challenge: *how long do you think you'll last?* Joke's on him: I made it the whole damn year. But based on his expression, I can see he doesn't expect me back for a second round.

My heart stutters as he reaches out and tangles some of my paint-splattered hair around his long fingers, giving the short rose gold locks a tug. The paint smears across his skin like blood as we stare each other down.

"I take it you won't be coming back next year, will you, Marnye?" Even after everything I've just been through, I can't stop a shiver from racing through me at the sound of his voice. He thinks he's the king here, but so does Zayd, so does Creed. One day, they're going to have it out and it's not going to be pretty. They'll destroy each other.

Their money can't buy them true friendship, and it won't buy them love. It definitely won't buy them me.

Filthy Rich Boys

My gaze moves past Tristan, to Zayd and Creed, but Tristan's standing so close that I can't help but look back at him. Has he enjoyed it this whole time, tormenting me? It's clear in his face that he has. He loves it. They all do.

"Just go home, Marnye, and it'll all be over," Tristan says, and even though his voice is soft, it's a deception. There's a razor's edge to his words, one that promises to cut if I don't heed its warning. On the inside, I'm breaking apart, but there's some stubborn bit of steel inside of me that won't let me crumble. "You don't belong here."

Zayd slides one of his inked arms around Becky Platter, and my stomach twists into a knot. I feel so sick I could throw up, but I won't, not here in front of them. Maybe when I get home, I'll let myself cry, let myself mourn, but not here. Never here. My hands curl into fists, and I grit my teeth.

Tristan meets my gaze one, last time, and then reaches out to pluck a tear from my cheek, bringing it to his lips for a lick, reveling in the taste of my pain. The knife of his betrayal cut close, but it didn't hit its target. I might be bleeding, but I'm not dead, not yet.

"I've already enrolled in my classes."

The courtyard is silent, watching this moment unfold in all its horrible glory.

There's not a person there that expects me to stand up for myself, to raise my chin in defiance. No, they thought I would crumble. Maybe they hoped that, like the girl in my essay, I'd run away and internalize my pain.

Not anymore.

All of this pain has changed me. Right now, it feels like it's changed me for the worst, cracked me in half and spit out broken pieces. But really, I've changed for the better. Their cruelty has shaped me into an immovable mountain, a force to stand against howling winds.

"Come September, I'll be the first in line for orientation."

"You wouldn't dare." Tristan is furious with me, but he's triumphant, too. He still believes he's won, his dark hair fluttering in the wind. He's gorgeous, but only on the outside. On the inside, he's a monster. They all are. "I'll make your life a living hell."

"You can try." My shaking hand reaches into my pocket and pulls out the registration form. I printed it out at the library last week after I filled out the online form to sign up for classes. If it kills me, I'll be back at Burberry Prep next year. This is *my* life, not theirs. I won't let them ruin it. "Because what you don't know ..." Sucking in a sharp breath, I bend down and grab the handle on my ratty, old duffle bag. Tristan is scowling at me, but he's already done his worst, wormed his way into my heart and tried to break me. What else is there? "Is that my life outside of these walls was already a living hell. This is just another level of Dante's inferno, and I'm not afraid—not of any of you."

My eyes meet Creed's, and then Zayd's, and then my feet start to move, taking me around Tristan and down the steps, toward the school gates and three months of freedom.

At the last minute, his hand curls around my arm and jerks me back. I look down at it, and then up at him. His smile ... it's painfully wicked.

"Challenge accepted." Tristan releases me with a small shove, but I don't stumble or fall. Instead, I head down the

Filthy Rich Boys

path toward the waiting line of academy cars, still dressed in my torn uniform, but with my chin up and my fears pushed back.

Challenge accepted is right.

I'm going to come back, and I'm going to give these assholes a taste of their own medicine. The girl these boys met on day one is not the same girl leaving now.

No matter what it takes, I'll make sure they know that.

I'll stay one step ahead, and I'll show them what happens when someone plays them at their own game.

EPILOGUE

The first few weeks of summer are hot and uncomfortable. The Train Car doesn't have air conditioning, and even though I have money in that account Tristan set up for me, the last thing I feel like doing is using it.

He betrayed me. Creed betrayed me. Zayd did

They systematically cut me off from Lizzie, from Miranda and Andrew, from Zack.

They humiliated me in front of my parents, and destroyed me in front of the entire school.

They made a bet ... and it worked. I was falling for them. Now I've fallen so hard that I'm not sure I can get up. For several days, all I do is lie facedown on my bed and cry, huge wracking sobs that drum up old memories of feeling lost and unwanted. But this time, the darkness doesn't call to me. I

Filthy Rich Boys

don't even consider it.

This time, when the tears dry up and my emotions have fizzled out, only one thing remains.

Revenge.

It burns like a distant star inside of me, white-hot and far away, but when I reach for it, it glows brighter.

Grabbing Miranda's list from the beginning of the year and a red Sharpie from inside my nightstand, I sit on the edge of my bed, and I make some changes to it.

Revenge On *The Bluebloods of Burberry Prep*
A list by ~~Miranda Cabot~~ *Marnye Reed*

*The Idols (guys): Tristan Vanderbilt (year ~~one~~ **two**), Zayd Kaiser (year ~~one~~ **two**), and Creed Cabot (year ~~one~~ **two**)*

*The Idols (girls): Harper du Pont (year ~~one~~ **two**), Becky Platter (year ~~one~~ **two**), ~~and Gena Whitley (year four)~~* **(graduated)**

The Inner Circle: Andrew Payson, Anna Kirkpatrick, Myron Talbot, Ebony Peterson, Gregory Van Horn, Abigail Fanning, John Hannibal, Valentina Pitt, Sai Patel, Mayleen Zhang, Jalen Donner ... ~~and, I guess, me!~~

Plebs: everyone else~~, sorry. XOXO~~

Zack Brooks

I put the cap on the pen and set it aside, exhaling as I stare down at my list. I'm not going to be chased away from a bright future by a bunch of bullies, not even by bullies I was starting to fall for. No way. So I dry my tears, fold the list up, and put it inside my bookbag for next year.

As soon as the summer is over, I'm going to go back to Burberry Prep, stronger than ever.

The hardest hearts are forged in fire; the weakest bend under their will.

And revenge … is wicked sweet.

To Be Continued ...

Coming April 2019

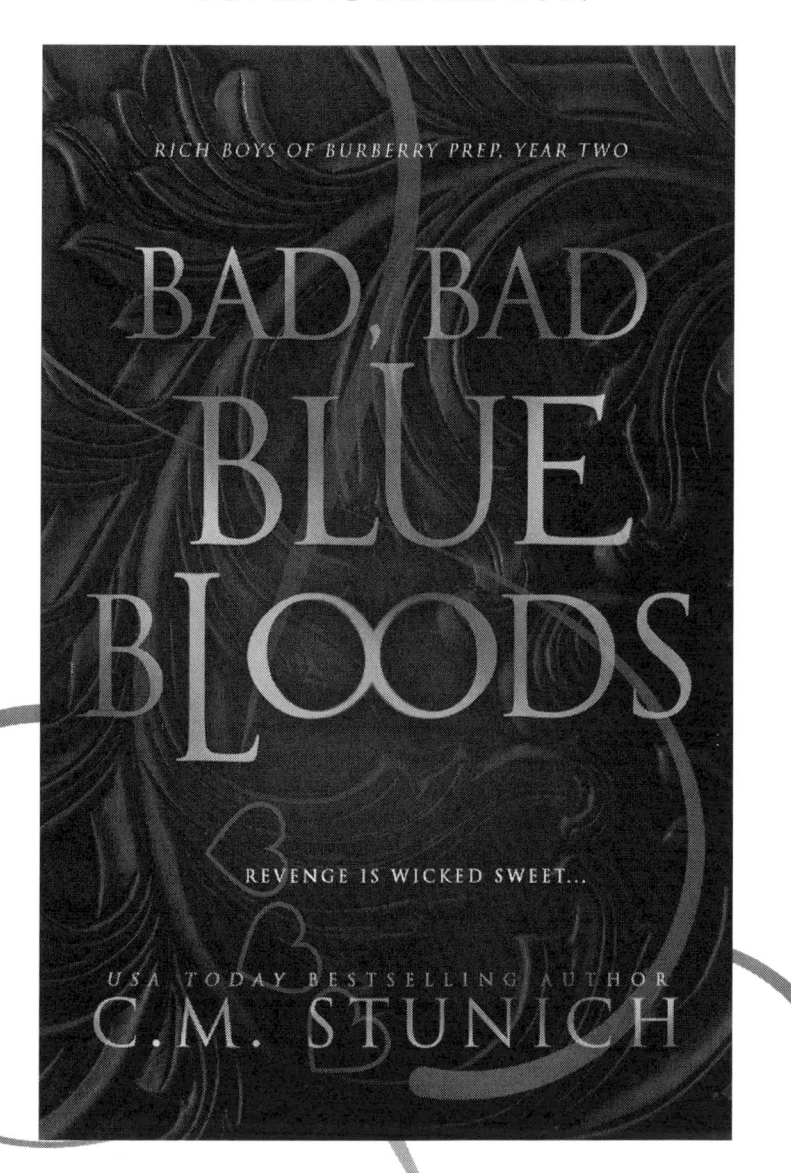

RICH BOYS OF BURBERRY PREP, YEAR TWO

BAD, BAD BLUE BLOODS

REVENGE IS WICKED SWEET...

USA TODAY BESTSELLING AUTHOR
C.M. STUNICH

Bad, Bad Blue Bloods
Rich Boys of Burberry Prep # 2

SIGN UP FOR
THE C.M. STUNICH

Newsletter

Sign up for an exclusive first look at the hottest new releases, contests, and exclusives from the author.

@

www.cmstunich.com

JOIN THE
C. M. STUNICH

Discussion Group

Want to discuss what you've just read?
Get exclusive teasers or meet special guest authors?
Join CM.'s online book clubs on Facebook!

@

www.facebook.com/groups/thebookishbatcave

Stalking Links

JOIN THE C.M. STUNICH NEWSLETTER – Get three free books just for signing up http://eepurl.com/DEsEf

TWEET ME ON TWITTER, BABE – Come sing the social media song with me https://twitter.com/CMStunich

SNAPCHAT WITH ME – Get exclusive behind the scenes looks at covers, blurbs, book signings and more http://www.snapchat.com/add/cmstunich

LISTEN TO MY BOOK PLAYLISTS – Share your fave music with me and I'll give you my playlists (I'm super active on here!) https://open.spotify.com/user/12101321503

FRIEND ME ON FACEBOOK – Okay, I'm actually at the 5,000 friend limit, but if you click the "follow" button on my profile page, you'll see way more of my killer posts https://facebook.com/cmstunich

LIKE ME ON FACEBOOK – Pretty please? I'll love you forever if you do! ;) https://facebook.com/cmstunichauthor & https://facebook.com/violetblazeauthor

CHECK OUT THE NEW SITE – (under construction) but it looks kick-a$$ so far, right? You can order signed books here! http://www.cmstunich.com

READ VIOLET BLAZE – Read the books from my hot as hellfire pen name, Violet Blaze http://www.violetblazebooks.com

SUBSCRIBE TO MY RSS FEED – Press that little orange button in the corner and copy that RSS feed so you can get all the latest updates http://www.cmstunich.com/blog

AMAZON, BABY – If you click the follow button here, you'll get an email each time I put out a new book. Pretty sweet, huh? http://amazon.com/author/cmstunich http://amazon.com/author/violetblaze

PINTEREST – Lots of hot half-naked men. Oh, and half-naked men. Plus, tattooed guys holding babies (who are half-naked) http://pinterest.com/cmstunich

INSTAGRAM – Cute cat pictures. And half-naked guys. Yep, that again. http://instagram.com/cmstunich

About the Author

C.M. Stunich is a self-admitted bibliophile with a love for exotic teas and a whole host of characters who live full time inside the strange, swirling vortex of her thoughts. Some folks might call this crazy, but Caitlin Morgan doesn't mind – especially considering she has to write biographies in the third person. Oh, and half the host of characters in her head are searing hot bad boys with dirty mouths and skillful hands (among other things). If being crazy means hanging out with them everyday, C.M. has decided to have herself committed.

She hates tapioca pudding, loves to binge on cheesy horror movies, and is a slave to many cats. When she's not vacuuming fur off of her couch, C.M. can be found with her nose buried in a book or her eyes glued to a computer screen. She's the author of over thirty novels – romance, new adult, fantasy, and young adult included. Please, come and join her inside her crazy. There's a heck of a lot to do there.

Oh, and Caitlin loves to chat (incessantly), so feel free to e-mail her, send her a Facebook message, or put up smoke signals. She's already looking forward to it.

Printed in Great Britain
by Amazon